GENERATION
WARRIORS

The Planet Pirate Series

Dinosaur Planet
Dinosaur Planet Survivors
Sassinak
The Death of Sleep
Generation Warriors

GENERATION WARRIORS

Anne McCaffrey
and
Elizabeth Moon

Chapter One

"We have resources they don't know about," Sassinak said, and not for the first time. It did not reassure her.

The convivial mood in which Sassinak and Lunzie had first made their plans to combine forces against the planet pirates had long since evaporated. They had been carried by the euphoria following the incredible Thek cathedral which had dispensed right justice to Captain Cruss who had illegally landed a heavyworlder colony transport ship on the planet Ireta, right under the bows of Sassinak's pursuing cruiser. The Thek conference had elicited considerable fascinating information about the Captain's superiors. Apart from sorting out the problem of which race "owned" Ireta, the Thek had departed without reference to bringing the perpetrators of planet pirating to a similar justice.

Neither Sassinak nor Lunzie felt they would be lucky enough to obtain more support from the Theks, even if that long-lived race were the oldest of the space-faring species. Theks rarely interfered with members of the various ephemeral species that they had discovered over the centuries. Only when, as on Ireta, some ancient plan of their own might be jeopardized would they intervene. As a rule, Thek permitted all their client races, from the lizard-like

Seti, the shape-changing Wefts, the marine Ssli down to humans, to "dree their ain weirds." No sooner than the Thek had resolved the matter of Ireta then they had departed, leaving Sassinak and Lunzie with an irresistible challenge: to seek out and destroy those who indulged in the most daring sort of piracy—the rape and pillage of entire planets and the mass enslavement of their legally resident populations. The problems were immense. Sassinak was too experienced a commander to ignore real problems, and Lunzie had seen too many good plans go wrong herself. Lunzie, sprawled comfortably on the white leather cushions in Sassinak's office, watched her distant offspring with amusement. She was so young to be so old.

"So are you," Sassinak retorted.

Lunzie felt herself reddening.

"There's no such thing as telepathy," she said. "It's never been demonstrated under controlled conditions."

"Twins do it," Sassinak said. "I read that somewhere. And other close relatives, sometimes. As for you and me . . . nobody knows what that many deepfreezes have done to your brain, and what my life's done to me. You were thinking I'm young to be so old, and I was thinking exactly the same thing about you. You're *younger* than I am . . ."

"Which doesn't give you the right to play boss," said Lunzie. Then she wished she hadn't. Sassinak's face had hardened . . . and of course to her, she did have the right. She was the captain of her ship, one step below her first star, and she had ten more years of actual, awake, living-experience age.

"I'm sorry," Lunzie said quickly. "You *are* older, and you *are* the boss . . . I'm just still adjusting."

Sassinak's quick smile almost reassured her. "Same here. But I do have to be the boss on this ship. Even if you are my great-great-great, you don't know which pipes hold what."

"Right. Point taken. I will be the good little civilian." And try, she thought to herself, to adjust to having a distant offspring not only older than herself but quite a bit tougher. She leaned forward, setting her mug down on the table. "What are you thinking of doing?"

"What we need," said Sass, frowning at nothing, "is a lot more information. The kind of proof we can bring before the Council meeting, for instance. Take the Diplo problem. Who's been contacting whom, and whose money paid for that heavyworlder seedship? Which factions of heavyworlders are involved, and do they all know what they're doing? Then there's the Paraden family. I have my own reasons to think they're guilty, root and branch, but no proof. If we could get someone into position, some social connection . . ."

Lunzie picked up her mug, gulped down the last of her drink, and tried to ignore the hollow in her belly. Was she about to do something stupid, or brave, or both?

"I . . . might be able to help with the Diplo bit."

"You? How?"

Sassinak had been thinking of her own heavyworlder friends, but she hated to use any of them that way. It would be too risky for them if some agent within Fleet caught on.

"They don't let many lightweights visit Diplo, but because of their continuing medical problems, genetic and adaptive, medical researchers and advisors are welcome. As welcome as lightweights ever are. I'd need a refresher course with a Master Adept . . ."

Sassinak pursed her lips. "Hmmm. That's reasonable, the refresher part. If anyone were watching you, they'd expect you to. You've gone a stage or so beyond your rating, haven't you? And you people go back fairly regularly, once you're in the Adept rating, so I've heard. . . ."

She let that trail away, in case Lunzie wanted to offer more information, but wasn't surprised when Lunzie simply nodded and went on to talk about Diplo.

"Doctors are expected to ask questions. If I were on a research team, perhaps statistical survey of birth defects, something like that, I'd have a chance to talk to lots of people as part of my job."

Sassinak cocked her head to one side; Lunzie barely stopped herself from making the same gesture.

"Are you sure you're not doing this just to exorcise your own heavyworld demons? From what you've said . . ."

Lunzie didn't want to go into that again. "I know. I have reason to hate and fear them. Some of them. But I've also known good ones; I told you about Zebara." Sassinak nodded, but looked unconvinced. Lunzie went on. "Besides, I'll have time to talk to the Master Adept renewing my training. You know enough about Discipline to know that's as good as any psych software. If a Master says I'm not stable enough to go, I'll let you know."

"You'll discuss it with him?" By Sassinak's tone, she wasn't entirely happy with that.

Lunzie sighed internally. "Not everything, no. But my going to Diplo, certainly. There are certain special skills which can make it easier on a lightweight."

"Just be sure a Master passes you. This is too important to risk on an emotional storm, and with the trouble you've had . . ."

"I can handle it." Lunzie let her voice convey the Discipline behind it, and Sassinak subsided. Not really impressed, Lunzie noticed, as most people would be, but convinced for the time being.

"That's Diplo, then," Sassinak gave a final minute shrug, and went on to the other problems. "You're going off. And you don't know how long that will take, either, do you? I thought not. You're going off for a refresher course and a visit to Diplo, and that leaves us with digging to be done among the suspect commercial combines, the Seti, and the inner workings of EEC, Fleet, and the Council. It would be handy if we had our own private counter-intelligence network, but . . ."

Lunzie interrupted, feeling smug. "You know Admiral Coromell, don't you?"

Sassinak's jaw did not drop because she would not let it, but Lunzie could tell she was surprised. "Do *you* know Admiral Coromell?"

"Quite well, yes." Lunzie watched Sassinak struggle with the obvious implications, and decide not to ask. Or perhaps the implications weren't obvious to her. By now Coromell would be as old as his father had been; Sassinak would have known him as an old man. Lunzie fought off yet another pang of sorrow, and concentrated on the present moment. "Coromell actually recruited me, temporarily, back before the Ambrosia thing."

"Recruited you!" Was that approval or resentment? Lunzie did not ask, but gave as brief a synopsis as possible of the circumstances of that recruitment, and what followed. Sassinak listened without interrupting, her eyes focussed on some distant vision, and shook her head slightly when Lunzie finished.

"My dear, I have the feeling we could talk for weeks and you'd still surprise me." There was nothing in the tone to indicate whether this most recent surprise had been pleasant or not; Lunzie suspected that respect for Coromell's stars might be part of Sassinak's reticence. To underscore that reticence, Sassinak pushed away from her desk. "I feel like stretching my legs, and you haven't really seen the ship yet. Want a tour?"

"Of course." Lunzie was as glad to take a break from their intense conversation. She followed Sassinak out into the passage that led nearly the length of Main Deck.

"It's so different," Lunzie said, as Sass led her down the aft ladder to Troop Deck. She wondered why the walls—bulkheads, she reminded herself —were green here, and gray above.

"Different?"

"I hadn't had time to mention it, but when we were rescued from Ambrosia that time, the Fleet cruiser that came was this one. The *Zaid-Dayan*. I never saw the captain, but it was a woman. That's why I used the name in the cover I gave Varian and the others back on Ireta. It was a *deja-vu* situation, you and this ship . . ."

Sassinak grunted. "Couldn't have been *this* ship. Wasn't the Ambrosia rescue before Ireta and your coldsleep? Forty years or so back? That must have been the '43 version . . . that ship was lost in combat the year I graduated from the Academy." She nodded to the squad of marines that had flattened themselves along the bulkhead to let her by, and waited for Lunzie to catch up.

Lunzie felt cold all over. Another reminder that she had not grown *naturally* older, when she would know things, but had simply skipped decades. "Are you sure? When I heard this was the *Zaid-Dayan*, with a woman captain, I thought maybe . . ."

Sassinak shook her head. "I'm not that much older than you. No—the Ambrosia rescue—we were taught that battle, in TacSim II. That was Graciela Vinish-Martinez, her first command and a new ship. She caught hell from a Board of Inquiry at first, bringing it back needing repairs like that, but someone on Ambrosia, some scout captain or something . . ."

"Zebara," said Lunzie, hardly breathing.

"Whoever it was wrote a report that got the Board off her neck. I thought of that when I had to go before a Board. I saw her." Sassinak's expression was strange, almost bemused. She punched a button on the bulkhead, and a hatch slid open: a lift. They entered, and Sassinak pushed another button inside before she said more. Lunzie waited. "She gave us—the female cadets—a lecture on command presence for women officers. We all thought that was a stupid topic. We were muttering about it, going in; the room was empty except for this little old lady in the corner, looked like the kind of retirement-age warrant officers that swarmed all around the Academy, doing various jobs no one ever explained. I hardly glanced at her. She had an old-fashioned clipboard and a marker. We sat down, wondering how late Admiral Vinish-Martinez was going to be. We knew better than to chatter, but I have to admit there was a lot of quiet murmuring going on, and some of it was mine." Sassinak grinned reminiscently. "Then this little old lady gets up. Nobody saw that; we figured she was taking roll. Walks around to the front, and we thought maybe she was going to tell us the Admiral was late or not coming. And then—I swear, Lunzie, not one of us saw her stars until she wanted us to, when she *changed* right there in front of us without moving a muscle. Didn't say a word. Didn't have to. We were out of our seats and saluting before we realized what had happened."

"And then?" Lunzie couldn't help asking; she was fascinated.

"And then she gave us a big bright smile, and said 'That, ladies, was a demonstration of command presence.' And then she walked out, while we were still breathless."

"Mullah!"

"Right. The whole lecture in one demonstration. We never forgot that one, I can tell you, and we spent hours trying it on each other to see if we'd learned anything yet. She said it all: it's not your size or your looks or your strength or how loud you can yell—it's something *else*, inside, and if you don't have that, no amount of size, strength, beauty, or bellowing will do instead." The lift opened onto a tiny space surrounded by differently colored pipes that gurgled and hissed. A sign said "ENVIRONMENTAL LEVEL ONE."

"Adept Discipline?" asked Lunzie, curious to know what Sass thought.

"Maybe. For some. You know we have basic classes in it in Fleet. But there has to be a certain potential or something has to happen later. Certainly the element of focus is the same . . ." Sassinak's voice trailed away; her brow furrowed.

"You have it," said Lunzie. She had seen the crew's response to Sassinak, and felt her own—an almost automatic respect and desire to please her.

"Oh . . . well, yes. Some, at least; I can put the fear of reality into wild young ensigns. But not like that." She laughed, putting the memory aside. "For years I wanted to do that . . . to be that . . ."

"Was she your childhood idol, then? Were you dreaming about Fleet even before you were captured?" Was that what had kept her sane?

"Oh, no. I wanted to be Carin Coldae." Lunzie must have looked as blank as she felt, for Sassinak said, "I'm sorry—I didn't realize. Forty-three years—she must not have been a vid star when you were last—I mean . . ."

"Don't worry." Another example of what she'd missed. She hadn't been one to follow the popularity of vid stars at any time, but the way Sassinak had said the name, Coldae must have been a household word.

"Just an adventure star," Sassinak was explaining. "Had fan clubs, posters, all that. My best friend and I dreamed of having adventures all over the galaxy, men at our feet . . ."

"Well, *you* seem to have made it," said Lunzie dryly. "Or so your crew let me know."

Sassinak actually blushed; the effect was startling. "It's not much like the daydreams, though. Carin never got a scratch on her, only a few artistically placed streaks of soot. Sometimes that soot was all she had on, but mostly it was silver or gold snugsuits, open halfway down her perfect front. She could toss twenty pirates over her head with one hand, gun down another ten villains with the other, and belt out her themesong without missing a beat. When I was a child, it never dawned on me that someone supposedly being starved and beaten in a thorium mine shouldn't have all those luscious curves. Or that climbing naked up a volcanic cliff does bad things to long scarlet fingernails."

"Mmm. Is she still popular?"

"Not so much. Re-runs will go on forever, at least the classics like *Dark of the Moon* and *The Iron Chain*. She's doing straight dramas now, and politics." Sassinak grimaced, remembering Dupaynil's revelations about her former idol. "I've been told she's behind some subversive groups, has been for years." Then she sighed, and said, "And I dragged you through Troop Deck without showing you much . . . well. This is Environmental, that keeps us alive."

"I saw the sign," said Lunzie. She could hear the distant rhythmic throbbing of pumps. Sassinak patted a plump beige pipe with surprising affection.

"This was my first assignment out of the Academy. Installing a new environmental system on a cruiser."

"I thought you'd have specialists—"

"We do. But officers in the command track have to be generalists. In theory, a captain should know every pipe and wire, every chip in every computer, every bit of equipment and scrap of supplies . . . where it is, how it works, who should be taking care of it. So we all start in one of the main ships' specialties and rotate through them in our first two tours."

"Do you know?" She couldn't, Lunzie was sure, but did she know she didn't know, or did she think she did?

"Not all of them, not quite. But more than I did. This one," and she patted it again, "this one carries carbon dioxide to the buffer tanks; the oxygen pipes, like all the flammables, are red. And no, you won't see them in this compartment, because some idiot coming off the lift could have a flame, or the lift could spark. Since you're a doctor, I thought you'd like to see some of this . . ."

"Oh, yes."

Luckily she knew enough not to feel like a complete idiot. Sassinak led her along low-ceilinged tunnels with pipes hissing and gurgling on either hand, pointing out access ports to still other plumbing, the squatty cylindrical scrubbers, the gauges and meters and status lights that indicated exactly what was where, and whether it should be.

"All new," Sassinak said, as they headed into the 'ponics section. "We had major trouble last time out, not just the damage, but apparently some sabotage of Environmental. Ended up with stinking sludge growing all along the pipes where it shouldn't, and there's no way to clean that out, once the sulfur bacteria start pitting the pipe linings."

Hydroponics on a Fleet cruiser looked much like hydroponics anywhere else to Lunzie, who recognized the basic configuration of tanks and feeder lines and bleedoff valves, but nothing special. Sassinak finally took her back to the lift and they ascended to Main again.

"How long does it take a newcomer to find everything?"

Sassinak pursed her lips. "Well . . . if you mean new crew or ensigns, usually a week or so. We start 'em off with errands in every direction, let 'em get good and lost, and they soon figure out how to use a terminal and a shipchip to stay found. You noticed that every deck's a different color, and the striping width indicates bow and stern; there's no reason to stay lost once you've caught on to that." She led the way into her office, where a light blinked on her board. "I've got to go to the bridge. Would you like to stay here, or go back to your cabin?"

Lunzie had hoped to be invited onto the bridge, but nothing in Sassinak's expression made that possible. "I'll stay here, if that's convenient."

"Fine. Let me give you a line out." Sassinak touched her terminal's controls. "There! A list of access codes for you. I won't be long."

Lunzie wondered what that actually meant in terms of hours, and settled down with the terminal. She had hardly decided what to access when she heard heavy steps coming down the passage. Aygar appeared in the opening, scowling.

"Where's Sassinak?"

"On the bridge." Lunzie wondered what had upset him this time. The Weft marine corporal behind him looked more amused than concerned. "Want to wait here for her?"

"I don't want to wait." He came in, nonetheless, and sat down on the white-cushioned chair as if determined to stay forever. "I want to know how much longer it will be." At Lunzie's patient look, he went on. "When we will arrive at . . . at this Sector Headquarters, whatever that is. When Tanegli's mutiny trial will be. When I can speak for my . . . my peers." He'd hesitated over that; "peer" was a new word to him, and Lunzie wondered where he'd found it.

"I don't know," she said mildly. "She hasn't told me, either. I'm not sure she knows." She glanced at the door, where the Weft stood relaxed, projecting no threat but obviously capable. "Does it bother you to be followed?"

Aygar nodded, and leaned closer to her. "I don't understand these Wefts. How can they be something else, and then humans? How does anyone know who is human and who isn't? And they tell me of other aliens, not only Wefts and Thek that I have seen, but Ryxi who are like birds, and Bronthin, and . . ."

"You saw plenty of strange animals on Ireta."

"Yes, but . . ." His brow furrowed. "I suppose . . . I grew up with them. But that so many are spacefaring races."

"'Many are the world's wonders,'" Lunzie found herself quoting, "'But none more wonderful than man . . .' Or at least, that's the way we humans think of it."

From his expression, he'd never heard the quotation—but she didn't think the heavyworlder rebels had been students of ancient literature. A Kipling rhyme broke into her mind and she wondered if Aygar's East would ever meet civilization's West, or if they were doomed to be enemies. She dragged her wandering mind back to the present (no quotes, she told herself) and found Aygar watching her with a curious expression.

"You're younger than she is," he said. No doubt at all who "she" was. "But she calls you her great-great-great grandmother . . . why?"

"Remember we told you about coldsleep? How the lightweight members of the expedition survived? That isn't the only time I've been in cold-sleep; my elapsed age is . . . older than you'd expect." She was not sure why she was reluctant to tell him precisely what it was. "Commander Sassinak is my descendant, just as you're descended from people who were young when I went into coldsleep on Ireta, people who are old now."

He looked more interested than horrified. "And you don't age at all, in coldsleep?"

"No. That's the point of it."

"Can you learn at the same time? I've been reading about the sleep-learning methods . . . would that work in coldsleep as well?"

"And let us wake up stuffed with knowledge and still young?" Lunzie shook her head. "No, it won't work, though it's a nice idea. If there were a way to feed in information that the person's missing, waking up forty or fifty years later wouldn't be so bad."

"Do you *feel* old?"

Aygar's question was lowest on Lunzie's list of things to think about. She was sure Sassinak had the same back-and-forth tug faced with someone that many generations removed, an uncertainty about what "age" really meant.

Lunzie put a touch of Discipline in her voice again. "Not old and feeble, if that's what you mean. Old enough to know my mind, and young enough to . . ." Now how was she going to finish that? "To . . . to do what I must," she finished lamely.

But Aygar subsided, asking no more in that difficult area. What he did ask about—and what Lunzie was prepared to answer cheerfully—was the psychological testing procedure that Major Currald, the marine commander, had recommended to him.

"It's a good idea," Lunzie said, nodding. "My field at one time was occupational rehab. With my experience, they felt I understood troubled spaceworkers better than most. And quite often the root of the problem is that someone's stuck in a job for which they're not suited. They feel trapped —and if they're on a spaceship or station, in a way they *are* trapped—and that makes for trouble when anything else goes wrong."

Aygar frowned thoughtfully. "But we were taught that we should not be too narrow—that we should learn to do many things, have many skills. That part of the trouble between heavyworlders and lightweights came from too much specialization."

"Yes, that can be true. Humans are generalists, and are healthier when they have varied activities. But their primary occupation should draw on innate abilities, should not require them to do what is hardest for them. Some individuals are naturally better at sit-down jobs, or with very definite routines to follow. Others can learn new things easily, but quickly become bored with routines. That's not the person you want running the 'ponics system, which needs the same routine servicing shift after shift."

"But what about me?" Aygar thumped his chest. "Will I fit in, or be a freak? I'm big and strong, but not as strong as Currald. I'm smart enough, you said, but I don't have the educational background, and I don't have any idea what's available."

Lunzie tried to project soothing confidence. "Aygar, with your background, both genetic and experiential, I'm sure you'll find—or make—a good niche for yourself. When we get to Sector Headquarters, you'll have direct access to various library databases, as well as testing and counseling services of FSP. I'll be glad to advise you, if you want . . ." She paused, assessing his expression.

His slow smile made her wonder if this was her idea or his. "I would like that. I will hope you are right." He stood up, still smiling down at her.

"Are you leaving? I thought you wanted to talk to the captain."

"Another time. If you are my ally, I will not worry about her."

With that he was gone. Lunzie stared after him. Ally? She was not at all sure she wanted Aygar for an ally, in whatever sense he meant it. He might be more trouble that way.

* * *

Sassinak returned shortly from the bridge, listened to Lunzie's report on Aygar's visit, and nodded.

"You put exactly the bee in his ear that I wanted. Good for you."

"But he said *ally* . . ."

"And I say fine. Better for us, better for what we want to do. Look, Lunzie, he's got the best possible reason for stirring around in the databases: he's entitled. His curiosity is natural. We said that." Sassinak put in a call to the galley for a snack, and started to say more, but her com buzzed. She turned to it. "Sassinak here."

"Ford. May I come in? I've had an idea."

"Come ahead."

Sassinak punched the door control and it slid aside. Ford gave Lunzie the same charming smile and nod as always, and lifted an eyebrow.

"You know you can speak in front of her," Sassinak told him. "She's my relative, and she's on the team."

"Did I ever tell you about Auntie Q?"

Sassinak frowned. "Not that I remember. Was that the one who paints birds on tiles?"

"No, that's Auntie Louise, my mother's sister. This is Auntie Quesada, who is actually, in her right name, Quesada Maria Louisa Darrell Santon-Paraden."

"Paraden!"

Sassinak and Lunzie tied on that one, and Sassinak glared at her Executive Officer in a way Lunzie hoped would never be directed at her.

"You never told me you were related to the Paradens," she said severely.

"I'm not. Auntie Q is my father's uncle's wife's sister, who married a Paraden the second time around, after her first husband died of—well, my *mother* always said it was an overdose of Auntie Q, administered daily in large amounts. My father always said it was gamboling debts, and I mean gambol," he said, accenting the last syllable.

"Go on," said Sassinak, a smile beginning to twitch in the corner of her mouth.

Ford settled one hip on her desk. "Auntie Q was considered a catch, even for a Paraden, because her first husband's older brother was Felix Ibarra-Jimenez Santon. Yes, *those* Santons. Auntie Q inherited about half a planet of spicefields and a gold mine: literal gold mine. With an electronics manufacturing plant on top. Then in her own right, she was a Darrell of the Westwitch Darrells, who prefer to call their source of income 'sanitary engineering products' rather than soap, so she wouldn't have starved if she'd run off with a mishi dancer."

"So what about this Paraden?"

"Minor branch of the family, sent out to find an alliance worth the trouble; supposedly he met her at an ambassadorial function, ran her through the computer, and the family said yes, by all means. Auntie Q was tired of playing merry widow and looking for another steady escort so they linked. She gave him a child by decree—it was in the contract—but he was already looking for more excitement or freedom or whatever, and ran off with her dressmaker. So she claimed breach of contract, dumped the child on the Paradens, kept the name and half his stocks and such, and spends her time cruising from one social event to another. And sending the family messages."

"Aha," said Sassinak. "Now we come to it. She's contacted you?"

"Well, no. Not recently. But she's always sending messages, complaining about her health, and begging someone to visit her. My father warned me years ago not to go near her; said she's like a black hole, just sucks you in and you're never seen alive again. He had been taken to meet her once. Apparently she cooed over him, rumpled his hair, hugged him to her ample bosom, and talked him out of the chocolates in his pocket, all in about twenty seconds. But what I was thinking was that I could visit her. She knows all the gossip, all the socialites, and yet she's not quite in the thick where they'd be watching her."

Sassinak thought about that. Wouldn't an efficient enemy know that Sassinak's Exec was related to an apparently harmless old rich lady? But she herself hadn't. They couldn't know everything.

"I'd planned to have you do the database searches at Sector HQ," she said slowly. "You're good at that, and less conspicuous than I am . . ."

Ford shook his head. "Not inconspicuous enough, not after this caper. But I know who can . . . either Lunzie here, or young Aygar."

"Aygar?"

Ford ticked off reasons on his fingers. "One, he's got the perfect reason to be running the bases: he's new to the culture, and needs to learn as much as he can as fast as he can. Two, no one's ever done a profile on him, so no one can say if any particular query is out of character. In that way, he's better than Lunzie; anyone looking for trouble would notice if she ran queries outside her field or the events of her own life. Three, even an attempt at a profile would cover exactly those fields we want him to be working on anyway."

"But is he trustworthy?" Lunzie asked it of Ford, as she had been about to ask it of Sassinak. Ford shrugged.

"What if he's not? He needs us to get access, and keep it; he's bright but he's not experienced, and you know how long it took any of us to learn to navigate through one of the big databases. And we can put a tag on him; it'll be natural that we do. We shouldn't seem to trust him."

Sassinak laughed. "I do like a second in command who thinks like I do. See, Lunzie? Two against one: both of us see why Aygar is ideal for that job."

"But he's expecting something more from us—from me, at least. If he doesn't get it . . ."

"Lunzie!" That was the command voice, the tone that made Sassinak no longer a distant relative but the captain of a Fleet cruiser on which Lunzie was merely a passenger. It softened slightly with the next words, but Lunzie could feel the steel underneath. "We aren't going to do anything to hurt Aygar. We know he's not involved in the plotting . . . of all the citizens of the Federation, he's one of the few who *couldn't* be involved. So he's not our enemy, not in any way whatever. Stopping the piracy will help everyone, including Aygar's friends and relatives back on Ireta. Including Aygar. We are on his side, in that way, and by my judgment—which I must remind you is ten years more experienced than yours—by my judgment that is enough. We can handle Aygar; we have dangerous enemies facing all of us."

Lunzie's gaze wavered, falling away from Sassinak's to see Ford as another of the same type. Calm, competent, certain of himself, and not about to change his mind a hairsbreadth for anything she said.

Chapter Two

Lunzie carried her small kit off the *Zaid-Dayan*, nodded to the parting salute of the officer on watch at the portside gangway, and did not look back as she crossed the line that marked ship's territory on the Station decking. It was so damnably hard to leave family again, even such distant family. She had liked Sassinak, and the ship, and . . . she did not look back.

Ahead were none of the barriers she'd have faced coming in on a civilian ship. She had Sassinak's personal authorization, giving her the temporary rank and access of a Fleet major, so exiting the Fleet segment required nothing but flashing the pass at the guard and walking on through. No questions to answer, no interviews with intrusive media.

Sassinak had made reservations for her on the first available shuttle to Liaka. Lunzie followed the directions she'd been given, in two rings and right one sector, and found herself in front of the ticketing office of Nilokis In-Line. Lunzie's name and Sassinak's reservation together meant instant service. Before she realized it, Lunzie was settled in a quiet room with video-relay views of the Station and a mug of something hot and fragrant on the table beside her. A few meters away, another favored passenger barely glanced up from his portable computer before continuing his work. The padded chair curved around her like warm hands; her feet rested on deeply cushioned carpet.

She tried to relax. She had not lost Sassinak forever, she told herself firmly. She was not going to have a disaster on every spaceflight for the rest of her life, and if she did she would just survive it, the way she'd survived everything else. Her steaming mug drew her attention, and she remembered choosing *erit* from the list of beverages. One sip, then another, quieted her nerves and settled her stomach. Four hours to departure and nothing to do. She thought of going back out into the Station but it was easier to sit here and relax. That's why she'd asked for *erit*. She closed her eyes, and let the steam clear her head. After all, if something happened this time, she'd know who'd come after her and with what vigor. Sassinak was not one to let someone muck about with her family, not now. Lunzie felt her mouth curving into a grin. Quite a girl, that Sassinak, even at her age.

She forced herself to concentrate, to think of the days she'd spent studying with Mayerd. With Sassinak's authority behind her, she'd been able to catch up a lot of the lost ground in her field. She knew which journals were current, what to read first, which areas would require formal instruction. (She was not about to try the new methods of altering brain chemistry from a cookbook—not until she had seen a demonstration, at least.) Her mind wandered to the time she had available for gathering information and she pulled out her calculator to check elapsed and Standard times. If Sassinak was right about the probable trial date, in the Winter Assizes (and *that* was an archaic term, she thought), then she had to complete her refresher course in Discipline, whatever medical refreshers were required for recertification, get to Diplo, and back to Sassinak (or the information back to Sassinak) in a mere eight months.

Another passenger came into the lounge, and then a pair, absorbed in each other. Lunzie finished her drink and eyed them benignly. They all looked normal, business and professional travelers (except the couple, who looked like two junior executives off on vacation). The shuttle flew a three-cornered route, to Liaka first and then Bearnaise and then back here; Lunzie tried to guess who was going where, and how many less favored passengers were waiting in the common lounge (orange plastic benches along the walls, and a single drinking fountain).

Even with the *erit*, and her own Discipline, Lunzie spent the short hop to Liaka in miserable anxiety. Every change in sound, every minute shift of the ship's gravity field, every new smell, brought her alert, ready for trouble. She slept lightly and woke unrested. On such short trips, less than five days, experienced passengers tended to keep to themselves. She was spared the need to pretend friendliness. She ate her standard packaged meals, nodded politely, and spent most of the time in her tiny cabin, claustrophobic as it was. Better that than the lounge, where the couple (definitely junior executives, and not likely to be promoted unless they grew up) displayed their affection as if it were a prizewinning performance, worth everyone's attention.

When the shuttle docked, Lunzie had been waiting, ready to leave, for hours. She took her place in the line of debarking passengers, checking out her guesses about which were going where (the lovers were going to Bearnaise, of course), and shifting her weight from foot to foot. Over the bobbing heads she could see the Main Concourse, and tried to remember the quickest route to the Mountain.

"Ah . . . Lunzie Mespil." The customs officer glanced at the screen in front of her, where Lunzie's picture, palm-print, and retinal scan should be displayed. "There's a message for you, ma'am. MedOps, Main Concourse, Blue Bay. Do you need a guide?"

"Not that far," said Lunzie, smiling, and swung her bag over her shoulder. MedOps had a message? Just how old was that message, she wondered.

Main Concourse split incoming traffic into many diverging streams. Blue was fourth on the right, after two black (to Lunzie) and one violet section. The blacks were ultraviolet, distinguishable by alien races who could see in those spectra, and led to services those might require. Blue Bay opened off the concourse, all medical training services of one sort or another; MedOps centered the bay.

"Ah . . . Lunzie." The tone was much the same, bemused discovery. Lunzie leaned on the counter and stared at the glossy-haired girl at the computer. "A message, ma'am. Will you take hardcopy, or would you prefer a P-booth?"

The girl's eyes, when she looked up, were brown and guileless. Lunzie thought a moment. The option of a P-booth meant the message had come in as a voice or video, not info-only.

"P-booth," she said, and the girl pointed to the row of cylinders along one side of the room. Lunzie went into the first, slid its translucent door shut, punched the controls for privacy, and then entered her ID codes. The screen blinked twice, lit, and displayed a face she knew and had not seen for over forty years.

"Welcome back, Adept Lunzie." His voice, as always, was low, controlled, compelling. His black eyes seemed to twinkle at her; his face, seamed with age when she first met him, had not changed. Was this a recording from the past? Or could he still be here, alive?

"Venerable Master." She took a long, controlling breath, and bent her head in formal greeting.

"You age well," he said. The twinkle was definite now, and the slight curve to his mouth. His humor was rare and precious as the millennia's-old porcelain from which he sipped tea. It was not a recording. It could not be a recording, if he noticed she had not aged. She took another deliberate breath, slowing her racing heart, and wondering what he had heard, what he knew.

"Venerable Master, it is necessary . . ."

"For you to renew your training," he said.

Interruptions were as rare as humor; part of Discipline was courtesy, learning to wait for others without hurrying them, or feeling the strain. Had that changed, along with the rest of her world? *Never hurry; never wait* had been one of the first things she'd memorized. It had always seemed odd, since doctors faced so many situations when they must hurry to save a life, or wait to see what happened. His face was grave, now, remote as a stone that neither waits nor hurries but simply exists where it is.

"The moment arrives," he said. Part of another saying, which she had no time to recite, for he went on. "Fourth level, begin with the Cleansing of the Stone."

And the screen blanked, leaving her confused but oddly reassured. Back to the MedOps desk, to see if Liaka's corridor plans had changed in the intervening years.

They had; she received a mapbug which chirped at her when she came to turns and crossings, and guided her into and out of droptubes. A few things looked familiar: the cool green doors that led to SurgOps, the red stripe that meant Quarantine. White-coated or green-gowned doctors still roamed the corridors in little groups, talking shop. She glanced after them, wondering if she'd ever feel at home with her colleagues again. Terminals for access to the medical databases filled niches along every wall. She thought of stopping to see if all the clone colony data had really been excised, then thought better of it. Later, when she felt calmer, would be soon enough.

Fourth level. She came out of the last droptube a little breathless, as always, facing a simple wood door, broad apricot-colored planks pegged together with a lighter wood. The wood glowed, as unmistakably real as Sassinak's desk. Lunzie took a deep breath, letting herself settle into herself, feeling that settling. She bowed to the door, and it swung open across a snowy white stone sill. A novice in brown bowed to her, stepped back to let her pass, and swung the door shut behind her. Then, bowing again, the novice took Lunzie's bag, and moved silently along the path toward the sleeping huts.

Here was a place unlike any other in this Station, or any Station. Ahead, on the left, a waist-high stone like a miniature mountain reared from a path artfully designed to lead the eye toward a pavilion. Lunzie stood where she was, looking at that stone, and the small, irregular pool behind it.

"Cleansing the stone" was an elementary exercise, but the foundation on which more striking ones were built. Empty the mind of all concerns, see the stone as it is . . . cleansed of associations, wishes, dreams, fantasies, fears. The word *stone* resonated in her mind, became all the hard things that had hurt her, because the mysterious Thek who confounded everyone's attempt to understand them. She stood quietly, relaxed, letting all these thoughts spill out, and then wiped them away. Again they came, and again, and once more she cleared them away from the stone before her. It had a certain beauty of its own, a history, a future, a *now*. She let her eyes wander over that irregular surface, not bothering to remember the glitter of mica, the glint of quartz . . . she did not need to remember, the stone was here and now, as solid as she, and as worthy of knowing.

When she had looked, she let her hand touch it, lightly, delicately, learning again (but not remembering) its irregular lumpy shape. She bent slowly to smell it, the curious and indescribable scent of stone, with behind it the smell of the water, and other stones. Something more sweet also scented the air, now that she was attending to smell, but she rested her attention on the stone.

When she was quite still, unhurried and unaware of waiting, he was there, in the pavilion. Venerable Master Adept, who had a name that no one spoke in this place, where names meant nothing and essence was all. When she became consciously aware of him, she realized he had been there for a time. What time she did not know, and it did not matter. What mattered was her mind's control of itself, its ability to engage or withdraw at her will. He would be ready when she was ready; she would be ready when he was ready. She heard a drop of water fall, and realized that the fountain was on. She bowed to the rock, her mind completely easy for the first time in too many years (for even in coldsleep she had been willing to worry, if not capable of it), and moved slowly along the path. Thoughts moved in her mind, like the carp in the pool. She let them move, let some rise almost to the surface, their scaled beauty clear, while others hung motionless, mere shapes below the surface.

This was the center of the world—of her world—of the world of every Adept, this place that was, in a physical sense, not the center of anything. Embarrassment had no place, with the Master Adept. She knelt across the little table from him, no longer aware that her worn workclothes from Ireta (however cleaned and smartened up by Sassinak's crew) were different from his immaculate white robe. His sash this day was aswirl with greens and blues and purples . . . a single thread of sulfur yellow. Her eye followed that thread, and then returned to his hands, as they gently touched petal-thin cups and saucers. He offered one, and she took it. Even in the subdued light within the pavilion, the cup seemed to glow. She could feel the warmth of the tea through it; that fragrance soothed.

After a time, he raised his cup, and sipped, and she did the same. They said nothing, for nothing needed to be said at this time. They shared the silence, the tea, the small pool where water fell tinkling from a fountain and carp dimpled the water from underneath.

Lunzie might have thought how very different this was, from the world she had just left, but such thoughts were unnecessary. What was necessary was recognition, appreciation, of the beauty before her. As she watched the carp, sipping her tea at intervals, a novice came silently to the pool and threw a handful of crumbs. The carp rose in a flurry of fins; a tiny splash broke the random song of the fountain. The novice retired.

The Master Adept spoke, his voice hardly louder than that splash. "It is what we identify as *lost* which brings us into concern, Adept Lunzie. When one knows that one owns nothing, nothing can be lost, and nothing mourned."

Her mind shied from that as from hot metal: instant rejection. He had never had a child, and they had had this discussion before.

"I am not speaking of your child," he said. "A mother's instinct is beyond training . . . so it must be. But the years you have lost, that you call yours: no one owns time, no one can claim even an instant."

Her heart steadied again. She could feel the heat in her face; it would have betrayed her. That shame made her blush again.

"Venerable Master . . . what I feel . . . is confusion."

It was safest to say what one felt, not what one thought. More than one tradition had gone into the concept of Discipline, and the Venerable Master had a Socratic ability to pursue a lame thought to its lair and finish it off. She dared to look at him; he was watching her with those bright black eyes in which no amusement twinkled. Not now.

"Confused? Do you perhaps believe that you *can* claim time as your own?"

"No, Venerable Master. But . . ."

She tried to sort out her thoughts. She had not seen him for so long . . . what would he know, and not know, about what had happened to her? How could he help if she did not explain everything? Part of her early training as a novice had been in organizing and relating memories and events. She called this up, and found herself reciting the long years' adventures calmly, softly, as if they had been written by someone else about a stranger's life.

He listened, not interrupting even by a shift of expression that might have affected her ability to recall and report what had happened. When she was through, he nodded once.

"So. I can understand your confusion, Adept Lunzie. You have been stretched and bent past the limits of your training. Yet you remained the supple reed; you did not break."

That was acceptance, and even praise. This time the warmth that rushed over her brought comfort to cramped limbs and to spaces of her mind still sore despite Cleansing the Stone. She had been sure he would say she had failed, that she was unfit to be an Adept.

"Our training," he was saying, "did not consider the peculiar strains of those with repeated temporal displacements, even though you brought the original problem to our attention. We should have foreseen the need, but . . ." he shrugged. "We are not gods, to know all we have not yet seen. Again, you have much to teach us, as we help you regain your balance."

"I live to learn, Venerable Master," said Lunzie, bowing her head.

"We learn by living; we live by learning."

She felt his hand on her head, the rare touch of approval, affirmation. When she looked up again, he was gone and she was alone in the pavilion with her thoughts.

Retraining, after that, was both more and less stressful than she had feared. Her pallet in the sleeping hut was comfortable enough after Ireta and she had never minded plain food. But it had been a long time since she'd actually done all the physical exercises; she spent the first days constantly sore and weary.

All the Instructors were perfectionists; there was only one right way (they reminded her) to make each block, each feint, each strike. Only one right way to sit, to kneel, to keep the inner center balanced. She had never been as good with the martial skills of Discipline; she had always thought them less fitting for a physician. But she had never been this bad. Finally one of them put her at rest, and folded herself down nearby.

"I sense either unwillingness or great resistance of the body, Lunzie. Can you explain?"

"Both, I think," Lunzie began slowly, letting her breathing slow. "As a healer, I'm committed to preserving health; this side of Discipline always seems a failure to me . . . something we haven't done right, that let things come to conflict. And then some physician—perhaps me, perhaps another— will have to work to heal what we break."

"That is the unwillingness," said the instructor. "What is the body's difficulty? Only that?"

"I'm not sure." Lunzie started to slump, and reminded herself to balance her spine properly. "I would like to think it is the many times in coldsleep—the long times, when I spent years in one position. Supposedly there's no aging, but there's such stiffness on waking. Perhaps it does something, some residual loss of flexibility."

The instructor said nothing for a long moment, her eyes half-closed. Lunzie relaxed, letting her sore muscles take the most comfortable length.

"For the unwillingness, you must speak to the Venerable Master," said the instructor finally. "For the body's resistance, you may be right—it may be the repeated coldsleep. We will try another approach on that, for a few days, and see what comes of it."

Another approach meant hours in hot and cold pools, swimming against artificial currents. Lunzie could feel her body stretching, loosening, then re-knitting itself into the confident, capable body she remembered, almost as if it had been a broken bone. Her conditioning included gymnastics, running, climbing, music, and finally—after several long conferences with the Venerable Master—renewed work with unarmed combat.

She would never be a figure of the Warrior, he had told her, but each aspect of Discipline had its place in every Adept, and she must accept the need to cause injury and even death, when failure meant the deaths of others.

But her dislike of conflict was not all they discussed. He had lived the years she had spent exiled in coldsleep; he remembered both her as she had been, and all she had missed of those years. He let her talk at length of her distress at the estrangements in her family, the guilt she felt for disliking some of her descendants and resenting their attitudes. About the pain of losing a lover, the fear that no relationship could ever be sustained. She told him about meeting Sassinak, and about the strains between them.

"She's the older one, really—she even said so—" her voice broke for an instant, and he insisted on hearing the whole conversation, every detail.

"That hurt you," he said afterwards. "You are older, you feel, and you want the respect naturally due to elders . . ." He let that trail away in a neutral tone.

"But I don't feel like an elder, either," Lunzie said, consciously relaxing her hands, which wanted to clamp into fists. "I feel . . . I don't know what I feel. I can't be young, it seems, or old: I'm suspended in life now just as much as when I was in coldsleep. I don't even know which child she is—did I see her and forget her? Is she one they never mentioned?"

"The leaf torn from the branch by wind," he said softly, smiling a little.

"Exactly."

"You must come to believe that the branch was no more yours than the wind is; you must come to see that we are each, in each moment, in the right place, the place from which all action and reflection come, and to which they go." He cocked his head, much like a bird. "What will you do if you must enter coldsleep again?"

She had not let herself think of that, forcing away the panic it brought with all the Discipline she could bring to bear. How had he known that she woke sweating some nights, sure that the terrifying numbness was once more spreading through her?

"I—I can't." She held her breath, stiff in every muscle, looking down and away from him. She heard the faintest sigh of breath.

"You cannot know that it will never happen." His voice was neutral.

"Not *again*—" It was as much plea as promise to herself; all the days of retraining might have been nothing for the rush of that emotion.

"I had hoped this would heal of itself," his voice said, musing. "But since it has not, we must confront it." A pause so long she almost looked up, and then he snapped, "Adept Lunzie!" and her eyes met his. "This is not beyond your strength or ability: this you will conquer. We cannot send you out still subject to such fears."

She wanted to protest, but knew it would do no good. The next several days tested her strength of will and body both: intense sessions of counseling, hours spent in a variety of cubicles resembling cold-sleep tanks of various types, even a couple of cold-sleep inductions, with the preliminary drugs taking her briefly into unconsciousness.

She thought at first she would simply go crazy, but the Venerable Master had been right: she could endure it, and come out sane. Valuable knowledge if she needed it, though she hoped she would not.

By the time her other instructors approved her skills, her mind had found a new balance. She could see her past uncertainties, her flurries of worry, her bouts with envy and guilt, as the struggles of a creature growing from one form to another. Most people had some emotional turmoil in their thirties; at least some of hers was probably just that: growing out of one stage of life. She had been that person; now she was someone else, someone who no longer envied Sassinak's power or Aygar's physical strength. Her life made sense to her, not as a tragic series of losses, but as challenges met, changes endured and even enjoyed.

The memory of her stuffier descendants no longer irritated her—poor darlings, she thought, they don't even know what fun they're missing—and Sassinak's potential for violence now seemed the appropriate foil for her own more pacific abilities. She could cherish Sassinak as a descendant, and respect her as an elder, at one and the same time, with a ruffle of amusement for the odd circumstance that made her both.

Her last sight of the Mountain was of that same quiet pool, that same boulder, the door opening now in the hands of another novice. She knew her own face expressed nothing but calm; inside she could feel her heart smiling, feel the excitement of another chance at life with all its difficulties.

Now the medical personnel in the corridors looked more like potential colleagues, and less like fortunate strangers who would never accept her. Lunzie checked into the Transient Physicians' Hostel at the first open terminal, and then entered the callcode the Venerable Master Adept had given her. The screen flashed briefly, then steadied as a line scrolled across it.

"Lunzie . . . good news. Level 7, Concourse B, 1300 tomorrow." And that was that, and she was on her way.

The Hostel, when she arrived at its door, gave her the clip to a single room with cube reader and datalink. She put her duffel on the single bed and touched the keypad. A menu of services available filled the wallscreen. She could find a partner for chess or sleep, purchase goods or information (to be included, with a service charge, in her hostel total), or roam the medical databases, all without leaving the room.

She was tempted to send a message to Sassinak; Fleetcom, the public access mail system for all Fleet personnel, would forward it. But that might bring attention they didn't want. Safer to wait. She had almost a full standard day before meeting someone (the Venerable Master had not said who) the next day at 1300. She would use that time to make predictable inquiries, things anyone would expect her to want to know.

She treated herself to a good meal at a cafe that occupied the space where, years before, she'd known a bar. The music now had a different sound, lots of chiming bells and some low woodwind behind a female trio. Back in her room, she fell asleep easily and woke without concern.

Level seven of Concourse B still sported the apricot striped walls that made Lunzie feel she had fallen into a layered dessert. Various names had been tried for this section, from Exotic Epidemiology to Nonstandard Colonial Medical Assistance. None had stuck; everyone called it (and still called it, she'd found out) the Oddball Corps. Its official designation, at the moment, was Variant Medical Concerns Analysis Division . . . not that anyone used it.

Lunzie presented her credentials at the front desk. Instead of the directions she expected, she heard a cheerful voice yelling down the corridor a moment later.

"Lunzie! The legendary Lunzie!" A big bearded man grinned as he advanced, his hands outstretched. She searched her memory and came up with nothing. Who was this? He went on. "We heard you were coming. Forty-three years, in this last coldsleep? And that makes how much altogether? We've got a lot of research we can do on you." His face fell slightly and he peered more closely at her. "You *do* remember me, don't you?"

She was about to say no, when a flicker of memory gave her the face of an enthusiastic teenager touring a hospital with a class. Now where had that been? She couldn't quite say . . . but he had been the most persistently curious in his group, asking questions long after his companions (and even his instructors) were bored. He had been pried loose only by the fifth reminder that their transport was leaving . . . *now.* She had no idea what his name was.

"You were younger," she said slowly, giving herself time to think. "I don't remember that beard."

His hands touched it. "Oh . . . yes. It does make a difference, I suppose. And it's been over forty years for you, even if most of that wasn't real time. I mean waketime. I was just so glad to see your name come up on the boards. I suppose you never knew that it was that hospital tour that got me into medicine, and beyond that into the Oddballs—"

"I'm glad," she said. What *was* his name? He had worn a big square nameplate that day; she could remember that it was green with black lettering, but not what the name was.

"Jerik," he said now, relieving her of that anxiety. "Doctor Jerik now, but Jerik to you, of course. I'm an epidemiologist, currently stranded in Admin because my boss is on leave."

He had the collar pin of an honor graduate and the second tiny chip of diamond which meant he was also an Adept. It was not something to speak of, but it meant he was not just out here blathering away for nothing. His pose of idle chatter and innocent enthusiasm was just that—a pose.

"You'll be wondering," he said, "why you were dragged into the Oddballs when you deserve a good long rest and chance to catch up on your education."

"Rather," said Lunzie. He must think the area was under surveillance, and it probably was. Only the Mountain would be certainly beyond anyone's ability to spy on.

"There are some interesting things going on—and you, with your experience of coldsleep, may be just the person we need. Of course, you will have to recertify . . ."

Lunzie grimaced. "I hate fast-tapes."

He was all sympathy. "I know. I hate them, too—it's like eating three meals in five minutes; your brain feels stuffed. But it's the only way, and unless you have two or three years to spare . . ."

"No. You're right. What will I need?"

What she would need, after 43 years out of date, was far more than Mayerd on Sassinak's ship had been able to give her. And she'd refused Mayerd's offer of fast-tape equipment. New surgical procedures, using new equipment: that meant not only fast-tape time, but actual in-the-OR work on "slushes," the gruesomely realistic androids used for surgical practice. New drugs, with all the attendant information on dosages, side effects, contraindications, and drug interferences. New theories of cognition that related to the coldsleep experience.

One of the neat things about her hop-skip-and-jump experiences, Lunzie realized partway through this retraining, was that it gave her an unusual overview of medical progress . . . and regress. She solved one diagnostic problem on the fourth day, pointing out that a mere 45 years ago, and two sectors away, that cluster of symptoms was called Galles Disease. It had been wiped out by a clever genetic patch, and had now reoccurred ("Probably random mutation," said the senior investigator with a sigh. "I should have thought of that") in an area where everyone had forgotten about it.

Differences between sectors, and between cultures within a sector, meant that what she learned might not be new in one place—or available in twenty others. Access to the best medical technology was at least as uneven as on Old Earth. Lunzie spent all her time in the fast-tape booths, or practicing procedures and taking the preliminary recertification exams. Basic and advanced life support, basic and advanced trauma first response, basic and advanced contagious disease techniques . . . her head would have spun if it could.

In her brief time "off," she tried to catch up with current research in her area, flicking through the computerized journal abstracts.

"What we really need is another team member for a trip to Diplo." Someone groaned, in the back of the room, and someone else shushed the groaner.

"Come on," the speaker said, half-angrily. "It's only a short tour, thirty days max."

"Because that's the medical limit," came a mutter.

"This comes up every year," the speaker said. "We have a contract pending; we have an obligation; whatever your personal views, the heavy-worlders on Diplo have significant medical problems which are still being researched."

"Not until you give us an allowance for G-damage."

Lunzie thought that was the same mutterer, someone a few seats to her left and behind.

"Pay and allowances are adjusted for local conditions," the speaker went on, staring fixedly at his notes. "This year's special topic is the effect of prolonged coldsleep on heavyworlder biochemistry, particularly the accumulation of calcium affecting cardiac function." He paused. Lunzie wondered when that topic had been assigned. Everyone would know, from her qualifications posted in the files, that she had special knowledge relevant to the research. But it would not do to show eagerness. The speaker went on. "We've already got a molecular biologist, and a cardiac physiologist—"

The names came up on the main room screen, along with their most recent publications. Very impressive, Lunzie thought to herself. Both Bias, the biologist, and Tailler, the cardiac physiologist, had published lead articles in good journals.

"Rehab medicine?" asked someone in back.

The speaker nodded. "If your Boards include a subspecialty rating in heavyworlder rehab, certainly. Clearly relevant to this year's special problem."

Another name went up on the screen, presumably the rehab specialist who'd spoken: Conigan, age 42, had published a textbook on heavyworlder rehabilitation after prolonged work undersea. Lunzie decided she'd waited long enough. What if someone else qualified for "her" slot?

"I've got a background in prolonged coldsleep, and some heavyworlder experience." Heads turned to look at her; Discipline kept her from flushing under that scrutiny. The speaker peered at what she assumed was her file on his podium screen. "Ah . . . Lunzie. Yes. I see you haven't yet taken your Boards recertification exam?"

"It's scheduled for three days from now." It had been scheduled for six months from now but Jerik had arranged for her to take the exam singly, ahead of time. "All the prelims are on file."

"Yes, they are. It's amazing you've caught up so fast, and your skills are well suited to this mission. Contingent on your passing your Boards, you're accepted for this assignment." He looked up, scanning the room for the next possible applicant.

The woman next to Lunzie nudged her.

"Are you sure you want to go to Diplo? I heard your last coldsleep was because heavyworlders went primitive."

Lunzie managed not to glare. She had not heard the rumors herself, but she'd known they would be flying around the medical and scientific community.

"I can't talk about it," she said, not untruthfully. "The case won't be tried for months, and until then—"

"Oh, I quite understand. I'm not prying, Doctor. It's just that *if* it was heavyworlders, I'm surprised you're signing up for Diplo."

Lunzie chuckled. "Well, there's this glitch in my pay records—"

The woman snorted. "There would be. Of course; I see. You'd think they could realize the last thing you need is worry about money, but the Feds have acute formitis."

"A bad case," Lunzie agreed.

With the others, she craned her head to see the last responder, a dark man whose specialty was heavyworlder genetics. From the heft of his shoulders, he might have heavyworlder genes of his own, she thought.

So it proved when the whole team met for briefing. Jarl was the smaller (and nonadapted) of twins born to a heavyworlder couple; he was fascinated by the unusual inheritance patterns of adaptation, and by the equally unusual inheritance patterns of tolerance or intolerance to coldsleep. Aside from his heavyworlder genes, he seemed quite normal, and Lunzie felt no uneasiness around him.

Bias, the volatile molecular biologist, was far more upsetting; he seemed ready to fly into pieces at any moment. Lunzie wondered how he would take the heavy gravity; he didn't look particularly athletic. Tailler, the cardiac physiologist, impressed Lunzie as a good team leader: stable, steady, but energetic, he would be easy to work with. She already knew, from a short bio at the foot of one of his papers, that he climbed mountains for recreation: the physical effort should be within his ability. Conigan, the rehab specialist, was a slender redheaded woman who reminded Lunzie of an older (but no less enthusiastic) Varian.

She was aware that she herself was the subject of just such curiosity and scrutiny. They would know little about her besides her file info: she had no friends or past associates they could question covertly. She wondered what they saw in her face, what they expected or worried about or hoped for. At least she had passed her Boards, and by a respectable margin, so Jerik had told her. She wondered, but did not ask, how he had gotten the actual raw scores, which supposedly no one ever saw.

And all the while, Bias outlined the project in excited phrases, pausing with his pointer aloft to see if they'd understood the last point. Lunzie made herself pay attention. Whatever information she could get for Sassinak and the trial aside, her team members deserved her best work.

By the time their ship came to the orbital station serving Diplo, they were all working easily together. Lunzie thought past the next few months, and Tanegli's trial, to hope that she would find such professional comraderie again. There were things you could not say to a cruiser captain, however dear to your heart she was, jokes she would never get, ideas beyond her scope. And here Lunzie had that kind of ease.

Chapter Three

"I did not need this." Sassinak waved the hardcopy of the Security-striped message at Dupaynil and Ford. "I've got things to do. We *all* have. And the last thing we need to do is waste time playing nursemaid to a senile conspirator." Things had gone too smoothly, she thought, when she'd sent Lunzie off. She should have expected some hitch to her plans.

Dupaynil had the suave expression she most disliked. "I beg your pardon, Commander?"

He could not be that suave unless he knew what was in the message: Ford, who clearly did not, looked worried.

"Orders," Sassinak said crisply. "New orders, sent with all applicable coding on the IFTL link. We are to transport the accused conspirator Tanegli and the alleged native-born Iretan Aygar to . . ." She paused, and watched them. Dupaynil merely waited, lips pursed; Ford spoke up.

"Sector HQ? Fleet HQ on Regg?"

"No. *Federation* Headquarters. For a full trial before and in the presence of the Federation High Council. We are responsible," and she glanced down at the message to check the precise wording, "responsible for the transportation and safe arrival of said prisoner, who shall be released to the custody of Council security forces only. The trial date has already been set, for a local date that translates to about eight standard months from now. Winter Assizes, as we were told before. Prisoner's counsel is given as Klepsin, Vigal, and Tollwin. And you know what that means."

"Pinky Vigal, Defender of the Innocent," said Dupaynil, almost chuckling. "That ought to make an exciting trial. You know, Commander, he can probably make you look like a planet pirate yourself, a villainous sort masquerading as a Fleet officer. Hmmm . . . you stole the uniform from Tanegli, bribed everyone else to testify against him."

"It's not funny," said Sassinak, glowering. She had never been one to follow the escapades of fashionable lawyers, but anyone in human space had heard of Pinky Vigal. It was another of the failings of civilian law, Sassinak thought, that someone everyone knew had done something could not be punished if a honeytongued defense counsel could convince even one member of a trial jury that some minute error had been made in procedure. Fleet had better methods.

"So," Ford broke in, clearly intending a distraction. "We're responsible for Tanegli until we get to Federation Central . . . and for Aygar as well? Why Aygar?"

"Witness for both sides, I suppose," Dupaynil said with a flourish of his hand. "Friendly to one, hostile to the other, but indispensable to both."

"*And* registered copies of all the testimony we took, and depositions from all bridge officers, and any other crew members having contact with the said Tanegli and Aygar," Sassinak continued to read. "Kipling's bunions! By now that's half the crew, the way Aygar's been roaming around. If I'd known . . ."

She knew from Ford's expression that she must look almost as angry as she felt. They would spend weeks getting in and out of the required transfer points for Federation Central, and then weeks being interviewed—*deposed*, she reminded herself—and no doubt Fleet Security would have its own band of interrogators there. In the meantime, the *Zaid-Dayan* would be sitting idle while the enemy continued its work. She would no doubt have umpteen thousand forms to fill out and sign: in multiple copies which had to be processed individually, rather than on computer, for security reasons.

She noticed that Dupaynil was watching her with alert interest. So he *had* read the message even before she'd seen it—which meant he had a tap on the IFTL link, or had somehow coerced one of her communications officers into peeling a copy to his quarters. What else did he know, or had he been told? She decided not to ask; he wouldn't tell her, and she'd just be angry when he refused.

"Dupaynil." The change in her tone surprised him; his smugness disappeared. "I want you to start finding out which crew Aygar has been in contact with. Marines, Wefts, officers, enlisted, everyone. You can have a clerk if you need one—"

"No . . . I can manage . . ." His voice was bemused; she felt a surge of glee that she was making him think.

"I suspect it's too late to restrict his contacts. And after all, we want him friendly to FSP policies. But if the crew know that they'll have to go through paperwork and interviews because they talk to him, some may pull back."

"Good idea . . . and I'd best get started." Dupaynil sketched a salute —to more than her rank, she was sure—and left.

Sassinak said nothing for a moment, engaging her own (surely still un-discovered?) privacy systems. Then she grinned at Ford.

"That *sneak*: he knew already."

"I thought so, too. But how?"

"He's Naval Intelligence—but I'm never sure with those types if he's Intelligence for someone else, or someones else, as well. The fact that he's planted his own devices—and too cleverly to reassure me of his ultimate aims —is distinctly unsettling because there's no telling *why* he's doing it. *I'm*—" and Sassinak pushed her thumb into her chest, grinning—"allowed to be that clever, but not my subordinates.

"At the moment, that's not the issue. Getting you away to find your dear great-aunt or whatever *is* the issue, because I don't want you tied up for the time this is going to take. We need information before that trial date." Sassinak pushed the orders over to Ford who noted the date and its conver-sion to Fleet standard notation on his personal handcomp. "If you can't find anything by then, be sure you're back to say so."

"But how can I leave when all—"

Sassinak hushed him with a gesture. "There are more tricks in that com shack than Dupaynil knows about. So far, he's the only one who knows that you were present when these orders arrived. And *he's* got priority orders he doesn't know about yet. But he soon will. Just follow my lead."

The bridge crew came to attention when Sassinak arrived, but she gave the helm to Ford and entered the communications alcove.

"Captain's orders," she said crisply to the officer on watch. "You re-ceived an IFTL a short time ago?"

"Yes, ma'am, to the captain's address with encryption."

Sassinak could not tell if the com officer's tension was normal or not. "The contents of that message require me to sit com watch myself for two hours." This was unusual, but not unheard of: sometimes extremely sensitive information was sent this way. "I expect incoming IFTL signals, encrypted, and by these orders," and she waved the paper, "only the ship's captain can receive them."

"Yes, ma'am. Will the captain need any assistance?"

Sassinak let herself glare, and the com officer vanished onto the bridge. What she was going to do was both illegal and dangerous . . . but so was what Dupaynil had done, and what the enemy had done. She logged onto the board and engaged her private comlink to the Ssli interface.

So far, normal procedure. But now . . . her fingers danced on the board, calling up the file of the original encrypted message. And there it was, the quadruple header code she had never forgotten, not in all the years. *Idiots*, she thought; they should have changed that long since, as she had changed from a naive ensign standing communications watch to an experienced and powerful ship captain.

With the right header code, it was easy to prepare an incoming message Dupaynil would have to believe was genuine. The other "incoming" message would be in regular Fleet fashion, Ford's detachment on "family compassionate leave" . . . but it would not arrive until Dupaynil was gone.

Where to send Dupaynil? Where would he be safely out of her way, and also, in his own mind, doing something reasonable? She wished she could send him to a Thek, preferably a large, old, very slow one . . . but that wouldn't work. Fleet Security had nothing to do with the pacifist Bronthins, or the Mrouxt.

Suddenly it came to her, and she fought back a broad grin which anyone glancing into the alcove might notice (why would the captain be grinning to herself in the com shack?): Ford would dig up dirt on the Paraden family's dealings, and Lunzie would find what she could on Diplo . . . and that, according to what they'd found on Ireta, left the alien Setis without an investigator. *That* would be Dupaynil's chore.

He had done a lot of diplomatic work, he'd said. He had bragged after dinner, once, about his ability to get along with any of the alien members of the Federation, and even said the Seti weren't as bad as everyone thought.

So, quickly, carefully, Sassinak wrote the orders. The Ssli had always shown her special considerations, above and beyond their usual shipboard duties. She owed her life to the sessile Ssli communications officer on her first tour of duty when Hssrho had located her in deep space after she'd had a "misadventure" in an evac pod. In gratitude she had always taken care to cultivate the Ssli communications officers on every other posting. Now she consulted the resident Ssli. She could not simply pretend that an IFTL had come in; the computer records would show it had not and Dupaynil probably had subverted computer security to some degree. But Dupaynil's actual shipboard experience was limited and Sassinak knew that he had never bothered to introduce himself to Dhrossh. Her favorite Wefts, such as Gelory, had mentioned in passing that Dupaynil's mind was not the right sort for direct contact. Whatever they meant by that.

The Ssli thought her scheme was delightful . . . an odd choice of adjective, Sassinak thought, and wondered if the speech synthesizer software was working correctly. She had never suspected the Ssli of any remotely human emotions. Ssli syntax tended toward the mathematical. But she entered her encrypted message, and the Ssli initiated IFTL communication with another Ssli on another Fleet vessel. Which one she would never know.

The Ssli, her own had informed her, felt no compunction about concealing such communications from human crew. Her own message bounced back, and appeared as a true incoming message on the computer and the board. Sassinak routed it to the decryption computer, peeled a copy for Dupaynil's file, and leaned out to call to the com watch officer, who had taken a seat on the bridge.

"Get me Dupaynil," she said, letting herself glower a bit.

Ford glanced at her but did not even let his brows rise. Dupaynil arrived in a suspiciously short time; this time Sassinak's glower was not faked at all.

"You," she said, pointing a finger at him. The rest of the bridge crew became very busy at their own boards. "You have an incoming IFTL, which not only requires decryption and states that I do not have access, but in addition to *that*, it carries initiation codes I remember all too well!"

He would have to know that, or he could find out—and perhaps her flare of anger would distract him from the unlikeliness of his own orders. At the moment, he looked confused, as well he might.

"This!" Sassinak pointed to the display she'd frozen onscreen. "The last time I saw that initiation code, that very one, in quad like that, someone smacked me over the head and dumped me in an evac pod. If you think you're going to do something like that, *Major*—take me out and take over my ship—you are very much mistaken!" She could hear the anger in her own voice, and the bridge was utterly silent.

"I . . . Commander Sassinak, I'm sorry, but I don't know what you're talking about. That code is known to me, yes—it's from the IG's office. But . . ."

"I don't like secrets on my ship, Dupaynil! I don't like junior officers receiving IFTL messages to which the captain is forbidden access. And encrypted messages at that. I don't like people going over my head to the IG's office. What's your gripe, eh?"

Dupaynil, she was sure, was not as upset as he looked. He was too smart by half. But he was responding to her obvious anger and had lost some of his gloss. "Commander, the IG's office might have reason to contact me about the Security work I've done here—if nothing else, about that—you know . . ." His voice lowered. Sassinak let herself calm down.

"I still don't like it," she grumbled, but softly. Someone smothered a cough, over in Weapons, and nearly choked from the effort. "All right. I see what you mean, and from what Lunzie said that whole thing was classified. Maybe there is a reason. But I don't like secrets. Not like this, at a time when we're all . . ." She let her voice trail away. Dupaynil's lids drooped slightly. Was he convinced? "Take your damned message, and unless you *like* causing me grief, tell me what's so important I can't even read it."

Dupaynil moved to the decryption computer and entered his password.

Sassinak turned to the communications watch officer, and said, "Take over. And make sure I know about any incoming or outgoing messages. From anyone." This last with a sidelong glance at Dupaynil.

The Security officer was staring at the screen as if it had grown tentacles; Sassinak controlled an impulse to laugh at him. He glanced at her, a shrewd, calculating look, and she spoke immediately.

"Well? Are you supposed to clap me in irons, or what?" He shook his head, and sighed.

"No, Commander, it's nothing like that. It is . . . odd. . . that is all. May we speak in your office? Privately?"

Sassinak nodded shortly and left the bridge with a final glower for everyone. She could feel the support of her crew—her *own* crew—like a warm blanket around her shoulders. In her office, she put her formal desk between herself and Dupaynil. His brows rose, recognizing that for what it was, and he sighed again.

"Captain, I swear to you . . ."

"Don't bother." Sassinak turned away, briefly, to glance at the hardcopy he offered her, then met his dark eyes squarely. "If you don't know what I'm talking about, then you don't—but I cannot ignore anything like that. It nearly cost me my life twenty years ago."

"I'm sorry. Truly sorry. But just as you received unwelcome orders a short while ago, I have now received unwelcome orders to leave this ship—unwelcome and even stranger than yours."

"Oh? And where are you supposed to go?" She saw Dupaynil wince at the unbending ice in that tone. She could care less, as long as she rid herself of a potential traitor.

"To the Seti—to the Sek of Fomalhaut, in fact. One of my past sins come to haunt me, I suppose. Apparently there's some kind of diplomatic

problem with the new human ambassador to the High Court, and I'm supposed to know someone who might be of assistance."

"But you can't," Sassinak said sharply. "You can't leave: we're all under
orders to proceed to Federation Central, you most of all. You were in on all of
it; your testimony . . ."

"Can be recorded, and will have to be. I'm sorry. Truly sorry, as I said,
but these orders take precedence. Have to." His finger tapped the authoriz-
ing seals and codes; in the labyrinthine regulations of Fleet and FSP, the IG's
signature outweighed even the Judge Advocate General's. "Besides, I might
still be of use to you. The Thek hinted that the Seti were involved, but they
had no solid data, or none they passed to us. That's something I can look
into, with my contacts in the Seti diplomatic subculture. They estimate the
assignment proper will take me only about six standard months; I can be back
in time to share what I've learned, and testify if called."

Sassinak heaved a dramatic sigh. "Well. I suppose, if you have to, you
have to. And maybe you *can* find something useful, although the Seti are the
least likeable bunch of bullies I've ever met."

"They do require careful handling," Dupaynil murmured, almost de-
murely.

Sassinak wondered what he was up to now. She did not trust him one
hairsbreadth. "Very well. Where are we supposed to drop you off?"

"It says your orders will be in shortly and I'm to leave at the next
transfer point. Wherever that is."

"Somebody's entirely too clever," Sassinak growled. She hoped she
hadn't been clever enough to trip herself with this—but so far Dupaynil
seemed convinced.

Just then the junior com officer tapped timidly on her door, and offered
a hardcopy of her second faked IFTL message, the one telling her to drop
out of FTL drive, and proceed to the nearest Fleet station. The nearest Fleet
station was a resupply center with only monthly tanker traffic and the occa-
sional escort or patrol craft dropping by. She remembered it well, from her
one previous visit fifteen years before. She showed Dupaynil the orders.

"Supply Center 64: says there's an escort in dock. You'll take that, I
imagine?" At his nod, she said, "I'll expect you back at 1500, to give your
deposition; we'll have the equipment set up by then, and an ETA for the
supply center."

The rest of that day Sassinak hardly dared look at Ford; she would have
burst out laughing. Dupaynil came back, gave his testimony while she asked
every question she could think of before she sent him off to pack his gear.

They popped out of FTL space within a few hours of the supply center.

Sassinak had already dispatched messages to it and the escort vessel (whose pilot had been planning an unauthorized three-day party with the supply center's crew). Escorts, not large enough to house a Ssli, were out of the IFTL links. Once aboard, Dupaynil would have only sublight ways of checking up on his orders.

Docking the *Zaid-Dayan* at the supply station was simple: the station had equipment to handle large transports of all shapes, and the small escort took up only a minute space at the far end of the station. Sassinak indulged herself, as she rarely could anymore, and brought the cruiser in herself, easing it to the gantry so gently that no one detected contact until the status lights changed color.

"Nice job!" said the station Dockmaster, a Weft. "We'll have air up in the tubes in a few minutes. Is your passenger ready to transfer?"

"Ready when you are."

Dupaynil would leave by one of the small hatches, an airlock on the second flight deck. Even with a Fleet facility, Sassinak didn't like opening up real interior space to a possible pressure loss. She glanced at Dupaynil, visible on one of the side screens, and flicked a switch to put him on-channel.

"They're airing up the tube. Sure you don't want a pressure suit?"

"No thank you."

He had already explained how he felt about pressure suits. Sassinak was tempted to teach him a lesson about that, but under the circumstances she wanted their parting to be as friendly as possible.

"Fine . . . we're standing by for your departure signal." She could see, in the monitor, the light above the hatch come on, flick twice, and steady to green.

"On my way," said Dupaynil. Then he paused, and faced the monitor-cam squarely. "Commander? I did *not* intend to cause you trouble and I have no idea what that initiation code means to you. You may not believe me, but I have no desire to see you hurt."

And I have a great desire to see your back going off my ship, thought Sassinak, but she smiled for his benefit. "I'd like to believe you, and if that's true, I hope we serve together again someday. Have a good trip. Don't let those Seti use you for nest padding."

When the status lights confirmed that Dupaynil was safely off the ship and into the station, Sassinak breathed a sigh of relief. *Now* she could tell Ford what she was up to—or enough for him to help her with the last of Dupaynil's maneuver. That involved a bit of straight talking to the escort captain, on the need for immediate departure, and the importance of keeping his mouth firmly shut. Sassinak kept the *Zaid-Dayan* linked to the station until the escort broke away.

"And just how did you manage *that*?" Ford had waited just long enough for her to engage her office's privacy circuits. Sassinak grinned at him. "And don't bother to look innocent," he went on. "I don't know how you did it, but you must have."

"Let's just say that someone who's spent her career on ships knows a bit more about them than a Security office rat."

"And you're not going to explain, eh?"

"Not entirely. Would you trust Dupaynil to have unclipped whatever bugs he's set out on this ship?"

"Mmm. I see."

"And you are smart enough to figure out everything you need to know. You can think about it while looking up your remarkable relative."

"But what about the depositions? I can't leave now!" His face changed expression suddenly. "Oh. The only one who knew about those orders is . . . Gods above, Captain, what did you *do*?"

"Used the resources available to make appropriate dispositions of personnel in a situation of extreme delicacy," said Sassinak crisply. "And that's all I'm going to say about it. Your assignment is to uncover whatever links you can between the suspect merchant families and planet piracy and the slave trade. On my orders, by my assessment that this need overrides any other orders you may have heard about."

"Ummm . . . yes, ma'am."

"Good. Dupaynil, meanwhile, is supposed to be investigating the Seti and their connection with all this nastiness. I have heard, from time to time, that the Seti expressed sympathy with the heavyworlders for having been the victims of genetic engineering. You remember that they believe all such activity is wrong and refuse any kind of bioengineering on their own behalf. They're also known to hate Wefts, although no one seems to know why, and the Wefts won't comment."

"I've never understood why the Seti came into the Federation at all," Ford said. He seemed glad enough of a detour.

"Let Dupaynil worry about that," Sassinak said. "Now, d'you think a direct call to your family will locate your great aunt?"

"No, probably not. Let me think. The family hears at least once a standard year at Homefaring, but that's five months away. And she travels, you know; she's supposed to have one of the most luxurious yachts in space. We might find her in one of the society papers."

"*Society* papers!"

Ford flushed. "She's that kind; I told you. Minor aristocracy, but considers herself well up there. Once we locate her, I can fake—I mean arrange—a message from the family to justify a visit."

Sassinak did not even know the names of the papers Ford called up on their next shift down into normal space. She glanced at the sheets as he passed them over: even in flat copy, the photographs fairly glittered with wealth. Women in jewels and glistening gowns, men in formal Court dress, ribbons streaming from one knee. The sumptuous interiors of "gracious homes" as they were called, homes that existed merely to show off their owners' wealth. Sassinak could not imagine actually sleeping in one of the beds shown, a "sculpted masterpiece" with a stream of moving water actually running through it. She could feel her lip curling.

"Ah! Here she is." Ford had his finger on the place. "Among the notable guests at the wedding—would you look at that so-called bride!—is my very own noble relative. Will travel on to participate in the Season at the usual Rainbow Arc events . . . which means she's somewhere between Zalaive and the Rainbow Arc. Permission to initiate search?"

"Go ahead." Sassinak was deep in a discussion of the reasons why cuulinda was destined to replace folsath as the newest sporting rage among the nobility. She hadn't heard of either, and the article didn't mention whether they were played with teams, animals, or computers. Ford busied himself at the terminal, checking Fleet's comprehensive database on vessel ownership and movement on the lowlink.

"Ah! She's en route to Colles, ETA two weeks, and there's a . . . Oh snarks!"

"A what?" asked Sassinak, looking up at his tone.

"Well. I can get to her by her next planetfall, but it means hitching a ride on a tanker-transport."

Sassinak grinned at him. Tankers had a reputation as bare-bones transportation, and they played out that game on visitors.

"It'll make the contrast all the greater." She looked at the route he'd found. "I'll cut your orders, get you on that patrol-class. Don't forget to arrange that family message somehow."

"I won't."

His routing didn't give them much time, but, with Lunzie and Dupaynil both out of the way, they enjoyed a last festive evening in Sassinak's cabin. Then he was gone, and Sassinak had the final planning to do as they approached the crowded inner sector of the Federation.

* * *

She wondered how Aygar would react to the publicity and culture shock of FedCentral. He had been using the data banks on the *Zaid-Dayan* several hours a day. Ford kept a record of his access. He'd talked to both Marines and Fleet enlisted personnel and word of that trickled back to Sassinak by channels she doubted Aygar knew about. He had asked to take some of the basic achievement tests, to gauge for himself where he stood educationally. Sassinak had given permission, even though Dr. Mayerd thought "the boy," as she called him, should have professional advice.

The test results lay in the computer files. Sassinak had not accessed them, out of respect for the little privacy Aygar had, but from his demeanor he seemed well pleased with himself. She was less certain.

He was a striking young man, attractive if you liked muscles and regular features, and she admitted to herself that she did. But except for that subtle sense of rivalry with Lunzie, she would not have been drawn to him. She liked men of experience, men with whom she could share her broad background. Fleet officers of her own rank, or near it. It was all very well to impress youngsters like that ensign Timran. No woman minded starry-eyed boys as long as they stayed respectful. But Aygar did not fit that category, or any other.

"Commander? Central Docks wants a word."

That brought her out of her reverie, and across the passage onto the bridge. She had never brought a ship in to Federation Central's Docking Station before. Few did; Fleet protected the center of Federation government services, but was not entirely welcome here in force. Some races, and some humans, feared military rebellion and takeover. Hence the slow approach, dropping to sublight drive well outside the system, zigging and zagging (at high cost in fuel and time) to make unhandy checkpoints where defense satellites scrutinized their appearance and orders.

"Commander Sassinak, FSP cruiser *Zaid-Dayan*," said Sassinak.

"Ah . . . Commander . . . ah . . . procedures for securing armament, as required by the Federation for all incoming warships, must be complete before your vessel passes the outer shell."

Sassinak frowned, catching Arly's eye. The *Zaid-Dayan* could, in fact, take on most planetary defenses; she could understand why the more nervous members of the Federation would not want a human-crewed, fully armed heavy cruiser over their heads. But her trust in Federation Security right now was severely limited. She did not want her ship vulnerable.

"Securing," she said, with a nod to Arly.

Arly was scowling, but more with concentration than discontent. They had already discussed what to do; it remained to see if it would work. As a technical problem, Sassinak thought, watching Arly's hands rove her control board, it was interesting.

The Federation had only one telepathic race, the Wefts. Since the Wefts usually got along with humans, and had nothing to gain by disarming Fleet ships, any Wefts were unlikely to complain. The Seti would certainly complain of anything they recognized, and the pacifist members of the Federation, the Bronthin, would drop their foals if they knew. But would they know? Would they consider weaponry the same way Sassinak and Arly did?

The more obvious armament, items specified in the ship's Fleet classification, had to be secured. In this context, that meant control circuits patched out, projectile weapons unloaded and projectiles secured in locked compartments, power detached from EM projectors and opticals. A FedCentral In-system Security team would be aboard, guarding access to these areas, to prevent anyone from launching a missile, or frying something with a laser.

But the *Zaid-Dayan*'s power did not reside only in its named armaments. The most dangerous weapon you will ever control, one of her instructors had said back in the Academy, is right here: between your ears. The weapons you can see, or hold in your hand, are only chunks of metal and plastic.

Arly and Sassinak together had worked out ways of bypassing the patchouts, producing readouts that looked clean, while the systems involved still functioned. Not the projectiles. Someone could look and actually see whether or not a launcher had anything in the tube. But the EM and opticals, and the locks on the missile and ammunitions storage bins, could appear to be locked.

"Admiral Coromell's office," said Sassinak, facing the ident screen squarely. She had no idea where on this planet the Admiral would be, but the comcomp would take care of that. Surely there was only one Admiral Coromell at this time.

"Admiral Coromell's office, Lieutenant. Commander Dallish speaking." Dallish looked like most Lieutenant Commanders stuck with shore duty: slightly bored but wary. When he'd had a moment to take in Sassinak's rank, his eyes brightened. "Commander Sassinak! A pleasure, ma'am. We've heard about your exciting tour!"

Sassinak let herself smile. She should have realized that, of course, rumor would have spread so far. Fleet kept no secrets from itself. "Not entirely my idea. Is the Admiral available?"

Dallish looked genuinely disappointed. "No, Commander, he's not.

He's gone rhuch hunting over on Six and won't be back for several weeks Standard. You could go and—"

Sassinak shook her head. "No, worse luck. Orders say to deliver my prisoner and stand by for pre-trial depositions and hearings."

"Kipling's copper corns! Sorry, Commander. That's too bad. This is no port for a cruiser."

"Don't I know it! Look, is there anywhere I can give leave to the crew who aren't involved? Someplace they can have a good time and not get into too much trouble?" She did not miss the change in Dallish's expression, a sudden cool wariness. Had she caused it, or something in his office outside the scan area?

"Commander, perhaps I'd better come aboard, and you can give me your message for Admiral Coromell in person."

Perfectly correct, perfectly formal, and completely wrong: she had said nothing yet about any message. Sassinak's experienced hackles rose. "Fine," she said. "What time shall we expect you?"

"Oh . . . sixteen hundred Fleet Standard; that's twenty-three fifty local."

Late, in other words. Late enough Fleet time that he wouldn't be going back to the Admiral's office afterwards; very late in local time.

"Very well. Fleet shuttle, or . . ."

"Federation Insystem Security shuttle, Commander. Fleet has no dedicated planetary shuttles."

Oho, Sassinak thought. So Fleet personnel onplanet are isolated unless Security lets them fly? She asked for, and got, an identification profile, and signed off. When she looked around, her bridge crew had clearly been listening.

"I don't like that," she said to Arly. "If—when—I go downside, I'll want one of our shuttles available, just in case."

Arly nodded, eyes twinkling. Sassinak knew she was thinking of the last shuttle expedition. And young Timran's unexpectedly lucky rashness.

"Weapons systems lockdown is supposed to include shuttle lockdown," Arly reminded her.

Sassinak did not bother to answer; Arly had had her orders. They understood each other. She hoped an unauthorized shuttle flight would not be necessary. But if it was, she trusted that Arly would arrange it somehow.

Lieutenant Commander Dallish, when he appeared in her office shortly after debarking from the Security shuttle, apologized for his earlier circumlocutions.

"The Admiral told me he considers you in a unique position to provide evidence against the planet pirates," he said. "For that reason, he warned me to take every precaution if you contacted his office. I don't really think that anyone there is a traitor, but with that much traffic . . . and one of them a Council bureaucrat . . . I decided not to take chances."

"Very wise," said Sassinak.

In person he looked just as he had on the screen: perhaps five years younger than she, professional without being stuffy, obviously intelligent.

"You asked about liberty for your crew. Frankly, you could not be in a worse place, particularly right now. You know the Grand Council's in session this year?"

Sassinak hated to admit that she had only the vaguest idea how the Federation Grand Council actually scheduled its work, and gave a noncommittal response. Dallish went on as if she'd said something intelligent.

"All the work gets done in the preliminary Section meetings, of course: the Grand Council's mostly a formality. But it does overlap the Winter Assizes; a convenience for delegates when a major intercultural case is on the schedule. As it is now. And that means the hotels are already filling up—yes, months early—with delegations from every member. Support staff arriving early. Your crew, since they've been involved in the case, will of course have to be debriefed by Fleet Intelligence *and* Federation Security. And if they go onplanet after that, they'll be harassed by the newsmedia."

Sassinak frowned. "Well, they can't stay locked up in the ship the entire time. We're not going anywhere and there's not enough to do." In the back of her mind, she was running over all the miserable long-hour chores that she could assign, but with the weapons systems locked, and flight decks supposedly off limits, nothing but cleaning the whole environmental system with toothbrushes would keep everyone busy.

"My advice, Captain, would be to see if those who've been deposed, and whose testimony is at best minor, couldn't be released to go on long liberty over on Six. That's a recreational reserve: hunting, fishing, sailing, a few good casinos. Fleet has a lodge in the mountains, too. They'd have to go by civilian carrier, but at least they'd be out of your hair."

"I don't like splitting my crew." Without calling up the figures, she couldn't be sure just how far away Six was: days of travel, anyway, on a civilian insystem ferry, perhaps more. If something did happen . . . She shut that line of thought down. Better to clean the whole environmental system with toothbrushes. Preparedness, she'd noticed, tended to keep trouble from happening. And there were worse problems than boredom.

Chapter Four

"Darling boy!" Auntie Q, Ford thought, was the archetypal spoiled rich widow. She had sparkling jewels on every exposed inch of flesh: rings, brace-lets, armlets, necklaces, earrings, and even a ruby implanted between her eyes. He hoped it was a ruby, and not a Blindeye, a medjewel. "You can't know how I've longed to meet you!" Auntie Q also had the voice his father had warned him about. Already he could feel his spine softening into an ingratiating curve.

"I'm so glad, too," he managed.

He hoped it sounded sincere. It had better. He'd spent a lot of time and money tracking Auntie Q down. Most of his immediate family had intention-ally lost her address and her solicitors were not about to give her yacht's private comcode to a mere great-nephew by marriage serving on a Fleet cruiser. He had finally had to go through Cousin Chalbert, a harrowing inquisition which had started with an innocent enough question, "But *why* do you want to see her? Are you short of funds, or anything like that?" and ended up with him confessing every venial and mortal sin he had ever com-mitted.

Then he'd had to endure that ride on a tank-hauler, whose bridge crew seemed delighted to make things tough for someone off a cruiser. They seemed to think that cruiser crews lived in obscene luxury and had all the glory as well. Ford was willing to admit that hauling supplies was less thrilling than chasing pirates, but by the third day he was tired of being dumped on for the luxuries he'd never actually enjoyed.

Auntie Q gave him a glance that suggested she had all oars in the water, and turned to speak into a grill. "Sam, my great-nephew arrived after all. So we'll be three for dinner and I want your very best."

"Yes, ma'am," came the reply.

Ford wished he had a way out, and knew he hadn't. The tank-hauler's crew had insisted he share their mess and his stomach was still rebelling.

"You did bring dress things, didn't you?" asked Auntie Q, giving Ford another sharp look.

But he'd been warned. Some of his outlay had been for the clothes which Auntie Q expected any gentleman to have at hand.

"Of course . . . although they may be a little out of date . . ."

She beamed at him. "Not at all, dear. Men's clothes don't go out of date like that. All this nonsense of which leg to tie the ribbons on. That's ridiculous. Black tie, dear, since no one's visiting."

Auntie Q's favorite era of male dress had been thirty years back: a revival of 19th century Old Earth European. Ford thought it was ridiculous, but then all dress clothes were, and were probably intended to be. Fleet taught you to wear anything and get the job done. He thought of that, checking himself in the mirror in his vast stateroom. It was as big as Sassinak's *Zaid-Dayans* tateroom and office combined, full of furniture as costly as her desk. His black tie, crisply correct, fitted between stiffly white collar points. Studs held the stiff front panels of his shirt together (buttons were pedestrian, daytime wear) and cufflinks held his cuffs. It was utterly ridiculous and he could not keep from grinning at himself. He shrugged on the close-fitting dinner jacket. Like his dress uniform, it showed off broad shoulders and a lean waist (if you had them) or an expanse of white shirt, if you did not. He already wore the slim black trousers, the patent-leather shoes. He looked, to himself, like a caricature of a Victorian dandy.

A face appeared in the mirror behind him: haughty, willful, her graying hair piled high in elaborate puffs and curls, a diamond choker around her wattled neck. Her gown, draped artfully to suggest what she no longer had to display, was a shimmering mass of black shot with silver-gray. From the top of her hairdo three great quills stuck up, quivering in shades of green and silver. Ford blinked. Surely they weren't *really*. . . ?

She winked at him, and he had to grin back. "Yes they are, dearie," she said. "Ryxi tailfeathers, every one, and you shall hear how I came by them."

Impossibly, this visit was going to be fun. No wonder his father had been overwhelmed; no male under thirty-five would stand a chance. Ford swept her a bow, which she received as her due, and offered his arm. Her hand on his was light but firm; she guided him unobtrusively to her dining room.

Three for dinner meant Ford himself, Auntie Q, and her "companion," introduced as Madame Flaubert. Ford's excellent education reminded him of all possible associations, and his Fleet-honed suspicions quivered. Madame Flaubert had excruciatingly red hair, a bosom even more ample than Auntie Q, and an ornate brooch large enough to conceal a small missile launcher. The two women exchanged raised eyebrows and significant nods and shrugs while Ford attempted to pretend he didn't notice. Then Madame Flaubert leaned over and laid her hand on Ford's. He managed not to flinch.

"You are Lady Quesada'a great-great-nephew?" Her voice was husky, with a resonance that suggested she might have been trained as a singer.

"Only by courtesy," said Ford smoothly, with a smiling nod to Auntie Q. "The relationship is by marriage, not by blood, on my father's side."

"I told you that, Seraphine," his aunt said, almost sharply.

"I'm sorry, but you know my mind wanders." Ford could not decide if the menace that weighted those words was intentional or accidental. But his aunt sat up straighter; she knew something about it. Madame Flaubert smiled at Ford, an obviously contrived smile. "Your aunt will not have told you, perhaps, that I am her spiritual advisor."

Despite himself, his eyes widened and shifted to his aunt's face. Two spots of color had come out on her cheeks. They faded slowly as he watched. Madame Flaubert pressed his hand again to get his attention, and he forced himself to meet her gaze.

"You do not believe in spirit guides? No. I see you are a *practical* young man, and I suppose your . . . Fleet . . . does not encourage a spiritual nature."

Ford tried to think of something innocuous to say. Of all the things he had thought about coming to meet his notorious Auntie Q, spiritualism had not entered his mind. Madame Flaubert finally patted his hand, as one would pat a child who had just proven a disappointment, and smiled sadly.

"Whether you believe or not, my dear, is of little consequence as long as your heart is filled with purity. But for you, for a man who makes his living by war, I see trouble ahead for you, if you do not seek a higher road." Her hand fell from his heavily, with a little thump on the table, and she lay back in her chair, eyes closed. Ford glanced at his aunt, who was sitting bolt upright, her lips folded tightly. She said nothing, staring past him down the table, until

Madame Flaubert moaned, sat up, and (as Ford by this time expected) said, "Oh! Did I say something?"

"Later, Seraphine." Auntie Q lifted the crystal bell and, in response to its delicate ring, a uniformed servant entered with a tray of food.

Whatever else Auntie Q had, Ford thought later that evening, she had a miracle of a cook. He was sure it was not just the contrast with the supply hauler's mess: he had eaten well enough on the *Zaid-Dayan*, and at plenty of elegant restaurants in several Sectors. No, this was special, a level of cuisine he had never even imagined. Nothing looked like what it was, or tasted the way he thought it would, and it all made "good" or "delicious" into inadequate words. If only his unsteady stomach had not suffered through the tanker crew's cookery, he'd have been in culinary heaven.

Conversation, on the other hand, was limited. Madame Flaubert kept giving Ford meaningful looks, but said nothing except to ask for the return of certain dishes. Spiritual advising was evidently hungry work; she ate twice as much as Auntie Q, and even more than Ford. Auntie Q asked Ford perfunctory questions about his family, and was satisfied with the barest outline of answers. He had the feeling that normally she'd want to know what color stockings his sister's bridesmaids had worn at her wedding, and who had given what gift, but something was distracting her. Suddenly, while Madame Flaubert still had a mouthful of food, Auntie Q pushed back her chair.

"We shall retire," she said, "while you enjoy your port."

Madame Flaubert flushed, swallowed gracelessly but without choking, and stood. Ford was already on his feet, and bowed them out. Port? After clearing away, the servant had returned, carrying a tray with bottle, glass, and a box of cigars. Ford eyed them. He did not smoke, and everything he'd read about cigars warned him not to start now. The port was something else. Would it settle his stomach or make things worse? And how long was he supposed to wait before rejoining the ladies? For that matter, what *did* the ladies do while waiting for the gentleman to finish his port?

He took a cautious sip, and smiled in spite of himself. Wherever Auntie Q had found this, it was grand stuff for a stomach-ache, warming all the way down. He stretched his legs beneath the table and tried to imagine himself lord of all he surveyed. With the exception of Auntie Q, who would rule whatever domain she happened to be in.

After a time, the same servant appeared to take away the tray, and direct Ford to "Madame's drawing room." Originally a *withdrawing* room, Ford recalled, to which the ladies withdrew while the menfolk made noise and rude smells with their cigars.

* * *

His aunt's drawing room was furnished with more restraint than Ford would have expected. A small instrument with black and white keys, reversed from the usual, and too small for a piano. Ford wondered what it was, but did not ask. Several elegant but sturdy chairs, each different. A low table of some remarkable wood, sawn across knots and knurls to show the intricate graining. A single tall cabinet, its polished doors closed, and two graceful etchings on the walls but none of the cluttered knick-knacks her other mannerisms had suggested.

Madame Flaubert lounged in a brocaded armchair, a pose he suspected of concealing more tension than she would admit. She fondled a furry shape he gradually recognized as a dog of some sort. Its coat had been brushed into fanciful whirls, and it had a jeweled collar around its tiny neck. Two bright black eyes glittered at him, and it gave one minute yip before subsiding into Madame Flaubert's ample lap. His aunt, on the contrary, sat upright before a tapestry frame.

"I remember your father," Auntie Q said. "Hardly more than a boy, he was then. Seemed afraid of me, for some reason. Very stiff."

Ford gave her the smile that had worked with other women. "If I'd been a boy, you'd have frightened me."

"I doubt that." She snipped the needle free and threaded a length of blue. "I know what your side of the family thinks of me. Too rich to be reasonable, too old to know what she's doing, troublesome. Isn't that right?" Her eye on him was as sharp as her needle's point.

Ford grinned and shrugged. "Spoiled, overbearing, arrogant, and tiresome, actually. As you, without doubt, already know."

She flashed a smile at him. "Thank you, my dear. Honesty's best between relatives, even when, as so often, it is inconvenient elsewhere. Now we know where we stand, don't we? You didn't come to see a spoiled, overbearing, arrogant, tiresome old lady for the fun of it."

"Not for the fun of it, no." Ford let himself frown. "It was actually curiosity."

"Oh?"

"To see if you were as bad as they said. To see if you were as sick and miserable as *you* said. To see what kind of woman could have married into both Santon and Paraden and then gotten free of them."

"And now?"

"To see what kind of woman would wear Ryxi tailfeathers to dinner. How could anyone resist *that*?"

"I can't tell you what you want to know," she said, sombre for an instant. "I can't tell you why. But, never mind, I can tell you about the Ryxi."

Ford was not surprised to notice that Madame Flaubert was back in the room, cooing to her dog, which had spent the interim curled on her chair.

"Even the Ryxi are fellow beings searching for the light," said Madame Flaubert. "Ridicule damages the scoffer . . ."

"I'm not scoffing," said Auntie Q tartly. "I'm merely telling Ford where I got these feathers."

She plunged into the tale without looking at Madame Flaubert again; her voice trembled at first, then steadied. Ford listened, amused by the story. He could have predicted it, what a high-spirited rich young wife might do at one of the fancy balls when her "incorrigibly stuffy" husband tried to insist that she be discreet. Discretion, quite clearly, had never been one of Auntie Q's strong points. He could almost see her younger (no doubt beautiful) self, capering in mock courtship with a Ryxi in diplomatic service . . . a Ryxi who had let himself get overexcited, who had plucked the jeweled pin from her turban, and crowed (as Ryxi sometimes did, when they forgot themselves).

He could imagine her shock, her desire to do something outrageous in return. When the Ryxi had gone into the final whirling spin of the mating dance, she had yanked hard on his tailfeathers. By the time the whirling Ryxi could stop, screeching with mingled pain and humiliation, she had run away, safely hidden by her own wild crowd. Ford glanced at Madame Flaubert, whose mouth was pinched into a moue of disgust. He could almost hear her mental comment: *vulgar*. Ford himself agreed, but not with any intensity.

Most of what he knew about the wealthy and powerful he considered vulgar, but it didn't bother him. He certainly didn't bother about the degrees of vulgarity they might assign to one another's actions. Tenuous as the family connection might be, he would pick Auntie Q over Madame Flaubert anytime. His aunt had finished her story, with a challenging, almost defiant lift of her chin. He could imagine her as a spoiled child, when she would have had dimples beside her mouth. He grinned as much at the memory as at her story.

"Didn't he file a protest?" asked Ford.

His aunt bridled. "Of course he did. But I had filed a protest, too. Because he still had my jewel and he'd made a public nuisance of himself by losing control and going into the mating sequence. It's quite unmistakable even if you've never seen it."

"I have." Ford fought to keep his voice under control. It must have been the spectacle of the year, he thought to himself.

"So there was a lot of buzzing around. My husband's attorneys got involved and eventually everyone withdrew charges. The Ryxi ambassador himself sent a note of apology. Everyone insisted I do the same. But both of us kept our trophies. I had to agree not to display them *then*—not in public, you know—but that was years back, and this is my own private yacht."

It sounded as if she expected an argument; another glance at Madame Flaubert suggested with whom. Ford felt protective, but realized that Auntie Q expected (and trained) her menfolk to feel protective.

"It's a wonderful story," he said, quite honestly. "I wish I'd been there to see it." He meant that, too. Formal diplomatic functions with multiple races were usually painfully dull, kept so by everyone's attempts not to break another culture's rules of etiquette. Fleet officers stuck with attendance expected to spend long hours standing politely listening to civilian complaints while all the good-looking persons of opposite sex enjoyed themselves across a crowded dance floor. He remembered Sassinak telling him about a little excitement once, but that was all.

His aunt leaned over and touched his cheek. "You'd have enjoyed it, I can tell. You might even have helped me."

"Of course I would."

His stomach rumbled, loudly and insistently, and he felt himself flush. His aunt ignored the unmentionable noise, turning instead to Madame Flaubert, who was staring at Ford's midsection as if she could see into it.

"Seraphine, perhaps you could find the cube with the newsstories from that event?" Her tone made it more command than request; Madame Flaubert almost jumped, but nodded quickly and set her lapdog back down.

"Of course."

But even as she rose to comply, Ford's stomach clenched, and he realized he was about to be sick. He felt cold, clammy, and his vision narrowed.

"Excuse me, please," he said, between gritted teeth.

Auntie Q glanced at him politely, then stiffened. "You've gone quite green," she said. "Are you ill?"

Another pang twisted him, and he barely whispered, "Something I ate on the tanker, perhaps."

"Of course. I'll have Sam find you some medicine." She rose, as imperious as she had been after dinner. "Come, Seraphine."

They swept out as Ford groped his way to the door. He was perversely irritated that she had seen him lose control, and at the same time that she had left him to find his own way back to his stateroom. He didn't want to throw up on her elegant silver and rose carpet, but if he had to wander far. . . .

He had hardly taken a few steps down the corridor when a strongly-built man in chef's whites (another uniform unchanged through the centuries) grasped him under the arm and helped him swiftly back to his quarters.

He had been very thoroughly sick in the bathroom, losing with regret that delicious dinner, hardly noticing the silent, efficient help of the cook. When he regained his sense of balance, he was tucked into bed, his dress clothes draped across a chair, and the cold clamminess had passed into a burning fever and aching joints. What a beginning to a social inquiry, he thought, and then lapsed into unrestful sleep.

He woke to a foul taste in his mouth, the sour smell of sickness, and the suspicion that something was very wrong indeed. He had had bad dreams, full of dire symbolism (a *black* Ryxi dancing around his aunt's casket waving her two stolen plumes in macabre triumph? Commander Sassinak handing him a shining medal that turned into a smoking fuse when he pinned it to his uniform? A scaly, clawed hand tossing a handful of Fleet vessels, including the *Zaid-Dayan*, like dice onto a playing board whose pieces were planets and suns?).

He was quite sure that Madame Flaubert could "explain" them all, in ways that would make him responsible if he didn't reform, but he felt too weak to reform. Even to get up. Someone tapped on his door, and he croaked a weak answer.

"Sorry, sir, to be so late with breakfast."

It was the man in white, the cook. Sam, he remembered. He had not expected anyone, but if he'd thought, he'd have expected the servant who served dinner. Sam carried a covered tray; Ford thought it probably smelled delicious, but whatever it was he didn't want it. He shook his head, but Sam brought it nearer anyway, and set it on a folding table he had had in his other hand.

"You're still not well. I can see that." Off came the tray cover, revealing a small plate with crisp slices of toast, small glasses of fruit juice and water, and a tiny cut-glass pillbox. "This may not sit well, but at least it'll give me an idea what to try next . . ."

"I don't want anything." That came out in a hoarse voice he hardly recognized for his own. "Something on the tanker . . ."

"Well, I didn't think it came out of *my* kitchen." That barely missed smugness, the certainty of a master craftsman. "Did you get a look in that tanker's galley?" Sam held out the glass of water, and Ford sipped it, hoping to lose the taste in his mouth. It eased the dryness in his throat, at least.

"They told me, boasted in fact, that they didn't have a galley. Cooked their own food, mostly just heated up whatever came out of the synthesizer."

"And didn't clean the synthesizer coils often enough, I daresay. It's not easy to make great meals from basic synth, but it doesn't have to be sickening, either." As he spoke, Sam offered the toast, but Ford shook his head again.

"Just the water, thanks. Sorry to cause you any inconvenience." Which was a mild way of apologizing for the night before, when he had done more than cause inconvenience. And what was he going to do now? In Auntie Q's circle, he was sure that one did not inflict one's illnesses on hosts. But he had no place to go. The *Zaid-Dayan* was on her way to FedCentral; the nearest Fleet facility was at least a month's travel away, even if the yacht was headed that direction, which it wasn't.

"Not at all, sir." Sam had tidied away the toast, replacing the tray's cover, while leaving the cold water on his bedside table. Ford wished he would go away soon. He no longer felt nauseated, but he could tell he was far from well. "Bowers will be in later, to help you with your bath. I will inform Madame that you are still indisposed; she inquired, of course."

"Of course," Ford murmured.

"She regrets that her personal physician is presently on vacation, but when we reach our destination, she will be able to obtain professional assistance for you from the local community."

"I shall hope not to need it by then." That had a double meaning, he realized after it came out. The cook—not quite what he would have expected from Auntie Q's cook, barring the expertise—smiled at him.

"Taking that the best way, sir, I hope not, too. We do have a fair assortment of medicines, if you're prone to self-medicate?"

"No thanks. I'll wait it out. These things never last long."

At last the cook was standing, tray in hand, giving a last smile as he went out the door. Ford sagged back against his pillows. What a bad start to his investigation! He was sure that Auntie Q liked him . . . that she would have told him all about her connection to the Paradens . . . but she would not be the sort to waste her time nursing a nastily sick invalid. He hoped the virus or whatever it was would be as brief as most such illnesses. Leaving aside his mission, he wanted to try more of Sam's marvelous cooking.

Two days later, after surviving a light breakfast with no aftershocks, he made his way to the dining room, once more clad in the formal daytime dress of a nineteenth century European. (He thought it was European—something

Old Earth, and the Europeans had been dominant that century.) Auntie Q
had sent him a couple of ancient books (real books, with paper leaves) for
amusement, had inquired twice daily about his welfare, but otherwise left
him alone. He had to admit it was better than having someone hovering,
whose feelings he would have had to respect.

Auntie Q greeted him with restrained affection; Madame Flaubert inquired volubly about his symptoms until Auntie Q raised a commanding
hand.

"Really, Seraphine! I'm sure dear Ford doesn't wish to discuss his shaky
inner organs, and frankly I have no interest in them. Certainly not before a
meal." Madame Flaubert subsided, more or less, but commented that Ford's
aura seemed streaky.

Luncheon, despite this, was another culinary masterpiece. Ford savored
every bite, aware that Sam had done a great deal with color and texture,
while keeping the contents easy on a healing stomach. Auntie Q led the
conversation to curiosities of collecting, something Ford knew nothing about.
He let her wrangle amiably with Madame Flaubert over the likelihood that a
certain urn in the collection of the Tsing family was a genuine Wedgwood,
from Old Earth, or whether it was (Madame Flaubert's contention) one of
the excellent reproductions made on Gaehshin, in the first century of that
colony.

They came up for air with dessert, as Madame Flaubert passed Ford a
tray of pastries and said, "But surely we're boring you . . . unless this
touches your fancy?"

Ford took the pastry nearest him, hoping from the leak of rich purple
that it might be filled with dilberries, his favorite. Madame Flaubert retrieved the plate, and set it aside; his aunt, he noticed, was dipping into a
bowl of something yellow. He bit into the flaky pastry, finding his hope
fulfilled, and swallowed before he answered.

"I'm never bored hearing about new things, although I confess you lost
me back where you were arguing about pressed or carved ornament."

As he had half-hoped, his aunt broke in with a quick lecture on the
difference and why it was relevant to their argument. When she wanted, she
could be concise, direct, and remarkably shrewd. No fool, and no spoiled
idler, he thought to himself. *If she appears that way, it's because she wants to
—because it works for her.* Except for the two hours that Auntie Q spent
lying down "restoring my youth," they spent the afternoon in the kind of
family gossip they'd missed the first night. Auntie Q had kept up with all the
far-flung twigs of her family tree, many of them unknown to Ford, including
the careers and marriages of Ford's own sibs and first cousins. She thought his

brother Asmel was an idiot for leaving a good job at Prime Labs to try his fortune raising liesel fur; Ford agreed. She insisted that his sister Tara had been right to marry that bank clerk, although Ford felt she should have finished graduate school first.

"You don't understand," Auntie Q said for the third time, and this time explained in detail. "That young man is the collateral cousin of Maurice Quen Chang; he was a bank clerk when Tara married him but he won't be one in ten years. Maurice is by far the shrewdest investor in that family. He will end with control of two key industries in the Cordade Cluster. Didn't your sister explain?"

"I didn't see her; I got this in the mails, from Mother."

"Ah yes. Your mother is a dear person; my old friend Arielle knew her as a girl, you know. Before she married your father. Very upright, Arielle said, and not at all inclined to play social games, but charming in a quiet way." Ford thought that was a fair description of his mother, although it left out her intelligence, her wit, and her considerable personal beauty. He had inherited her smooth bronze skin, and the bones that let him pass in any level of society. True enough, even if his mother had known that the bank clerk was someone's cousin, she would not have approved of such calculation in one of her daughters. Auntie Q went on, "I'm sure, though, that any daughter of your mother's would have had a genuine affection for the young man, no matter what his connections."

"Mother said so." Interesting, too, that Mother had never mentioned knowing a friend of Auntie Q's, all those times his father had talked about her. Had she known that Arielle was Auntie Q's friend? Or not cared? He tried to puzzle it out, aware of a growing fuzziness in his head. He blinked to clear his vision, and realized that Auntie Q was peering at him, her mouth pursed.

"You're feeling ill again." It was not a question. Nor did he question it: he was feeling ill again. This time the onset was slower, more in the head than the stomach, a feeling of swooping and drifting, of being smothered in pale flowers.

"Sorry," he said. He could see in her eyes that he was being tiresome. Visiting relatives were supposed to be entertaining. They were supposed to listen to her stories and provide the material for new ones she could tell elsewhere. They were not supposed to collapse ungracefully in her exquisitely furnished rooms, fouling the air with bad smells.

He realized he had fallen sideways off his chair onto the floor. A disgrace. She did not say it aloud and he did not need her to say it. He knew it. He lay there remembering to breathe, wishing desperately that he were back on the *Zaid-Dayan*, where someone would have whisked him to sickbay, where the diagnostic unit would have figured out what was wrong, and what to do, in a few minutes, and a brusque but effective crew of Fleet medics would have supervised the treatment. And Sassinak, more vivid in her own way than Auntie Q at her wildest, would have come to see him, not walked out of the room in a huff. He remembered, with the mad clarity of illness, the jeweled rosettes on the toes of Auntie Q's shoes as she pushed herself from her chair, pivoted, and walked away.

This time he came to himself back in bed, but with the feeling that some catastrophic conflict was happening overhead. He felt bruised all over, his skin flinching from the touch of the bedclothes. The space between his ears, where his mind should have been ticking along quietly, seemed to be full of a quiet crackling, a sensation he remembered from five years before, when he'd had a bout of Plahr fever.

"I assure you, Sam, that Madame's nephew is in need of my healing powers." That syrupy voice could only be Madame Flaubert.

Ford tried to open his eyes, but lacked the strength. He heard something creak and the rustle of layers of clothes.

"His aura reveals the nature of his illness: it is seated in the spiritual house of his darkest sin. Through study and prayer, I am equipped to deal with this. I will need quiet, peace, and absolutely no interference. You may go."

Ford struggled again to open his eyes, to speak, but could not even twitch. Had he been hypnotized somehow? Given a paralytic drug? Panic surged through him, but even that did not unlock his muscles. For the first time, he realized that he might actually *die* here, in a luxurious statcroom in a private yacht, surrounded by rich old women and their servants. He could not imagine a more horrible death.

Even as he thought that, he felt a plump, moist hand on his forehead. Fingernails dug into the skin of his right temple just a little. His mind presented a vision from his nightmares: a scaly clawed hand about to dig in and rip his head open. The scent of Madame Flaubert's cologne mingled with the imagined stench of a reptilian, toothy maw; he wanted to retch and could not move.

"You may *go*," she said again, somewhere near his left shoulder. Evidently Sam had not gone; Ford hoped fervently he would stay, but he could not move even a toe to signal him.

"Sorry, Madame," said Sam, sounding more determined than sorry. "I think it would be better for us all if I stayed." Something in his tone made

Ford wish he could smile, a hint of staunch rectitude that implied Madame Flaubert had known—proclivities, perhaps? At the thought of her hands on his body, he actually shuddered.

"Your voice hurts him," Madame Flaubert said. Quietly, venomously, a voice to cause the same shudders. "You saw that twitch. You had better go, or I will be compelled to speak to your mistress."

No sound of movement. Ford struggled again with his eyelids, and felt one almost part. Then that hand drifted down his forehead and he felt a thumb on his lid.

"Madam gave me permission; *she* agreed it was best."

An actual hiss followed, a sound he had read about but never heard a woman make. The thumb on his eyelid pressed; he saw sparkling whorls. Then it released, with a last little flick that seemed a warning, and the hand fell heavily on his shoulder.

"I can't imagine what she means by it." Now Madame Flaubert sounded almost petulant, a woman wronged by false suspicions.

"She has such . . . such *notions* sometimes." A soft scrape, across the room; the sound of someone settling in a chair. "She has not forgotten why you are here. Nor have I."

Madame Flaubert sniffed, a sound as literary as the hiss, and as false. "You forget yourself, Sam. A servant—"

"Madam's cook." The emphasis was unmistakable. Madam's cook—her loyal servant. Not Madame Flaubert's. And she was someone he tolerated on his mistress's behalf?

Ford wished he could think clearly. He knew too little about whatever loyalties might exist in such situations. If this were Fleet, those overtones in Sam's voice would belong to the trustworthy NCO of a good officer. But he could hardly imagine his Auntie Q as a good officer. Or could he? And why *was* Madame Flaubert here, if neither Auntie Q nor her faithful servant wanted her?

"Well. You can scarcely object to my seeking healing for him."

"As long as that's all it is." Sam's voice had flattened slightly. Warning? Fear?

"Those who live by violence die of its refuse," Madame Flaubert intoned. Ford felt something fragile touch his face, and had just decided it was a scarf or veil when Madame Flaubert drew it away. "I see pain in this aura. I see violence and grief. I see the shadow of wickedness in the past, and its unborn child of darkness . . ." Her voice had taken on a curious quality, not quite musical, that seemed to bore into Ford's head and prevent thought. He could almost feel himself floating on it, as if it were a heavy stream of honey.

"What're you trying to do, make him feel guilty?" Sam's voice cut through hers and Ford felt as if he'd been dropped bodily from several feet up. A spasm went through his foot; he felt the covers drag at it. Before Madame Flaubert could move, Sam's strong hands were kneading it, relaxing the cramp.

"Don't touch him!" she said. "You'll interfere with the healing flow, if it comes at all with you here."

"He's been still too long. He needs massage." Where Sam's hands rubbed, Ford felt warmth, felt he could almost move himself.

"Impossible!" Her hand left his shoulder; he heard the rustle as she stood. "I can't be expected to do anything with you treating his legs like bread dough, stirring his aura, mixing the signs. *When* you're quite finished, you will have the kindness to inform me! If he's still alive, that is." An odd sound followed, a complex rustle, then she said, "And I'll leave this protective symbol with him."

It was cold on his forehead, icy cold that struck straight into his brain; his breath came short. But she was leaving, the rustle diminishing, and he heard the door open and close. Instantly a warm hand removed the thing, whatever it was, and a warm finger pried up one eyelid. He could see, somewhat to his surprise. Sam's face stared down at him. The man shook his head.

"You're a sick man, and no mistake. You should never have tried to outfox your great-aunt, laddie . . . you aren't in her league."

Chapter Five

"This was *not* a good idea," muttered one of the medical team as they stumped wearily off the shuttle at Diplo's only fully-equipped port. Lunzie didn't care who'd said it: she agreed. Her variable-pressure-support garment clasped her like an allover girdle. When the control circuitry worked correctly, it applied a pressure gradient from toes to neck without impeding joint movement . . . much. Over it, she wore the recommended outerwear for Diplo's severe winter, light and warm on a one-G world, but (she grumbled to herself) heavy and bulky here. She could feel her feet sinking into the extra-thick padded bootliners they had to wear, every separate bone complaining slightly of the extra burden.

"Winter on Diplo," said Conigan, waving a padded arm at the view out the round windows of the terminal. Wind splashed a gout of snow against the building and it shuddered. Snow, Lunzie reminded herself, would feel more like sleet or hail. Their shuttle had slewed violently in the storm coming in. She had heard something rattle on the hull.

At least they were through Customs. First on the orbiting Station, and then in the terminal, they'd been scrutinized by heavyworlders who might have been chosen to star in lightweight nightmares. Huge, bulky, their heavy faces masks of hostility and contempt, their uniforms emphasizing bulging muscle and bulk, they'd been arrogantly thorough in their examination of the team's authorization and equipment. Lunzie felt a momentary rush of terror when she realized how openly arrogant these heavyworlders were, but her Discipline reasserted itself, and she had relaxed almost at once. They had done nothing yet but be rude, and rudeness was not her concern.

But that rudeness made the minimal courtesy shown them now seem almost welcoming. A cargo van for their gear, the offer of a ride to the main research facility. None of them felt slighted that their escort was only a graduate student and not, as it should have been, one of the faculty.

If Lunzie had hoped that Diplo had not yet heard about her experience on Ireta, she was soon undeceived. The graduate student, having checked their names on a list, actually smiled at her.

"Dr. Lunzie? Or do you use Mespil? You're the one who's had all the coldsleep experience, right? But the heavyworlders in that expedition put *you* under, didn't they?"

Lunzie had not discussed her experience much with the others on the team; she was conscious of their curiosity.

"No," she said, as calmly as if discussing variant ways of doing a data search. "I was the doctor; I put our lightweights under."

"But there were heavyworlders on Ireta . . ." the student began. He was young, by his voice, but his bulky body made him seem older than his years.

"They mutinied," Lunzie said, still calmly. If he had heard the other, he should have heard that. But perhaps the Governor had changed the facts to suit his people.

"Oh." He gave her a quick glance over his shoulder before steering the van into a tunnel. "Are you sure? There wasn't some mistake?"

The others were rigidly quiet. She could tell they wanted her version of the story, and didn't want her to tell it here. The graduate student seemed innocent, but who could tell?

"I can't talk about it," she said, trying for a tone of friendly firmness. "It's going to trial, and I've been told not to discuss it until afterwards."

"But that's *Federation* law," he said airily. "It's not binding here. You could talk about it here, and they'd never know."

Lunzie suppressed a grin. Graduate students everywhere! They never thought the law was binding on them, not if they wanted to know something. Of course, it might be that the rest of Diplo felt that way about Federation law, which was something the FSP suspected, but just as likely it was pure student curiosity.

"Sorry," she said, not sounding sorry at all. "I promised, and I don't break promises." Only after it was out, did she remember something Zebar had repeated as a heavyworlder saying: *Don't break promises! Break bones!* She shivered. She had no intention of breaking bones—or having her own broken—if she could avoid it.

Their first days on Diplo were a constant struggle against the higher gravity and the measures they took to survive it. Lunzie hated the daily effort to worm her way into a clean pressure garment, the intimate adjustments necessary for bodily functions, the clinging grip that made her feel trapped all the time. Discipline could banish in her some of the fatigue that her colleagues, Tailler and Bias felt, at least for awhile, so that her fingers did not slip on the instruments or tremble when she ate. But by the end of a working day they were all tired, and trying not to be grumpy.

To add to their discomfort, Diplo's natural rotation and political "day," were just enough longer than standard to exhaust them, without justifying adherence to Standard measures.

Lunzie found the research fascinating, and had to remind herself that her real reason for coming had nothing to do with heavyworlder response to coldsleep. Especially as she only had a limited time to make contact with Zebara. She had been able to establish that he was still alive, and on Diplo. Contacting him might be difficult and enlisting his aid was problematic. But Zebara was the only option. He'd be at least 80, she reminded herself, even if living on ships and low-G worlds would have improved his probable life expectancy. They had trusted each other at one point: would that old trust suffice for the information she required of him? If, that is, he was in a position to help at all.

At the end of the first week, the team had its first official recognition: an invitation to a formal reception and dance at the Governor's Palace. The team quit work early. Lunzie spent an hour soaking in a hot tub before she dressed. The need to wear pressure garments constantly meant that "formal dress" for the women would be more concealing than usual. Lunzie had packed a green gown, long-sleeved and high-necked, that covered the protective garment but clung to her torso. Wide-floating skirts hung unevenly in Diplo's heavy gravity. She'd been warned, so this had only enough flare to make walking and dancing easy. She looked in her mirror and smiled. She looked more fragile than she was, less dangerous: exactly right.

The team gathered in Tailler's room to await their transport to the festivities. Lunzie asked about the Governor's compound.

"It *is* a palace," said Tailler, who had been there before. "It's under its own dome, so they could use thinner plexi in the windows. With the gardens outside, colorful even in this season. It's a spectacle. Of course, the resources used to make it all work are outrageous, considering the general poverty."

"It wasn't so bad before," Bias interrupted. "After all, it's the recent population growth that makes resources so short."

Tailler frowned. "They've been hungry a long time, Bias. Life on Diplo's never been easy."

"But you have to admit they don't seem to mind. They certainly don't blame the Governor."

"No, and that's what's unfair. They blame *us*, the Federation, when it's their own waste—"

"Shhh." Lunzie thought she heard someone in the corridor outside. She waited; after a long pause, someone knocked on the door. She opened it to find a uniformed heavyworlder, resplendent in ribbons and medals and knots of gold braid. She could read nothing on that expressionless face, but she had a feeling that he had heard at least some of what had been said.

"If you're ready, we should leave for the Palace," he said.

"Thank you," said Lunzie. She could hear the others gathering their outer wraps. Her own silvery parka was in her hand.

Within the dome, the Governor's Palace glittered as opulently as promised. Around it, broad lawns and formal flowerbeds glowed in the light of carefully placed spotlights. The medical team walked on a narrow strip of silvery stuff that looked like steel mesh, but felt soft underfoot, like carpet. A news service crew turned blinding lights on them as they came to the massive doors and the head of the receiving line.

"Smile! You're about to be famous," muttered Bias.

Lunzie had not anticipated this, but smiled serenely into the camera anyway. Others blinked away from the light and missed the first of many introductions. Lunzie grinned to herself, hearing them stumble in their responses. Such lines were simple, really, as long as you remembered to alternate any two of the five or six acceptable greeting phrases and smile steadily. By the time she was halfway down the line, well into the swing of it, with "How *very* nice" and "*So* pleased to meet you," tripping easily off her lips, the back of her mind was busy with commentary.

Why, she wondered, did the heavyworlder women try to copy lightweight fashions *here*, when everywhere else on Diplo they wore garments far better suited to their size and strength. Formal gowns could have been designed for them, taking into account the differences in proportion. But no heavyworlder should wear tight satin with flounces at the hip, or a dress whose side slit looked as if it had simply given way from internal pressure.

* * *

One of the men—the Lieutenant Governor, she noted as she was introduced and put her hand into his massive fist—had also opted for lightweight high fashion. And if there was anything sillier than a massive heavyworlder leg with a knot of hot pink and lime-green ribbons at the knee, she could not imagine it. The full shirt with voluminous sleeves made more sense, but those tight short pants! Lunzie controlled herself with an effort and moved on down the line. The Governor himself wore more conservative dark blue, the sort of coverall that she'd seen so much of since she arrived.

Refreshments covered two long tables angled across the upper corners of the great hall. Lunzie accepted a massive silver goblet of pale liquid from a servant and sipped it cautiously. She'd have to be careful, nurse it along, but she didn't think it was potent enough to drop her in her tracks. She took a cracker with a bit of something orange on it and two green nubbins that she hoped were candy, and passed on, smiling and nodding to the heavyworlders around her. Besides the medical team, the only lightweights were the FSP consul and a few consulate staff.

She recognized some of the heavyworlders: scientists and doctors from the medical center where they'd been working. These clumped together to talk shop, while the political guests—high government officials, members of the Diplo Parliament (which Lunzie had heard was firmly under the Governor's broad thumb)—did a great deal of "mingling."

The green nubbins turned out to be salty, not sweet, and the orange dollop on the cracker was not cheese at all, but some kind of fruit. Across the room a premonitory squawk from an elevated platform warned of music to come. Lunzie could not see over the taller shoulders around her. As the room filled, she felt more and more like a child who had sneaked into a grownup party.

"Lunzie!" That was the Lieutenant Governor, his wide white sleeves billowing, the ribbons at his knee jiggling. He took her free hand in his. "Let me introduce you to my niece, Colgara."

Colgara was not as tall as her uncle, but still taller than Lunzie, and built along the usual massive lines. Her pale yellow dress had rows of apricot ruffles down both sides and a flounce of apricot at the hem. She bowed over Lunzie's hand. The Lieutenant Governor went on, patting his niece on the shoulder.

"She wants to be a doctor, but of course that's just adolescent enthusiasm. She'll marry the Governor's son in a year, when he's back from . . ." His voice trailed away as someone tapped him on the shoulder. He turned away, and the two men began to talk.

Lunzie smiled at the girl who towered over her. "So? You're interested in medicine?"

"Yes. I have done very well at my studies." Colgara swiped at the ruffles down the side of her dress, a nervous gesture that made her seem a true adolescent. "I—I wanted to come see your team at work, but you are too busy, I know. Uncle said you must not be bothered, and besides I am not to go to medical school." She glowered at that, clearly not through fighting for it.

Lunzie was not sure how to handle this. The last thing she needed was to get involved in a family quarrel, particularly a family of this rank. But the girl looked so miserable.

"Perhaps you could do both," she said.

"Go to school *and* marry?" Colgara stared. "But I must have children. I couldn't go to school and have babies."

Lunzie chuckled. "People do," she said. "Happens all the time."

"Not here." Colgara lowered her voice. "You don't understand how it is with us. It's so difficult, with our genes and this environment."

Before Lunzie realized it, she was being treated to a blow-by-blow account of heavyworlder pregnancy: Colgara's mother's experience, and then her aunt's, and then her older sister's. It would have been interesting, somewhere else, but not at a formal reception, with all the gory details mingling with other overheard conversations about politics, agricultural production, light and heavy industry, trade relations. Finally, at great length, Colgara ended up with "So you see, I couldn't possibly go to medical school and have babies."

"I see your point," said Lunzie, wondering how to escape. The Lieutenant Governor had disappeared into a sea of tall heavy shoulders and broad backs. She saw no one she knew and no one she could claim a need to speak to.

"I've bored you, haven't I?" Colgara's voice was mournful; her lower lip stuck out in a pout.

Lunzie struggled for tact, and came up short. "Not really, I just . . ." She could not say, *just want to get away from you.*

"I thought since you were a doctor you'd be interested in all the medical problems . . ."

"Well, I am, but . . ." Inspiration came. "You see, obstetrics is really not my field. I don't have the background to appreciate a lot of what you told me." That seemed to work; Colgara's pouting lower lip went back in place. "Most of my work is in occupational rehab. That's why I focus on making it possible to do the work you want to do. People always have reasons why they can't. We look for ways to make it possible."

Colgara nodded slowly, smiling now. Lunzie wasn't sure which of the things she'd said had done the trick, but at least the girl wasn't glowering at her. Colgara leaned closer.

"This is my first formal reception—I begged and begged Uncle, and he finally let me come because his wife's sick." Lunzie braced herself for another detailed medical recitation but fortunately Colgara was now on a different tack. "He insisted that I had to wear offworld styles. This is really my cousin Jayce's dress. I think it's awful but I suppose you're used to it."

"Not really." Lunzie didn't want to explain to this innocent that she'd been forty-three years in one suit of workclothes, coldsleeping longer than Colgara had been alive. "I have few formal clothes. Doctors generally don't have time to be social."

She could not resist looking around, hoping to find something—someone, anything—in that mass of shoulders and backs, to give her an excuse to move away.

"Want something more to eat?" asked Colgara. "I'm starved." Without waiting for Lunzie's response, she turned and headed for the refreshment tables.

Lunzie followed in her wake. At least on this side of the room, people were sitting down at tables and she could see around. Then Lunzie was caught up by the ornate center arrangement on the nearest table, pink and red whorls surrounded by flowers and fruit. Surely it wasn't? But her nose confirmed that it was and some was uncooked. She glanced at Colgara. The girl had reached across and was filling her plate with the whorls. Didn't she know? Or was it deliberate insult? Slightly nauseated by such a blatant display, Lunzie fastidiously took a few slices of some yellowish fruit, more crackers, and moved away.

"Is it true you lightweights can't eat meat?" asked Colgara. Her tone held no hidden contempt, only curiosity. Lunzie wondered how to answer *that one*.

"It's a philosophical viewpoint," she said finally. Colgara, her mouth stuffed with what had to be slices of meat, looked confused. Lunzie sighed, and said "We don't think it's right to eat creatures that might be sentient."

Colgara looked even more confused as she chewed and swallowed. "But . . . but muskies aren't people. They're animals and not even smart ones. They don't talk, or anything." She put another slice of meat into her mouth and talked through it. "Besides, we need the complex proteins. It's part of our adaptation."

Lunzie opened her mouth to say that any protein compound could be synthesized without the need to kill and eat sentient creatures, but realized it would do no good. She forced a smile. "My dear, it's a philosophical position, as I said. Enjoy your . . . uh . . . muskie."

She turned away and found herself face to face with a white-haired man whose great bulk had twisted with age, bringing his massive face almost down to her level. For a moment she simply saw him as he was, exceptionally old for a heavyworlder in high-G conditions, someone of obvious intelligence and wit (for his eyes twinkled at her), and then her memory retrieved his younger face.

"Zebara!"

It was half joy and half shock. She had halfway wanted to find him, had not wanted to search the databases and find that he'd died while she slept, had not wanted to see what was now before her: a vigorous man aged to weakness. He smiled, the same warm smile.

"Lunzie! I saw your name on the list, and hardly dared believe it was you. And then there you were on the cameras! I had to come down and see you."

Conflicting thoughts cluttered her mind. She wanted to ask him what he'd done in the years she'd lost. She wanted to tell him all that had happened to her. But she had no time for a long, leisurely chat, even if he'd been able to join her. She was here with two missions already, and at the moment, she had to concentrate on Sassinak's needs.

"You're looking surprisingly . . . well . . ." he was saying.

"Another forty-three years of coldsleep," said Lunzie, wondering why he didn't know already, when some of the heavyworlders certainly did. "And you, you look . . ."

"Old," said Zebara, chuckling. "Don't try to flatter me. I'm lucky to be alive but I've changed a lot. It's been an interesting life and I wish we had time to discuss it." Lunzie looked a question at him and one of his heavy eyebrows went up. "You know we don't, dear girl. And yes, I can condescend to you because I have *lived* those forty-three years." He reached out and took the plate from her hand. "Come here."

Lunzie looked around, seeing only the same roomful of massive bodies, none of the other lightweights in sight. Across the serving table, one of the servants was watching her with a smirk.

"Come on," said Zebara, with a touch of impatience. "You don't really think I'm going to rape you."

She didn't, of course. But she wished she could find someone, a lightweight on the Team, to let them know she was going with him. She managed not to flinch when Zebara took her wrist and led her along the serving table toward the short end of the hall. The servant was still smirking, grinning openly finally, as Zebara led her through a double doorway into a wide, carpeted passage. Here the crush was less, but still heavyworlder men and women walked by in both directions.

"Restrooms," said Zebara, still holding her wrist and leading her right along a side corridor, then left along another. He opened a door, and pulled Lunzie into a room lined with glass-fronted shelves. Broad, heavy couches clustered around a massive glass-topped table. "Here! Sit down and we'll have a chat."

"Are you sure this is a good idea?" Lunzie began, as Zebara turned to look around the room, his eyelids drooping. He waved a hand, which she took as a signal for silence.

The couch was too deep for her comfort; her feet did not reach the floor if she relaxed against the backrest. She felt like a child in an adult's room. Zebara walked around the room slowly, obviously intent on something Lunzie could neither see nor hear. She could not relax while he was so tense. Finally he sighed, shrugged, and came to sit beside her.

"We must take the chance. If anyone comes, Lunzie, pretend to be struggling with me. They'll understand *that*. They know I was fond of you, that I considered you a 'pet' lightweight. That is their term for it."

"But . . ."

"Don't argue that with me. We haven't time." He kept scanning the room. This close, Lunzie could recognize the slight tremor that age had imposed on him; she grieved for the man he had been. "I know about Ireta, though I didn't know beforehand, and couldn't have stopped it anyway. Please believe that."

"I do, of course. You aren't the kind . . ."

"I don't know what kind I am any more." That stopped her cold, not only the words but the deadly quiet tone of voice. "I am a heavyworlder, I am dying. Yes, within the year, they tell me, and nothing to be done. I've been luckier than most. My children and grandchildren are heavyworlders, who face the same constraints I do. So while I agree that mutiny is wrong, and piracy is wrong, that we must not make enemies of all you lightweights, I wish the Federation would face facts about us. We are not dumb animals, just as you say that the subhuman animals that all once ate are not 'dumb animals.' How can I convince my children that they should watch their children starve, just to preserve the sensitivities, the 'philosophical viewpoint' of those who don't *need* meat but do want our strength to serve them?"

Shaken, Lunzie could only stare at him. She had been so sure, for so long, that Zebara was the best example of a good heavyworlder: trustworthy, idealistic, selfless. Had she been wrong?

"You didn't mistake me," Zebara said, as if she'd spoken aloud. Was her expression that obvious? But he wasn't really looking at her; he was staring across the room. "Back then, I was what you saw. I tried! You can't know how hard, to change others to my viewpoint. But you don't know what else I've seen since, while you were sleeping the years away. I don't want war, Lunzie, as much because my people would lose it as because I think it is wrong." He sighed, heavily, and patted her arm as a grandfather might pat a child. "And I don't like being that way. I don't like thinking that way."

"I'm sorry," said Lunzie. It was all she could think of. She had trusted Zebara; he had been a good man. If something had changed him, it must have been a powerful force. She let herself think it might have convinced her if she'd been exposed to it.

"No, *I'm* sorry," said Zebara, smiling directly at her again. "I often wished to talk with you, share my feelings. You would have understood and helped me stay true to my ideals. So here I've poisoned our meeting, a meeting I dreamed of, with my doubts and senile fears, and you're sitting there vibrating like a harpstring, afraid of me. And no wonder. I always knew you were a brave woman, but to come to Diplo when you'd had such vicious treatment from heavyworlders? That's incredible, Lunzie."

"You taught me that all heavyworlders were not alike," said Lunzie, managing a smile in return.

He mimed a flinch and grinned. "A palpable hit! My dear, if trusting me let you be hurt by others, I'm sorry indeed. But if you mean that it helped you gather courage to come here and help our people, after what you'd been through, I'm flattered." His face sobered. "But seriously, I need your help on something, and it may be dangerous."

"You need *my* help?"

"Yes, and that . . ." He suddenly lunged toward her, and flattened her to the couch.

"What!" His face smothered her. She beat a tattoo on his back. Behind her, she heard a chuckle.

"Good start, Zebara!" said someone she could not see. "But don't be *too* long. You'll miss the Governor's speech."

"Go away, Follard!" Zebara said, past her ear. "I'm busy and I don't care about the Governor's speech."

A snort of laughter. "Bedrooms upstairs, unless you're also working on blackmail."

Zebara looked up. Lunzie couldn't decide whether to scream or pretend acquiescence. "When I need advice, Follard, I'll ask for it."

"All right, all right; I'm going."

Lunzie heard the thump of the door closing and counted a careful five while Zebara sat back up.

"I'm glad you warned me! Or I'd be wondering why you wanted my help."

"I do." Zebara was tense, obviously worried. "Lunzie, we can't talk here, but we must talk. I do need your help and I need you to pretend your old affection for me."

"Here? For Follard's benefit?"

"Not his! This is important, for you and the Federation as well as for me. So, *please*, just act as if you . . ." A loud clanging interrupted him. He muttered a curseword Lunzie had not heard in years, and stood up. "That does it. Someone's hit the proximity alarm in the Governor's office and this place'll be swarming with police and internal security guards. Lunzie, you've got to trust me, at least for this. As we leave, lean on me. Act a little befuddled."

"I am."

"And then meet me tomorrow, when you're off work. Tell your colleagues it's for dinner with an old friend. Will you?"

"It won't be a lie," she replied with a wry smile.

Then he was pulling her up, his arms still stronger than hers. He put one around her shoulders, his fingers in her hair. She leaned back against him, trying to conquer a renaissant fear. At that moment the door opened, letting in a clamor from the alarm and two uniformed police. Lunzie hoped her expression was that of a woman surprised in a compromising position. She dared not look at Zebara.

But whatever he was, whoever he was in his own world, his name carried weight with the police, who merely checked his ID off on a handcomp and went on their way. Then Zebara led her back to the main hall where most of the guests were clumped at one end, with the lightweights in a smaller clump to one side. The other members of the medical team, Lunzie noticed, were first relieved to see her, then shocked. She was trying to look like someone struggling against infatuation, and she must be succeeding.

Zebara brought her up to that group, gave her a final hug, and murmured, "Tomorrow. Don't forget!" before giving her a nudge that sent her toward them.

"Well!" That almost simultaneous huff by two of the team members at once made Lunzie laugh. She couldn't help it.

"What's the alarm about?" she asked, fighting the laugh back down to her diaphragm where it belonged.

"Supposedly someone tried to break into the Governor's working office." Bias's voice was still primly disapproving. "Since you didn't show up at once, we were afraid you were involved." A pause, during which Lunzie almost asked why *she* would want to break into the Governor's office, then Bias continued. "I see you *were* involved, so to speak."

"Meow," said Lunzie. "I've told you about Zebara before. He saved my life, years ago, and even though it's been longer for him, I was glad to see him . . ."

"We could tell." Lunzie had never suspected Bias of prudery, but the tone was still icily contemptuous. "I might remind you, Doctor, that we are here on a mission of medical research, not to reunite old lovers. Especially those who should have the common sense to realize how *unsuited* they are." The word unsuited caught Lunzie's funnybone and she almost laughed again. That showed in her face, for Bias glowered. "You might *try* to be professional!" he said, and turned away.

Lunzie caught Conigan's eye, and shrugged. The other woman grinned and shook her head: no accounting for Bias, in anything but his own field. Brilliancy hath its perks. Lunzie noticed that Jarl was watching her with a curious expression that made him seem very much the heavyworlder at the moment.

As the guards moved through the crowd, checking IDs, Jarl shifted until he was next to her, between her and the other team members. His voice was low enough to be covered by the uneven mutter of the crowd.

"It's none of my business, and I have none of the, er, scruples of someone like Bias, but . . . you *do* know, don't you, that Zebara is now head of External Security?"

She had not known; she didn't know how Jarl knew.

"We were just *friends*," she said as quietly.

"Security has no friends," said Jarl. His face was expressionless, but the statement had the finality of death.

"Thanks for the warning," said Lunzie.

She could feel her heart beating faster and controlled the rush of blood to her face with a touch of Discipline. Why hadn't he told her himself? Would he have told her if they'd had more time? Would he tell her at their next meeting? Or as he killed her?

She wanted to shiver, and dared not. What was going on here?

* * *

By the end of the workshift the next day, she was still wondering. All the way back to their quarters, Bias had made barbed remarks about over-sexed female researchers until Conigan finally threatened to turn him in for harassment. That silenced him, but the team separated in unhappy silence when they arrived. The morning began with a setback in the research; some-one had mistakenly wiped the wrong data cube and they had to re-enter it from patient records. Lunzie offered to do this, hoping it would soothe Bias, but it did not.

"You are not a data entry clerk," he said angrily. "You're a doctor. Unless you are responsible for the data loss, you have no business wasting your valuable time re-entering it."

"Tell you what," said Tailler, putting an arm around Bias's shoulders, "why don't we let Lunzie be responsible for scaring up a data clerk? You know you don't have time to do that. Nor do I. I've got surgery this morning and you're supposed to be checking the interpretation of those cardiac mus-cle cultures. Conigan's busy in the lab, and Jarl's already over at the archives, while Lunzie doesn't have a scheduled procedure for a couple of hours."

"But she shouldn't be wasting her time," fumed Bias. Tailler's arm grew visibly heavier and the smaller biologist quieted.

"I'm not asking her to *do* it," said Tailler, giving Lunzie a friendly but commanding grin. "I'm asking her to see that it's done. Lunzie's good at administrative work. She'll do it. Come on. Let's leave her with it; you don't want to be late."

And he steered Bias away even as the biologist said, "But she's a *doctor* . . ." one last time. Tailler winked over his shoulder at Lunzie, who grinned back.

It was easy enough to find a clerk willing to enter the data. Lunzie stayed to watch long enough to be sure the clerk really understood his task, then went on to her first appointment. She waited until well after the local noon to break for her lunch, hoping to miss Bias. Sure enough, he'd already left the dining hall when she arrived, but Conigan and Jarl were eating together. Lunzie joined them.

"Did you get the data re-entered?" asked Jarl, grinning.

Lunzie rolled her eyes. "I did not, I swear, enter it myself. Thanks to Tailler, and a clerk out of the university secretarial pool, it was no problem. Just checked, and found that it's complete, properly labelled, and on file."

Jarl chuckled. "Tailler told us when we came in for lunch about Bias's little fit. He says Bias is like this by the second week of any expedition, to Diplo or anywhere else. He's worked with him six or seven times."

"I'm glad to know it's not just my aura," said Lunzie.

"No, and Tailler says he's going to talk to you about last night. Seems there's some reason Bias is upset by women associates having anything to do with local males."

"Alpha male herd instinct," muttered Conigan.

Jarl shook his head. "Tailler says not. Something happened on one of his expeditions, and he was blamed for it. Tailler wouldn't tell us, but he said he'd tell you, so you'd understand."

Lunzie did not look forward to that explanation. If Bias had peculiar notions, she could deal with them; she didn't have to be coaxed into sympathy. But she suspected that avoiding Tailler would prove difficult. Still, she could try.

"I'm having dinner with Zebara tonight," she said. "Bias will just have to live with it."

Jarl gave her a long look. "Not that I agree with Bias, but is that wise? You know?"

"I know what you told me, but I also know what Zebara did for me over forty years ago. It's worth embarrassing Bias, and worth risking whatever *you* fear."

"I don't like *anyone's* Security, external, internal, or military. Never been one yet that didn't turn into someone's private enforcement agency. You've had a negative contact with heavyworlders before. You have a near relative in Fleet: reason enough to detain and question you if they're so minded."

"Not Zebara!" Lunzie hoped her voice carried conviction. Far below the surface, she feared precisely this.

"Just be careful," Jarl said. "I don't want to have to risk my neck on your behalf. Nor do I want to answer a lot of questions back home if you disappear."

Lunzie almost laughed, then realized he was being perfectly honest. He had accorded her the moderate respect due a fellow professional, but he felt no particular friendship for her (for anyone?) and would not stir himself to help if she got into trouble. She could change quickly from "fellow professional" to "major annoyance" which in his value system would remove her from his list of acquaintances.

To add to her uneasiness, Tailler did indeed manage to catch her before she left the center and insisted on explaining at length the incident which had made Bias so sensitive to "relationships" between research staff and locals. A sordid little tale, Lunzie thought: nothing spectacular, nothing to really justify Bias's continuing reaction. He must have had a streak of prudery before that happened to give him the excuse to indulge it.

Chapter Six

Dupaynil, hustled through the scarred and echoing corridors of the transfer station to the control center where the *Claw*'s captain met him with the suggestion that he "put a leg in it" and get himself out to the escort's docking bay, had no chance to think things over until he was strapped safely into the escort's tiny reserve cabin. He had not been passenger on anything smaller than a light cruiser for years; he had never been aboard an escort-class vessel. It seemed impossibly tiny after the *Zaid-Dayan*. His quarters for however long the journey might be was this single tiny space, a minute slice of a meager pie, hardly big enough to lie down in. He heard a loud clang, felt something rattle the hull outside, and then the escort's insystem drive nudged him against one side of his safety restraints. The little ship had artificial gravity, of a sort, but nothing like the overriding power that made Main Deck on the *Zaid-Dayan* feel as solid as a planet.

The glowing numbers on the readout overhead told him two standard hours had passed when he felt a curious twinge and realized they'd shifted into FTL drive. Although he'd had basic training in astrogation, he'd never used it, and had only the vaguest idea what FTL travel really meant. Or where, in real terms, they might be. Somewhere behind (as he thought of it) was the cruiser he had left, with its now-familiar crew and its most attractive captain. Its *very angry* and most attractive captain. He wished she had not been so transparently suspicious of his motives. *She* was no planet pirate nor agent of slavers. She had nothing to fear from him. And he would gladly have spent more time with her. He let himself imagine the nights they could have shared.

"Sir, we're safely in FTL, if you want to come up to Main."

Dupaynil sighed as the voice over the com broke into that fantasy and thumbed the control.

"I'll be there."

He had messages to send, messages he had had no time to send from the transfer station. And with the angry Commander Sassinak sitting on the other end of the block, so to speak, he would not have sent them from the station anyway. He re-discovered what he had once been taught about escort-class vessels in a few miserable minutes. They were small, overpowered for their mass, and understaffed. No one bunked on Main but the captain who was the pilot. Crew consisted of a round dozen: one other officer, the Jig Executive, eleven enlisted, from Weapons to Environmental. No cook: all the food was either loaded prepackaged, to be reconstituted and heated in automatic units, or synthesized from the Environmental excess.

Dupaynil shuddered; one of the best things about the *Zaid-Dayan* had been the cooking. With full crew and one supercargo, the escort had to ration water: limited bathing. The head was cramped: the slots designed to discourage meditation. There was no gym but the uneven artificial gravity and shiplong access tubing offered opportunity for informal exercise. For those who liked climbing very long ladders against variable G. Worst of all, the ship had no IFTL link.

" 'Course we don't have IFTL," said the captain, a Major Ollery whose face seemed to brighten every time Dupaynil found something else to dislike. "We don't have a Ssli interface, do we?"

"But I thought . . ." He stopped himself in mid-argument. He had seen a briefing item, mention of the ship classes that had IFTL, mention of those which would not get it because of "inherent design constraints." And escorts were too small to carry a Ssli habitat. "That . . . that *stinker!*" he said, as he realized suddenly what Sassinak had done.

"What?" asked Ollery.

"Nothing." Dupaynil hoped his face didn't show how he felt, torn between anger and admiration. That incredible woman had fooled *him*. Had fooled an experienced Security officer whose entire life had been spent fooling others. He had had a tap on her communications lines, a tap he was sure she'd never find, and somehow she'd found out. Decided to get rid of him.

And *how* in Mulvaney's Ghost had she managed to fake an incoming IFTL message? With that originating code?

He sank down on the one vacant seat in the escort's bridge, and thought about it. Of course she could fake the code, if she could fake the message. That much was easy, if the other was possible. But nothing he'd been taught, in a long and devious life full of such instruction, suggested that an IFTL message could be faked. It would take . . . he frowned, trying to think it through. It would take the cooperation of a Ssli: of *two* Ssli, at least. How would the captain of one ship enlist the aid of the Ssli on another? What kind of hold did Sassinak have on her resident Ssli? It had never occurred to him that the Ssli were capable of anything like friendship with humans. Once installed, the sessile Ssli never experienced another environment, never "met" anyone except through a computer interface. Or so he'd thought.

He felt as if he'd sat down on an anthill. He fairly itched with new knowledge and had no way to convey it to anyone. Ssli could have relationships with humans beyond mere duty. Could they with other races? With Wefts? Were Ssli perhaps telepathic? No one had suspected that. Dupaynil glanced around the escort bridge and saw only human faces, now bent over their own work. He cleared his throat, and the captain looked up.

"Do you . . . mmm . . . have any Wefts aboard?"

An odd expression in reply. "Wefts? No, why?" Then before he could answer, Ollery's face cleared. "Oh! You've been with Sassinak, I know. She's got a thing about Wefts, doesn't she? They say it started back in the Academy. She had a Weft lover or something. That true?" Ollery's voice had the incipient snigger of those who hope the worst about their seniors.

Dupaynil suppressed a surge of rage. As a Security officer, he listened to gossip professionally; idle gossip, malicious gossip, juicy gossip, boring gossip. He found it generally dull, and sometimes disgusting: a necessary but unpleasant part of his career. But here, applied to Sassinak, it was infuriating.

"So far as I know," he said as smoothly as he could, "that story was started by a cadet expelled for stealing and harassing women cadets." He knew the truth of that; he'd seen the files. "*Commander* Sassinak, and"—he emphasized the rank a little, intentionally, and enjoyed seeing Ollery's face pale—"keeps her sex life in her own cabin, where it belongs, and where I intend to leave it."

A muffled snort behind him meant that either someone else thought the captain had been out of line, or that Dupaynil's defense implied personal knowledge. He left that alone, too, and hoped no one would ask.

Silence settled over the bridge; he went on with his thoughts. *Telepathic* Wefts, and a ship's captain who could sometimes talk that way with them.

He'd seen the reports on Sassinak's first tour of duty. A Ssli who—he suddenly remembered something from the tour before he joined the *Zaid-Dayan*. Sassinak had reported it as part of her testimony before the Board of Inquiry. Her Ssli, this same Ssli, had taken control of the ship momentarily and flipped it in and out of FTL space. A move which she had described as "unprecedented, but undoubtedly the reason I am here today."

He was beginning to think that Fleet knew far too little about the capabilities of Ssli. But he had no way to find out more at the moment so he moved his concentration to Sassinak herself. When he thought of it, her actions were entirely probable. He could have kicked himself for not realizing that she would react quickly and strongly to any perceived threat. She had never liked having him aboard; she had never really trusted him. So his interception of her classified messages, once she found out, would naturally result in some action. Her history suggested a genius for quick response, for instantly recognizing danger and reacting effectively in novel ways.

And so he was here, out of communication until the escort reached its destination. No way to check the validity of his orders (though he was quite sure now where they had come from) and no way to tell anyone what he'd found out. It occurred to him then, and only then, that Sassinak might have planned even more than getting him off her ship before he could "do something." Perhaps she had other plans. Perhaps she was not going to take the *Zaid-Dayan* tamely into Federation Central space, with all its weaponry disabled and all its shuttles locked down.

For a long moment he fought off panic. She might do *anything*. Then he settled again. The woman was brilliant, not crazy: aggressive in defending her own, responsive to danger, but not disloyal to Fleet or Federation, not likely to do anything stupid, like bombing FedCentral. He hoped.

"Panis, take the helm." Ollery pushed himself back, gave Dupaynil a challenging glance, and stretched.

"Sir." Panis, the Executive Officer, had slid forward to the main control panel. He, too, glanced at Dupaynil before looking back at the screen.

"I'm going on a round," Ollery said. "Want to come along, Major?" A round of inspection, through all those long access tubes.

Dupaynil shook his head. "Not this time, thanks. I'll just . . ." *What?* he wondered. There was nothing to do on the tiny bridge but stare at the back of Panis's head or the side of the Weapons Control master mate's thick neck. A swingaway facescreen hid his face as he tinkered delicately with something in the weapons systems. At least, that's what Dupaynil assumed he was doing with a tiny joystick and something that looked like a silver toothpick. Maybe he was playing a game.

"You'll get tired of it," warned Ollery. Then he was gone, easing through the narrow hatch.

A lengthy silence, in which Dupaynil noted the scuffmarks on the decking by the captain's seat, the faded blue covers of the Fleet manuals racked for reference below the Exec's workstation. Finally Jig Panis looked over his shoulder and gave Dupaynil a shy smile.

"The Captain's ticked," he said softly. "We got into the supply station a day early."

"Ollery reporting: Environmental, section 43, number-two scrubber's up a half-degree."

"Logged, sir." Panis entered the report, thumbed a control, and sent "Spec Zigran" off to check on the errant scrubber. Then he turned back to Dupaynil. "We'd had a long run without liberty," he said. "The Captain said we'd have a couple of days off-schedule, sort of rest up and then get ready for inspection."

Dupaynil nodded. "So . . . my orders upset your party-time, eh?"

"Yes. *Playtak* was supposed to be in at the same time."

With a loud click, the Weapons Control mate flicked the facescreen back into place. Dupaynil caught the look he gave the young officer; he had seen senior noncoms dispense that "You talk too much!" warning glance at every rank up to admiral.

Panis turned red, and focussed on his board. Dupaynil asked no more; he'd heard enough to know why Ollery was hostile. Presumably *Playtak*'s captain was a friend of Ollery's and they'd agreed to meet at the supply station and celebrate. Quite against regulations, because he had no doubt that they had stretched their orders to make that overlap. It might be innocent, just friendship, or it might have been more. Smuggling, spying, who knows what? And he had been dumped into the middle of it, forcing them to leave ahead of schedule.

"Too bad," he said casually. "It certainly wasn't my idea. But Fleet's Fleet and orders are orders."

"Right, sir." Panis did not look up. Dupaynil looked over at the Weapons Control mate whose lowering expression did not ease although it was not overtly hostile.

"You're Fleet Security, sir?" asked the mate.

"That's right. Major Dupaynil."

"And we're taking you into Seti space?"

"Right." He wondered who'd told the man that. Ollery had had to know, but hadn't he realized those orders were secret? Of course they weren't really secret, since they were faked orders, but . . . He pushed that away. It was too complicated to think about now.

"Huh. Nasty critters." The mate put the toothpick-like tool he'd been using into a toolcase, and settled back in his seat. "Always get the feeling they're hoping for trouble."

Dupaynil had the same feeling about the mate. Those scarred knuckles had broken more than a few teeth, he was sure. "I was there with a diplomatic team once," he said. "I suppose that's why they're sending me."

"Yeah. Well, don't let the toads sit on you." The mate lumbered up, and with a casual wave at the Exec, left the bridge.

Dupaynil looked after him, a little startled. He had not considered Sassinak strict on etiquette, but no one would have left *her* bridge without a proper salute to the officer in charge, and permission to withdraw. Of course, this was a smaller ship than he'd ever been on. Was it *healthy* to have such a casual relationship?

Then the term "toads" which wasn't at all an accurate description of the Seti, but conveyed the kind of racial contempt that put Dupaynil on alert. Everyone knew the Federation combined races and cultures that preferred separation, that some hardly-remembered force had compelled the Seti and humans both to sign agreements against aggression. And, for the most part, abide by them. As professional keepers of this fragile peace, Fleet personnel were expected to have a more dispassionate view. Besides, he always thought of the Seti as "lizards."

" 'Scuse me, sir." That was another crewman, squeezing past him to get to a control panel on his left.

Dupaynil felt very much in the way, and very much unwanted. Blast Sassinak! The woman might at least have dumped him onto something *comfortable*. He looked over at Panis who was determinedly not looking at him. If he remembered correctly, the shortest route to Seti space was going to take weeks and he could not endure this kind of thing for weeks.

The crew had worked off their bad humor in less than a week. Dupaynil exerted his considerable charm, let Ollery win several card games, and entertained them with some of the safer racy anecdotes from his last assignment in a political realm. He had read Ollery correctly; the man liked to find flaws in those above him; preferably blackmailable flaws. Given a story about an ambassador's lady addicted to drugs or a wealthy senior bureaucrat who preferred cross-cultural divertissements, his eyes glistened and his cheeks flushed.

Dupaynil concealed his own contempt. Those who best liked to hear such things usually had their own similar appetites to hide.

Panis, however, was of very different stripe. He had tittered nervously at the story about the bureaucrat and turned brick red when Ollery and the senior mate sneered at him. It was clear that he had no close friends among the crew. When Dupaynil checked, he found that Panis had replaced the previous Exec only a few months before, while the rest of the crew had been unchanged for almost five years. And the previous Exec had left the ship because of an injury in a dockside brawl. It was odd, and more than odd: regular rotation of crew was especially important on small ships. Fleet policy insisted on it. No matter how efficient a crew seemed to be, they were never left unchanged too long.

Dupaynil had not been able to bring all his tools along, but he always had some. He placed his sensors carefully, as carefully as he had in the larger ship, and slid his probe into the datalinks very delicately indeed. He had the feeling that carelessness here would get him more trouble than a chewing out by the captain.

In the meantime, as the days wore on, the crew loosened up with him and played endless hands of every card game he knew, and a few he'd never seen. Crutch was a pirate's game, he'd been told once by the merchanter who taught it to him; he wondered where this crew had learned it. Poker, blind-eye, sin on toast, at which he won back all he'd lost so far, having learned that on Bretagne, where it began.

He sweated up and down the access tube ladders, learning to respond quickly to the shifting artificial-G, keeping his muscles supple. He discovered a storage bay full of water ice which made the restrictions on bathing ridiculous. There was enough to last a crew twice that size all the way to Seti space and *back* but he kept his mouth shut. It seemed safer.

For all their friendliness, all their casual demeanor, he'd noticed that Ollery or the senior mate were always in any compartment he happened into. Except his own tiny cabin. And he was sure they'd been there when he found evidence that his things had been searched. He had time to wonder if Sassinak had known just what kind of ship she'd sent him to. He thought not. She had probably done a fast scan of locations, looking for the nearest docked escort vessel, some way to keep him from communicating while he was in FTL.

"I say he's spying on *us*, and I say dump him." That was the mate. Dupaynil shivered at the quietly deadly tone.

"He's got IG orders. They'll want to know what happened." That was Ollery, not nearly so sure of himself.

"We can't just space him. We have to figure out a way."

"Emergency drill. Blow the pod. Say it was an accident." The mate's voice carried the shrug he would give when questioned later.

"What if he figures it out?"

"What can he do? Pod's got no engine, no decent long-range radio, no scan. Dump him where he'll fall down a well, into a star or something else big. Disable the radio and beacon. That way no one'll know he's ever been there. 'Sides, I don't think his orders are real. Think about it, sir. Would the IG haul someone off a big cruiser like the *Zaid-Dayan*—an IFTL message, that'd have to be—and stick 'em on a little bitty escort? To go to Seti space? C'mon. You send a special envoy to the Seti, you send a damn flotilla in with 'em, not an escort. No, you mark my words, sir, he's here to spy on *us* and this proves it."

Dupaynil could not tell through the audio link which of his taps had been found, but he wished ardently that he had not planted it, whatever it was. Once again he had out-smarted himself, as he had with Sassinak. Never underestimate the enemy and be damned sure you know who the enemy is; a very basic rule he had somehow violated.

He felt a trickle of sweat run down his ribs. Sassinak had been dumped in an evac pod, rescued by the combined efforts of Wefts and a Ssli. He had no Wefts or Ssli to back him up; he would have to figure this out himself.

"You're sure he hasn't got the good stuff out of comp yet?"

"Pretty sure." The mate's voice was even grimmer. "Security's got good tools, though. Give him all the time between here and Seti space, and he'll have not only the basics but enough to mind-fry the lot of us, all the way up to Lady Luisa herself."

Dupaynil almost forgot his fear. *Lady* Luisa? Luisa *Paraden*? He had always been able to put two and two together and find more interesting things than four. Now he felt an almost physical jolt as his mind connected everything he'd ever heard or seen; including all the information Sassinak had gathered.

As bright as a diagram projected on the screen of a strategy meeting, all connections marked out in glowing red or yellow . . . Luisa to Randolph, who had ample reason to loathe Sassinak. That had been *Randolph* Paraden's vengeance, through his aunt's henchman, a brainwashed Fleet officer once held captive on the same slaver outpost as an orphan girl. Dupaynil spared a moment to pity that doomed lieutenant: Sassinak never would, even if she learned the whole story. Luisa would never do something that potentially dangerous just for Randolph, though. It must have been vengeance for Abe's part in disrupting her operation, a warning to others. Perhaps fear that he would cause her more trouble.

Abe to Sassinak, Sassinak to Randolph, Randolph to Luisa, whose first henchman partially failed. Where was Randolph *now*, Dupaynil wondered suddenly. He should know and he did not know. He realized that he had not ever seen one bit of information on Randolph in the system since that arrogant young man had left the Academy. Unnatural. A Paraden, wealthy, with connections: he should have done *something*. He should have been in the society news or been an officer in one of Aunt Luisa's companies.

Unless he had changed his identity some way. It could be done, though it was expensive. Not that that would bother a Paraden. And why had they stopped with one attack on Sassinak? Dupaynil wished he had her file in hand. They would have been covert attempts, but knowing what to look for he might be able to see it. But of course! The Wefts. The Wefts she had saved from Paraden's accusations in the Academy; the Wefts who had saved her from death in the pod. Wefts might have foiled any number of plots without bothering to tell *her*.

Or perhaps she knew, but never made the connection, or never bothered to report it, rules or no. She was not known for following the rules. He leaned on the wall of his cubicle, sweating and furious, as much with himself as the various conspirators. This was his *job*, this was what he had trained for, what he had thought he was good at; finding things out, making connections, sifting the data, interpreting it. And here he was, with all the threads woven into the pattern and no possible way to get that information *out*.

You're so smart, he thought bitterly. *You're going to your death having won the war but lost the brawl.* He knew—it was in her file and she had confided it as well—that Sassinak still wondered about the real reason Abe had been killed. She had never forgotten it, never laid it to rest. And he had that to offer her, more than enough to get her forgiveness for that earlier misunderstanding. But too late!

Thinking of Sassinak reminded him again of her experience in the escape pod. It had made chilling reading, even in the remote prose her captain had used. She had gone right up to the limit of the pod's oxygen capacity, hoping to be conscious to give her evidence. He shuddered. He would have put himself into coldsleep as soon as he realized what happened, and he'd probably have died of it. Or, like Lunzie, been found decades later. He didn't like that scenario either. He fairly itched to get his newly acquired insights where they could do the most good.

Sassinak, now. What would she do, cooped in an escort full of renegades? He had trouble imagining her on anything but the bridge of the *Zaid-Dayan*, but she had served in smaller ships. Would she find a weapon (where?) and threaten them from the bridge? Would she take off in an escape pod before she was jettisoned, with a functioning radio, and hope to be found in time? (In time for what? Life? The trial?) The one thing she wouldn't do, he was sure, was slouch on a bunk wondering what to do. She would have thought of something, and given her luck it would probably have worked.

The idea, when it finally came to him hours later (miserable, sweaty hours when he was supposed to be sleeping), seemed simple. Presumably they would have a ship evacuation drill as the occasion of his murder. The others would be going into pods as well, just to make it seem normal. They had found one of his taps, but not all (or surely they'd have blocked the audio so he couldn't hear). And therefore he could tap the links again, reset the evac pod controls, and trap *them*—or most of them—in the pods. They would not be able to fire his pod; he could fire theirs.

He was partway through the reprogramming of the pod controls when he realized why this was not such a simple solution. Fleet had a name for someone who took illegal control of a ship and killed the captain and crew. An old, nasty name leading to a court martial which he might well lose.

I am not contemplating mutiny, he told himself firmly. *They are the criminals*. But they were not convicted yet, and until then what he planned was, by all the laws and regulations, not merely mutiny but also murder. And piracy. And probably a dozen or so lesser crimes to be tacked onto the charge sheet(s), including the things Sassinak might say about his tap into her com shack. And his present unauthorized reprogramming of emergency equipment. Not to mention his supposed orders to proceed into Seti space: faked orders, which no one (after he pirated a ship and killed the crew) would believe he had not faked for himself.

What would Sassinak do about *that*, he wondered. He remembered the holo of the *Zaid-Dayan* with its patched hull, with the scars of the pirate boarding party. She had let the enemy onto her ship to trap them. Could he think of anything as devastating? All things considered, forty-three years of coldsleep might be the easy way out, he thought, finishing off the new switching sequences.

Sassinak's great-great-great might complain but a little time in the freezer could keep you out of big trouble. His mind bumped him again, hard. Of course. Coldsleep *them*, the nasties. Drop the charges to mere mutiny and piracy and et cetera, but not murder (mandatory mindwipe for murder), and he might merely spend the next twenty years cleaning toilet fixtures with a bent toothbrush.

Of course it still wasn't simple. For all his exercise up and down the ladders, he had no more idea than a space-opera hero how to operate this ship. He'd had only the basics, years back; he'd flown a comp-desk, not a ship. He could chip away at that compartment of water ice and not die of thirst, but he couldn't convert it and take a shower. Or even get the ship down out of FTL space. Sassinak could probably do it, but all he could do was trigger the Fleet distress beacon and hope the pickup ship wasn't part of the same corrupt group. He wouldn't even do that, if he didn't quit jittering and get to it.

Chapter Seven

Diplo

Zebara led her through the maze of streets around the university complex at a fast pace. For all his age and apparent physical losses, he was still amazingly fit. She was aware of eyes following them, startled glances. She could not tell if it was Zebara himself, or his having a lightweight companion. She was puffing when he finally stopped outside a storefront much like the others she'd seen.

"Giri's Place," Zebara said. "Best chooli stew in the city, a very liberal crowd, *and* a noisy set of half-bad musicians. You'll love it."

Lunzie hoped so. Chooli stew conformed to Federation law by having no meat in it, but she had not acquired a taste for the odd spices that flavored the mix of starchy vegetables.

Inside, hardly anyone looked at her. The "liberal crowd" were all engrossed in their own food and conversation. She smelled meat, but saw none she recognized. The half-bad musicians played with enthusiasm but little skill, covering their blats and blurps with high-pitched cries of joy or anguish. She could not tell which, but it did make an effective sonic screen. She and Zebara settled into one of the booths along the side, and ordered chooli stew with figgerunds, the green nuts she'd had at the reception, Zebara explained.

"You need to know some things," he began when the chooli stew had arrived, and Lunzie was taking a first tentative bite of something yellowish.

"I heard you were head of External Security," she said quietly.

He looked startled. "Where'd you hear? No, it doesn't matter. It's true, although not generally known." He sighed. "I can see this makes it more difficult for you . . ."

"Makes what more difficult?"

"Trusting me." His eyes flicked around the room, as anyone's might, but Lunzie could not believe it was the usual casual glance. Then he looked back at her. "You don't, and I can't blame you, but we must work together or. Or things could get very bad indeed."

"Isn't your involvement with an offworlder going to be a little conspicuous?" She let a little sarcasm edge her voice; how naive did he think she was?

"Of course. That doesn't matter." He ate a few bites while she digested the implications of that statement. It could only "not matter" if policymakers knew and approved. When he looked up and swallowed, she nodded at him. "Good! You understand. Your name on the medical team was a little conspicuous, if you'd had any ulterior motive for coming here . . ." He let that trail away, and Lunzie said nothing. Whatever motives she had had, the important thing now was to find out what Zebara was talking about. She took another bite of stew; it was better than the same dish in the research complex's dining hall.

"I saw the list," Zebara went on. "One of the things my department does is screen such delegations, looking for possible troublemakers. Nothing unusual. Most planets do the same. There was your name, and I wondered if it was the same Lunzie. Found out that it was you and then the rocks started falling."

"Rocks?"

"My . . . employers. They wanted me to contact you, renew our friendship. More than friendship, if possible. Enlist your aid in getting vital data offplanet."

"But your employers . . . that's the Governor, right?" Lunzie was not sure, despite having read about it, just where political power was on this planet.

"Not precisely. The Governor knows them, and that's part of the problem. I have to assume that you, with what's happened to you, are like any normal Federation citizen. About piracy, for instance."

His voice had lowered to a muffled growl she could barely follow. The half-bad musicians were perched on their tall stools, gulping some amber liquid from tall glass mugs. She hoped it would mellow their music as well as their minds.

"*My* ethics haven't changed," she said, with the slightest emphasis on the pronoun.

"Good. That's what they counted on, and I, in my own way, counted on the same thing." He took a long swallow of his drink.

"Are you suggesting," Lunzie spoke slowly, phrasing it carefully, "that your goals and your employers' goals both depend on my steadfast opinions, even if they are . . . divergent?"

"You could say it that way." Zebara grinned at her, and slightly raised his mug.

And what other way, with what other meaning, could I say it? Lunzie wondered. She sipped from her own mug, tasting only the water she'd asked for, and said, "That's all very well, but what does it mean?"

"That, I'm afraid, we cannot discuss here. I will tell you what I can, and then we'll make plans to meet again." At her frown, he nodded. "That much is necessary, Lunzie, to keep immediate trouble at bay. We are watched. Of course we are, and I'm aware of it so we must continue our friendly association."

"Just how friendly?"

That slipped out before she meant it. She had not meant to ask that until later, if ever. He chuckled, but it sounded slightly forced.

"You know how friendly we *were*. You probably remember it better than I do since you slept peacefully for over forty of the intervening years."

She felt the blood rushing to her face and let it. Any watchers would assume that was genuine emotion.

"You! I have to admit that I haven't forgotten you, not one . . . single . . . thing."

This time, he was the one to blush. She hoped it satisfied whoever was doing the surveillance but she thought the actual transcript would prove deadly.

As if he could read her thoughts, he said "Don't worry! At this stage they're still letting me arrange the surveillance. We're relatively safe as long as we don't do something outside their plans."

Their plans or your plans, she wondered. She wanted to trust Zebara: she *did* trust the Zebara she'd known. But this new Zebara, this old man with the hooded eyes, the grandchildren he wanted to save, the head of External Security, could she trust *this* Zebara? And how far?

Still, when he reached for her hand, she let him take it. His fingers stroked her palm and she wondered if he would try something as simple as dot code. Cameras might pick that up. Instead, a fingernail lightly drew the logo on the FSP banner, then letter by letter traced her name. She smiled at him, squeezed his hand, and hoped she was right.

The next day's work at the Center went well. Whatever Bias thought, he managed not to say and no one else asked uncomfortable questions. Lunzie came back to her quarters, feeling slightly uneasy that she hadn't heard from Zebara but her message light was blinking as she came in. She put in a call to the number she was given, and was not surprised to hear his voice.

"You said once you'd like to hear our native music," he began. "There's a performance tonight of Zilmach's epic work. Would you come with me?"

"Formal dress, or informal?" asked Lunzie.

"Not formal like the Governor's reception, but nice."

She was sure he was laughing underneath at her interest in clothes. But she agreed to be ready in an hour without commenting on it. Dinner before the performance was at an obviously classy restaurant. The other diners wore expensive jewels in addition to fancy clothes. Lunzie felt subdued in her simple dark green dress with the copper-and-enamel necklace that served her for all occasions. Zebara wore a uniform she did not recognize. Did External Security really go for that matte black or did they intend it to intimidate offworlders? He looked the perfect foil for Sassinak. She let herself remember Sassinak in her dress whites, with the vivid alert expression that made her beautiful. Zebara sat there like a black lump of rough stone, heavy and sullen. Then he smiled.

"Dear Lunzie, you're glaring at me. Why?"

"I was thinking of my great-great-great-granddaughter," she said, combining honesty and obliqueness at once. "You have grandchildren, you said? Then surely they cross your mind at the oddest times, intruding, but you'd never wish them away."

"That's true." He shook his head with a rueful smile. "And since mine are here in person, they can intrude physically as well. Little Pog, the youngest, got loose from his mother in my office one time. Darted past my secretary, straight through the door and into my conference room. Set off alarms and thoroughly annoyed the Lieutenant Governor and the Chiefs of Staff. He'd grabbed me by the leg and was howling because the alarm siren scared him. He made so much noise the guards were sure someone was really hurt." His smile had broadened; now he chuckled. "By the time I had peeled him off my leg, found his mother, and convinced the guards that it was not an exceptionally clever assassination scheme using a midget or a robot, none of us could get our minds back on the problem. Worst of all, I had to listen to a lecture by the Lieutenant Governor on the way he disciplines *his* family. What he didn't know, and I couldn't tell him, was that his eldest son was about to be arrested for sedition. This is, as you might suspect, the *former* Lieutenant Governor, not the one you met the other night."

The revelation about his job did nothing to quiet Lunzie's nerves. Anyone who could pretend not to know that someone's child was about to be arrested had more than enough talent in lying to confuse *her*. She forced herself to concentrate on his feelings for his children and grandchildren. That, at least, she could understand and sympathize with.

"So what happened to little . . . Pog, was it?"

"Yes, short for Poglin. Family name on his mother's side. Well, I counseled leniency since he'd been frightened so badly by the alarms and the subsequent chaos, but his mother felt guilty that he'd gotten away from her. She promised him a good thrashing when they got home. I hope that was mostly for my benefit. She's very . . . aware of rank, that one." It was obvious that he didn't like his daughter-in-law much. Lunzie wondered if he'd meant to reveal that to her. "And have you caught up with all your family after your long sleep?" he was asking.

Lunzie shook her head, and sipped cautiously at the steaming soup that had appeared in front of them. Pale orange, spicy, not bad at all.

"My great-great, Sassinak, gave me Fleet transport to Sector Headquarters. She's an orphan. She's never met the others."

"Oh. Isn't that unusual? Wouldn't they take her in?" His eyelids had sagged again, hiding his expression. Lunzie suspected he knew a lot more about her and her family, including Sassinak, than he pretended.

"They didn't know." Quickly, she told him what little Sassinak had told her and added her own interpretation of Sassinak's failure to seek out her parents' relatives. "She's still afraid of rejection, I think. Fleet took her in. She considers it her family. I had one grandson, Dougal, in Fleet, and I remember the others complaining that he was almost a stranger to them. Even when he visited, he seemed attached somewhere else."

"Will you introduce her?"

"I've thought about that. Forty-three more years. I don't know who's alive, where they are, although it won't be hard to find out. But she may not want to meet them, even with me. I'm still trying to figure out whose she is, for that matter. I haven't really had time." At the startled look on his face, she laughed. "Zebara, you've been *with* your family all this time. Of course nothing is more important to you. But I've had one long separation after another. I've had to make my connections where and when I could. The first thing was to get my certification back, get some kind of job."

"Surely your great-great, this Sassinak, wouldn't have tossed you out to starve!"

"She's Fleet, remember? Under orders. I'm civilian." *Sort of*, she thought to herself, wondering just what status she did have. Coromell had recruited her: was that official? The Venerable Master Adept seemed to have connections to Fleet she had never quite understood. But surely *he* wasn't a Fleet agent? Sassinak had sent her to Liaka with the same assurance she'd have sent one of her own officers. "I wouldn't have starved, no. You're right about that. But by the time I left Liaka, I still didn't have my accumulated back pay. It would come, they assured me, but it was sticking in someone's craw to pay me for forty-three years of coldsleep. All I really wanted was the credit for time awake, but . . ." She shrugged. "Bureaucrats."

"We are difficult sometimes." He was smiling, but she wondered why he had intruded his position again.

They finished dinner with little more conversation, then went to the concert. Zebara's rank meant excellent seats, a respectful usher, and a well of silence around them, beyond which Lunzie could just hear curious murmurs. She glanced down at the program. She had never heard of Zilmach or his (her?) epic work. The program cover showed two brawny heavyworlders lifting a spaceship overhead. She didn't know if that was a scene from the work she would hear or the logo of the Diplo Academy of Music. She nudged Zebara.

"Tell me about this."

"Zilmach, a composer you won't have heard of, spent twenty years on this, working from the series of poems Rudrik wrote in the first Long Freeze on Diplo. Rudrik, by the way, died of starvation, along with some forty thousand of those early colonists. It's called *Bitter Destiny* and the theme is exploitation of our strength to provide riches for the weak. You won't like the libretto, but the music is extraordinary." He nuzzled her neck and Lunzie managed not to jump. "Besides, it's loud, and we can talk if we're careful."

"It's not rude?"

"Yes," he said quietly into her ear, "But there are segments in which almost everyone gets affectionate; you'll know."

Zilmach's epic work began with a low moaning of strings and woodwinds, plus a rhythmic banging on some instrument Lunzie had never heard before: rather like someone whacking a heavy chain with a hammer. She ventured a murmured question to Zebara who explained that it represented the pioneers chipping ice off their machinery. Zilmach had invented the instrument in the course of writing the music.

After the overture, a massed chorus marched in singing. Lunzie felt goosebumps break out on her arms. Although she had told herself that the heavyworlders must have creative capacity, she had never truly believed it. She had never seen any of their art, or heard their music. Now, listening to those resonant voices filling the hall easily, she admitted to herself just how narrowminded she'd been. The best she'd been able to imagine was "kind" or "gentle." But this was magnificent.

She did not enjoy the staged presentation of the lightweight "exploiters." Although seeing massive heavyworlders pretending to be tiny fragile lightweights cringing from each other had the humor of incongruity. She remembered having seen a cube of an Old Earth opera in which a large lady with sagging jowls was being serenaded as a "nymph."

But the voices! She had imagined heavyworlder music as heavy, thumping, unmelodic . . . and she'd been wrong.

"It's *beautiful*," she murmured to Zebara, in a pause between scenes.

"You're surprised." It was not a question. She apologized with her expression as the music began again. He leaned closer. "Don't worry. I thought you'd be surprised. And there's more."

"More" included a display of gymnastics representing shifting alliances in the commercial consortium that had (according to the script) dumped ill-prepared heavyworlder colonists on a planet that suffered predictable, but infrequent, "triple winters." Complex gong music apparently intimated the heartless weighing of profit and loss (a balance loaded with "gold" bars on one side and limp heavyworlder bodies on the other) while the corporate factions pushed on the balance and each other, and leapt about in oddly graceful contortions.

Diplo's gravity prevented any of the soaring leaps of classical ballet but quick flips were possible and used to great effect. A scene showing the luxurious life of lightweights in space was simply ludicrous. Lunzie had never seen anyone aboard a spaceship lounging in a scented fountain while a heavyworlder servant knelt with a tray of fruit. But overall she remained amazed with the lush, melodic sound and the quality of the voices.

Those segments in which, as Zebara promised, "everyone gets affectionate" depicted the colonists fighting off the depression of that long winter with song and love. Or lust. Lunzie wasn't sure. Perhaps the colonists hadn't been sure, either. But they had been determined to survive and have descendants.

Duet followed duet, combined into a quartet praising "love of life that warms the heart." Then a soprano aria from a singer whose deep, dark, resonant voice throbbed with despair before rising slowly, impossibly, through three octaves to end in a crystalline flourish which the singer emphasized by a massive fist, shaking at the wicked lightweights in their distant ships.

Finally the male chorus of colonists, who had chosen to starve voluntarily so that children and pregnant women might have a chance to survive, made their final vows, led by a tenor whose voice soared to nearly the same dynamic height as the soprano.

"To you, the children of our dreams, we leave the bread of life!" Lunzie felt tears stinging her eyes. "We ask but this! That you remember . . ."

The voices faded, slowly dropping to a complex chant. The music and the rich incense flowing from the censers onstage were enough to get anyone's hormones moving. She let her head sag toward Zebara's shoulder.

"Good girl," he murmured.

Around them, rustling indicated that others, too, were changing their positions. Suddenly Lunzie felt something bump her legs, and realized that the seats in this section reclined *completely*. The armrest between hers and Zebara's retracted. Onstage, the music swelled as the lights dimmed. Clearly, an invitation to Zilmach's epic meant more than just listening to the music.

At the same moment that she wondered how she was going to get out of what was clearly intended, she remembered her pressure garment, and sniggered.

"What?" he asked. His arm lay heavily on her shoulders; his broad hand stroked her back.

"An element of lightweight weakness your producers forgot to show," Lunzie said, trying to control her laughter. "This thing we have to wear. Very inefficient at moments like this."

Zebara chuckled. "Dear Lunzie, I have no intention of forcing you. You might get pregnant. You're young enough. You don't want my child, and I don't want the responsibility. But we *are* expected to whisper sweet nothings in each others' ears. If the sweets are not nothings, who's to know?"

This was no time to ask if Diplo External Security had the same kinds of electronics Fleet used, which could have picked up the rumbles from dinner in her stomach, let alone anything she and Zebara might whisper. If they didn't, they didn't need to know about it. If they did, she had to hope Zebara had only one doublecross in mind.

"So, how long does this last?"

"Several *looong* minutes. Don't worry. We'll have plenty of warning before it's over. There's the funeral scene coming up and the decision whether or not to eat the bodies. So let's use this interval to find out the things I must know. Who sent you here and what are you trying to find?"

Lunzie could not answer at once. She had not thought that even a heavyworlder could mention cannibalism so calmly. Another blow to her wish to trust him. His tongue flicked her ear, gaining all her attention easily.

"Lunzie, you cannot expect me to believe you came here just to get over your fear of heavyworlders. Ireta would have left you even worse. You could not care that much how we experience coldsleep or what it does to us. You are here for a purpose. Either your own, or someone else's, and I must know that if I am to keep you safe."

"You've told me your government wants you to use our old relationship. How can you ask me to confide in you first?" That was lame, but the best she could do with cannibalism still on her mind.

"I want my grandchildren to live! Really live. I want them to have enough food, freedom to travel, to get education, to work where they want. You want that for your descendants. In that we agree. If war breaks out between our peoples, none of our descendants will have the lives we want for them. Can't you see that?"

Lunzie nodded slowly. "Yes, but unless your people quit working with planet pirates I don't see what's to stop it."

"Which they won't do, unless they see a better future. Lunzie, I want you to be our advocate, our spokeswoman to the Council. You have suffered from us but you have also seen, perhaps understood, what we are, what we could be. I want you to say 'Give the heavyworlders hope! Give them access to normal-G worlds they can live on, worlds like Ireta. Then they won't have reason to steal them.' But as long as you are here to collect evidence proving how bad we are."

"Not all of you."

Lunzie caught a flicker of movement near them, above them, and curled into Zebara's embrace. Perhaps someone needed the restrooms, sidling along between the seat sections. Or perhaps someone wanted to know what they were saying.

"You're different. The patients I've met here are not like those who hurt me." She felt under her hands his slight tension. He, too, had noticed that shadowy form edging past them.

"Dear Lunzie." That ended in a kiss, a curiously grandfatherly kiss of dry lips. Then he sighed, moved as if slightly cramped, and laid his hand back on her hair.

"Who? Please tell me!"

She decided to give him a little, what he might have tapped from Fleet communications if his people were good enough.

"Sassinak. She wanted to know if the Governor were officially involved in Ireta. Captain Cruss, the heavyworlder on that colony ship, thought so. The Theks got it out of him. With Tanegli's trial coming up, she wanted to know whether to suggest that the Fleet subpoena the Governor."

"Ahhh. About what we thought. But how were you, a physician, supposed to find out such things?"

"I'd told her about you. She said I should come." That wasn't quite accurate, but if he believed she had been pushed into it, he might be sympathetic.

"I see. Your descendant, being a professional, does not consider your feelings, your natural reluctance. Not very sensitive, your Sassinak."

"Oh, she is," Lunzie said quickly. "She is sensitive, she just . . . She just thinks of duty first."

"Commendable in a Fleet officer, no doubt, but not in a great-great-great-granddaughter. She should have more respect."

"It's a problem," Lunzie admitted. "But she's actually older than I am —real time, at least—and she has trouble seeing me as her elder. We both do." She squirmed a little getting a stiff wrinkle out from under her hip. "But that's why I came . . . really."

"And I am to offer you just the information you seek, and ask you to smuggle out more. But you will be found to have instead information of great commercial value. You will be discredited as a commercial spy, detained long enough that you cannot testify against Tanegli. Your taped evidence will not be nearly as effective, and if Kai and Varian are not there . . ."

"Why shouldn't they be?"

"Contract scientists with EEC? Easy enough to send an all too special ship to collect them to attend the Assizes. It should not be hard for those with adequate resources to be sure they arrive late. Or not at all."

Lunzie shivered. How could she warn Kai and Varian? Why hadn't she thought of them before? She had assumed that, as civilians, they would be allowed to go about their new responsibilities on Ireta. She should have known better.

"It is not just heavyworlders," Zebara murmured, as if he'd read her mind. "You know there are others?" Lunzie nodded.

Any of the commercial entities would find greater profit in resource development without regulation. Humans and aliens both. She had heard of no society so idealistic that it had no criminals among it. Perhaps the Ssli, she amended: once sessile, how could they do anything wrong, in anyone's terms? But here and now?

"Seti!" came Zebara's murmur. "They've used us, pretended sympathy for our fate, for having been genetically altered. But they despise us for it, as well."

She nodded against his chest, trying to think. The Seti predated human membership in the FSP, though not by much. They were difficult, far more alien-seeming, and less amusing, than the Ryxi or Wefts. They had destroyed a Weft planet and later claimed to have done so accidentally, not knowing of the Wefts they killed. And the Thek!

"It's three-cornered, really." Zebara nuzzled her hair a long moment and she felt the draft of someone's movement past them again. "Our Governor's worked for the Pralungan Combine for over twenty years. He's been paid off in money, shares, and positions for his relatives. The Combine gets strong backs for its internal security forces, industrial enforcers. Even private troops. Crew for illegally armed vessels to fight Fleet interference. Your Sassinak's been a major problem for us, by the way. She gets along too well with her heavyworlder marines. That word's spread and we have too many youngsters thinking of Fleet as a future. Not to mention the number of ships she's blown up in her career. Also, the Seti have some gain of their own we haven't quite figured out. They want some of the planets we've taken: mostly those unsuitable for human settlement. They're funneling money into the Combine and the Combine funnels some, as little as they can, to us."

It was almost too much to take in. "What do you want me to do?" asked Lunzie.

"Get the real data out. Not the faked stuff you're supposed to be caught with. You'll have to leave before your team. It's supposed to look as if you're fleeing with stolen information. And if you don't, they'll know I didn't convince you. But you can leave before even they expect it. I can say you double-crossed me, used the pass you were given too soon."

It sounded most unlikely. No lightweight could get offplanet unnoticed. Surely they would be watching her. If she tried to bolt, they would simply call Zebara to check. And then find on her the real data, dooming both of them. She said this, very fast and very softly, into his ear. He held her close, a steady grip that would have been calming if her mind had not gone on ahead to the obvious conclusion.

He did not mean her to escape as a lightweight: as someone walking up the ramp, opening her papers for inspection at the port, climbing into her seat in the shuttle. He had something else in mind, something that would not be so obvious. The possibilities scrolled through her mind as if on a screen.

As cargo? But an infrared scan would find her. As— She stiffened, pulled her head back, and tried to see his face in the darkened hall.

"*Not* in coldsleep." She meant it to be non-negotiable.

"I'm sorry," he said, into her hair.

"No." Quietly, but firmly, and with no intention of being talked into it. "Not again."

At that very inopportune moment, the softly passionate music stopped, leaving the hall in sudden silence interspersed with rustling clothing. The silence lengthened. A single drumbeat, slow, inexorable, signalled a dire event, and the back of her seat shoved her up, away from Zebara. The armrest slid upward between them. The footrest dropped. Another drum joined the first, heavy, sodden with grief. Muted brass, one grave note after another followed the drums. Onstage, lights showed the barest outline of a heap of bodies, of sufferers still alive and starving. The sacrifice had not been enough. They would all die after all. A child's soprano, piercing as a needle, cried out for food, and Lunzie flinched. The alto's voice replying held all history's bitterness.

Surely it had not really been this bad! It could not have been! The rigid arm of the man beside her insisted it was, it had been. He believed it so, at least, and he believed the future might be as bleak. Lunzie swallowed, fighting nausea. If they actually *showed* cannibalism onstage . . . but they did not. A chorus of grieving women, of hungry children. One suggested, the others cried out in protest, and this went on (as so often in operas) somewhat longer than was necessary to convince everyone that both sides were sincere.

One after another came over to the side of horror, for the children's sake, but it was, in the end, a child who raised a shaking arm to point at the new element in the crisis. The new element, presented onstage as a fur-coated robot of sorts, was the native grazer of the tundra. Shaggy, uncouth, and providentially stupid, it had been drawn by the warmth of the colonists' huts from its usual path of migration. The same woman who had been ready to put the dead into a synthesizer now wrestled the shaggy beast and killed it: not without being gored by two of its six horns. Whereupon the survival of the colony was assured so long as they were willing to kill and eat the animals.

One alone stood fast by the Federation's prohibition, and threatened to reveal what they'd done. She was prevented from sending any message and died by her own hand after a lengthy aria explaining why she was willing to kill not only herself but her unborn child.

"That none of my blood shed sentient blood, so precious is to me . . ."

Lunzie found herself more moved by this than she had expected. Whether it was true or not, whether it had happened at all, or for these reasons, the story itself commanded respect and pity. And it explained a *lot* about the heavyworlders. If you believed this, if you had grown up seeing this, hearing this gorgeous music put to the purpose of explaining that the lightweights would let forty thousand people die of cold and starvation because it was inconvenient to rescue them, because it would lower the profit margin, then you would naturally distrust the lightweights, and despise their dietary whims.

Would I have eaten meat even after it had been through the synthesizer? she asked herself. She let herself remember being pregnant, and the years when Fiona had been a round-faced toddler. She would not have let Fiona starve.

In a grand crashing conclusion, the lightweights returned in a warm season to remonstrate with the colonists about their birthrate and their eating habits. The lead soprano, now white-haired and many times a grandmother, the children clustered around her as she sang, told them off in ringing phrases, dizzying swoops of melody that seemed impossible to bring from one throat. The colonists repudiated the lightweights' claims, refused to submit to their rules, their laws, demanded justice in the courts or they would seek it in their own way.

The lightweights flourished weapons and two heavyweights lifted them contemptuously overhead, tossing them—the smallest cast members Lunzie had yet seen—until they tumbled shaken to the ground. Then the two picked up the "spaceship," stuffed the lightweight emissaries inside, and threw the whole assemblage into space. Or so it appeared. Actually, Lunzie was sure, some stage mechanism pulled it up out of sight.

Curtain down! Lights up! Zebara turned to her.

"Well? What do you think of Zilmach?" Then his blunt finger touched her cheek. "You cried."

"Of course I did." Her voice was still rough with emotion. To her own ears she sounded peevish. "If that's true . . ." She shook her head, started again. "It's magnificent, it's terrible, and tears are the only proper response." What she wanted to say would either start a riot or make no sense. She said, "What voices! And to think I've never heard of this. Why isn't it known?"

"We don't export this. It's just our judgment that your people would have no interest in it."

"Music is music."

"And politics is politics. Come! Would you like to meet Ertrid, the one who brought those tears to your eyes?"

Clearly the only answer was yes, so she said yes. Zebara's rank got them backstage quickly, where Ertrid proved to have a speaking voice as lovely as her singing. Lunzie had had little experience with performers. She hardly knew what to expect. Ertrid smiled, if coolly, and thanked Lunzie for her compliments, with an air of needing nothing from a lightweight. But she purred for Zebara, almost sleeking herself against him. Lunzie felt a stab of wholly unreasonable jealousy. Ertrid's smile widened.

"You must not mind, Lunzie. He has so *many* friends!"

She fingered the necklace she wore, which Lunzie had admired without considering its origins. Zebara gave the singer a quick hug and guided Lunzie away. When they were out of earshot, he leaned to speak in her ear.

"I could have said, so does she, but I would not embarrass such a great artist on a night like this. She does not like to see me with another woman, and particularly not a lightweight."

"And particularly not after that role," said Lunzie, trying to stifle her jealousy and be reasonable. She didn't want Zebara now, if she ever had. The emotion was ridiculous.

"And I *didn't* buy her that necklace," Zebara went on, as if proving himself to her. "That was the former Lieutenant Governor's son, the one I spoke of."

"It's all *right*."

Lunzie wished he would quit talking about it. She did not care, she told herself firmly, what Zebara had done with the singer, or who had bought what jewelry seen and unseen, or what the Lieutenant Governor's son had done. All that mattered was her mission, and his mission, and finding some other way to accomplish it than enduring another bout of coldsleep.

Chapter Eight

FedCentral, Fleet Headquarters

"And that's the last of the crew depositions?" Sassinak asked. The 'Tenant behind the desk nodded.

"Yes, ma'am. The Prosecutor's office said they didn't need anyone else. Apparently the defense lawyers aren't going to call any of the enlisted crew as witnesses either."

So we've just spent weeks of this nonsense for nothing, Sassinak thought. Dragging my people up and down in ridiculous civilian shuttles, for hours of boring questioning which only repeats what we taped on the ship before. She didn't say any of this. Both the Chief Prosecutor's office and the defense lawyers had been furious that Lunzie, Dupaynil, and Ford were not aboard. For one thing, Kai and Varian had also failed to appear for depositions. No one knew if the fast bark sent to collect them from Ireta had found them on the planet's surface for no message had been received on either count.

She herself was sure that Ford and Lunzie would be back in time. Dupaynil? Dupaynil might or might not arrive, although she considered him more resourceful than most desk-bound Security people. If he hadn't made her so furious, she'd have enjoyed more of his company.

She would certainly have preferred him to Aygar as an assistant researcher. True, Aygar could go search the various databases without arousing suspicion. Anyone would expect him to. The Prosecutor's office had arranged a University card, a Library card, all the access he could possibly want. And he was eager enough.

But he had no practice in doing research; no background of scholarship. Sassinak had to explain exactly where he should look and for what. Even then he would come back empty-handed, confused, because he didn't understand how little bits of disparate knowledge could fit together to mean anything. He would spend all day looking up the genealogy of the heavyworlder mutineers, or haring after some interest of his own. Dupaynil, with all his smug suavity, would have been a relief.

She strolled back along the main shopping avenues of the city, in no hurry. She was to meet Aygar for the evening shuttle flight. She had time to wander around. A window display caught her eye, bright with the colors she favored. She admired the jeweled jacket over a royal-blue skirt that flashed turquoise in shifts of light. She glanced at the elegant calligraphy above the glossy black door. No wonder! "Fleur de Paris" was only the outstanding fashion designer for the upper classes. Her mouth quirked: at least she had good taste.

The door, its sensors reporting that someone stood outside it longer than the moment necessary to walk past, swung inward. A human guard, in livery, stood just inside.

"Madame wishes to enter?"

The sidewalk burned her feet even through the uniform shoes. Her head ached. She had never in her life visited a place like this. But why not? It could do no harm to look.

"Thank you," she said, and walked in.

Inside, she found a cool oasis: soft colors, soft carpets, a recording of harp music just loud enough to cover the street's murmur. A well-dressed woman who came forward, assessing her from top to toe, and, to Sassinak's surprise, approving.

"Commander . . . Sassinak, is it not?"

"I'm surprised," she said. The woman smiled.

"We do watch the news programs, you know. How serendipitous! Fleur will want to meet you."

Sassinak almost let her jaw drop. She had heard a little about such places as this. The designer herself did not come out and meet everyone who came through the door.

"Won't you have a seat?" the woman went on. "And you'll have something cool, I hope?" She led Sassinak to a padded chair next to a graceful little table on which rested a tall pitcher, its sides beaded, and a crystal glass. Sassinak eyed it doubtfully. "Fruit juice," the woman said. "Although if you'd prefer another beverage?"

"No, thank you. This is fine."

She took the glass she was offered and sipped it to cover her confusion. The woman went away, leaving her to look around. She had been in shops, in some very good shops, with elegant displays of a few pieces of jewelry or a single silk dress. But here nothing marked the room as part of a shop. It might have been the sitting room of some wealthy matron: comfortable chairs grouped around small tables, fresh flowers, soft music. She relaxed, slowly, enjoying the tart fruit juice. If they knew she was a Fleet officer, they undoubtedly knew her salary didn't stretch to original creations. But if they were willing to have her rest in their comfortable chair, she wasn't about to walk out.

"My dear!" The silver-haired woman who smiled at her might have been any elegant great-grand-mother who had kept her figure. Seventies? Eighties? Sassinak wasn't sure. "What a delightful surprise. Mirelle told you we'd seen you on the news, didn't she? And of course we'd seen you walk by. I must confess," this with a throaty chuckle that Sassinak could not resist, "I've been putting one thing after another in the window to see if we could entice you." She turned to the first woman. "And you see, Mirelle, I was right: the jeweled jacket did it."

Mirelle shrugged gracefully. "And I will wager that if you asked her, she'd remember seeing that sea-green number."

"Yes, I did," said Sassinak, half-confused by their banter. "But what . . ."

"Mirelle, I think perhaps a light snack." Her voice was gentle, but still commanding. Mirelle smiled and withdrew, and the older woman smiled at Sassinak. "My dear Sassinak, I must apologize. It's . . . it's hard to think what to say. You don't realize what you mean to people like us."

Thoroughly confused now, Sassinak murmured something indistinct. Did famous designers daydream about flying spaceships? She couldn't believe that, but what else was going on?

"I am known to the world as Fleur," the woman said, sitting down across the table from Sassinak. "Fleur de Paris, which is a joke, although very few know it. I cannot tell you what my name was, even now. But I can tell you that we had a friend in common. A very dear friend."

"Yes?" Sassinak rummaged in her memory for any wealthy or socially prominent woman she might have known. An admiral, or an admiral's wife? And came up short.

"Your mentor, my dear, when you were a girl, Abe."

She could not have been more startled if Fleur had poured a bucket of ice over her. "Abe? You knew *Abe*?"

The older woman nodded. "Yes, indeed. I knew him before he was captured, and after. Although I never met you, I would have, in time. But as it was . . ."

"I know." The grief broke over her again, as startling in its intensity as the surprise that this woman—this old woman—had known Abe. But Abe, if he'd lived, would be old. That, too, shocked her. In her memory, he'd stayed the same, an age she gradually learned was not so old as the child had thought.

"I'm sorry to distress you, but I needed to speak to you. About Abe, about his past and mine. And about your future."

"My future?" What could this woman possibly have to do with her future? It must have shown on her face, because Fleur shook her head.

"A silly old woman, you think, intruding on your life. You admire the clothes I design, but you don't need a rich woman's sycophant reminding you of Abe. Yes?"

It was uncomfortably close to what she'd been thinking. "I'm sorry," she said, apologizing for being obvious, if for nothing else.

"That's all right. He said you were practical, tenacious, clear-headed, and so you must be. But there are things you should know. Since we may be interrupted at any time—after all, this is a business—first let me suggest that if you find yourself in need of help, in any difficult situation in the city, mention my name. I have contacts. Perhaps Abe mentioned Samizdat?"

"Yes, he did." Sassinak came fully alert at that. She had never found any trace of the organization Abe had told her about once she was out of the Academy. Did it still exist?

"Good. Had Abe lived, he would have made sure you knew how to contact some of its members. But, as it was, no one knew you well enough to trust you, even with your background. This meeting should remedy that."

"But then you . . ."

Fleur's smile this time had an edge of bitterness. "I have my own story. We all do. If there's time, you'll hear mine. For now, know that I knew Abe, and loved him dearly, and I have watched your career, as it appears in the news, with great interest."

"But how . . ." As she spoke, the door opened again, and three women came in, chattering gaily. Fleur stood at once and greeted them, smiling.

Sassinak, uncertain, sat where she was. The women, it seemed, had come in hopes of finding Fleur free. They glanced at Sassinak, then away, saying that they simply *must* have Fleur's advice on something of great importance.

"Why of course," she said. "Do come into my sitting room." One of them must have murmured something about Sassinak, for she said, "No, no. Mirelle will be right back to speak to the commander."

Mirelle reappeared, as if by magic, bearing a tray with tiny sandwiches and cookies in fanciful shapes.

"Fleur says you're quite welcome to stay, but she doesn't think she'll be free for several hours. That's an old customer, with her daughters-in-law, and they come to gossip as much as for advice. She's very sorry. You will have a snack, won't you?"

For courtesy's sake, Sassinak took a sandwich. Mirelle hovered, clearly uneasy about something. When Sassinak insisted on leaving, Mirelle exhibited both disappointment and relief.

"You will come again?"

"When I can. Please tell Fleur I was honored to meet her, but I can't say when I'll be able to come onplanet again."

That should give Sassinak time to think, and if she hadn't made a decision by the next required conference, she could always go by a different street. Outside again, she found herself thinking again of Dupaynil, simply because of his specialties. She wished she had some way of getting into the databases herself, without going through Aygar, and without being detected. She would like very much to know who "Fleur de Paris" was, and why her name was supposed to be a joke.

In his days on the *Zaid-Dayan*, Dupaynil would have sworn that he was capable of intercepting any data link and resetting any control panel on any ship. All he had to do was reconfigure the controls on the escort vessel's fifteen escape pods so that he could control them. It should have been simple. It was not simple. He had not slept but for the briefest naps. He dared not sleep until it was done. And yet he had to appear to sleep, as he appeared to eat, to play cards, to chat idly, to take the exercise that had become regular to him, up and down the ladders.

He had no access to the ship's computer, no time to himself in the compartments where his sabotage would have been easiest. He had to do it all from his tiny cabin, in the few hours he could legitimately be alone, "sleeping."

And they had already found one of his taps. It frightened him in a way he had never been frightened before. He was good at the minutiae of his work, one of the neatest, his instructors had said, a natural. To have a lout like Ollery find one of his taps meant that he had been clumsy and careless. Or he had misjudged them, another way of being clumsy and careless.

He would not have lived this long had he really been clumsy or careless, but he had depended on the confusion, the complexity, of large ships. Fear only made his hands shake. Coldly, he considered himself as if he were a new trainee in Methods of Surveillance. *Think,* he told himself, the nervous trainee. You have the brains or they wouldn't have assigned you here. Use your wits. He set aside the odds against him. Beyond "high," what good were precise percentages? He considered the whole problem. He simply had to get those escape pods slaved to his control.

A crew which had spent five years together on a ship this small would know everything, would notice everything, especially as they now suspected him. But since they were already planning to space him, would they really worry about his taps? Wouldn't they, instead, snigger to each other about his apparent progress, enjoy letting him think he was spying on them, while knowing that nothing he found would ever be seen? He thought they would.

The question was, when would they spring their trap, and could he spring his before? And assuming he did gain control of the escape pods, so that they could not eject his, and he could eject theirs, he still had to get them all *into* the pods. They would know—at least the captain and mate would know—that the evacuation drill was a fake. So there was a chance, a good chance, that they would not be in pods at all. But thinking this far had quieted the tremor in his hands and cured his dry mouth.

Wiring diagrams and logic relays flicked through his mind, along with the possible modifications a renegade crew might have made. His audio tap into the captain's cabin still functioned. Listening on a still operative tap, he learned that the one that the mate had discovered had fallen victim to a rare bout of cleaning. As far as he knew, and as far as they said, they had not found any of the others. On the other hand, he had found two of theirs. He left them alone, unworried.

The personal kit he always had with him included the very best antisurveillance chip, bonded to his shaver. Through his own taps, he picked his way delicately toward control functions. Some were too well guarded for his limited set of tools. He could not lock the captain in his cabin, or shut off air circulation to any crew compartment. He could not override the captain's control of bridge access. He knew they were watching, suspecting just such a trick. He could not roam the computer's files too broadly, either. But he could get into such open files as the maintenance and repair records, and find that the galley hatch had repeatedly jammed. As an experiment, to see if he could do it without anyone noticing, Dupaynil changed the pressure on the upper hatch runner. It should jam, and be repaired, with only a few cuss-words for the pesky thing.

Sure enough, one of the crew complained bitterly through breakfast that the galley hatch was catching again. It was probably that double-damned pressure sensor on the upper runner. The mate nodded and assigned someone to fix it.

On such a small vessel, the escape pods were studded along either side of the main axis: three opening directly from the bridge, and the others aft, six accessed from the main and six from the alternate passage. Escape drill required each crew member to find an assigned pod, even if working near another. Pod assignments were posted in both bridge and galley.

Dupaynil tried to remember if anyone had actually survived a hull-breach on an escort, and couldn't think of an instance. The pods were there because regulations said every ship would carry them. That didn't make them practical. Pod controls on escort ships were the old-fashioned electro-mechanical relays; proof against magnetic surges from EM weapons which could disable more sophisticated controls by scrambling the wits of their controlling chips.

This simplicity meant that the tools he had were enough. Although, if someone looked, the changes would be more obvious than a reprogrammed or replacement chip. Fiddling with the switches and relays also took longer than changing a chip, and he found it difficult to stay suave and smiling when a crew member happened by as he was finishing one of the links.

The final step, slaving all the pod controls to one, and that one to his handcomp, tested the limits of his ability. He was almost *sure* the system would work. Unhappily, he would not know until he tried it. He was ready, as ready as he could be. He would have preferred to set off the alarm himself, but he dared not risk it. He played his usual round of cards with Ollery and the mate, making sure that he played neither too well nor too badly, and declined a dice game.

"Tomorrow," he said, with the blithe assurance of one who expects the morrow to arrive on schedule. "I can't stand all this excitement in one night."

They chuckled, the easy chuckle of the predator whose prey is in the trap. He went out wondering when they'd spring it. He really wanted a full shift's sleep.

The shattering noise of the alarm and the flashing lights woke him from the uneasy doze he'd allowed himself. He pulled on his pressure suit, lurched into the bulkhead, cursing, and staggered out into the passage. There was the mate, grinning. It was not a friendly grin.

"Escape pod drill, Lieutenant Commander! Remember your assignment?"

"Fourteen, starboard, next hatch but one."

"Right, sir. Go on now!" The mate had a handcomp, and appeared to be logging the response to the drill.

It could not be that. The computer automatically logged crew into and out of the escape pods. Dupaynil moved quickly down the passage, hearing the thumps and snarled curses of others on their way to the pods. He let himself into the next hatch but one, the pod he hoped was not only safely under his control, but now gave him control of the others.

On such a small ship, the drill required everyone to stay in the pods until all had reported in. Dupaynil listened to the ship's com as the pods filled. He hoped that the captain would preserve the fiction of a real drill. If nothing else, to cover his tracks with his Exec, and actually enter and lock off his own pod.

Things could get very sticky indeed if the captain discovered before entering his own pod, that Dupaynil had some of his crew locked away. Four were already "podded" when Dupaynil checked in. He secured their pods. It might be better to wait until everyone was in. But if some came out, then he'd be in worse trouble. If they obeyed the drill procedures, they wouldn't know they were locked in until he had full control.

One after another, so quickly he had some trouble to keep up with them, the others made it into their pods and dogged the hatches. Eight, nine (the senior mate, he was glad to notice). Only the officers and one enlisted left.

"Captain! There's something . . ."

The senior mate. Naturally. Dupaynil had not been able to interfere with the ship's intercom *and* reconfigure the pod controls. The mate must have planned to duck into his pod just long enough to register his presence on the computer, then come out to help the captain space Dupaynil.

Even as the mate spoke, Dupaynil activated all his latent sensors. Detection be damned! They knew he was onto them, and he needed all the data he could get. His control locks had better work! He was out of his own escape pod, with a tiny button-phone in his ear and his hand-held control panel.

Ollery and Panis were on the bridge. Even as Dupaynil moved forward, the last crewman checked into his pod and Dupaynil locked it down. Apparently he hadn't heard the mate.

That left the captain and that very new executive officer who would probably believe whatever the captain told him. He dogged down the hatch of his escape pod manually. From the corridor, it would look as if he were in it.

Go forward and confront the captain? No. He had to ensure that the others, especially the mate, stayed locked in. His fix might hold against a manual unlocking, but might not. So his first move was to the adjoining pods where he smashed the control panels beside each hatch. Pod fourteen, his own, was aftmost on the main corridor side, which meant he could ensure that no enemy appeared *behind* him. He would have to work his way back and forth between corridors though. Luckily the fifteenth pod was empty, and so was the thirteenth. Although the pods were numbered without using traditionally unlucky thirteen, most crews avoided the one that would have been thirteen. Stupid superstition, Dupaynil thought, but it helped him now.

Although he was sure he remembered which crew members were where, he checked on his handcomp and disabled the mate's pod controls next. Pod nine was off the alternate passage. He'd had to squeeze through a connecting passage and go forward past "14A" (the unlucky one) and pod eleven. From there he went back to disable pod eleven and checked to be sure the other two on that side were actually empty. It was not unknown for a lazy crewmember to check into the nearest unassigned pod.

He wondered all the while just what the captain was doing. Not to mention the Exec. If only he'd been able to get a full-channel tap on the bridge! He had just edged into the narrow cross passage between the main and alternate passages when he heard a faint noise and saw an emergency hatch slide across in front of him. Ollery had put the ship on alert, with full partitioning.

I should have foreseen that, Dupaynil thought. With a frantic lurch, he got his hands on its edge. The safety valve hissed at him but held the door still while he wriggled through the narrow gap. Now he was in the main corridor. Across from him he could see the recesses for pods ten and eight. He disabled their manual controls, one after another, working as quickly as he could but not worrying about noise. Just aft, another partition had come down, gray steel barrier between him and the pods further aft. But, when he first got out, he had disabled pod twelve. Just forward, another.

A thin hiss, almost at the edge of his hearing, stopped him just as he reached it. None of the possibilities looked good. He knew that Ollery could evacuate the air from each compartment and his pressure suit had only a two-hour supply. Less, if he was active. Explosive decompression wasn't likely, though he had no idea just how fast emergency decomp was. He had not sealed his bubble-helmet. He'd wanted to hear whatever was there to be heard. That hiss could be Ollery or Panis cutting through the partition with a weapon, something like a needler.

In the short stretch of corridor between the partitions, he had no place to hide. All compartment hatches sealed when the ship was on alert. Even if he had been able to get into the galley, it offered no concealment. Two steps forward, one back. What would Sassinak have done in his place? Found an access hatch, no doubt, or known something about the ship's controls that would have let her get out of this trap and ensnare Ollery at the same time. She would certainly have known where every pipe went and what was in it, what each wire and switch was for. Dupaynil could think of nothing.

It was interesting, if you looked at it that way, that Ollery hadn't tried to contact him on the ship's intercom. Did he even know Dupaynil was out of the pod? He must. He had normal ship's scans available in every compartment. Dupaynil's own sensors showed that the pods he had sealed were still sealed, their occupants safely out of the fight. Two blobs of light on a tiny screen were the captain and Panis on the bridge, right where they should be. Then one of them started down the alternate passage, slowly. He could not tell which it was, but logic said the captain had told Panis to investigate. Logic smirked when Ollery's voice came over the intercom only moments later.

"Check every compartment. I want voice report on anything out of the ordinary."

He could not hear the Jig's reply. He must be wearing a pressure suit and using its comunit to report. Didn't the captain realize that Dupaynil could hear the intercom? Or didn't he care? Meanwhile there was his own problem: that emergency partition. Dupaynil decided that the hissing was merely an air leak between compartments, an ill-fitting partition, and set to work to override its controls.

Several hot, sweaty minutes later, he had the thing shoved back in its recess, and edged past. The main passage forward looked deceptively ordinary, all visible hatches closed, nothing moving on the scarred tiles of the deck, no movement shimmering on the gleaming green bulkheads. Ahead, he could see another partition. Beyond it, he knew, the passage curved inboard and went up a half-flight of steps to reach Main Deck and access to the bridge and three escape pods there.

Dupaynil stopped to disable the manual controls on pods six and four. Now only three pods might still be a problem: five and seven, the two most forward on the alternate passage, and pod three, accessible from the bridge and assigned to the weapons tech. That one he could disable on his way to the bridge, assuming he could get through this next partition. Five and seven? Panis might be able to open them from outside, although the controls would not work normally.

How long would it take him? Would he even think of it? Would the captain try to free the man in pod three? At least the odds against him had dropped. Even if they got all three out, it would still be only five to one, rather than twelve to one. With this much success came returning confidence, almost ebullience. He reminded himself that he had not won the war yet. Not even the first battle. Just a preliminary skirmish, which could all come undone if he lost the next bit.

"I don't care if it looks normal," he heard on the intercom. "Try to undog those hatches and let Siris out."

Blast. Ollery was not entirely stupid. Panis must be looking at pod five. Siri: data tech, the specialist in computers, sensors, all that. Dupaynil worked at the forward partition, hoping Ollery would be more interested in following his Exec's progress, would trust to the partition to hold him back. A long pause, in which his own breathing sounded ragged and loud in the empty, silent passage.

Then: "I don't care what it takes, *open it*!"

At least some of his reworking held against outside tampering. Dupaynil spared no time for smugness, as the forward partition was giving him more trouble than the one before. If he'd only had his complete kit . . . But there, it gave, sliding back into its slot with almost sentient reluctance to disobey the computer. Here the passage curved and he could not get all the way to the steps. Dupaynil flattened himself along the inside bulkhead, looking at the gleaming surface across from him for any moving reflections. Lucky for him that Ollery insisted on Fleet-like order and cleanliness. Dupaynil found it surprising. He'd always assumed that renegades would be dirty and disorderly. But the ship would have to pass Fleet inspections, whether its crew were loyal or not.

He waited. Nothing moved. He edged cautiously forward, with frequent glances at his handcomp. The captain's blob stayed where it had been. Panis's was still in the alternate passage near the hatch of pod five. At the foot of the steps, he paused. Above was the landing outside the bridge proper, with the hatches of three pods on his left. One and two would be open: the assigned pods for captain and Exec. Three would be closed, with the weapons tech inside. The hatch to the bridge would be closed, unless Panis had left it open when he went hunting trouble. If it was open, the captain would not fail to hear Dupaynil coming. Even if he weren't monitoring his sensors, and he would be, he'd know exactly where Dupaynil was. And once Dupaynil came to the landing, he could see him out the open hatch. If it was open.

Had Panis left the bridge hatch open? Had he left the partition into the alternate corridor open? It would make sense to do so. Even though the captain could control the partitions individually from the bridge, overriding the computer's programming, that would take a few seconds. If the captain suspected he might need help, he would want those partitions back so that Panis and any freed crewmen had easy access.

He started up the steps, reminding himself to breathe deeply. One. Two. No sound from above, and he could not see the bridge hatch without being visible from it. Another step, and another. If he had had time, if he had had his entire toolkit, he would have had taps in place and would know if that hatch . . .

A clamor broke out on the other side of the ship, crashing metal, cries. And, above him and around the curve, the captain's voice both live and over the intercom.

"Go *on*, Siris!"

Then the clatter of feet, as the captain left the bridge (no sound of the hatch opening: it had been open) and headed down the alternate passage. Dupaynil had no idea what was going on, but he shot up the last few steps, and poked his head into the upper end of the alternate corridor. And saw the captain's back, headed aft, with some weapon, probably a needler, in his clenched fist. There were yells from both Panis and the man he had freed.

It burst on Dupaynil suddenly that the Ollery intended to kill his Exec. Either because he thought he was in league with Dupaynil or was using this excuse to claim he'd mutinied. Dupaynil launched himself after the captain, hoping that the crewman wasn't armed. Panis and Siris were still thrashing on the floor. Dupaynil could see only a whirling confusion of suit-clad bodies. Their cries and the sound of the blows covered his own approach. Ollery stood above them, clearly waiting his chance to shoot. Dupaynil saw the young officer's face recognize his captain, and his captain's intent. His expression changed from astonishment to horror.

Then Dupaynil flipped his slim black wire around the captain's neck and *pulled*. The captain bucked, sagged, and dropped, still twitching but harmless. Dupaynil caught up the needler that the crewman reached for, stepping on the man's wrist with deceptive grace. He could feel the bones grate beneath his heel.

"But what? But who?" Panis, disheveled, one eye already blackening, had the presence of mind to keep a firm controlling grip on the crewman's other arm.

Dupaynil smiled. "Let's get this one under control first," he said.

"I don't know what happened," Panis went on. "Something's wrong with the escape pod hatches. It took forever to get this one open, and then Siris jumped me, and the captain—" His voice trailed away as he glanced at the captain lying purple-faced on the deck.

Siris tried a quick heave but the Jig held on. Dupaynil let his heel settle more firmly on the wrist. The man cursed viciously.

"Don't do that," Dupaynil said to him, waving the needler in front of him. "If you should get loose from Jig Panis, I would simply kill you. Although you might prefer that to trial. Would you?"

Siris lay still, breathing heavily. Panis had planted a few good ones on him, too. His face was bruised and he had a split lip which he licked nervously. Dupaynil felt no sympathy. Still watching Siris for trouble, he spoke to Panis.

"Your captain was engaged in illegal activities. He planned to kill both of us." Even as he spoke, he wondered if he could possibly convince a Board of Inquiry that the entire scheme, including the rewired escape pod controls, had been the captain's. Probably not, but it was worth considering in the days ahead.

"I can't believe . . ." Again Panis's voice trailed away. He *could* believe; he had seen that needler in his captain's hand, heard what the captain said. "And you're?"

"Fleet Security, as you know. Apparently that spooked Major Ollery, convinced him that I was on his trail. I wasn't, as a matter of fact."

"Liar!" said Siris.

Dupaynil favored him with a smile that he hoped combined injured innocence with predatory glee. It must have succeeded for the man paled and gulped.

"I don't bother to lie," he said quietly, "when truth is so useful." He went on with his explanation. "When I found that the captain planned to kill me and that you were not part of the conspiracy, I assumed he'd kill you, too, so he wouldn't have to worry about any unfriendly witness. Now! As the officer next in command, you are now technically captain of this ship, which means that *you* decide what we do with Siris here. I would not recommend just letting him go!"

"No." The Jig's face had a curious inward expression that Dupaynil took to mean he was trying to catch up to events. "No, I can see that. But," and he looked at Dupaynil, taking in his rank insignia. "But, sir, you're senior."

"Not on this vessel." Curse the boy! Couldn't he see that he had to take command? Sassinak would have, in a flash.

"Right." It had taken him longer, but he came to the same decision; Dupaynil had to applaud that. "Then we need to get this fellow—Siris—into confinement."

"May I suggest the escape pod he just came out of? As you know, the controls no longer respond normally. He won't be able to get out, and he won't be able to eject from the ship."

"NO!" Dupaynil could not tell if it was fury or fright. "I'm not going back in there. I'd die before you get anywhere!"

"Frankly, I don't much care," Dupaynil said. "But you will have access to coldsleep. You know there's a cabinet built in."

Siris let fly the usual stream of curses, vicious and unimaginative. Dupaynil thought the senior mate would have done better, although he had no intention of letting him loose to try. Panis squirmed out of his awkward position, half-under the crewman, without losing his grip on the man's shoulder and arm or getting between Dupaynil's needler and Siris. Then he rolled clear, evading a last frantic snatch at his ankles. Dupaynil put all his weight on the trapped wrist for an instant, bringing a gasp of pain from Siris, then stepped back, covering him with the weapon. In any event, Siris went into the escape pod without more struggle, though threatening them both with the worst that his illicit colleagues could do.

"They'll get you!" he said, as Panis closed the hatch, Dupaynil aiming through the narrowing crack just in case. "You don't even know who it'll be. They're in the Fleet, all through it, all the way up, and you'll wish you'd never . . ."

With a solid chunk, the hatch closed and Panis followed Dupaynil's instructions in securing it. Then he met Dupaynil's eyes, with only the barest glance at the needler still in Dupaynil's hand.

"Well, Commander, either you're honest and I'm safe, or you're about to plug me and make up your own story about what happened. Or you still have doubts about *me*."

Dupaynil laughed. "Not after seeing the captain ready to kill you, I don't. But I'm sure you have questions of your own and will be a lot more comfortable when I'm not holding a weapon on you. Here." He handed over the needler, butt first.

Panis took it, thumbed off the power, and stuck it through one of the loops of his pressure suit.

"Thanks." Panis ran one bruised hand over his battered face. "This is not . . . quite . . . like anything they taught us." He took another long breath, with a pause in the middle as if his ribs hurt. "I suppose I'd better get to the bridge and log all this." His gaze dropped to the motionless crumpled shape of Ollery on the deck. "Is he?"

"He'd better be," said Dupaynil, kneeling to feel Ollery's neck for a pulse. Nothing, now. That solved the problem of what to do if he'd been alive but critically injured. "Dead," he went on.

"You . . . uh . . ."

"Strangled him, yes. Not a gentlemanly thing to do, but I had no other weapon and he was about to kill you."

"I'm not complaining." Panis looked steadier now and met Dupaynil's eyes. "Well. If I'm in command? And you're right, I'm supposed to be, I'd best log this. Then we'll come back and put his body . . ." he finished lamely, "somewhere."

Chapter Nine

Diplo

Although Zebara had said that few offworlders knew about, had ever seen or heard, Zilmach's opera, Lunzie found the next morning that some of the medical team had heard more than enough. Bias waylaid her in the entrance of the medical building where they worked. Before Lunzie could even say "Good morning," he was off.

"I don't know what you think you're doing," he said in a savage tone that brought heads around, though his voice was low. "I don't know if it's an aberration induced by your protracted coldsleep or a perverse desire to appease those who hurt you on Ireta . . ."

"Bias!" Lunzie tried to shake his hand away from her arm but he would not let go.

"I don't care *what* it is," he said, more loudly. Lunzie felt herself going red. Around them people tried to pretend that nothing was going on, although ears flapped almost visibly. Bias pushed her along, as if she weren't willing, and stabbed the lift button with the elbow of his free arm. "But I'll tell you, it's disgraceful. Disgraceful! A medical professional, a researcher, someone who ought to have a minimal knowledge of professional ethics and proper behavior . . ."

Lunzie's anger finally caught up with her surprise. She yanked her arm free.

"Which does *not* include grabbing my arm and scolding me in public as if you were my father. Which you're not. May I remind you that I am considerably older than you, and if I choose to . . ."

To what? She hadn't done what Bias thought she had done. In some respect, she agreed with him. If she *had* been having a torrid affair with the head of External Security, it would have been unprofessional and stupid. In Bias's place, in charge of a younger (older?) woman doing something like that, she'd have been irritated, too. She'd been irritated enough when she thought Varian was attracted to the young Iretan, Aygar. Her anger left as quickly as it had come, replaced by her sense of humor. She struggled for a moment with these contradictory feelings, and then laughed. Bias was white-faced, his mouth pinched tight.

"Bias, I am not sleeping with Zebara. He's an old friend."

"Everyone *knows* what happens at that opera!"

"I didn't." That much was true. "And how did you know?"

This time it was Bias who reddened, in unattractive blotches. "The last time I came I . . . ah. Um. I've always liked music. I try to learn about the native music anywhere I go. A performance was advertised. I bought a ticket, I went. And they didn't want to let me in. No one admitted without a partner, they said."

Lunzie hadn't known that. After a moment's shock, she realized that it made sense. Bias, it seemed, had argued that he had already paid for the ticket. He had been given his money back, with the contemptuous suggestion that he put his ticket where it would do him more good than the performance would. He finally found a heavyworlder doctor, at the medical center, willing to explain what the opera was about, and why no one wanted him there.

"So you see I know that no matter what you say . . ."

Lunzie stopped that with a laugh. They entered the lift with a crowd of first-shift medical personnel and Bias kept silence until they reached their floor. He opened his mouth but she waved him to silence.

"Bias, it came as a surprise to me, too. But they don't . . . mmm. Check on it. Besides which," and she cocked her head at him, "there's the problem of a pressure suit."

Bias turned beet-red from scalp to neck. His mouth opened and closed as if he were gasping for air, but formed no words.

"It's all right, Bias," she said, patting his head as if he were a nervous boy about to go onstage. "I'm over a hundred years old and I didn't live this long by risking an unexpected pregnancy."

Then, before she lost control of her wayward humor, she strode quickly down the corridor to her own first chore.

But Bias was not the only one to broach the subject.

"I've heard that heavyworlder opera is really something, hmm? *Different* . . ." said Conigan. She did not quite smirk.

Lunzie managed placidity. "Different is hardly the word, but you may have heard more than I saw."

"Or felt?"

"Please. I may be ancient and shriveled by coldsleep but I know I don't want to have a half-heavyworlder child. The opera re-enacts a time of great tragedy. I'm an outsider, an observer, and I have the sense to know it."

"That's something, at least. But is it really that good?"

"The music is. Unbelievable; I'm ashamed to admit I was so surprised by the quality."

Conigan appeared satisfied. If not, she had the sense to let Lunzie alone. More troubling were the odd looks she now got from the other team members, and from one of the heavyworlder doctors they'd been working with. She could not say she had no feeling for Zebara. Even had it been true, their tentative cooperation required that she appear friendly. She wondered if she should have feigned a more emotional response to the opera.

And on the edge of her mind, kept firmly away from its center during the working day, was the question of coldsleep. *Not again!* she wanted to scream at Zebara and anyone else who thought she should use it. *I'd rather die.* But that was not true. More particularly, she did not want to die on Diplo, in the hands of their Security or in their prisons. In fact, with the renewed strength and health of her refresher course in Discipline, she did not want to die anywhere, any time soon. She had a century of healthy life ahead of her, if she stayed off high-G worlds. She wanted to enjoy it.

The Venerable Master Adept had said she might need to use coldsleep again. She had trained for that possibility. She knew she *could* do it. *But I don't want to*, wailed one part of her mind to another. She squashed that thought down and hoped it would not be necessary. Surely she and Zebara could find some other way. That night she had no message, and slept gratefully, catching up on much-needed rest.

The next step in Zebara's campaign came two days later, when he invited her to spend her next rest day with him.

"The team's supposed to get together for a progress evaluation." Lunzie wrinkled her nose; she expected it to be a waste of time. "If I go off with you, I'll get in trouble with them."

She was already in trouble with them, but saw no reason to tell Zebara. And that kind of trouble would make it seem his employers' plot was working well. Surely a lightweight alienated from her own kind would be easier to manipulate. She shivered, wondering who was manipulating whom.

Zebara's image grimaced. "We have so little time, Lunzie. Your research tour is almost half over. We both know it's unlikely you'll come back and even if you did, I would not be here."

"Bias has told me, very firmly, that the purpose of this medical mission was *not* to reunite old lovers."

"*His* purpose, no. And I respect your professional work, Lunzie. I always did. We know it could not be a real relationship. You must go and I will not live long. But I want to see you again, for more than a few minutes in public."

Lunzie flinched, thinking of the agents who would, no doubt, snicker when they got to that point in the tapes being made of this conversation. If they weren't listening now, in real-time surveillance. She glanced at the schedule on her wall. Only one rest day after this one. Time had fled away from them, and even if she had not had the additional problem of Zebara and her undercover assignment, she would have been surprised at how short a 30 day assignment could be.

"Please," Zebara said, interrupting her thoughts. Was he really that eager? Did he know of some additional reason she must meet him now, and not later. "I can't wait."

"Bias will have a flaming fit," Lunzie said. His face relaxed, as if he'd heard more in her voice than she intended. "I'll have to talk to Tailler. I don't see why you couldn't wait until the next rest-day. Only eight days."

"Thank you, Lunzie. I'll send someone for you right after breakfast."

"But what about?" That was to an empty screen. He had cut the connection. Damn the man. Lunzie glowered at the screen and let herself consider ignoring his messenger in the morning. But that would be too dangerous. Whatever was going on, in his mind, or that of his employers, she had to play along.

When she told him, Tailler heaved a great sigh and braced his arms against his workbench.

"Are you trying to give Bias a stroke, or what? I thought you understood. Granted he's not entirely rational, but that makes it our responsibility to keep from knocking him loopsided."

Lunzie spread her hands. If the whole team turned against her, she could lose any chance of a good position after the mission. *And after the mission you could be one frozen lump of dead meat*, she reminded herself.

"I'm sorry," she said and meant it. That genuine distaste for hurting others got through to Tailler. "I think they should have studied me for the effects of prolonged coldsleep, instead of stuffing *me* full of current trends in medicine and shipping me out here. But they said they were desperate, that no one else had my background. Perhaps my reaction to Zebara is partly that, although I think no one who hasn't been through it *can* understand what it's like to wake up and find that thirty or forty years have gone by. Did you know I have a great-great-great-granddaughter who's older than I am in elapsed time? That makes us both feel strange. Zebara knew me *then*. Though to me that's the self I am *now*. Yet he's dying of old age. I know that personal feelings aren't supposed to intrude on the mission, but these are, in a sense, relevant to the work I'm doing. My normal lifespan, without coldsleep, would be twelve to fourteen decades, right?"

"Yes. Perhaps even longer, these days. I think the rates for women with your genetic background are up around fifteen or sixteen decades."

Lunzie shrugged. "See? Even the lifespans have changed since I was last awake. But my point is that each time I've come out of a prolonged cold-sleep, I've battled severe depression over the relationships I've lost. The kind of depression which we know impairs the immune system, makes people more susceptible to premature aging and disease. This depression, this despair and chaos, will affect the heavyworlders even more, because their life-span is naturally shorter, especially on high-G worlds. My feelings—my personal experiences—are what got me scheduled for this mission. While I can't claim that I consciously chose to consider Zebara as part of a research topic, his reaction to my lack of aging and my reaction to his physical decay, are not matters I can ignore."

Tailler stood, stretched, and leaned against the bench behind him. "I see your point. Emotions and intellect are both engaged and so tangled that you can't decide which part of this is most important. Would you say, on the whole, that you are an intuitive or a patterned thinker?"

"Intuitive, according to my early psych profiles, but with strong logical skills as well."

"You must have or I'd have said intuitive without asking. It sounds as if your mind is trying to put something together which you can't yet articulate. On that basis, meeting Zebara, spending a day with him, might give you enough data to come to some conclusions. But the rest of us are going to have a terrible time with Bias."

"I know. I'm sorry, truly I am."

"If I didn't believe you were, I'd be strongly tempted to play heavy-handed leader and forbid your going. I presume that if your mind finds its gestalt solution in the middle of the night, you will stay with us instead?"

"Yes—but I don't think it will."

Tailler sighed. "Probably not. Some rest-day this is going to be. At least stay out of Bias's way today and let me tell him tomorrow. Otherwise, we'll get nothing done."

When she answered the summons early the next morning, Zebara's escort hardly reassured her. Uniformed, armed—at least she assumed the bulging black leather at his hip meant a weapon—stern-faced, he checked her identity cards before leading her to a chunky conveyance almost as large as the medical center's utility van. Inside, it was upholstered in a fabric Lunzie had never seen, something smooth and tan. She ran her fingers over it, unable to decide what it was, and wishing that the broad seat were not quite so large. Across from her, the escort managed to suggest decadent lounging while sitting upright. The driver in the front compartment was only a dark blur through tinted plex.

"It's leather," he said, when she continued to stroke the seat.

"Leather?" She should know the word, but it escaped her. She saw by the smirk on the man's face that he expected to shock her.

"Muskie hide," he said. "Tans well. Strong and smooth. We use a lot of it."

Lunzie had her face well under control. She was not about to give him the satisfaction of knowing that she was disgusted.

"I thought they were hairy," she said. "More like fur."

His face changed slightly; a glimmer of respect came into the cold blue eyes.

"The underfur's sometimes used, but it's not considered high quality. The tanning process removes the hair."

"Mmm." Lunzie made herself touch the seat again, though she wished she didn't have to sit on it. "Is it all this color? Can it be dyed?"

Contempt had given way now to real respect. His voice relaxed as he became informative.

"Most of it's easily tanned this color; some is naturally black. It's commonly dyed for clothing. But if you dye upholstery, it's likely to come off on the person sitting on it."

"Clothing? I'd think it would be uncomfortable, compared to cloth."

Lunzie gave herself points for the unconcerned tone of voice, the casual glance out the tinted window.

"No, ma'am. As boots, now," and he indicated his own shining boots. "They're hard to keep polished, but they don't make your feet sweat as bad."

Lunzie thought of the way her feet felt in the special padded boots she wore most of the day. By evening, it was as if she stood in a puddle. Of course it was barbaric, wearing the skins of dead sentient creatures. But if you were going to eat them, you might as well use the rest of them, she supposed.

"Less frostbite," the man was saying now, still extolling the virtues of "leather" over the usual synthetic materials.

Outside the vehicle, an icy wind buffeted them with chunks of ice. Lunzie could see little through the windows; the dim shapes of unfamiliar buildings, none very tall. Little vehicular traffic: in fact, little sign of anyone else on the streets. Lunzie presumed that most people used the underground walkways and slideways she and Zebara had used their two previous meetings.

"The ride takes more than an hour," the escort said. "You might as well relax." He was smirking again, though not quite so offensively as before.

Lunzie wracked her brain to think of some harmless topic of conversation. Nothing was harmless with a heavyworlder. But surely it couldn't hurt to ask his name.

"I'm sorry," she began politely, "but I don't know what your insignia means, nor what your name is."

The smirk turned wolfish. "I doubt you'd really want to know. But my rank would translate in your Fleet to major. I'm not at liberty to disclose my name."

So much for that. Lunzie did not miss the significance of "*your* Fleet." She did not want to think what "not at liberty to disclose my name" might mean.

Did Zebara not trust her, after all? Or was he planning to turn her over to another branch of his organization and wanted to keep himself in the clear?

Time passed, marked off only by the slithering and crunching of the vehicle's wheels on icy roadway.

"The Director said he knew you many years ago. Is that true?" There could be no harm in answering a question to which so many knew the answer.

"Yes, over forty years ago."

"A long time. Many things have changed here in forty years."

"I'm sure of it," Lunzie said.

"I was not yet born when the Director knew you." The escort said that as if his own birth had been the most significant change in those decades. Lunzie stifled a snort of amusement. If he still thought he was that important, he wouldn't have much humor. "I have been in his department for only eight years." Pride showed there, too, and a touch of something that might have been affection. "He is a remarkable man, the Director. Worthy of great loyalty."

Lunzie said nothing; it didn't seem needed.

"We need men like him at the top. It saddens me that he has lost strength this past year. He will not say, but I have heard that the doctors are telling him the snow is falling." The man stared at her, obviously hoping she knew more, and would tell it. She fixed on the figure of speech.

"Snow is falling? Is this how you say sickness?"

"It is how we say death is coming. You should know that. You saw *Bitter Destiny*."

Now she remembered. The phrase had been repeated in more than one aria, but with the same melodic line. So it had come to be a cultural standard, had it?

"You are doing medical research on the physiological response of our people to longterm coldsleep, I understand. Hasn't someone told you what our people call coldsleep, how they think of it?"

This was professional ground, on which she could stand firmly and calmly.

"No, and I've asked. They avoid it. After the opera, I wondered if they associated coldsleep with that tragedy. It's one of the things I wanted to ask Zebara. He said we would talk about it today."

"Ah. Well, perhaps I should let him tell you. But as you might expect, death by cold is both the most degrading and the most honorable of deaths we know: degrading because our people were forced into it. It is the symbol of our political weakness. And honorable because so many chose it to save others. To compel another to die of cold or starvation is the worst of crimes, worse than any torture. But to voluntarily take the White Way, the walk into snow, is the best of deaths, an affirmation of the values that enabled us to survive." The man paused, ran a finger around his collar as if to loosen it, and went on. "Thus coldsleep is for us a peculiar parody of our fears and hopes. It is the little cold death. If prolonged, as I understand you have endured, it is the death of the past, the loss of friends and family as if in actual death—except that you are alive to know it. But it also cheats the long death of winter. It is like being the seed of a chranghal—one of our plants that springs first from the ground after a Long Winter. Asleep, not dreaming, almost dead! And then awake again, fresh and green.

"When our people travel, and know they will be placed in coldsleep, they undergo the rituals for the dying and carry with them the three fruits we all eat to celebrate spring and rebirth."

"But your death rate in coldsleep, for anything beyond a couple of months, is much higher than normal," said Lunzie. "And the lifespan after tends to be shorter."

"True. Perhaps you are finding out why, in physical terms. I think myself that those who consent to prolonged coldsleep have consented to death itself. They are reliving that first sacrifice and, even if they live, are less committed to life. After all, with our generally shorter lifespans, we would outlive our friends sooner than you. And you, the Director has told me, did not find it easy to pick up your life decades later."

"No."

Lunzie looked down, then out the blurred windows, thinking of that first black despair when she realized that Fiona was grown and gone, that she would never see her child as a child again. And each time it had been a shock, to find people aged whom she'd known in their youth. To find a great-great-great-granddaughter older than she herself.

He was silent after that. They rode the rest of the way without speaking, but without hostility. Zebara's place, when they finally arrived and drove into the sheltered entrance, was a low mound of heavy dark granite, like a cross between a fortress and a lair.

Zebara met her as she stepped out, said a cool "Thank you, Major," to the escort, and led her through a double-glass door into a circular hall beneath a low dome. Its floor was of some amber-colored stone, veined with browns and reds; the dome gleamed, dull bronze, from lights recessed around the rim. All around, between the four arching doorways, were stone benches against the curving walls. In the center two steps led down to a firepit in which flames flickered, burning cleanly with little smoke.

She followed Zebara down the steps, and at his gesture sat on the lowest padded seat; she could feel the heat of that small fire. He reached under the seat on his side, and brought out a translucent bead.

"Incense," he said, before he put it on the fire. "Be welcome to our hall, Lunzie. Peace, health, prosperity to you, and to the children of your children."

It was so formal, so strange, that she had no idea what to say, and instead bowed her head a moment. When she looked up, a circle of heavy-worlders enclosed her, on the floor of the hall above. Zebara raised his voice.

"My children and their children. You are known to them, Lunzie, and they are known to you."

They were a stolid, lumpish group to look at, Zebara's sons and their wives, the grandchildren, even the youngest, broad as wrestlers. She wondered which was the little boy who had interrupted his meeting. How long ago had that been? But she could not guess.

He was introducing them now. Each bowed from the waist, without speaking, and Lunzie nodded, murmuring a greeting. Then Zebara waved them away and they trooped off through one of the arched doorways.

"Family quarters that way," he said. "Sleeping rooms, nurseries, schoolrooms for the children."

"Schoolrooms? You don't have public schooling?"

"We do, but not for those this far out. And anyone with enough children in the household can hire a tutor and have them schooled. It saves tax money for those who can't afford private tutors. You met only the older children. There are fifty here altogether."

Lunzie found the thought disturbing, another proof that the heavyworlder culture diverged from FSP policy. She had known there was overcrowding and uncontrolled breeding. But Zebara had always seemed so *civilized*.

Now, as he took her arm to guide her up the steps from the firepit and across the echoing hall to a door, she felt she did not know him at all. He was wearing neither the ominous black uniform nor the workaday coverall she had seen on most of the citizens. A long loose robe, so dark she could not tell its color in the dimly lit passage, low boots embroidered with bright patterns along the sides. He looked as massive as ever, but also comfortable, completely at ease.

"In here," he said at last, and ushered her into another, smaller, circular room. "This is my private study."

Lunzie took the low, thickly cushioned seat he offered, and looked around. Curved shelving lined the walls; cube files, film files, old-fashioned books, stacks of paper. There were a few ornaments: a graceful swirl of what looked like blue-green glass, stiff human figures in brown pottery, an amateurish but very bright painting, a lopsided lump that could only be a favorite child's or grandchild's first attempt at a craft. A large flatscreen monitor, control panels. Above was another of the shallow domes, this one lined with what looked like one sheet of white ceramic. The low couch she sat on was upholstered with a nubbly cloth. She was absurdly glad to be sure it was not leather. Fluffy pillows had been piled, making it comfortable for her shorter legs.

Zebara had seated himself across from her, behind a broad curving desk. He touched some control on it and the desk sank down to knee height, becoming less a barrier and more a convenience. Another touch, and the room lights brightened, their reflection from the dome a clear unshadowed radiance like daylight.

"It's . . . lovely," said Lunzie.

She could not think of anything else. Zebara gave her a surprisingly sweet smile, touched with sadness.

"Did your team give you trouble about visiting me?"

"Yes." She told him about Bias and found herself almost resenting Zebara's obvious amusement. "He's just trying to be conscientious," she finished up. She felt she had to make Bias sound reasonable, although she didn't think he was.

"He's being an idiot," Zebara said. "You are not a silly adolescent with a crush on some muscular stud. You're a grown woman."

"Yes, but, in a way, he's right, you know. I'm not sure myself that my encounters with coldsleep have left me completely . . . rational." She wondered whether to use any of what the young officer had told her, and decided to venture it. "It's like dying, and being born, only not a real start—everything over birth. Leftovers from the past life keep showing up. Like missing my daughter . . . I told you about that, before. Like discovering Sassinak. People say 'Get on with your life, just put it behind you.' And it *is* behind me, impossibly past. But it's also right there with me. Consequences that most people don't live to see, don't have to worry about."

"Ah. Just what I wanted to talk to you about. For I will take the long walk soon, die the death that has no waking, and it occurs to me that for you my younger self—the self you knew—is still alive. Still young. That self no one here remembers as clearly as you do. Tell me, Lunzie, will *this* self," and he thumped himself on the chest, "destroy in your memory the self I was? The self you knew?"

She shook her head. "If I only squint a little, I can see you as you were. It's hard to believe, even now, that you . . . I'm sorry . . ."

"No. That's all right. I understand, and this is what I wanted." He was breathing a little faster, as if he'd been working hard, but he didn't look distressed, only excited. "Lunzie, it is a sentimental thing, a foolish wish, and I do not like myself for revealing it. For having it. But I know how fast memories fade. I had thought, all these years, that I remembered you perfectly. The reality of you showed me I had not. I had forgotten that fleck of gold in your right eye, and the way you crook that finger." He pointed, and Lunzie looked down, surprised to see a gesture she had never noticed. "So I know I will be forgotten—myself, my present self—as my younger self has already been forgotten. This happens to all, I know. But . . . but you, you hold my younger self in your mind, and you will live . . . what? Another century, perhaps? Then I will be only a name to my great-grandchildren, and all the stories will be gone. Except with you."

"Are you . . . are you asking me to remember you? Because you must know I will."

"Yes . . . but more, too. I'm asking you to remember me as I was, the young heavyworlder you trusted, the younger man you loved, however briefly and lightly. I'm asking you to hold that memory brightly in mind whenever you consider my people. Coldsleep has a special meaning for our people."

"I know. The escort you sent was telling me."

Zebara's eyebrows rose, then he shook his head. "I shouldn't be surprised. You're a very easy person to talk to. But if anyone had asked me whether Major Hessik would discuss such things with a lightweight, I'd have said never."

"I had to do something to get away from the subject of leather," said Lunzie, wrinkling her nose. "And from there, somehow . . ."

She went on to tell him what Hessik had explained. Zebara listened without interrupting.

"That's right," he said, when she finished. "A symbolic death and rebirth, which you have endured several times now. And which I ask you to endure once more, for me and my people."

The absolute *no* she had meant to utter stuck in her throat.

"I . . . never liked it," she said, wondering if it sounded as ridiculous to him as it did to her.

"Of course not. Lunzie, I brought you here today for several reasons. First, I want to remember you . . . and have you remember me . . . as I near my own death. I want to relive that short happy time we shared, through your memories. That's indulgence, an old man's indulgence. Second, I want to talk to you about my people, their history, their customs, in the hope that you can feel some sympathy for us and our dilemma. That you will speak for us where you can do so honestly. I'm not asking you to forget or forgive criminal acts. You could not do it and I would not ask. But not all are guilty, as you know. And finally, I must give you what we talked of before, if you are willing to carry it."

He sat hunched slightly forward, the dark soft robe hiding his hands. Lunzie said nothing for a moment, trying to compare his aged face, with all the ugly marks of a hard life in high G, to the younger man's blunt but healthy features. She had done that before. She would do it, she thought, even after he died, trying to reconcile what he had lost in those forty-odd years with her own losses.

He sighed, smiled at her, and said, "May I sit with you? It is not . . . what you might think."

Even as she nodded, she felt a slight revulsion. As a doctor, she knew she should not. That age did not change feelings. But *his* age changed *her* feelings, even as a similar lapse had changed Tee's feelings for her. What she and Zebara had shared, of danger and passion, no longer existed. With that awareness, her feelings about Tee changed from resignation to real understanding. How it must have hurt him, too, to have to admit that he had changed. And now Zebara.

He sat beside her, and reached for her hands. What must it be like for him, seeing her still young, feeling her strength, to know his own was running out, water from a cracked jug?

"The evidence you would believe, about our people's history," he began, "is far too great to take in quickly. You will either trust me, or not, when I say that it is there, incontrovertible. Those who sent the first colonists knew of the Long Winters that come at intervals: knew, and did not tell the colonists. We do not know all their reasons. Perhaps they thought that two years would be enough time to establish adequate food stores to survive. Perhaps those who made the decision didn't believe how bad it would be. I like to think they intended no worse than inconvenience. But what *is* known is that when our colony called for help, no help came."

"Was the call received?"

"Yes. No FTL communications existed in those days, you may recall. So when the winter did not abate and it became obvious it would not, the colonists realized that even an answered call might come too late. They expected nothing soon. But there was supposed to be a transfer pod only two light months out, with an FTL pod pre-programmed for the nearest Fleet sector headquarters. That's how emergency calls went out: sublight to the transfer point, which launched the pod, and the pod carried only a standard message, plus its originating transfer code."

Lunzie wrinkled her nose, trying to think when they might have expected an answer. "Two months, then. How long to the Fleet headquarters?"

"Should have been perhaps four months in all. An FTL response, a rescue attempt, could have been back within another two or three. Certainly within twelve Standard months, allowing decel and maneuvering time on both ends. The colonists would have had a hard time lasting that long. They'd have to eat all their seed grain and supplies. But most of them would have made it. Instead," and he sighed again, spreading his big gnarled hands.

"I can't believe Fleet ignored a signal like that." Unless someone inter-cepted it, Lunzie thought suddenly. Someone within Fleet who for some reason wanted the colony to fail.

"It didn't!" Zebara gave her hands a squeeze, then stood, the robe swirling around him. "Let me fix you something. I'm thirsty a lot these days." He waved at the selection revealed behind one panel of his desk. "Fruit juices? Peppers?"

"Juice, please." Lunzie watched as he poured two glasses, and gave her the choice of them. Did he really think she worried about him drugging her? And if he did, should she be worried? But she sipped, finding nothing but the pleasant tang of juice as he settled beside her once more.

He took a long swallow, then went on. "It was not Fleet, as near as we can tell. At least, not they that ignored an emergency pod. There was no emergency pod."

"What!"

"We did find, buried in the file, the notation that the expense of an FTL emergency pod was not justified since Diplo was no more than twelve Standard light months from a major communications nexus which could pass on any necessary material. Colonists had wasted, the report said, such expen-sive resources before on minor matters that required no response. If colonists could not take care of themselves for twelve months, and I can just hear some desk-bound bureaucrat sniff at this point, they hardly qualified as colonists." He took another swallow. "You see what this means."

"Of course. The message didn't arrive somewhere useful in four months. It arrived at a commercial telecom station in twelve months by which time the colonists were expecting a rescue mission."

"And from there," Zebara said, "it was . . . re-routed. It never reached Fleet."

"But that's . . ."

"It was already embarrassing. The contract under which the colonists signed on specified the placement of the emergency pod. When that message arrived at the station, it was proof that no pod had been provided. And twelve months already? Suppose they had sent a mission then. What would they have found? From this point we have no direct proof, but we expect that someone made the decision to deepsix the whole file. To wait until the next scheduled delivery of factory parts, which was another two standard years, by which time they expected to find everyone dead. So sad, but this happens to colonies. It's a dangerous business!"

Lunzie felt cold all over, then a white-hot rage. "It's . . . it's *murder.* Intentional murder!"

"Not under the laws of FSP at the time. Or even now. We couldn't prove it. I say 'we,' but you know I mean those in Diplo's government at the time. Anyway, when the ships came again, they found the survivors; the women, the children, and a few young men who had been children in the Long Winter. The first ship down affected not to know that anything had happened. To be surprised! But one of the Company reps on the second ship got drunk and let some of this out."

She could think of nothing adequate to say. Luckily he didn't seem to expect anything. After a few moments, he went back to family matters, telling her of his hopes for them. Gradually her mind quieted. By the time they parted, she carried away another memory as sweet as her first. It had no longer seemed perverse to have an old man's hands touching her, an old man's love still urgent after all those years.

Chapter Ten

FSP Escort Claw

Dupaynil led the way back toward the bridge, walking steadily and slowly. The young officer would still be wondering, might still wish he had Dupaynil under guard. Except that there was no guard. He would feel safer with Dupaynil in front of him, calm and unhurried. At the landing outside the bridge, Dupaynil said over his shoulder, "If you don't mind, I'd like to finish disabling the pod locks on pod three."

"Who's in there?"

"Your weapons tech. So far as I know, all the crew were in this with Ollery. They're all dangerous, but this one particularly so."

Panis frowned. "Suppose we run into something we need to fight?"

"We'd better not. We can't trust him. I don't think he can get out by himself. At least not without your help. But he and Siris had the best chance of figuring out what I did and undoing it, even with the minimal toolkits standard in pods."

"You may be right, but, look, I want to log at least some of this first. And I want you with me."

Dupaynil shrugged and moved onto the bridge. He thought it would be hours before the weapons tech could possibly get out. At the moment, gaining Panis's confidence took precedence. They settled in uneasy silence, Panis in the command seat and Dupaynil in the one in which he'd first seen the master mate.

He said nothing while Panis made a formal entry in the ship's computer, stating the date and time that he assumed command, and the code under which he would file a complete report. The computer's response to change of command, Dupaynil noticed, was to recheck Panis's retinal scans, palmprint, and voiceprint against its memory of him. Dupaynil would have had a hard time taking over if something had happened to Panis. He asked about that.

"Not as ship commander, no sir. You might have convinced it that you were a disaster survivor. You were logged in as a legitimate passenger. But you wouldn't have been given access to secure files or allowed to make any course changes. It would've given you lifesupport access: water, food, kept the main compartments aired up. That's all. And the ship would have launched an automatic distress signal when it dropped out of FTL."

"I see. There are files in the computer, Captain, which will provide evidence needed to confirm Ollery's treachery."

Dupaynil noticed that Panis reacted to the use of his new title with a minute straightening; a good sign. He did not mention that he had penetrated some of the computer's secure files already. Maintenance wasn't what he would call secure. Panis glanced over.

"I suppose you'd like me to access them. Although I'd think that would be a matter for Fleet Security." Dupaynil said nothing and waited. Panis suddenly grimaced. "Of course. *You are* Fleet Security, at least part of it. Or so you say." Wariness became him. He seemed to mature almost visibly as Dupaynil watched.

"Yes, I am. On the other hand, since I am the officer involved, the one who killed Ollery, you have a natural reluctance to let me meddle in the files, just in case. Right?"

"Right." Panis shook his head. "And I thought I was lucky to be yanked off a battle platform where I was one of a hundred Jigs, to be executive officer on an escort! Maybe something will happen, I said."

"Something did." Dupaynil grinned at him, the easy smile that had won over more than one who had had suspicions of him. "And you survived, acquitted yourself well. I assure you, if you can bring in the *evidence* that shows just where the agents of piracy are in Fleet, you'll have made your mark."

"Piracy!" Panis started to say more, then held up his hand. "No, not this moment. Let me log the first of it, and we'll get into that later."

This was a ship's captain speaking, however inexperienced. Dupaynil nodded and waited. The Jig's verbal report was surprisingly orderly and concise for someone who had narrowly escaped death and still had ripening bruises on his face. Dupaynil's opinion of him went up another two notches, and then a third when Panis waved him over to the command input station.

"I'd like your report, too, sir. Lieutenant Commander Dupaynil, taken aboard *Claw* on resupply station 64, Fleet Standard dating . . . Computer?" The computer checked the date and time, and flashed it on Panis's screen. "Right! 23.05.34.0247. Transfer from the cruiser *Zaid-Dayan*, Commander Sassinak commanding, with orders from Inspector-General Parchandri to proceed to Seti space on a secret mission. Is that right, sir?"

"Right," said Dupaynil. Was this the time to mention that he thought those orders were faked? Probably not. At least, not without thinking about it a bit more. He didn't think Sassinak had intended to tangle him with planet pirates or their allies. If he said his orders were faked, that would drag her into it.

"Then if you'll give your report, Commander," and Panis handed him the microphone.

Carefully, trying to think ahead to the implications of his report, Dupaynil told how his suspicions had been aroused by the length of time the crew had been together and the captain's attitude.

"Escort and patrol crews are never left unshuffled for more than one 24 month tour," he said. "Precisely because these ships are hard to track and very dangerous, and small enough for one or two mutineers to take over. Five years without a shuffle is simply impossible. Someone in Personnel had to be in the plot, to cover the records." He went on to tell about setting some surveillance taps and hearing the senior mate and captain discuss his murder. "They said enough about their contacts in both Fleet and certain politically powerful families to convince me that information we've been seeking for years could well be on this ship. Agents aren't supposed to write things down, but they all do it. Names, dates, places to meet, codes: no one can remember all of it. Either in hardcopy or in the computer. And they knew it, because they were afraid I'd get access to those files." He finished with a brief account of his sabotage of the escape pods, and his actions during and after the drill.

"Do you have any evidence now to support these allegations?" asked Panis.

"I have the recording from that audio tap. There may be data in the other taps. I haven't had time to look at them."

"I'd like to hear what you have," Panis said.

"It's in my cabin." At Panis's expression, Dupaynil shrugged. "Either I would make it through alive to retrieve it or I'd be dead and it might, just might, survive me. Not on my body, which they'd search. May I get it for you?"

He could see uncertainty and sympathized. Panis had had a lot to adjust to in less than an hour. And to him, Dupaynil was still a stranger, hardly to be trusted. But he made the decision and nodded permission. Dupaynil left the bridge quickly, noting that all the partitions were retracted. He went directly to his cabin, retrieved the data cube, and returned. Panis was waiting, facing the bridge hatch. Without saying anything, Dupaynil slipped the cube into a player and turned it on. As it played, Panis's expression changed through suspicion to surprise to, at the end, anger.

"Bastards!" he said, when the sound ceased and Dupaynil picked up the cube again. "I knew they didn't like you, but I never thought . . . And then to be in league with planet pirates! Who's that Lady Luisa they were talking about?"

"Luisa Paraden. Aunt, by the way, of the Randolph Paraden who was expelled from the Academy because Commander Sassinak proved he was involved in theft, sexual harassment, and racial discrimination against Wefts. They were cadets at the same time."

"I never heard that."

Dupaynil smiled sardonically. "Of course not. It wasn't advertised. But, if you ever wonder why Commander Sassinak has a Weft following, that's one reason. When Ollery was trying to get me to gossip about her, that's one of the things he mentioned. And it made me suspicious: he shouldn't have known. It was kept very quiet."

"And you think there's more evidence in the ship's computer?"

"Yes, you heard what they said. Probably even more in their personal gear. But you're the captain, Panis. You're in legal command. I believe that you recognize we're both in a very tricky situation. We have one dead former captain and eleven live crew imprisoned in escape pods. If we should run into some of the other renegades, especially some of Ollery's friends, we could be shot for mutiny and murder before we ever got that evidence to a court martial."

Panis touched his swelling face gingerly, then grinned. "Then we'd better not get caught."

In the time it took to lug Ollery's body to a storage bay and to disable the controls on the last occupied pod, Dupaynil figured out what to do about his faked orders. He could blame them on the traitor in the Inspector General's office. Sassinak would never reveal the real source. He was fairly sure he could never get Ssli testimony incriminating *her*. In fact, it was only a guess that she had done it. It was not in the interest of Fleet or the FSP that she be blamed, even though she'd done it. But it was entirely in the interests of the Fleet to bring as many charges as possible against those guilty of conniving at planet piracy.

He thought through the whole chain of events. Would it have made sense for such a traitor to assign him to *Claw* and get him killed? Certainly, if they considered Sassinak a threat and they knew he'd been working with her. They'd disrupted a profitable scam on Ireta. He'd uncovered one of their agents on the *Zaid-Dayan*. He was dangerous to them in himself, and they'd taken the opportunity to get him away from Sassinak.

He could almost believe that. It made sense, criminal sense. But if it were true, Ollery or the mate who he suspected of being the senior within the criminal organization, should have known from the beginning about him, should not have needed to discover his taps to suspect him. Of course, there were always glitches in the transfer of data within an organization. Perhaps the message explaining him to Ollery was even now back at the supply station.

Panis had let him do a bit of first aid, a sign of trust that Dupaynil valued. The Jig's bruised face wasn't all the damage. He had a massive bruise along his ribs on one side.

"Ollery," he said when Dupaynil raised his eyebrows at it. "That's when I realized, or at least, I didn't know what was going on. Siris had me down, and then I saw the captain with the needler. He yelled for Siris to roll aside, and kicked me, and then you . . ."

"Yes," said Dupaynil, interrupting that. "And it's going to hurt you to breathe for awhile. We'll have to keep an eye on your color, make sure you don't start collecting fluid in that lung. Why don't you start teaching me what I need to know to do the heavy work while we're going wherever we're going? You don't need to be hauling up and down ladders."

He had had Panis fetch a clean uniform from his quarters, and now helped him into it. Ice for the bruises. At least they had plenty of that. He mentioned the bay full of water ice and suggested thawing some for showers.

"I'll tell you another thing that bothers me," Dupaynil said with disarming frankness when they were back on the bridge. "I'm no longer sure that my orders to leave the *Zaid-Dayan* and board this ship were genuine."

"What? You think someone sent false orders?" Dupaynil nodded. "My orders carried an initiation code that really upset Commander Sassinak. She claimed she'd seen it before, years ago, right before someone tried to kill her, on her first cruise. I always thought that initiation code simply meant the

Inspector General's office. One particular comp station, say, or a particular officer. But even she thought it was strange that she had to put in at a supply station. That I was being yanked off her ship when she had previous orders that all of us were to appear as witnesses in the Ireta trial." He had explained the bare outline of that to Panis. "I could hardly believe it, but they'd come by IFTL link. No chance of interference. But you heard what they said on tape and what Siris said. If there are high-placed traitors in Fleet, especially in Personnel Assignment, and there'd almost have to be for this crew to have stayed together so long, it would be no trick at all to have me transferred."

"Hard to prove," Panis said, sipping a mug of hot soup.

"Worse than that." Dupaynil spread his hands. "Say that's what happened and they expected me to be killed, with a good excuse, like that malfunctioning escape pod. They still might take the precaution of wiping all records of those orders out of the computers. Suppose they try to claim Commander Sassinak or I faked those orders. Then, if I turn up alive, they can get me on that. If I don't, they can go after her. She's caused them a lot of trouble over the years, and I'd bet Randy Paraden still holds a big, prickly grudge where she's concerned. Faking orders or interfering with an IFTL link is big enough to get even a well-known cruiser captain in serious trouble."

"I see. It does make sense they'd want you away from her, with the evidence you'd gathered. And if they could discredit her later . . ."

"I wonder how many other people they've managed to finagle away from her crew," Dupaynil went on, embroidering for the mere fun of it. "If we find out that one officer's been called away for a family crisis, and another's been given an urgent assignment? Well, I think that would prove it."

Panis, he was glad to see, accepted all this without difficulty. It did, after all, make sense. Whereas what Sassinak had done, and Dupaynil was still convinced she had done it, made sense only in personal terms: he had trespassed on her hospitality. At least his new explanation might clear her and laid guilt only on those already coated with it.

"So what do you think we should do, aside from avoiding all the unknown friends of the late Major Ollery?"

Dupaynil smiled at him. He liked the way the young man referred to Ollery, and he liked the dry humor.

"I think we should find out who they are, preferably by raiding Ollery's files. And then it would be most helpful if we'd turn up at the Ireta trial. Tanegli's trial, I should say. Then we ought to do something about your prisoners before their pod air supplies run out."

"I forgot about that." Panis's eyes flicked to the computer. "Oh, they're still on ship's air. Unless you did something to that, too."

"Didn't have time. But they don't have recycling capacity for more than a hundred hours or so, do they? I don't think either of us wants to let them out, even one by one."

"No. But I can't . . . ."

"You can offer them coldsleep, you know. The drugs are there, and the cabinets. They'd be perfectly safe for as long as it takes us to get them to a Fleet facility."

Panis nodded slowly. "That's a better alternative than what I thought of. But what if they won't do it?"

"Warn them. Wait twelve hours. Warn them again and cut them off ship's air. That'll give them hours to decide and prepare themselves. Are these the standard pods, with just over 100 hours of air?"

"Yes. But what if they still refuse?"

Dupaynil shrugged. "If they want to die of suffocation rather than face a court martial, that's their choice. We can't stop it without opening the pods and I can't advise that. Only Siris has any injuries, and his aren't bad enough to prevent his taking the induction medications."

When push came to shove, though most of them blustered, only three waited until the ship ventilators cut out. The senior mate, Dupaynil noticed, was one of them. All the crew put themselves into coldsleep well before the pod air was gone. When the last one's bioscans went down, Dupaynil and Panis celebrated with the best the galley offered.

Dupaynil had found that the crew kept special treats in their quarters. Nothing as good as fresh food, but a tin of sticky fruitcake and a squat jar of expensive liquor made a party.

"I suppose I should have insisted on sealing the crew quarters," Panis said around a chunk of cake.

"But you needed to search them for evidence."

"Which I'm finding." Dupaynil poured for both of them with a flourish. "The mate kept a little book. Genuine pulp paper, if you can believe that. I'm not sure what all the entries mean . . . yet . . . but I doubt very much they're innocent. Ollery's personal kit had items far out of line for his Fleet salary, not to mention that nonissue set of duelling pistols. We're lucky he didn't blow a hole in you with one of those."

"You sound like a mosquito in a bloodbank," Panis grumbled. "Fairly gloating over all the data you might find."

"I am," Dupaynil agreed. "You're quite right; even without this," and he raised his glass, "I'd be drunk with delight at the possibilities. Do you have any idea how hard we normally work for each little smidgen of information? How many times we have to check and recheck it? The hours we burn out our eyes trying to find correlations even computers can't see?"

"My heart bleeds," said Panis, his mouth twitching.

"And you're only a Jig. Mulvaney's Ghost, but you're going to make one formidable commodore."

"If I survive. I suppose you'll want to tap into the computer tomorrow?"

"With your permission." Dupaynil sketched a bow from his seat. "We have to hope they were complacent enough to have only simple safeguards on the ticklish files. If Ollery thought to have them self-destruct if a new officer took command . . ."

Panis paled. "I hadn't thought of that."

"I had. But then I thought of Ollery. That kind of smugness never anticipates its own fall. Besides, you had to log a command change. It was regulation."

"Which you always follow." Panis let that lie, a challenge of sorts.

Dupaynil wondered what he was driving at, precisely. They'd worked well together so far. The younger man had seemed to enjoy his banter. But he reminded himself that he did not really *know* Panis. He let his face show the fatigue he felt, and sag into its age and his usually-hidden cynicism.

"If you mean Security doesn't always follow the letter of regulations, then you're right. I freely admit that planting taps on this ship was both against regulations and discourteous. Under the circumstances . . ." Dupaynil spread his hands in resignation to the inevitable.

Panis flushed but pursued the issue. "Not that so much. You had reasons for suspicion that I didn't know. Anyway it saved our lives. But I'd heard about Commander Sassinak, that she didn't follow regulations as often as not. If this is some ploy of hers?"

Blast. The boy was too smart. He'd seen through the screen. Dupaynil let the worry he felt edge his voice.

"Who'd you hear that from?"

"Admiral Spirak. He captained the battle platform I . . ."

"Spirak!" Relief and contempt mixed gave that more force than he'd intended. Dupaynil lowered his voice and kept it even. "Panis, your admiral is the last person who should complain of someone else's lack of respect for regulations. I won't tell you *why* he's still spouting venom about Sassinak, even though she saved his career once. Gossip was Ollery's specialty. But if you ever wondered why he's got only two stars at his age and why he's commanding Fleet's only *non*operational battle platform, there's a damn good reason. I've seen Commander Sassinak's files, and it's true she doesn't always fight an engagement by the book. But she's come out clean from encounters that cost other commanders ships. The only regulations she bends are those that interfere with accomplishing the mission. She's far more a stickler for ship discipline than anyone on this ship was."

Now Panis looked as if he'd been dipped in boiling water.

"Sorry, sir. But he'd said if I ever *did* end up serving with one of her officers, look out. That she had a following, but more loyal to her than to Fleet."

"I don't suppose he told you about the promotion party he gave himself? And nobody came? It's useless to tell you, Panis. You'll have to decide for yourself. She's popular, but she's also smart and a good commander. As for regulations, I felt that my duties entitled me to bend a few on her ship and she straightened me out in short order."

"What'd you do? Put a tap on *her?*"

Dupaynil gave that a hard look, and Panis suddenly realized what that could mean and turned even redder than before.

"I didn't mean . . . That's not what . . ."

"Good." Dupaynil gave no ground with that tone. "I did attempt to monitor some communications traffic without giving her proper notice. We were looking for a saboteur, as I told you. I thought a little snooping along the corridors, in the crew's gym, and so on, wouldn't hurt. She felt differently." That this was only distantly related to what had really happened bothered him not at all. She had been angry. He had put in surveillance devices without her permission. That much was true. "I don't consider myself one of Commander Sassinak's officers," Dupaynil went on. "My assignment to her ship was temporary duty only, a special mission to unearth this saboteur."

He could not tell if this satisfied Panis, and he didn't really care. He had liked the younger officer but suggestive questions about Sassinak rubbed him the wrong way. Why? He wasn't sure. He had not been tempted to involve himself with her. Her relationship with Ford was clear enough. So why did he feel such rage when someone criticized? It was worth thinking over later, when they'd found or not found the evidence he needed, and decided what to do with it.

Dupaynil's excursions into the ship's computers yielded all he could have wished for. He knew his satisfaction showed. He insisted on sharing his findings with Panis so the younger officer would know why.

"Besides," he said, "if someone scrags me successfully, you'll still have a chance to break up the conspiracy."

"How?" Panis looked up from the hardcopy of one of the more startling files, and tapped it with his finger. "If all these people are really part of it, then Fleet itself is hopeless."

"Not at all." Dupaynil put his fingertips together. "Do you know how many officers Fleet has? This is less than five percent. Your reaction is as dangerous as they are. If you assume that five percent rotten means the whole thing's rotten, then you've done their work for them."

"I hadn't thought of it that way."

"No. Most people don't. But let's be very glad we have to evade only five percent. And let's figure out how to get this information back to some of the 95% who *aren't* involved in it."

Panis had an odd expression on his face. "I'm not really . . . I mean, my skills in navigation are only average. And the computer in this ship holds only a limited number of plots."

"Plots?"

"Pre-programmed courses between charted points. I'm not sure I could drop us out of FTL, and then get us somewhere else that's not in the computer."

Dupaynil had assumed that all ship's officers were competent in navigation. He opened his mouth to ask what was Panis's problem, and shut it again. *He* wasn't able to pilot the ship, or even maintain the environmental system without Panis's instructions, so why should he expect everything of a young Jig?

"Does this mean we're stuck with the course and destination Ollery put in?" A worse thought erupted into his mind with the force of an explosion. "Do we even *know* where we're going?"

"Yes, we do. The computer's perfectly willing to tell me that. We're headed for Seti space, just as your orders specified." Panis frowned. "Where did you think we might be going?"

"It suddenly occurred to that Ollery might never have entered that course, or might have changed it, since he was planning to kill me. Seti space! I don't know whether to laugh or cry," Dupaynil said. "Assuming my orders were faked, was that chosen as a random destination, or for some reason?"

Panis fiddled with his seat controls and glanced at something on the command screen next to him.

"Well . . . from where we were, that gives the longest stretch in FTL. Time enough for Ollery to figure out what to do with you and how. Perhaps it was that. Or maybe they had a chore for him in Seti space, in addition to scragging you."

"So, you're saying that we have to go where we're going before we can go anywhere else?"

"If you want to be sure of getting anywhere anytime soon," Panis said. "We've been in undefined space—FTL mode—for a long time, and if we drop out before the mode, I have no idea where we might end up. We do have the extra supplies that the crew would have needed, but . . ."

"All right. On to Seti space. I suppose I could find something to do there, in the way of digging up dirt, although what we have already is more than enough." Dupaynil stretched. "But you do realize that while the personnel listed as on duty with the embassy to the Sek are *not* on Ollery's list of helpers, this means nothing. They could be part of the same conspiracy without Ollery having any knowledge of it."

The outer beacon to the Seti systems had all the courteous tact of a boot in the face.

"Intruders be warned!" it bleated in a cycle of all the languages known in FSP. "Intruders not tolerated. Intruders will be destroyed, if not properly naming selves immediately."

Panis set *Claw*'s transmitter to the correct setting and initiated the standard Fleet recognition sequence. He was recovering nicely, Dupaynil thought, from the shock of his original captain's treachery and the necessity of helping in a mutiny. He did not blurt out everything to the Fleet officer who was military attache at the embassy nor did he request an immediate conference with the Ambassador. Instead, he simply reported that he had an officer with urgent orders insystem and let Dupaynil handle it from there.

"I'm not sure I understand, Commander Dupaynil, just what your purpose here is."

That diplomatic smoothness had once seemed innocuous. Now, he could not be sure if it was habit or conspiracy.

"My orders," Dupaynil said, keeping his own tone as light and unconcerned as the other's, "are to check the shipping records of the main Seti commercial firms involved in trade with Sector Eighteen human worlds. You know how this works. I haven't the foggiest notion what someone is looking at, or for, or why they couldn't do this long distance."

"It has nothing to do with that Iretan mess?"

Again, it might be only ordinary curiosity. Or something much more dangerous. Dupaynil shrugged, ran his finger along the bridge of his nose and hoped he passed for a dandified Bretagnan.

"It might, I suppose. Or it might not. How would I know? There I was happily ensconced on one of the better-run cruisers in Fleet, with a woman commander of considerable personal ah . . . charm . . ." He made it definitely singular, but with a tonal implication that the plural would have been more natural, and decided that a knowing wink would overdo his act. "I would have been quite satisfied to finish the cruise with her . . . her *ship*." He shrugged again, and gave a deep sigh. "And then I find myself shipped out here, just because I have had contact with the Seti before, without arousing an incident, I suppose, to spend days making carefully polite inquiries to which they will make carefully impolite replies. That is all I know, except that if I had an enemy at headquarters, he could hardly have changed my plans in a way I would like less."

That came out with a touch more force than he'd intended, but it seemed to convince the fellow that he was sincere. The man's face did not change but he could feel a subtle lessening of tension.

"Well. I suppose I can introduce you to the Seti Commissioner of Commerce. That's a cabinet level position in the Sek's court. It'll know where else you should go."

"That would be very kind of you," said Dupaynil. He never minded handing out meaningless courtesies to lubricate the daily work.

"Not at all," the other said, already looking down at the pile of work on his desk. "The Commissioner's a bigot of the worst sort, even for a Seti. If this is a plot of your worst enemy at headquarters, he's planning to make you suffer."

The conventions of Seti interaction with other races had been designed to place the inferior of the universe securely and obviously in that inferior position and keep them there. To Seti, the inferior of the universe included those who tampered with "Holy Luck" by medical means (especially including genetic engineering), and those too cowardly (as they put it) to gamble. Humans were known to practice genetic engineering. Many of them changed their features for mere fashion—the Seti view of makeup and hair styling. Very few wished to gamble, as Seti did, by entering a room through the Door of Honor which might, or might not, drop a guillotine on those who passed through it . . . depending on a computer's random number generator.

Dupaynil did not enjoy his crawl through the Tunnel of Cowardly Certainty but he had known what to expect. Seated awkwardly on the hard mushroom shaped stool allowed the ungodly foreigner, he kept his eyes politely lowered as the Commissioner of Commerce continued its midmorning snack. He didn't want to watch anyway. On their own worlds, the Seti ignored FSP prohibitions and dined freely on such abominations as those now writhing in the Commissioner's bowl. The Commissioner gave a final crunch and burp, exhaled a gust of rank breath, and leaned comfortably against its cushioned couch.

"Ahhh. And now, Misss-ter Du-paay-nil. You wish to ask a favor of the Seti?"

"With all due respect to the honor of the Sek and the eggbearers," and Dupaynil continued with a memorized string of formalities before coming to the point. "And, if it please the Commissioner, merely to place the gaze of the eye upon the trade records pertaining to the human worlds in Sector Eighteen."

Another long blast of smelly breath; the Commissioner yawned extravagantly, showing teeth that desperately needed cleaning, although Dupyanil didn't know if the Seti ever got decay or gum disease.

"Ssector Eighteen," it said and slapped its tail heavily on the floor.

A Seti servant scuttled in bearing a tray piled with data cubes. Dupaynil wondered if the Door of Honor ignored servants or if they, too, had to take their chances with death. The servant withdrew, and the Commissioner ran its tongue lightly over the cubes. Dupaynil stared, then realized they must be labelled with chemcodes that the Commissioner could taste. It plucked one of the cubes from the pile, and inserted it into a player.

"Ah! What the *human*-dominated Fleet calls Sector Eighteen, the Flower of Luck in Disguise. Trade with human worlds? It is meager, not worth your time."

"Illustrious and most fortunate scion of a fortunate family," Dupaynil said, "it is my unlucky fate to be at the mercy of admirals."

This amused the Commissioner who laughed immoderately.

"Sso! It is a matter of luck, you would have me think? Unlucky in rank, unlucky in the admiral who sent you? But you do not believe in luck, so your people say. You believe in . . . What is that obscenity? Probabilities? Statistics?"

The old saying about "lies, damn lies, and statistics" popped into Dupaynil's mind, but it seemed the wrong moment. Instead, he said "Of others I cannot speak, but *I* believe in luck. I would not have arrived without it."

He did, indeed, believe in luck. At least at the moment. For without his unwise tapping of Sassinak's com shack, he would not have had the chance to find the evidence he had found. Now, if he could just get through with this and back to FedCentral in time for Tanegli's trial . . . That would be luck indeed! Apparently even temporary sincerity was convincing. The Seti Commissioner gave him a toothy grin.

"Well. A partial convert. You know what we say about your statistics, don't you? There are lies, damn lies, and . . ."

And I'm glad I didn't use that joke, Dupaynil thought to himself, since I don't believe this guy thinks that it is one.

"I will save your eyes the trouble of examining our faultless, but copious, records regarding trade with the Flower of Luck in Disguise. If you were unlucky in your admiral, you shall be lucky in my support. Your clear unwillingness to struggle with this unlucky task shall be rewarded. I refuse permission to examine our records, not because we have anything to conceal, but because this is the Season of Unrepentance, when no such examination is lawful. You are fortunate in my approval for I will give you such refusal as will satisfy the most unlucky admiral."

Again, a massive tail-slap, combined with a querulous squealing grunt, and the servitor scuttled in with a rolling cart with a bright green box atop. The Commissioner prodded it and it extruded a sheet of translucent lime green, covered with Seti script. Then another, and another.

"This is for the human ambassador, and this for your admiral, and this, o luckiest of humans, is your authorization to take passage in a human-safe compartment aboard the *Grand Luck* to human space. To attend a meeting of the Grand Council, in fact. You will have the great advantage of enjoying the superiority of Seti technology first-hand, an unprecedented opportunity for one of your . . . ah . . . luck."

It reached out, with the sheets and Dupaynil took them almost without thinking, wondering how he was going to get out of *this*.

"My good fortune abounds," he began. "Nonetheless, it is impossible that I should be honored with such a gift of luck. A mere human to take passage with Seti? It is my destined chance to travel more humbly."

A truly wicked chuckle interrupted him. The Commissioner leaned closer, its strong breath sickening.

"Little man," it said, "I think you will travel humbly enough to please whatever god enjoys your crawl through the Tunnel of Cowardly Certainty. With choice, always a chance. But with chance, no choice. The orders are in your hand. Your prints prove your acceptance. You will report to your ambassador, and then to the *Grand Luck* where great chances await you."

Chapter Eleven

Private Yacht Adagio

Ford woke to an argument overhead. It was not the first time he'd wakened, but it was the first time he'd been this clear-headed. Prudence kept his eyelids shut as he listened to the two women's voices.

"It's for his own good," purred Madame Flaubert. "His spiritual state is simply ghastly."

"He looks ghastly." Auntie Quesada rustled. He couldn't tell if it was her dress or something she carried.

"The outward and visible sign of inward spiritual disgrace. Poison, if you will. It must be purged, Quesada, or that evil influence will ruin us all."

A sniff, a sigh. Neither promised him much. He felt no pain, at the moment, but he was sure that either woman could finish him off without his being able to defend himself. And why? Even if they knew what he wanted, that should be no threat to them. Auntie Quesada had even seemed to like him and he had been enchanted by her.

He heard a click, followed by a faint hiss, then a pungent smell began to creep up his nose. A faint yelp, rebuked, reminded him of Madame Flaubert's pet. His nose tickled. He tried to ignore it and failed, convulsing in a huge sneeze.

"Bad spirits," intoned Madame Flaubert.

Now that his eyes were open to the dim light, he could see her fantastic draperies in all their garishness; purples, reds, oranges, a flowered fringed shawl wrapped around those red tresses. Her half-closed eyes glittered at him as she pretended, and he was sure it was pretense, to commune with whatever mediums communed with. He didn't know. He was a rational, well-educated Fleet officer. He'd had nothing to do with superstitions since his childhood, when he and a friend had convinced themselves that a drop of each one's blood on a rock made it magic.

"May they fly away, the bad spirits, may they leave him safe and free . . ."

Madame Flaubert went on in this vein for awhile longer as Ford wondered what courtesy required. His aunt, as before, looked completely miserable, sitting stiffly on the edge of her chair and staring at him. He wanted to reassure her, but couldn't think how. He felt like a dirty wet rag someone had wiped up a bar with. The pungent smoke of some sort of a floral incense blurred his vision and made his eyes water. Finally Madame Flaubert ran down and simply sat, head thrown back. After a long, dramatic pause, she sighed, rolled her head around as if to ease a stiff neck and stood.

"Coming, Quesada?"

"No . . . I think I'll sit with him a bit."

"You shouldn't. He needs to soak in the healing rays."

Madame Flaubert's face loomed over his. She had her lapdog in hand and it drooled onto him. He shuddered. But she turned away and waddled slowly out of his cabin. His great-aunt simply looked at him.

Ford cleared his throat, more noisily than he could have wished, and said, "I'm sorry, Aunt Quesada . . . this is not what I had in mind."

She shook her head. "Of course not. I simply do not understand."

"What?"

"Why Seraphine is so convinced you're dangerous to me. Of course you didn't really come just to visit. I knew that. But I've always been a good judge of men, young or old, and I cannot believe you mean me harm."

"I don't." His voice wavered, and he struggled to get it under control. "I don't mean you any harm. Why would I?"

"But the BLACK KEY, you see. How can I ignore the evidence of my own eyes?"

"The black key?" Weak he might be but his mind had cleared. She had said those words in capital letters.

His aunt looked away from him, lips pursed. In that pose, she might have been an elderly schoolteacher confronted with a moral dilemma outside her experience.

"I suppose it can't hurt to tell you," she said softly.

The Black Key was, it seemed, one of Madame Flaubert's specialties. It could reveal the truth about people. It could seek out and unlock their hidden malign motives. Ford was sure that any malign motives were Madame Flaubert's, but he merely asked how it worked.

His aunt shrugged. "I don't know. I'm not the medium. But I've *seen* it, my dear. Sliding across the table, rising into the air, turning and turning until it . . . it pointed straight at the guilty party."

Ford could think of several ways to do that, none of them involving magic or "higher spirits." He himself was no expert but he suspected that Dupaynil could have cleared up the Black Key's actions in less than five minutes.

"One of my servants," Auntie Q was saying. "I'd been missing things, just baubles really. But one can't let it go on. Seraphine had them all in and questioned them, and the Black Key revealed it. The girl confessed! Confessed to even more than I'd known about."

"What did the authorities say, when you told them how you'd gotten that confession?"

Auntie Q blushed faintly. "Well, dear, you know I didn't actually *report* it. The poor girl was so upset and, of course I had to dismiss her, and she had had so many troubles in her life already. Seraphine said that the pursuit of vengeance always ends in evil."

I'll bet she did, Ford thought. Just as she had probably arranged the theft in the first place, for the purpose of showing the Black Key's power, to convince Auntie Q.

"As a matter of fact," Auntie Q said, "Seraphine felt a bit guilty, I think. She had been the one to suggest that I needed another maid, with the Season coming on, and she'd given me the name of the agency."

"I see." He saw, indeed. What he did not know yet was just why Seraphine perceived him as a threat—or why his aunt had taken in Madame Flaubert at all. "How long has Madame Flaubert been your companion?"

Auntie Q shifted in her seat, unfolded and refolded her hands. "Since . . . since a few months after . . . after . . ." Her mouth worked but she couldn't seem to get the words out. Finally she said, "I . . . I can't quite talk about that, dear, so please don't ask me."

Ford stared at her, his own miseries forgotten. Whatever else was going on, whatever Auntie Q knew that might help Sassinak against the planet pirates, he had to get Madame Flaubert away from his aunt.

He said as gently as he could, "I'm sorry, Aunt Quesada. I didn't mean to distress you. And whatever the Black Key may have intimated, I promise you I mean you no harm."

"I want to believe you!" Now the old face crumpled. Tears rolled down her cheeks. "You're the first—the only family that's come to see me in years —and I *liked* you!"

He hitched himself up in bed, ignoring the wave of blurred vision.

"My dear, please! I've admitted my father was wrong about you. I think you're marvelous."

"She said you'd flatter me."

Complex in that were the wish to be flattered, and the desire not to be fooled.

"I suppose I have, if praise is flattery. But, dear Aunt, I never knew *anybody* with enough nerve to get two Ryxi tailfeathers! How can I not flatter you?"

Auntie Q sniffed, and wiped her face with a lace-edged kerchief. "She keeps telling me that's a vulgar triumph, that I should be ashamed."

"Poppycock!" The word, out of some forgotten old novel, surprised him. It amused his aunt, who smiled through her tears. "My dear, she's jealous of you, that's all, and it's obvious even to me, a mere male. She doesn't like me because . . . Well, does she like any of the men who work for you?"

"Not really." Now his aunt looked thoughtful. "She says . . . she says it's indecent for an old lady to travel with so many male crew, and only one female maid. You know, I used to have a male valet who left my ex-husband's service when we separated. Madame Flaubert was *so* scathing about it I simply had to dismiss him."

"And then she found you the maid who turned out to be a thief," Ford said. He let that work into her mind. When comprehension brightened those old eyes, he grinned at her.

"That . . . that *contemptible* creature!" Auntie Q angry was as enchanting now as she must have been sixty years back. "Raddled old harridan. And I took her into my bosom!" Metaphorically only, Ford was sure. "Brought her among my friends, and *this* is how she repays me!"

It sounded like a quote from some particularly bad Victorian novel and not entirely sincere. He watched his aunt's face, which had flushed, paled, and then flushed again.

"Still, you know, Ford, she really does have powers. Amazing things, she's been able to tell me, and others. She knows all our secrets, it seems. I . . . I have to confess I'm just a little afraid of her." She tried a giggle at her own foolishness, but it didn't come off.

"You really *are* frightened," he said and reached out a hand. She clutched it, and he felt the tremor in her fingers.

"Oh, not really! How silly!" But she would not meet his eye, and the whites of hers showed like those of a frightened animal.

"Auntie Q, forgive my asking, but . . . but do your friends ever come visit? Travel with you? From what my father said, I'd had the idea you traveled in a great bevy, this whole yacht full to bursting."

"Well, I used to. But you know how it is. Or I suppose you don't. In the Navy you can't choose your companions. But there were quarrels, and upsets, and some didn't like this, and others didn't like that . . ."

"And some didn't like Madame Flaubert," Ford said very quietly. "And Madame Flaubert didn't like anyone who got between you."

She sat perfectly still, holding his hand, the color on her cheeks coming and going. Then she leaned close and barely whispered in his ear.

"I can't . . . I can't tell you how horrible it's been. That woman! But I can't do anything. I . . . I don't know why. I c-c-can't . . . say . . . anything she doesn't. . . want me to." Her breathing had roughened; her face was almost purple. "Or I'll die!" She sat back up, and would have drawn her hands away but Ford kept his grasp on them.

"Please send Sam to help me to the . . . uh . . . facilities," he said in the most neutral voice he could manage.

His aunt nodded, not looking at him, and stood. Ford felt his strength returning on a wave of mingled rage and pity. Granted, his aunt Quesada was a rich, foolish old lady, but even foolish old ladies had a right to have friends, to suffer their own follies, and not those of others. Sam, when he appeared, eyed Ford with scant respect.

"You going to live? Or make us all trouble by dying aboard?"

"I intend to live out my normal span and die a long way from here," Ford said.

With Sam's help, he could just make it up and into the bath suite. The face he saw in the mirror looked ghastly, and he shook his head at it.

"Looks don't kill," he said.

Sam gave an approving nod. "You might be getting sense. You tell Madam yet the real reason you came to visit?"

"I've hardly had a chance." He glared at Sam, without effect. "For people who can't believe in my idle curiosity, you're all curious enough yourselves."

"Practice," said Sam, helping him into clean pajamas. "Madame Flaubert keeps us on our toes."

Ford snorted. "I'll bet she does. How long has she been around?"

"Since about six months after Madam and her Paraden husband had the final court ruling on their separation. The one that gave Madam some major blocks of shares in Paraden family holdings," Sam said. At Ford's stare, he winked. "Significant, eh?"

"She's a . . . ?" Ford mouthed the word Paraden without saying it.

Sam shook his head. "Not of the blood royal, so to speak. Maybe not even on the wrong side of the blanket. But in her heart, she does what she's paid to."

"Does my aunt know?"

Sam frowned and pursed his lips. "I've never been sure. She's got some hold on your aunt, but that particular thing, I don't know."

"They want her quiet and out of their way. No noise, no scandals. I'm surprised she's survived this long."

"It's been close a few times." Sam shook his head, as he helped Ford brush his teeth, and handed him a bottle of mouthwash. "It's funny. Your aunt's real cautious about some things but she won't *do* anything, if you follow me."

Scared to do anything, Ford interpreted. Scared altogether, as her friends dropped away year by year, alienated by Madame Flaubert. He smiled at Sam in the mirror, heartened to find that he could smile, that he looked marginally less like death warmed over.

"I think it's about time," he drawled, "that my dear aunt got free of Madame Flaubert."

Sam's peaked eyebrows went up. "Any reason why I should trust *you*, sir?"

Ford grimaced. "If I'm not preferable to Madame Flaubert, then I deserved that, but I thought you had more sense."

"More sense than to challenge where I can't win. Your aunt trusts me as a servant but no more than that."

"She should know better." Ford looked carefully at Sam, reminded again of the better NCOs he'd known in his time. "Are you *sure* you didn't start off in Fleet?"

A flicker in the eyes that quickly dropped before his. "Perhaps, sir, you're unaware how similar some of the situations are."

That was both equivocal, and the only answer he was going to get. Unaccountably, Ford felt better.

"Perhaps I am," he said absently, thinking ahead to what he could do about Madame Flaubert. His own survival, and Auntie Q's, both depended on that.

"Just don't let her touch you," Sam said. "Don't eat anything she's touched. Don't let her put anything on you."

"Do you know what it is, what she's using?"

Sam shook his head, refusing to say more, and left the cabin silently. Ford stared moodily into the mirror, trying to think it through. If the Paradens were that angry with his aunt, why not just kill her? Were her social and commercial connections *that* powerful? Did she have some kind of hold on them, something they thought to keep at bay, but dared not directly attack? He knew little about the commercial side of politics, and nothing of society except what any experienced Fleet officer of his rank had had to meet in official circles. It didn't seem quite real to him. And that, he knew, was his worst danger.

The confrontation came sooner than he'd expected. He was hardly back in his bed, thinking hard, when Madame Flaubert oozed in, her lapdog panting behind her. She had a net bag of paraphernalia which she began to set up without so much as a word to him. A candlestick with a fat green candle, a handful of different colored stones in a crystal bowl and geometric figures of some shiny stuff. He couldn't tell if they were plastic or metal or painted wood. Gauzy scarves to hang from the light fixtures, and drape across the door.

"Don't you think all that's a little excessive?" Ford asked, arms crossed over his chest. He might as well start as he meant to go on. "It's my aunt who believes in this stuff."

"You can't be expected to understand, with the demonic forces still raging within you," she answered.

"Oh, I don't know. I think I understand demonic forces quite well." That stopped her momentarily. She gave him a long hostile stare.

"You're unwell," she said. "Your mind is deranged."

"I'm sick as a dog," he agreed. "But my mind is clear as your intent."

Red spots showed under her makeup. "Ridiculous. Your wicked past merely asserts itself, trying to unnerve me."

"I would not try to unnerve you, Madame Flaubert, sweet Seraphine, but I would definitely try to dissuade you from actions which you might find unprofitable . . . even . . . dangerous."

"Your aura is disgusting," she said firmly, but her eyes shifted.

"I could say the same," he murmured. Again that shifting of the eyes, that uncertainty.

"You came here for no good! You want to destroy your aunt's life!" Her plump hands shook as she laid out the colored stones on the small bedside table. "You are danger and death! I saw that at once."

Quick as a snake's tongue, her hand darted out to place one of the stones on his chest. Wrapping his hand in the sheet, Ford picked it up and tossed it to the floor. Her face paled, as her dog sniffed at it.

"Get *away*, Frouff! It's contaminated by *his* evil."

The dog looked at Ford, its tail wagging gently. Madame Flaubert leaned over, never taking her eyes off Ford, and picked up the stone. He watched, eerily fascinated, as she held it up before her, crooned to it, and placed it back with the others.

If he had not watched so closely, he would not have seen it. Her hands were hardly visible, what with ruffles drooping from her full sleeves, dozens of bracelets, gaudy rings on every finger. But they *were gloved*. Her fingertips were too shiny, and when she held the stone, one of them *wrinkled*. Ford hoped his face did not reveal his feelings as he watched her fondle the stones, squeeze them. And watching with that dazed fascination, he saw the squeeze that sent something from one of those massive rings, to be spread on the stones.

Contact poison. He had thought of injections, when Sam warned against letting her touch him. He had thought of poison in his food, but not of contact poison working through intact skin. Had *that* been the paralyzing agent that had held him motionless before while she claimed to commune with spirits over him? He was no chemist or doctor so he had no idea what kinds of effects could be obtained with poisons working through the skin.

He tried to let his eyelids sag, feigning exhaustion, but when Madame Flaubert reached out, he could not help flinching away from her. Her predatory smile widened.

"Ah! You suspect, do you? Or think you know?"

Ford edged farther away, telling himself that even in his present state he had to be a match for any woman like Madame Flaubert. He didn't believe it. She was big and probably more powerful than she looked. As if she'd read his thoughts, she nodded slowly, still smiling.

"Silly man," she said. "You should have had the sense to wait until you were stronger. Of course, you weren't *going* to be stronger."

He couldn't think of anything to say. His back was against the cabin bulkhead. She was between him and the door, holding up a purple stone and rubbing it slowly. He could feel every square centimeter of his bare skin. After all, how much protection were pajamas?

"All I have to decide," she gloated, "is whether it should look like a heart attack or a stroke. Or perhaps a final spasm of that disgusting intestinal ailment you brought aboard."

He was supposed to be able to kill with his bare hands. He was supposed to be able to take command of any situation. He was not supposed to be cowering in his pajamas, terrified of the touch of an overdressed fake spiritualist with a poison ring. It would sound, if anyone ever heard about it, like something out of the worst possible mass entertainment.

He clenched one hand in the expensively fluffy pillow Auntie Q had provided the invalid. He could use that to shield his hand. What if this murderous old bag had put poison on his bedclothes, too? He felt cold and shaky. Fear? Poison?

"It's a pity," Madame Flaubert said, letting her eyes rove over him. "You're the handsomest young man we've had aboard in years. If you'd only been reasonably stupid, I could have had fun with you before. Or even let you live."

"Fun? With you?" He could not hide his disgust, and she glared at him.

"Yes, me. With you. And you'd have enjoyed it, my pretty young man, with the help of my . . . my *special* arts." She waved, indicating all her paraphernalia. "You'd have been swooning at my feet."

Ford said nothing. He could not reach any of the call buttons without coming within her reach, and he knew the cabins were well sound-proofed. Could he make it to the bath suite and hold the door shut? No. Too far, and around furniture. She'd get there first. If he'd been well and strong, he was sure he could do *something*. But another look at those glittering eyes made him wonder.

Her dog yipped suddenly and dashed to the door. Ford drew breath to yell, if it opened. Madame Flaubert backed slowly from the bed, to press the intercom button.

"Not now," she said. "No matter what . . . ignore!"

Ford leapt and yelled at once. His feet tangled in the bedclothes and he fell headlong to the floor between the bed and the ornate wardrobe with its mirrored doors. He saw Madame Flaubert's triumphant grin, distorted by the antique mirrors, and rolled aside in time to avoid one swipe with the stone. Her dog broke into a flurry of yips, dancing around her feet with its fluff of a tail wagging. Ford threw his weight against her knees, whirled, and tried again for the bath suite. White-hot pain raked his back, then his vision darkened.

"Idiot!" She stood above him, those over-red curls askew. Then lifted them off to show the bald ugliness of her . . . his? . . . head. "Too bad I can't keep you alive to see what happens to your captain Sassinak."

The wig plopped back down, still askew. Ford writhed, trying to move away, but one leg would not work. The little dog, wildly excited, bounced up and down, still yipping. The stone she'd used lay on the floor, just out of his reach, Not that he wanted to touch it.

"The green, I think. It has a certain appeal . . ." She had picked up another stone, and without any attempt to hide her act, dripped an oily liquid on it from another of her rings. "Of course, your poor aunt may suffer a shock of her own—even a fatal one—when she sees you lying there, and picks this off your chest."

She sauntered back across the small cabin, smiling that pitiless smile. Ford strained against the effects of the first poison. Sweat poured down his face, but he could *not* move more than a few inches. Then the cabin door opened and his aunt put her head in.

"Ford, I was thinking . . . Seraphine! Whatever are you doing!"

The little dog skittered toward her, still barking, then came back. With a curse, Madame Flaubert whirled, arm cocked.

Ford said, "Look out!" in the loudest voice he could and someone's muscular arm hauled his aunt back out of sight. Madame Flaubert whirled back to him, took a step, and tottered as her lapdog tripped her neatly. She fell in a tangle of skirts and shawls, arms wide to catch herself.

Ford prayed for someone to come in before she could get up. But she didn't get up. She lay sprawled, facedown, that murderous stone still clutched in one hand. The little dog trembled, crouched with its nose to the floor, and then lifted it to howl eerily.

I don't believe this, Ford thought muzzily. He thought it as Sam came in and as he was put back in his bed. As he drifted off, he was convinced it was a last dream in the course of dying.

But he believed it when he woke.

Auntie Q out from under the influence of Madame Flaubert was even more herself than Ford would have guessed. It had taken him three days to shake off the effects of that poison. In that period she had sacked most of her crew and staff except for Sam. In fact, anyone hired since Madame Flaubert's arrival.

Now Auntie Q spent her hours engaged in tapestry, gossip, and reminiscence. She refused to talk much about Madame Flaubert on the grounds that one should put unpleasantness out of one's mind as quickly as possible.

Ford had found out from Sam that Madame Flaubert's ornate rings had torn her surgical gloves, allowing the poison to contact her bare skin. Exactly what she deserved, but he still had cold chills when he thought about his close call. No wonder his aunt didn't want to talk about that.

But Auntie Q had plenty to say about the Paraden Family. Ford had confessed his official reason for visiting her and she took it in better part than he expected.

"After all," she said with a shrug that made the Ryxi tailfeathers dance above her head, "when you get to be my age, handsome young men don't come visiting for one's own sake. And you *are* good company, and you did get that . . . that *frightful* person out of my establishment. Ask what you will, dear. I'll be glad to tell you. Only tell me more of that captain of yours, the one that makes your blood move. Yes, I can tell. I may be old, but I'm a woman still, and I want to know if she's good enough for you."

When Ford was done, having told more about Sassinak than he'd intended, his aunt nodded briskly.

"I want to meet her, dear. When all this is over, bring her to visit. You say she likes good food. Well, as you know, Sam's capable of cooking for an emperor."

Ford tried to imagine Sassinak and Auntie Q in the same room and failed utterly. But his aunt waited with her bright smile for his answer and, at last, he agreed.

Chapter Twelve

FedCentral

Lunzie heard someone scolding her, or so it seemed, before she could even get her eyes open. Bias, she decided. Furious that I stayed too late with Zebara. Why can't that man understand that a woman over two hundred years old is capable of making her own decisions? Then she felt a prick in her arm and a warm surge of returning feeling.

With it came memory, and than rage. That liar, that cheat, that conniving bastard Zebara had sold her! Probably literally and gods only knew where she was! She opened her eyes to find a tired-faced man in medical greens leaning over her, saying, "Wake up, now. Come on. Open your eyes . . ."

"They *are* open," said Lunzie. Her voice was rough and it sounded almost as grouchy as she felt.

"You'd better drink this," he said in the same quiet voice. "You need the fluid."

Lunzie wanted to argue, but whatever it was she might as well drink it, or they could pump it in a vein. It tasted like any one of the standard restoratives: fruity, sweet, with an undertaste of bitter salt. She could feel her throat slicking back down. The next time she spoke, she had control of her tone.

"Since I've been informed that you don't exist," the man went on, his mouth quirking now in a half-grin, "I won't check your response to the standard mental status exam: no person, place, and time. I'm authorized to tell you that you are presently in a secure medical facility on FedCentral, that you have been in coldsleep approximately four Standard months, and that your personal gear, what there is of it, is in that locker!" He pointed. "You will be provided meals in your quarters until you have satisfied someone . . . I'm not supposed to ask who . . . of your identity and the reason you chose to arrive as a shipment of muskie-fur carpets. *Do* you remember who you are? Or are you suffering disorientation?"

"I know who I am," said Lunzie, grimly. "And I know who got me into this. Is this a Fleet facility, or civilian FSP?"

"I'm sorry. I'm not allowed to say. Your physical parameters are now within normal limits. Telemetry has transmitted that fact to . . . to those making decisions and I am required to withdraw." He sketched a wave and smiled, this time with no apparent irony. "I hope you're feeling better and that you have a happy stay here." Then he was gone, closing behind him a heavy door with a suspiciously decided clunk-click.

Lunzie lay still a moment, trying to think her way through it all. Telemetry? That meant she was still being monitored. She had on not the outfit she last remembered, the pressure suit and coverall she had worn on Diplo, but a hospital gown with ridiculous yellow daisies, printed white crinkled stuff that felt like plastic. Someone's idea of cheerful: it wasn't hers. She saw no wires, felt no tubes, so the telemetry must be remote. A "smart" hospital bed could keep track of a patient's heart and respiration rate, temperature, activity, and even bowel sounds, without anything being attached to the patient.

She sat up, carefully easing her arms and legs into motion again. No dizziness, no nausea, no pounding headache. She wasn't sure why she was surprised. After all, they'd had forty-three years to come up with better drugs than the ones she'd had available on Ireta.

Wherever she was, her quarters included a complete array of refreshment options. She chose the shower, yelping when the mysterious control handle switched to cold pulses when she tried to turn it off. *That* was an effective final wake-up step, to be sure. She wrapped herself in the thick, heavy towelling provided and looked around the small room. Her own personal kit, the green fabric no more scuffed than she remembered, still contained her own partly-used containers of cosmetics and scents and lotions. Drawers beneath the counter held others and remedies for any minor illness or emergency. She frowned thoughtfully. It would be difficult to commit suicide with the variety of medications provided, but possible if you took them all at once on an empty stomach. Weren't people in confinement usually kept without drugs?

Drawers on one side held neatly folded garments she did not recognize even when she shook them out. Pajamas, lounging wear, all her size, and in colors she favored, but she'd never bought these. She chose an outfit she could even have worn in public, loose plush pants and a pullover top—and felt much better. That ridiculous hospital gown made anyone feel helpless and submissive. Dressed, with her hair clean and brushed, and her feet in sensible shoes, she was ready to take on the world. Whatever world this happened to be.

Back in the other room, she found the bed remade and rolled to one side. Now a small table centered the room, with a meal laid ready on it. Soup, fruit, bread: exactly what she would have chosen. But the room was empty, silent. Had she taken that long to clean up? She looked but found no clock.

She wondered whether the food was drugged, and then realized that it made no difference. If they . . . whoever they were . . . wanted to drug her, it would be easy enough to do it in other ways. She ate the excellent meal with full appreciation of its excellence. Then she investigated the locker the attendant had first pointed out. There were the rest of her clothes from the Diplo trip and all the other personal gear she'd taken along. Everything seemed to be freshly cleaned, but otherwise untouched.

FedCentral. The man had said she was on FedCentral. She'd never been there and knew nothing of it except for the standard media shots of the Council sessions. *Who* had secure medical facilities on FedCentral? Fleet? But if she was in Fleet's hands, surely Sassinak could identify her and get her out of here? Unless something had happened to Sassinak . . . and she didn't even want to think about that possibility.

Instead she tried to add up the elapsed time since she'd left the *Zaid-Dayan*. It must be very close to Tanegli's trial date when she would be called to give evidence. Unless, of course, she was still cooped up here. Was that what someone wanted? Had that been Zebara's plan all along? She rooted through her personal gear, looking for anything that might be the proof Zebara had promised her of the Diplo end of the conspiracy, but found nothing. Her clothes were all there and the one or two pieces of jewelry she had taken to Diplo.

Her little computer held only its software. Nothing stored in files with mysterious names and nothing new in the files she'd initiated. No mysterious lumps in her clothing, nothing tucked into a pocket of her duffel. Even the clutter was still there. She wondered why no one had tossed out the copy of the program from *Bitter Destinies* or the baggage claim receipt from Diplo or the ragged scrap on which she'd jotted the room number on Liaka where the medical team would assemble. An advertising card from a dress shop she'd never had time to visit. She couldn't even remember if that was from before Ireta or after. Another torn scrap of paper with the numbers of the cases that needed to be re-entered on cubes, the ones Bias had thrown that fit about. But nothing resembling Zebara's promised evidence. Finally, frustrated, she threw herself into the softly padded chair and glared at the door. With suspicious quickness, it opened.

She did not recognize the old man who stood there. He clearly knew her, but waited, at ease, until she acknowledged him with a nod.

"May I come in?" he asked then.

As if I could stop you, she thought, but tried for a gracious smile and said, "Of course. Do come in."

Her voice carried more edge than she intended, but it didn't bother him. He shut the door carefully behind him as she tried to figure out who, or what, he was.

Although he wore no uniform, she felt a uniform would look more natural on him. With that bearing, he would be an officer. At that age, for his silvery hair and lined brow put him into his sixties at least, he should have stars. Tall, much taller than average, piercing blue eyes. If his hair had been yellow or black or brown . . . a warm honey-brown . . .

It was always a shock, and it was going to stay a shock, as it had with Zebara. At least this man was healthy, his white hair a sign of age, but not decay.

"Admiral Coromell," she murmured softly. He smiled, the same charming smile she remembered on a much younger face. Not in his sixties, but upper eighties, at least. "Your father?" He must be dead, but . . .

"He died about two decades ago, painlessly in his sleep," Coromell said. "And you have survived another long sleep! Remarkable."

Not remarkable, Lunzie thought, but disgusting. "I'm beginning to think myself that those superstitious sailors were right! I'm a Jonah."

He snorted, a curiously youthful snort. "Ireta's a planet. It doesn't count. My dear, much as I'd like to chat with you and play verbal games, I can't allow either of us the luxury. We have a problem."

Lunzie contented herself with a raised eyebrow. As far as she was concerned they had many more than one problem. He could say what he would.

"It's your descendant."

She had not expected *that*. "Descendant?" Fiona must be dead by now. Who could he mean? But of course! "Sassinak?" He nodded. She felt a surge of fear. "What's happened to her? Where is she?"

"That's what we don't know. She was here. I mean, on FedCentral, while I was on leave over on Six, hunting. Unfortunately. Now she's gone. Disappeared. She and an Iretan native, by the name of Aygar . . ."

"Aygar!"

Lunzie felt foolish, repeating it, but could think of nothing else to say. Why was Sassinak going anywhere with Aygar? Unless she . . . but Lunzie did not believe that for a moment. Sassinak had never, for one moment, thought of anything but her ship first and Fleet second. She would not take off on a recreational jaunt with Aygar when Tanegli's trial was coming up.

"According to the ranking officer aboard the *Zaid-Dayan*, Arly . . ." He paused to see if she knew the name. She nodded. "Commander Sassinak sent you to Diplo to some source you knew about, to get information on Diplo's connection to the Iretan mess. Is that right?"

"Yes, it is."

Quickly, Lunzie outlined Sassinak's thoughts, and her decision to offer to go to Diplo.

"I was best suited, in many ways . . ."

"I wouldn't have thought so, not after your experience with the heavy-worlders on Ireta," said Coromell. "The last person who should have had to go . . ."

"But I'm glad I did."

She stopped, wondering if she should tell him everything, and filled in with a brief account of her retraining on Liaka and the early part of the expedition.

"I presume, then, that you do have the information you sought?" When she didn't answer at once, he cocked his head and grinned, "Or did they catch you snooping and send you home in a coldsleep pod just to frustrate us?"

"I . . . I'm not sure."

He waited, quiet but curious, in just the attitude of the experienced interrogator who knows the suspect will incriminate herself, given enough rope. She did *not* want to explain Zebara to a Fleet admiral, especially not *this* Fleet admiral, but there was no other way. How best to do it? She remembered Sassinak, chewing out one of the junior officers who had tried to conceal a mistake . . . "When all else fails, Mister, tell the truth." She didn't think she'd made that big a mistake, but she'd still better tell the truth, and all of it.

It took longer than she expected. Although Coromell didn't ask questions until she finished, she could tell by his expression when she'd lost him and needed to backtrack and explain. And her leftover indignation at Bias, plus a natural reluctance to go into her emotional ties to Zebara, kept her ranting at the team leader's prudery far too long. At last she came to an end, trailing off with, ". . . and then I felt terribly sleepy in that stuffy car and, when I woke up, I was here."

A long pause, during which Lunzie endured the gaze of his brilliant blue eyes. Age had not fogged them at all. She felt they were seeing things she had not said. She had not said anything about the opera *Bitter Destinies* except that Zebara had taken her to an opera. He sighed, at last, the first thing he'd done that sounded old.

"So. And did Zebara give you the information he promised? Or will you go to Tanegli's trial with your testimony alone?"

"He hadn't when I left his home," Lunzie said. "He said I was to get it by messenger. And then . . . it was over."

"But he had you put in coldsleep, and safely aboard a transport that brought you here in a cargo of muskie-wool carpets. And I hear that was quite a scene, when Customs found a metallic return on the scan and unrolled the whole mess of them. Your little pod came rolling out like . . . Who was that Old Earth queen? Guinevere or Catherine or Cleopatra . . . someone like that. Rolled in a carpet to present herself to a king she'd fallen in love with. Anyway. So you don't know, do you, whether he passed that information with you or not?"

Lunzie shook her head. "I've looked through my things and found nothing. Surely your people looked, too?"

"I'm afraid they did." His lips pursed. "We found nothing we recognized. We thought perhaps when you woke, you would know what to look for. You don't?"

"No. If he included it, I don't recognize it."

"He gave you nothing at all?" Coromell's voice had a querulous edge now, age roughening it with impatience. He gave me a very good time, Lunzie thought to herself, *and a lot of worries.*

"Nothing." Then she frowned. He started to speak but she waved him to silence. "No, I think he did after all."

Quickly, she went to the locker and pulled out the duffel, pawing through it. She had not kept her copy of the *Bitter Destinies* program. She had not felt she needed it to remember that powerful work and she had not wanted to chance being teased by the team members if they saw her with it. She had not even been sure that Diplo customs would let her take it out. So Zebara must have put that program among her things. She found it, and brought it to Coromell.

"This isn't mine. I threw mine away. And this is signed. Look! All the singers autographed it."

Thick dark ink, in many different calligraphies, most of them extravagantly individual. Coromell took it gingerly from her hand.

"Ah! Perfect for a rather old-fashioned technology. It would take a dot only this size," and he pointed to one of the ellipsis dots between a performer's name and role, "to hold a great deal of information. We'll have to see . . ."

He stood, then shook his head at her. "I'm sorry, dear Lunzie, but you must stay here, unknown, awhile longer. Without Sassinak, we must not lose your testimony, no matter what this gives us."

"But I . . ."

He had moved even as he spoke, more swiftly and fluidly than she would have supposed possible, and abruptly she faced a closed door again.

"Blast you!" she said, to that impassive surface, "I am not a stupid child, even if you are an arrogant old goat."

That got the response it deserved! Nothing. But she felt better. She felt considerably better when Coromell returned very shortly to report that the program had none of the expected microdots.

"I find myself annoyed with your Zebara," he said, slapping the program down on the table between them. "If there's a message in this thing, no one's found it yet. Do you have any idea how many little specks there are in an opera program? Every single person credited with anything in the production has a row of them, and we had to check every one."

"But it has to be this," said Lunzie. She picked up the program, and flipped through it. She still thought the cover design looked pretentious. Even with heavyworlder pride at full blast on this thing, she noticed that the opera had needed corporate sponsorship. The ads covered the inside front and back pages. Then came photographs of the lead singers, then scenes from the opera itself, then the outline of the libretto, and the cast list. More photographs, an interview with the conductor. She realized she was reading the Diplo dialect much better than she ever had. It almost seemed natural. She found herself humming the aria of the suicide who refused to eat even re-synthesized meat. Coromell looked at her oddly.

"I don't know . . ." she said. She didn't want to speak Standard! She wanted to sing! Sing? Something fluttered in her mind like great feathered wings and the alternative slang meaning of "sing" popped up, along with the anagram "sign." Suddenly she knew. "Sing a song of sixpence . . . sing a sign . . . good heavens, that man is so devious a corkscrew would get lost in him."

"What!" Coromell fairly barked at her, his patience gone, looking now very like his boisterously bossy father.

"It's here, but it's . . . it's in my head. It's a key . . . an implant, keyed to this program. I think . . . Just be patient!"

She looked a bit longer, let her mind drift with the internal forces. Zebara had known she was a Disciple. She had eased his pain, she had touched his mind just a little, and his heart somewhat more. She looked on through the program, not knowing exactly what she was to find, but knowing she would find it. On the final page, the star's sprawling signature half covered her face, her broad bosom, the necklace . . . the necklace Zebara had . . . had *not* given her. So he said. The necklace . . . nearly priceless, he'd said. She'd said. A gift of the former lieutenant governor's son . . . no . . . that was not the link.

The necklace Zebara had not given her . . . her! He had not given *her* a necklace, and the necklace he had not given her lay innocently among her things. Cheap but a good design, she'd bought it . . . she'd bought it before the Ireta voyage, hadn't she? She couldn't remember, now. Did it matter? It did.

She snapped out of that near-trance and without a word to Coromell dove back into her duffel, coming up with the necklace. An innocent enough accessory, itemized among her effects on her way *into* Diplo. She remembered filling out the form. Not expensive enough to require duty on any world, but handy for formal occasions, a pattern of linked leaves in coppertoned metal, with streaks of enamel in blues and greens.

She laid it on the table, and pushed Coromell's hand back when he reached for it. She gave it her whole attention. Did it have the same number of links? She wasn't sure. Was it the same clasp? She wasn't sure. She prodded it with a finger, hoping for inspiration. She had worn it that last day. It had caught on something in Zebara's house. That fluffy pillow? He had unsnagged it for her, unhooking the clasp and refastening it later. She remembered being afraid of his hands so near her neck, and hating herself for that fear. The clasp it had how screwed together, making a little cylinder. Before, it had had an elegant hook, shaped like a tendril of the vine those leaves were taken from.

"The clasp," she said, quietly, without looking up at Coromell. "It's the clasp. It's not the same."

"Shall I?" he asked, reaching.

She shook her head. "No. I want to see." Carefully, as if it might explode for she felt a trickle of icy fear, she took it up and worked at the tiny clasp. Most such things unscrewed easily, two or three turns. This one was stuck, cross-threaded or not threaded at all. She heard Coromell shift restlessly in his chair. "Patience," she said.

Discipline focussed her attention. The real join was not in the middle, where a groove suggested it, but at the end. It required not a twist, but a pull —a straight pull, pinching the last link hard—and out came a delicate pin with its tip caught in a lump of something dark. She pulled the pin free and held on her hand that tiny, waxy cylinder.

"This has to be it. Whatever it is."

What it was, she heard later, was a complete record of Diplo's dealings with the Paradens and the Seti for the past century: names, dates, codes, the whole thing. Everything that Zebara had promised, and more.

"Enough," Coromell said, "to bring their government down . . . even revoke their charter."

"No." Lunzie shook her head. "It's not just the heavyworlders. They were the victims first. We can't take vengeance on the innocent, the ones who aren't part of it."

"You know something I don't?" He was giving her a look that had no doubt quelled generations of junior officers. Lunzie felt what he intended her to feel, but fought against it.

"I do," she said firmly, against the pressure of the stars on his uniform and his age. "I've been there myself. I've been to their opera!"

"Opera!" That came out as a bark of amusement.

Lunzie glared and he choked it back. "Their very, very beautiful opera, Admiral Coromell. With singers better than I've heard in most systems. Composed by heavyworlders to dramatize poems written by heavyworlders, and for all its political bias, we don't come off very well. Tell me! What do you know about the early settlement of Diplo?"

He shrugged, clearly baffled at the intent of the question. "Not much. Heavyworlders settled it because it was too dense for the rest of us without protective gear. It's cold, isn't it? And it was one of the first pure-heavyworlder colony worlds. It still is the richest." The lift of his eyebrows said *so what?*

"It's cold, yes." Lunzie shivered, remembering that cold, and what it had meant. "And in the first winter, the colonists had heavy losses."

He shrugged again. "Colonies always have heavy casualties at first."

She was furious. Zebara had reason for his bitterness, his anger, his near despair! Coromell had no reason for this complacency but ignorance.

"Forty thousand casualties, Admiral, out of ninety thousand."

"What?" That had his attention. He stared at her.

"Forty thousand *men*, who died of starvation and cold because their death was the only hope for the women and children to survive. And even so, not all of them did. Because no one bothered to warn the colonists about the periodic long winter cycles, or provide food for them."

"Are you . . . are you *sure*? Didn't they complain to FSP?"

"To the best of my knowledge, it happened, and what I was told, what I believe is also on that chip along with Paraden and Seti conspiracy, is why the FSP never heard about it officially. Major commercial consortia, Admiral, found it inexpedient to bother about Diplo. And then, because the colonists had turned in desperation to eating indigenous animals, these same consortia threatened to have Fleet down on them. Blackmailed them, to put it simply. The whole long conspiracy, the conscription of heavyworlders into private military forces by Paraden and Parchandri families . . . all that results from the original betrayal."

"But why didn't anyone ever tell us? It's been decades . . . centuries . . . no one can keep a secret that long!"

"They can if they're frightened enough. Once begun, it suited the power-hungry on both sides to keep Diplo's population convinced that the FSP would be nothing but trouble. Think of it. Those the consortia dealt with had power. Had that power as long as those they ruled believed no one else could intervene, or would intervene, to bring justice. These chose others, equally ambitious and unscrupulous, to follow them. It was to no one's advantage in the Diplo government *or* the guilty families to have Diplo citizens confiding in the FSP. No one could come out of the Diplo educational system believing FSP would do anything but interdict the planet for meat-eating and lack of population control." She paused, watching Coromell's face change as he thought about it. "Of course, they *do* eat meat, and they *don't* control their population." His eyes widened again.

"You don't mean? You're serious! But that means . . ."

"It means they remember that only meat-eating saved them, and that they'd promised the men who died to carry on their names. They are as serious, as *devout*, I suppose you'd say, as any upright citizen of FSP who gags at the thought of eating a sentient being. They've broken the law, and they expect all of us to despise them. But they see the law as a weapon which nearly killed them all—for some died rather than eat the muskies—and which we use merely to keep them down."

"But not all the heavyworlder troublemakers are from Diplo."

"No, that's true. Though I have no direct evidence, I would imagine that the one place the *secret* did get out was to other heavyworlders in the form of a warning. Some would believe it, and some wouldn't. And so you have Separationists, Integrationists, the whole complicated mess that we have here."

"I think I see." He stared past her for a long moment. "If you're right, Lunzie—and I must say you present a compelling case—then we are dealing not only with today's conspirators, but with long-developed plans out of the past. If only Sassinak hadn't disappeared!"

"And you still haven't told me how that happened."

"Because we don't know." Coromell smacked his fist into his other hand. "I wasn't here and no one admits to knowing anything about it. She told her Weapons Officer that she had an appointment with me, that she was taking Aygar along, and, in essence, not to wait up for her. No one on my staff knows of any such appointment. She had been informed that I was on leave and was not due back for three more days. The last anyone saw—anyone whose accounts I trust—she and Aygar walked off the down shuttle and into the usual crowd at the shuttleport. Passed customs, their prints are on file, and then nothing."

Chapter Thirteen

Sassinak frowned at the carefully worded communication. She did not need to consult the codebook to figure out what it meant. It was in the common senior officers' slang that made its origin very definitely Fleet. Almost impossible to fake slang and the topical references. She had used something like this herself, though rarely. Not something a junior would send to a senior but a senior's discrete way of hinting to the more alert junior.

If she could believe a senior admiral would want a clandestine meeting, would return from leave early, this would be a likely way to signal the officer he wanted to meet. Padalyan reefed her sails, indeed! The reference to the ship she'd served on before the *Zaid-Dayan* almost removed her doubts. But it meant leaving the *Zaid-Dayan* again, and she had not expected to go back onplanet until Coromell returned just before the trial. There was nothing illegal about it, with her ship secured in the FedCentral Docking Station. She still didn't like it.

If Ford had been here . . . but Ford was not only not here, he had not reported anything, anything at all. She should have heard from him by now. Another worry. It had seemed so neat, months ago, sending Ford to find out about the Paradens from a social contact, and Lunzie to Diplo, and dumping

Dupaynil on the Seti. Her mouth quirked. She would bet on Dupaynil to come through with something useful, even if he did figure out his orders were faked. He was too smart for his own good, but a challenge would be good for him.

She realized she was tapping her stylus on the console and made herself put it down. She could think of a dozen good reasons why neither Ford nor Lunzie had shown up yet. And two dozen bad ones. She flicked on one of the screens, calling up a view of the planet below. The fact was that she simply did not want to leave her ship. Here she felt safe, confident, in control. Down on a planet—any planet—she felt lost and alone, a potential victim.

Once recognized, the fear itself drove her to action. She wasn't a frightened child any more. She was a Fleet commander who would finish with more than one star on her shoulders. Earned, not inherited. And she could not afford to be panicked by going downside. Admirals couldn't spend all their time in space. Besides, she had promised to share her memories of Abe with that remarkable designer woman.

Even after all these years, thinking of Abe made her feel safer. She shook her head at herself, then went to the bridge to give Arly her orders.

"I can't tell you more than what I know," she said, keeping her voice low. She trusted her crew, but no sense in their having to work to keep secrets. "Coromell wants a meeting out of his office. I'm taking Aygar along as being less obvious than one of the crew. Don't know how long it will take, or when we'll surface, but stay alert. If you can, monitor their longscans. I have an uneasy feeling that something may be out there, 'way out, and if that happens, you know what to do."

Arly looked unhappy. "I'm not breaking the *Zaid-Dayan* out of here without you, Captain."

"Don't expect you'll have to. But it won't do me any good if someone slams the planet while I'm on it. I'll carry a comunit, of course. Buzz me on the ship's line if Ford or Lunzie show up."

"You're wearing a link?"

"No! They're too easy for someone else to track. I know the com's signal is hard to home on, but it's better than advertising where the admiral is, since he wants the meeting secret."

"Are you sure?"

"Sure enough to risk my neck." Sassinak glanced around the bridge, and leaned closer. "To tell you the truth, *something's* got my hackles up straight, but I can't tell what. Ford's overdue. Lunzie, too. I don't know. Something. I hate to leave the ship, but I can't ignore the message. Just be careful."

"And you." Arly snapped a salute. Sassinak went back to her quarters and changed into civilian clothes, as requested. Another worry; in civilian clothes, she had no excuse for the "ceremonial" weapons she could carry in uniform.

She was aware that her bearing would hint Fleet to any really good observer. Why not simply wear her uniform? But orders, assuming these to be genuine, were orders. She stopped by her office and picked up the things she could carry in one of the pouches currently in style. Aygar should be waiting at the access port. He, at least, had sounded eager enough to go back to the planet. Of course, he had spent only these few months in space; he was a landsman at heart.

She was surprised to see Ensign Timran waiting with Aygar when she came into the access bay. She nodded in answer to his swift salute.

"Ensign." That should send him away quickly. To her surprise, it did not. Her brows raised.

"Captain . . . ma'am . . ."

"Yes, Ensign?"

"Is there any chance that . . . uh . . . that Aygar and I could . . ."

Now what was *this*?

"Spit it out, Ensign, and hurry. We have a shuttle to catch."

"Could go downside together? I mean, you're going to be busy, and he really needs someone along who . . ."

She saw in his face that her expression had changed.

"And just how do you know that I will be 'busy'?"

He reddened and said nothing, but his eyes flicked to Aygar. Sassinak sighed.

"Ensign, if our guest has shared confidential information, you should have the wit to pretend he did not. You surely heard the announcement I made: no liberty, no leaves. Not my decision, but FedCentral regulations. They don't trust Fleet here. And, if by some mischance you *did* end up on the surface, that very distrust could get you in serious trouble."

"Yes, ma'am."

"Nor was I aware that you and Aygar were friends."

This time Aygar spoke up, with almost Tim's eagerness.

"He's stronger than he looks, this little one. We began working out in the gym together, at the marine commander's suggestion." Clever Currald, Sassinak thought. These two might even do each other good.

"Even so, he can't come downside. Sorry. And you're going with me. You'll be busy enough yourself."

Timran still looked disconsolate. Sassinak grinned at him.

"Come now. I need the best shuttle-jockeys up *here*, just in case something breaks loose."

He brightened at once and Sassinak led Aygar through the access tube toward the Station shuttle bay.

They had met nothing to arouse suspicion, but Sassinak felt as tight-drawn as a strangling wire. Aygar had long since quit pointing out interesting shops or odd costumes. He'd lapsed into an almost sullen silence. Sassinak was more annoyed by this than she wanted to be. He was not, after all, Fleet. He could not be expected to react as a trained sailor or marine would.

They had walked out of the shuttleport with no visible tail, into a stifling afternoon made worse by the stinging brown haze over the city. Sassinak was no expert but she had made full use of the gleaming show windows of the shuttleport shopping mall. No one seemed to be following them. No one paused repeatedly to look in the windows when she did. She had been down-side with Aygar before. Unless someone knew specifically of the meeting with Coromell, this ought to look very much like the previous trips.

She would be expected to take him to one of the monotonous gray buildings in which the prosecution attorneys were working up the case against Tanegli, or to Fleet's own gray precincts. Then on yet another walking tour of the sights, such as they were.

She had started as if for the Fleet offices, then, as instructed, boarded one of the express subways bound for Ceylar East, one of the suburbs. None of those who boarded with them were still in their module when they got off and transferred to another line. They had zigged and zagged back and forth under the vast city until Sassinak herself was hardly sure exactly where they were.

Now, only a short distance from the designated meeting place, she wished she'd been born a Weft, with the ability to make eyes in the back of her head. The hot sun and smog made her head ache. She wanted to call Engineering and complain. There. Eklarik's Fantasies and Creations. Its sign was purple curlicues on green with mythical beasts in the corners. Not the sort of place she would ever go on her own; a signal to any follower, as far as she was concerned.

Did Admiral Coromell have a secret passion for historical costumes or antique musical instruments? She gave Aygar a nudge. His shoulders twitched, but he moved across the slideway traffic that way. Sassinak pushed aside the bead curtain and let it rattle closed behind her.

Inside, the shop smelled of potpourri and incense. A thread of smoke rose to a blue haze overhead. Close on either hand were two suits of armor, one smoothly burnished as if it were but iron skin, and the other worked into fantastic peaks and points, decorated with red silk tassels. Racks of costumes, topped with what Sassinak supposed were the appropriate headgear. Floppy hats, spiked helms, flat straw circles, bonnets drowned in ruffles and bows, a row of tiny red enameled cylinders like oversized pillboxes.

She took a step forward, kicked something that clattered, and realized that she had bumped a tall ceramic jar filled with swords. Swords? She lifted one, then realized it had neither edge nor point—a stage sword? It was not steel; the metal made a flat, unpromising sound when she tapped it with her finger. Cluttering the narrow aisles were toppling piles of boots, shoes, sandals; the footgear for the racked costumes, no doubt. Suspended overhead were masks, dozens—no, hundreds—in shapes and colors Sassinak had never imagined. She blinked. Aygar bumped into her from behind.

"What *is* this?" he began, as Sassinak caught a glimpse of someone moving toward them from the back of the shop. She raised her hand, and he quieted, though she could practically feel his resentment.

"May I help?" asked a breathy voice from the dimness. "I'm afraid Eklarik's not here right now, but if it's just normal rental?"

"I'm . . . not sure." The message from Coromell had not specified whether Eklarik's shop assistant would do as well as the man himself. "It's about the *Pirates of Penzance*," she said, feeling like an idiot.

Her knowledge of musical productions was small. She'd had to look up that reference, and although it told her Gilbert and Sullivan were contemporaneous with Kipling, she knew nothing of the work itself. Or what result should follow from the mention of it.

"Ah," said the colorless little person who now came into view between another pair of mounted costumes, these obviously meant for the female form. One was white, a clinging drapery that left one shoulder bare; the other, a vast pouf of pale blue, heavily ornamented with bows, braid, ruching, buttons as if the maker had to prove that he knew how to do all that, bulged halfway across the aisle.

The assistant, between the two, looked so meek and unimportant, that Sassinak was instantly alarmed. No one could be that self-effacing.

"A policeman's lot . . ." said the assistant.

"Is not a happy one," Sassinak replied dutifully, thinking the same thing about the lot of Fleet commanders stuck onplanet in civilian clothes trying to play spy.

"You are the dark lady," said the assistant. Sassinak was still not sure what sex—and was beginning to wonder what race—the assistant might be. Short, slim, dressed in something darkish that rippled. "Your star is shining."

That had to refer to Admiral Coromell. She opened her mouth to say something, but found herself confronted with a crystal sphere slightly larger than she could have held in one hand. The assistant had two hands under it. The crystal gleamed.

"The star you follow," the assistant was saying in a tone that Sassinak would have assumed meant drunk, if one of her crew had used it. "It is dimly seen, in dark places, and often occluded by maleficent planets."

"You have a message for me?" prompted Sassinak when a long silence had followed that after the crystal globe had vanished again into the dimness.

"That *was* your message." A quizzical expression crossed that face, followed by: "You are familiar with the local bars, aren't you? You are a sailor?"

Behind her, Aygar choked and Sassinak barely managed not to gulp herself.

"No," she said gently. "I'm not any more familiar with local bars than with . . . uh . . . costumes."

"Oh." Another long silence, during which Sassinak realized that the assistant's pupils were elliptical, and that the dark costume was actually fur. "I thought you would be. Try the Eclipse, two blocks down, and order a Planetwiper."

That was clear enough, but Sassinak wasn't sure she believed it was genuine.

"You . . ." she began.

The assistant withdrew behind the billowing blue satin skirt, and opened its mouth fully, revealing a double row of pointed teeth.

"I'm an orphan, too," it said, and vanished.

Sassinak shook her head.

"What *was* that?" breathed Aygar.

"I don't know. Let's go."

She didn't like admitting she'd never seen an alien like that before. She didn't like this whole setup.

The Eclipse displayed a violently pink and yellow sign, which at night must have made sleep difficult for anyone across the street. Sassinak glanced that way and saw only blank walls above the street-level shops. No beaded curtain here but a heavy door that opened to a hard shove and closed solidly behind them. A heavyworlder in gleaming gray plastic armor stood at one side—evidence of potential trouble, and its cure, all in one. A glance around showed Sassinak that her clothes did not quite fit in. Except for the over-dressed trio at one table, clearly there to prey on customers, the women wore merchant-spacers' coveralls, good quality but not stylish. Most of the men wore the same, although two men had on business clothes, one with the crumpled gown of an attorney at court piled on the seat beside him. Sassinak supposed the little gray coil atop it was his ceremonial wig.

She was aware of sideways glances, but conversation did not stop. These people were too experienced for that. She led Aygar to one of the booths and dialled their order. Planetwipers had never been her favorite but, of course, she didn't have to drink the thing. Aygar leaned massive elbows on the table.

"Can you tell me what is going on, or are you trying to drive me crazy?"

"I'm not, and I don't know. I presume that at some point our party will arrive. At least I know what he looks like."

She was trying not to be too obvious about looking around. No one here of Coromell's age, or close to it. Surely they wouldn't have a third meeting-place to find. Aygar took a long swallow of his drink.

"That's potent," she said quietly. "Best be careful."

He glowered at her. "I'm not a child. I don't even know why you . . ."

He stopped as someone stopped by their table. Tall, silver-haired, erect. If Sassinak had not known Coromell, she might have believed this was he.

"Commander," he said quietly. "May I sit down?"

"Do join us," Sassinak said. She gestured to Aygar. "The young Iretan you may have heard so much about."

The older man nodded, but did not offer to shake hands. He wore an impeccable blue coverall, what she would have expected of a merchanter captain off-duty. One hand bore a ring that might have been an Academy ring, but the face was turned under where she could not see it. And his movements, his assurance, came from years of command, some kind of command. If he was not Admiral Coromell—and he wasn't—then who or what was he?

"There's been a slight misunderstanding," he said. "It is necessary to stay out of reach of compromised surveillance devices until . . ."

Sassinak never saw the flicker of light, only the surprised look on his face and the neat, crisped holes, five of them, in his face.

Instinct had her under the table and scrambling before the first blood oozed out. She heard a bellow and crash as Aygar tossed the table aside and came after her. Something sizzled and Aygar yelped. Then the whole place erupted in noise and motion.

Like all fights, it was over in less time than she could have described it. The experienced hit the floor and scuttled for shelter. The inexperienced screamed, flailed, and threw things that crashed and tinkled. Fumes from the shattered bottles stung her nose and eyes. Glass shards pricked her palms and knees.

Sassinak bumped into other scuttlers, caught sight of Aygar and yanked him down just as a pink streak ripped the air where he'd been and burst the windows out. She jerked hard on his wrist, trusting him to follow, as she worked her way through the undergrowth of the fight. Table standards, chair legs, bodies. Through the service door, and into a white-tiled kitchen. She was surprised to realize that the place sold food as well. More noise behind her, following. She slipped on the greasy wet floor, staggered, and yanked Aygar again.

"Come *on*, dammit!"

"But . . ." He threw a last glance over his shoulder, and whatever he saw propelled him in a great leap that ended with Aygar and Sassinak tangled out the back door, and flames bursting out behind them.

"Snarks in a *bucket!*"

Sassinak struggled out from under the younger man and shook her head. Screams, more sounds of mayhem. She looked down the alley they'd landed in. She hated planets . . . living on them, at least. No one to keep things really shipshape. On the other hand, this filthy and disreputable bit of real estate offered hiding places no clean ship would. Aygar, she noted, had a bleeding gash down his face and several rips in his coverall, but no serious injury.

He was already up on one knee, looking surprisingly relaxed and comfortable for someone who had narrowly escaped death. He had probably saved her life with that last lunge for the back door.

"Thanks," she said, trying to figure out what to do with him. She'd thought of him more as deterrence than serious help if things turned nasty. And at the moment, they were about as nasty as she had seen in awhile.

"We should go," he pointed out. "I was told only Insystem had that sort of weaponry."

"We're going."

Another quick glance, and she chose the shorter end of the alley. Nothing happened on the first quick dash to cover behind a stinking trash bin with rusty streaks down its sides. Sassinak eyed the other back doors opening on the alley. Surely someone should have peeked? Unless the neighborhood were really that tough, in which case . . .

"There's someone behind the next one of these," Aygar said softly in her ear.

She eyed him with respect. "How d'you know?"

He shrugged. "I lived by hunting, remember? On Ireta, the things you didn't notice would hunt you. I heard something wrong."

"Great."

No weapons. No armor. And all her tricks were back in childhood, the tricks that worked on screen, and not in real life. Real life worked a lot better with real weapons.

"I can take them," Aygar went on.

She looked at him: all the eagerness appropriate to a young male in the prime of his pride and no military training whatever. And he wasn't hers, the way young Timran would have been. He was a civilian, under her oath of protection. She started to shake her head, but he hadn't waited.

Even knowing about the great strength his genes and his upbringing had developed, she was still surprised. Aygar picked up the entire trash bin with all its clinking, rattling, dripping, smelly contents, and hurled it down the alley to crash into the next. Someone yelped. Sassinak heard the flat crack of small arms fire, then nothing.

Aygar was moving, rushing the barrier of the two trash bins crunched together. With a quick shrug, she followed, vaulting neatly into the mash of rotten vegetables and fruit peels on the far side. Aygar had neatly broken the neck of the ambusher. Sassinak picked herself out of the disgusting mess carefully and smiled at Aygar.

"Try not to kill them unless you have to," she heard herself say.

"I did," he said seriously. "Look!"

And sure enough, the Insystem guard had managed to hang onto his weapon even with a trash bin pinning him by the legs.

"Right. There are times . . . good job." At least she wouldn't have to worry about this one having post-combat hysterics. "Let's get out of this."

Aygar hesitated. "Should I take his weapon?"

"No, it's illegal. We'll be in enough trouble." *We're already in enough trouble, she thought.* "On second thought, yes. Take it. Why should the bad guys have all the advantages?"

Aygar pried it out of the man's hand and courteously offered it to her. Surprised, Sassinak let her eyebrows rise as she took it and tucked it into a side pocket. Then, swiping futilely at the stains on her coverall, she led them down the alley to the street.

By this time, sirens wailed nearby. With any luck, they would be on the other street. Sassinak motioned Aygar back. With that blood dripping down his face, he'd be better in hiding. Cautiously, she put her head around the corner. As if he'd been waiting for her, a stocky man in bright orange uniform bellowed and then blew a piercing whistle. Sassinak muttered a curse, and yanked Aygar into a run. No good going back into the alley. They'd have someone at the other end.

They pelted down the street, dodging oncoming pedestrians. Sassinak expected at least one of them to try stopping them, but none did. Behind them, the whistleblower fell steadily behind. Sassinak led them right at the first corner, slowing to an almost-polite jog as she stepped on the first slideway. Aygar, beside her, wasn't even breathing hard.

Then he gripped her wrist. Across the street they were on, ahead, was a cordon of orange-uniforms on the pedestrian overpass above the slideways. They carried something that looked uncomfortably like riot-control weapons. Sassinak and Aygar edged back off the slideway. This street, like the other, had a miscellany of small shops and bars.

No time to choose. Sassinak ducked into the first she saw, hoping it had a useful back entrance.

"You look terrible, dearie," said someone out of the dimness.

Sassinak started to answer when she realized the young woman was looking at Aygar. Who was looking at her.

"We don't have time for this," she said, tugging at Aygar's suddenly immobile bulk.

"Men always have time for this," said the young woman, setting her various fringes in motion. "As for you, hon, why don't you take a look in the other room."

Someone from there had already come to the archway. Sassinak ignored him and tried the only thing she could think of.

"We need to find Fleur. Now. It's an emergency."

"Fleur! What do you know about her?"

An older woman stormed through the draperies of another archway. Somewhat to Sassinak's surprise, she had the trim, brisk appearance of a successful professional which, in a sense, she was. "Who are you, anyway?"

"I need to find her. That's all I can say."

"Security after you?" When Sassinak didn't answer immediately, the woman moved past them to peer through the outer window. "They're after somebody and you've got bloodstains and gods know what stinking up your clothes. Tell me now! You?"

"Yes. I'm . . ."

"Don't tell me."

Sassinak obeyed. Here, in this place, someone else commanded.

"Come." When Aygar cast a last look after the young woman who had greeted him, their guide snorted. "Listen, laddy-o, you're looking at a week's salary, unless you're ranked higher than I think, and you'd be dead before you enjoyed it if we don't get you under cover."

Then, as she led them down a passage, she shouted back to her household, "Lee, get yourself in three with Ell. I don't think the locals know you yet. Pearl, you saw Lee come in. The woman with him, if they think they saw one, was our street tout." She muttered over her shoulder to Sassinak. "Not that that'll hold five minutes if they really saw you, but they might not have. It's getting to our busy time of day, so there's a chance. In here."

In here was a tiny square office, crowded with desk and two chairs. The woman pulled open a drawer and slapped an aid kit down on the surface.

"He won't pass anywhere, with all that blood. Clean him up. I'll be back with another coverall for you."

Aygar sat in one of the chairs while Sassinak cleaned the shallow gash and put a sticker over it. He did look less conspicuous with the blood off his face. She used several more stickers to hold the rents in his coverall together. The scratches under them had long stopped bleeding.

The woman came back with a cheap working coverall of tough tan fabric and tossed it to Sassinak.

"Get that smelly thing off so I can run it through the shredder in the kitchen. What'd you do, camp out in a grocer's trash bin?"

"Not exactly." Sassinak didn't want to explain. She handed Aygar the gun out of her pocket before peeling off her coverall and slipping into the other one. Aygar, she noticed, was trying not to watch while the woman stared at her.

"You must be Fleet," she said, more quietly. "You've got muscles, for a woman your age. Over forty, aren't you?"

"A little, yes."

The tan coverall was a bit short in the arms and legs, but ample in the body. Sassinak transferred her ID and the handcom into its pockets and then took the gun back from Aygar.

"Ever heard of Samizdat?" The woman's voice was even lower, barely above a murmur.

Sassinak stared, remembering that bleak afternoon when Abe had told her a tiny bit about that organization.

"A little," she said cautiously.

"Hmm. Fleet. Samizdat. Fleur. Tell you what, honey, you'd better be honest, or I swear I'll hunt you to the last corner of the galaxy, my own self, and stake your gizzard in the light of some alien sun, so I will. That Fleur's a lady, saved my life more'n once, and never thinks the worse of a girl for doing what she has to."

"She's a Fleet captain," said Aygar.

Both women glared at him.

"I didn't want to know that," said the woman. "A Fleet captain with undisciplined crew . . ."

Before Aygar could say anything, Sassinak said, "He's not crew; he's civilian, an important witness against planet pirates, and they're trying to silence him. We were supposed to have a quiet meeting but it didn't stay quiet."

"Ah. Then you *do* know about Samizdat. Well, we'll have to get you out of here later, and I'll send word to Fleur . . ." She stopped, as voices erupted down the passage. "Rats. Up out of that chair, laddy-o, and quick about it."

Aygar stood, and the woman shoved until he flattened against the wall. Sassinak, guessing what she wanted, lifted the chairs onto the desk. Beneath the worn carpet was the outline of a trapdoor. The woman didn't have to urge quickness, not with the words "search" and "illegal aliens" and "renegade posing as Fleet" booming down the hall.

First came a straight drop down five feet to a landing above a short stair. Aygar had scarcely bent to get his head below floor level when the trap banged down, leaving them in complete darkness. Sassinak could hear muffled thumps and scrapes as the rug and chairs went back atop it. She had made it almost to the next level, but stopped where she was, afraid to move in the darkness lest she trip and make a noise. Aygar crept down three steps and touched her shoulder.

"What now?" he asked.

"Shhh. We hope the searchers don't know about the trapdoor."

For the first time since trouble started, Sassinak had leisure to think about it and about her ship. She had been fooled by the original communication because it was in Fleet slang. That implied, but did not prove, that someone in Fleet was trying to get her killed. Whoever it was knew enough about Coromell to suspect that his name would lure her and that she would know only his general appearance. He was famous enough. It wouldn't be hard for anyone to know his height, his age, and find someone reasonably close to impersonate him.

But why all the complexity? Why not simply have someone assassinate her, or Aygar, or both, as they were on their way out of the shuttleport, or any place between? And, assuming those orange uniforms were the police, why were the authorities on the side of the attackers?

She tried to think what someone might have said to convince the local police that she and Aygar were dangerous criminals causing trouble. Fleeing a bar fight was only common sense. She'd originally thought to call in to Coromell's office as soon as she found a telecom booth. And what was happening to her ship, topside? She wanted to pull out the comunit and find out, but dared not with searchers after them.

Time waiting in the darkness had strange dimensions. Endless, seamless, compressed by fear and stretched by anticipation: she had no idea how long it was before she dared extend a cautious foot to the next lower step. She edged down, drawing Aygar after her. Just in case they found the trapdoor, she'd rather be around a corner, behind something, under something. Another step, and another.

When the lights went on, her vision blanked for a moment. Aygar gasped. Now she could see the long narrow room. She ran down the last few steps, Aygar behind her, and looked for a place to hide. There? An angle of wall, perhaps a support for something overhead? She ducked around it, out of sight of the stairs. Then a voice crackled from some hidden speaker.

". . . know you have a basement, Sera Vanlis, and you'd better cooperate. This is nothing to play games about."

"I still don't see a warrant." Not quite defiance, but not quite calm confidence, either. "I've nothing to hide, but I'm not setting precedent by letting you search without one."

"I'll call for one."

A pause, then the sound of speech Sassinak could not distinguish. Did the sound go both ways? She had to trust not, had to hope the woman had hit some hidden switch to give them both warning and a way out. But nothing looked like a way out. No doors, in the long opposite wall, or the far end. No door at either end. A fat column of cables and pipes came out of the ceiling, entered and exited a massive meter box covered with dials, and disappeared into a grated opening in the floor.

Aygar nodded toward it. Sassinak looked closer. Not big enough for Aygar and she wasn't sure she could slither alongside the bundled utilities, but it gave her an idea. If this were a ship, there'd be some kind of repair access to the utility conduits. She couldn't find it, and the conversation overhead could have only one ending.

Then Aygar picked up a filing cabinet, one of a row along the far wall, but in line with the path of the cables, and there it was. A flat circle of metal, with a pop-up handle, and under it a vertical shaft with a ladder fixed to one side. She would have had trouble getting the cover free, and up, but Aygar's powerful fingers lifted it as easily as a piece of toast on a tray.

Sassinak eeled into the hole, slipped easily down the ladder to give Aygar room, and murmured "How're you going to cover it after us?"

"Don't worry."

Nonetheless, she did worry as he slipped the access cover behind the next file cabinet over, and backed down into the hole, dragging the file cabinet with him. Surely he couldn't possibly move it all the way into place, just with his hands? He could.

They were in the dark again, the top of the shaft sealed with the file cabinet, but she could hear the proud grin in his voice when he said, "Unless they heard that, they won't know. And I think it's been used that way before. That cabinet's not as heavy as a full one would be."

"Good job."

She patted his leg and backed on down the ladder. They ought to come to a cross-shaft . . . and her foot felt nothing below, then something uneven. She ran her foot over it in the dark, momentarily wondering why she'd been stupid enough not to bring along a handlight. Lumpy, long, slick . . . probably the bundled utilities. She couldn't quite reach them with her hand while clinging to the ladder. She'd have to drop. Aygar's foot tapped her head, and she touched his ankle, a slight sideways shove that she hoped he would understand as "Wait!"

Chapter Fourteen

"What about a light?" asked Aygar softly.

Sassinak counted to ten, reminding herself that he was not, despite his talents, a trained soldier. He would not have thought to tell her before that he had a light.

"Fine."

Above her, a dim light came on, bright enough to dark-adapted eyes. Shadows danced crazily as he passed it down. Below, the cross tunnel was twice the diameter of theirs, its center full of pipes, with a narrow catwalk along one side. Sassinak eased down, swung her legs onto the catwalk, and guided Aygar's feet. She had to crouch a little; he was bent uncomfortably. She touched his arm and jerked her head to one side. They would move some distance before they dared talk much.

Twenty meters down the tunnel, Sassinak paused and doused the handlight. No sound or sight of pursuit. She closed her eyes, letting them adapt to darkness again, and wishing she had even the helmet to her armor. Even without the link to the cruiser's big computers, the helmet onboard with sensors could have told her exactly what lay ahead, line-of-sight.

She opened her eyes to darkness. Complete . . . no. Not complete. Ahead, so dim she could hardly make it out, a distant red-orange point. She squinted, then remembered to shift her gaze off-center and back across. *Two* red-orange points. She leaned out to peer back past Aygar. Another, and another beyond that.

Marker lights for maintenance workers. That would be the most harmless. Alternatives included automatic cameras that could send their images straight to some police station without ever giving them enough light to see. Or automatic lasers, linked to heat and motion sensors, designed to rid the tunnels of vermin.

She hated planets. There might even *be* vermin in these tunnels. But when there were no choices, only fools refused chances . . . so Abe had said. She edged sideways along the catwalk, moving with ship-trained neatness in that unhandy space. Aygar had more trouble. She could hear him thumping and stumbling, and had to hope that there were no sound sensors down here. She used the handlight as seldom as she could.

Moving past the first dim light in the tunnel's roof set off no alarms she could sense, but then a good system wouldn't tell *her*. She was sweating now in the tunnel's unmoving air, and wondering just how good that air was. Between the first and second lights, she felt a sudden draft along her side, and turned the light on the tunnel wall. Waist high, another grill, this one rectangular. A silent, slightly cooler breath came from it. She could hear no fan, not even the hiss of air movement. Then for an instant it changed, sucking against the back of her hand, then stilled, then returned as before.

Nothing but a pressure-equalizing connector, probably from the subway system, she thought. Nice to know they were connected to something else with air, though she'd rather have found a route to the surface. She tapped Aygar's arm, and they crouched beneath the vent to rest briefly.

"I'm not sure who's after us," she said. "That wasn't the man I was supposed to meet, back there, just someone the right age and size, but not the same."

Aygar ignored this. "Do you know where we are? Can we get back?"

"Not the right questions. To get back, we have to figure out who's trying to kill us. At this point we don't know if they're after you, me, or both. And why."

She could think of reasons both ways. All three ways, and even a few more. Why send her to meet a fake Coromell and then kill *him*? It could hardly have been a mistake; the difference between a white-haired old man and a dark-haired woman was clear to the stupidest assassin. It couldn't have been bad marksmanship, not with the cluster that had destroyed the man's face. Had there been two different sets of conspirators whose plots intersected in wild confusion?

"You said that wasn't Coromell." Aygar's voice was quiet, his tone alert but not anxious. "Did the one who killed him know that?"

"I'm not sure." She was not sure of a lot, except that she wished she'd stayed on her ship. So much for confronting old fears. "If that had been Coromell, and if I'd also been killed, perhaps the next round of fire, you'd have been the ranking witness for Tanegli's trial. And, as you've said often enough, you don't know anything about the dealings Tanegli had with the other conspirators. All you could do is testify that he lied to you, led you to believe that Ireta was yours. If there were some way Coromell's death could be blamed on me . . ."

"And why were all those other people waiting for us outside?" Aygar asked.

Clearly his mind ran on a different track. Natural, with his background. But it was still a good question.

"Hmm. Suppose they plan to kill Coromell in the bar. They expect me to run, with you, just as I did. The only smart thing to do in something like that is get out. So they've got others outside, to kill us. Or me. Then they could pin Coromell's death on me, discredit Fleet, and any testimony I bring to the trial."

"What would happen to the *Zaid-Dayan*? Who is your heir?"

"Heir? Ships aren't personal property! Fleet would assign another . . ." She stopped short, struck by another possibility. "Aygar, you're a genius, and you don't even know it. Testimony is one thing: a ship of the line is another. My *Zaid* is possibly the most dangerous ship of its class. If it's the *ship* they fear and want to render helpless, then by taking me out or even keeping me onplanet while Coromell's death is investigated, that would do it. It would be Standard weeks before another captain arrived. They might even seal the ship in dock."

And why would someone be that upset about a cruiser at the orbital station, a cruiser whose weapons were locked down? What did someone fear that cruiser could do? Cruisers weren't precision instruments. Despite her actions on Ireta, cruisers were designed as strategic platforms, capable of dealing with, say, a planetary rebellion, or an invasion from space. Or both.

Sassinak was up again before she realized she was going to move. "Come on," she said. "We've got to get back to the ship."

As if that were going to be easy. She started looking for another access port. Soon enough this tunnel would come to someone's attention, even if they didn't find the escape hatch from that . . . place. Her mind was working now, full-speed, running the possibilities of several sets of plotters. It could reduce to one set, if they had some way to interfere with Coromell's return and thought the singed corpse could pass as his for long enough to get her in legal trouble. Or suppose they'd captured the real Coromell and could produce his body.

Not her problem. Not now. Now all she had to do was find a way out, to the surface, call Arly and get a shuttle to pick them up. She longer cared about the legal aspects of action.

The next access port led them down, deeper into the city's underground warren of service tunnels. This one was lighted and the single rail down the middle of the floor indicated regular maintenance monorail service. Plastic housings covered the bundled cables along one wall, the pipes running along the other. Sassinak noted that the symbols seemed to be the same as those used in Fleet vessels, the colored stripes and logos she knew so well, but she didn't try to tap a water pipe to make sure. Not yet. They could walk along the catwalk beside the monorail without stooping. With the light, they could move far more quickly.

That didn't help if they didn't know where they were going, Sassinak thought grimly. The port they'd come out of had a number on the reverse: useless information without the map reference.

"We're still going the same way," Aygar said.

She stared at him, surprised again. He was taking all this much better than she would have predicted.

"It's easy to lose one's way without references," she began, but he was holding up a little button. "What's that?"

"It's a mapper," Aygar said. "One of the students I met at the Library said I should have one or I'd get lost."

"A locator transmitter?" Her heart sank. If he was carrying that, their unknown enemies could simply wait, watching the trace on a computer, until they came up again.

"No. He said there were two kinds, the kind that told people where you were so they could find you and help you, and the kind that told you where you were for yourself. Tourists carry the first kind, he said, and rich people who expect their servants to come pick them up, but students like the second. So that's what I bought."

She had not realized he'd been on his own long enough to do anything like that. Thinking back . . . there were hours and hours in which he'd been left at the Library entrance. She'd taken him there, or the FSP prosecutors had, between depositions or conferences. She hadn't even known he'd met anyone else.

"How does it work?"

"Like this." He flicked it with a thumbnail and a city map, distorted by the casing of the cables, appeared on the wall of the tunnel. A pulsing red dot must be their position. The map seemed to zoom closer, and letters and numbers replaced part of the criss-cross of lines. "E-84, RR-72." Aygar flicked the thing again and a network of yellow lines appeared. There they were, in what was labelled *Maintenance access tunnel* 66-43-V. "Where do we want to go?"

"I'm . . . not sure." Until she knew who their enemies were, she didn't know where it might be safe to surface and call Arly. Or if even that would be a good idea. "Where's the nearest surface access?"

The red dot distorted into a line that crept along the yellow of their tunnel, then turned orange.

"That means go up," Aygar said. "If we have to go down to get somewhere, our line will turn purple." It made sense, in a way.

"Let's go, then."

She let him lead the way. He seemed to know how the mapper worked. She certainly did not. She wanted to ask about scale, but they'd been in one place too long already. Her neck itched with the certainty that pursuit was close behind.

"If you have any more little goodies, like the light, or the mapper, why not tell me now?" It came out a bit more waspish than she intended.

"I'm sorry," he said. He actually sounded abashed. "I didn't know . . . There hasn't been time."

"Never mind. I'm just very glad you opted for this kind of mapper and not the other."

"I didn't think I'd need it, really," he said. "I don't get lost easily. But Gerstan was being so friendly." He shrugged.

Sassinak felt another bubble of worry swell up beside the cluster that already filled her head. A friendly student who just happened to take an interest in the well-being of a foreigner?

"Tell me more about Gerstan," she said as calmly as she could.

Gerstan, it seemed, was "a lot like Tim." Sassinak managed not to say what she thought and hoped Aygar had made a mistake. Gerstan had been friendly, open, helpful. He had sympathized with Aygar's position. Because, of course, Aygar had explained all about Ireta. Sassinak swallowed hard and let Aygar go on talking as they walked. Gerstan had helped him use the Library computers to access the databases, and he had even said that it was possible to bypass the restriction codes.

"Really?" said Sassinak, hoping her ears weren't standing right straight out. "That's pretty hard, I'd always heard."

Aygar's explanation did not reassure her. Gerstan, it seemed, had friends. He had never explained just who they were: just friends whose specialty was intercepting data transmissions and diverting them.

"What kind of transmissions?"

"He didn't say, exactly." Aygar sounded slightly grumpy about that, as if in retrospect Gerstan didn't seem quite as helpful. "He just said that if I ever needed to get into the databases, or . . . or slip a loop, whatever that is, he could help. Said it was easy, if you had the knack. All the way up to the Parchandri, he said."

An icy spike went straight down Sassinak's back at that. "Are you sure?" she said, before she could stop it.

"Sure of what?" Aygar was lolloping ahead, apparently quite relaxed.

"That he said 'all the way up to Parchandri?' "

"The *Parchandri*. Yes, that's what he said. Why?"

He glanced back over his shoulder and Sassinak hoped her face revealed nothing but calm interest. Parchandri. Inspector General Parchandri? Who should not be here anyway, but at Fleet Headquarters. As if they were printed in the fiery letters in the air before her, she could see that initiation code, supposedly coming from the Inspector General's office . . .

"I'm just trying to figure things out," she said to Aygar who had glanced back again.

Should she explain any of this to Aygar? His own problems were complicated enough, and besides he had no real right to Fleet's darker secrets. But if something happened . . . She shook her head fiercely. What was going to happen was that she would be laughing at The Parchandri's funeral. If, in fact, The Parchandri was guilty of Abe's murder.

At intervals they passed access ports on either side, above, below. Each had a number stenciled on it. Each looked much the same as the others. Had it not been for Aygar's mapper, Sassinak would have had no idea which way to go.

She had been hearing the faint whine for some moments before it registered, and then she jumped forward and tapped Aygar's shoulder. "Listen."

He shrugged. "This whole planet makes noise," he said. "No one can hear anything in a city. Nothing that means anything, that is."

"How far to where we go up?" asked Sassinak. The whine was marginally louder.

"Half a kilometer, perhaps, if I'm reading this right."

"Too far." She looked around and saw an access hatch less than twenty meters ahead, on their side of the monorail, below the cable housing. "We'll take that one."

"But why?"

The whine had sharpened and a soft brush of air touched his face. He whirled at once and raced for the hatch. Sassinak caught up with him, helped wrestle it open. At once, an alarm rang out, and a flashing orange light. Sassinak bit back a curse. If she ever got off this planet, she would never, under any circumstances, go downside again! Aygar was dropping his legs through the hatch, but Sassinak spotted another, only five meters farther on.

"I'll open that one, too. Then they won't know which."

She could not hear the whine of the approaching monorail car over the clamoring alarm, but the air pressure shifts were clear enough. She ran as she had not had to run for years, scrabbled at the hatch cover, threw it back, and winced as another alarm siren and light came on. Then back to the first, and in. Aygar had wisely retreated down the ladder, giving her room. A quick yank and the hatch closed over them. They were in darkness again. She could still hear the siren whooping. From this one? From the other? Both?

All the way down that ladder, much longer than any they'd taken before, she scolded herself. She didn't even know the monorail car was manned. It might have no windows, no sensors. They might have been able to stand quietly, watch it go by, and then walk out following Aygar's mapper. Then again maybe not. Second-guessing didn't help deal with consequences. She took a long, calming breath, and reminded herself not to tighten up. Although one thing after another had gone wrong, they *were* alive, unwounded, and uncaught. That had to be worth something. Her foot touched Aygar's head. He had reached the bottom of the ladder.

"I can't find a hatch," he said. His voice rang softly in the echoing dark chamber. "I'll try light."

Sassinak closed her eyes, and opened them when she saw pink against her lids. They were at the bottom of a slightly curving, near-vertical shaft, and nothing marked the sides at the bottom. Not so much as a roughly welded seam. Aygar's breath was loud and ragged.

"We . . . have to find a way out. There has to be a way out!"

"We will."

She felt almost comfortable in shafts and tunnels, but Aygar had had a wilderness to run in until he boarded the *Zaid-Dayan*. He'd done remarkably well for someone with no ship training, but this dead end in a narrow shaft was too much. She could smell his sudden nervous sweat; his hand on her leg trembled.

"It's all right," she said, the voice she might have used on a nervous youngster on his first cruise. "We passed it, that's all. Follow me up but *quietly*."

It was not that far up, a circular hatch in the shaft across from the ladder, easily reached. Sassinak just had her hand firmly on the locking ring, ready to turn it, when it was yanked away from her, and she found herself pinned in a beam of brilliant light.

"Well." The voice was gruff, and only slightly surprised. "And what have we here? Not the Pollys, this time."

Squinting against the brilliance, Sassinak could just see a dark form outlined by more light beyond, and the gleam of light down a narrow tube; a weapon, no doubt.

"How many?" demanded the voice.

Sassinak wondered if Aygar could hide below, but realized he couldn't, not in the grip of claustrophobia.

"Two," she said crisply.

"Y'all come on outa there, then," said the voice.

The light withdrew just enough to give them room. Sassinak slid through feet-first, and found herself coming out of a waist-high hatch in a horizontal tunnel. Aygar followed her, his tanned face pale around mouth and eyes, and dripping with sweat. Carefully, as if she were doing this on her own ship, Sassinak closed the hatch and pushed the locking mechanism.

Facing them were five rough-looking figures in much-patched jumpsuits. Two held obvious weapons that looked like infantry assault rifles: one had a long knife spliced to a section of metal conduit and one held the light that still blinded them. The last lounged against the tunnel wall, eyeing them with something between greed and disgust.

"Y'all rang the doorbell, up there?" that one asked. The same husky voice, from a stocky frame that might be man or woman—impossible to tell, with layers of ragged clothes concealing its real shape.

"Didn't mean to," said Sassinak. "Got a little lost."

"More'n a little. Douse the light, Jemi."

The spotlight blinked off, and Sassinak closed her eyes a moment to let them adjust. When she opened them again, the woman who had held the spotlight was stuffing it in a backpack. The two rifles had not moved. Neither had Sassinak. Aygar made an indeterminate sound behind her, not quite a growl. She suspected that he liked the look of the homemade spear. The person who had spoken pushed off the wall and stood watching them.

"Can you give me one good reason why we shouldn't slit and strip you right now?"

Sassinak grinned; that had been bravado, not decision.

"It'd make a big mess next to the shaft we came out of," she said. "If someone does follow down here . . ."

"They will," growled one of the rifle-bearers. The muzzle shifted a hair to one side. "Should be goin', Cor . . ."

"Wait. You're not the usual trash we get down here, and there's plenty of trouble up top. Who are you?"

"Who are the Pollys?" Sassinak countered.

"You got the Insystem Federation Security Police after you, and you don't know who they are?"

A twin of the jolt she'd felt hearing Parchandri's name went down her spine. Insystem Security's active arm was supposed to confine itself to ensuring the safety of governmental functions. She'd assumed their pursuers were planet pirate hired guns, or (at worst) a section of city police.

"I didn't know that's who we had after us. Orange uniforms?"

"Riot squads. Special action teams. Sheee! All right. You tell us who you are or you're dead right here, mess and all."

The rifles were steady again, and Sassinak thought the one with the spear probably knew how to use it.

"Commander Sassinak," she said. "Fleet, captain of the heavy cruiser *Zaid-Dayan*, docked in orbit . . ."

"And I'm Luisa Paraden's hairdresser! You'll do better than that or . . ."

"She really is," Aygar broke in. The other's eyes narrowed as she heard his unfamiliar accent. "She brought me . . ."

Sassinak had a hand on the hatch rim; a distant vibration thrummed in her fingers.

"Silence," she said, not loudly but with command.

All movement ceased. The silence seemed to quiver.

"They're coming. I can feel a vibration." The one who'd spoken growled out a low curse, then said, "Come on, then! Hurry! We'll straighten you later."

They followed along the tunnel, a bare chill tube of gray-green metal floored with something resilient. Under that, Sassinak thought, must be whatever the tunnel was actually for. She was aware of the man behind her with a rifle, of Aygar's growing confusion and panic, of the ache in her own legs.

She quickly lost track of their backtrail. They moved too fast, through too many shafts and tunnels, with no time to stop and fix references. She wondered if Aygar was doing any better. His hunting experience might help. Her ears popped once, then again, by which she judged they were now deep beneath the planet's surface. Not where she wanted to be, at all. But alive. She reminded herself of that; they might easily have been dead.

Finally their captors halted. They had come to a well-lit barnlike space opening off one of the smaller tunnels. Crates and metal drums filled one end to the low ceiling. In the open space, ragged blankets and piles of rags marked sleeping places on the floor; battered plastic carriers held water and food. Several huddled forms were asleep, others hunched in small groups, a few paced restlessly. The murmur of voices stopped and Sassinak saw pale faces turn toward them, stiff with fear and anger.

"Brought us in some uptowners," said the leader of their group. "One of 'em claims to be a Fleet captain."

Raucous laughter at that, more strained than humorous.

"That big hunk?" asked someone.

"Nah. The . . . *lady.*" Sassinak had never heard the word used as an insult before, but the meaning was clear. "Got the Pollys after her, and didn't even know what an orange uniform meant."

A big-framed man carrying too little flesh for his bones shrugged and stepped forward. "An offworlder wouldn't. Maybe she is . . ."

"Offworlder? Could be. But Fleet? Fleet don't rummage in the basement. They don't come off their fancy ships and get their feet dirty. Sit up in space, clean and free, and let us rot in slavery, that's Fleet!" The leader spat juicily past Sassinak's foot, then smirked at her.

"I suspect I know as much about slavery as most of you," Sassinak said quietly.

"From claiming to chase slavers while taking Parchandri bribes?" This was someone else, a skinny hunched little man whose face was seamed with old scars.

"From being one," said Sassinak. Silence, amazement on those tense faces. Now they were all listening; she had one chance, she reckoned. She met each pair of eyes in turn, nodding slowly, holding their attention. "Yes, it's true. When I was a child, the colony I lived in was raided. I saw my parents die. I held my sister's body. I never saw my little brother again. They left him behind. He was too young . . ." Her voice trembled; even now, even here. She forced steadiness into it. "And so I was a slave." She paused, scanning those faces again. No hostility now, less certainty. "For some years, I'm not sure how many. Then the ship I'd been sold to was captured by Fleet and I had a chance to finish school, go to the Academy, and chase pirates myself. That's why."

"*If* that's true, that's why the Pollys are after you," said the group's leader.

"But how can we know?"

"Because she's telling the truth," said Aygar. Everyone looked at him, and Sassinak was surprised to see him blush. "She came to my world, Ireta. She brought me here on cruiser for the trial."

"And you were born incapable of lying?" asked the leader.

Aygar seemed to swell with rage at such sarcasm. Sassinak held up her hand and hoped he'd obey the signal.

"This is my Academy ring," she said, stripping it from her finger and holding it out. "My name's engraved inside, and the graduation date's on the outside."

"Sas-sin-ak," the leader said, reading it slowly. "Well, it's evidence, though I'm not sure of what."

Sassinak took the ring back, and the leader might have said more, but a newcomer jogged into the room from the tunnel, carrying a flat black case that looked like a wide-band communications tap. Without preamble, he came up to the leader and started talking.

"The Pollys have an all-stations out for a renegade Fleet captain, name of Sassinak, and a big guy, civilian. They've murdered an Admiral Coromell . . ."

The leader turned to Sassinak. The messenger seemed to notice them for the first time, and his eyes widened.

"Is that true?"

"No."

"No which? You didn't murder anyone, or you didn't murder Coromell?"

"We didn't murder anyone and the dead man isn't Admiral Coromell."

"How do you—oh."

Sassinak smiled. "We were there, supposedly meeting Admiral Coromell, when someone of his age and general appearance sat down with us and promptly got holes in the head. We left in a hurry, and trouble followed us. Whoever killed him may think that was Coromell. It'll take a careful autopsy to prove it's not. Or the real Coromell showing up. I don't know who sent us a fake Coromell, or why, or who killed the fake Coromell, or why. Unless they just wanted to get us into trouble. Aygar's testimony, and mine, could be crucial in the trial coming up."

Blank looks indicated that no one had heard of, or cared about, any trial coming up.

"His name Aygar?" asked the messenger. " 'Cause that's who they're after, besides Sassinak."

Now a buzz of conversation rose from the others; no one would meet Sassinak's eyes. She could feel their fear prickling the air.

"You mentioned Parchandri," she said, regaining their attention. "Who is this Parchandri?"

To her surprise, the leader relaxed with a bark of laughter. "Good question! Who is *this* Parchandri? Who is *which* Parchandri would do as well. If you're Fleet, and have never been touched . . ."

"Well, she wouldn't, if she'd been a slave," said the big man. "They'd know better." He turned to Sassinak. "Parchandri's a family, got rich in civil service and Fleet just like the Paradens did in commerce. *Just* like takin' bribes and giving 'em, blackmailing, kidnapping, slicin' the law as thin as they could, and pilin' the profits on thick."

"I know there was a Parchandri Inspector General," Sassinak said slowly.

"Oh, that one. Yeah, but that's not all. Not even in Fleet. You got three Parchandris in the IG's staff alone, and two in Procurement, and five in Personnel. That's main family: using the surname openly. Doesn't count the cousins and all who use other names. There's a nest of Parchandri in the EEC, controls all the colony applications, that sort of thing. There's a Parchandri in Insystem Security, for that matter. And the head of the family is right here on FedCentral, making sure that what goes on in Council doesn't cause the family any trouble."

His casual delivery made it more real. Sassinak asked the first question that popped into her head.

"Are they connected to the Paradens?"

"Sure thing. But not by blood. They're right careful not to intermarry or anything that would show up on the computers. Even though they've got people in Central Data. Say a Paraden family company wants to open a colony somewhere but they're down the list. Somehow those other applications get lost, or something's found wrong with 'em. Complaints against a Paraden subsidiary get lost real easy, too."

"Are other families involved?" Sassinak noticed the sudden shifting of eyes. She waited. Finally the leader nodded.

"There have been. Not all the big families. The Chinese stay out of it; they don't need it. But a few smaller ones, mostly in transport. Any that gets in a little ways has to stay in for the whole trip. They don't like whistleblowers, the Parchandri. Things happen." The leader took a deep breath. "You're getting into stuff I can't answer unless I know . . . something more. You say you were a slave, and Fleet got you out so you joined Fleet . . ."

"That's right."

"Well, did you ever hear, while you were a slave, of a . . . a kind of group? People that . . . knew things?"

Sassinak nodded. "Samizdat," she said very softly.

The leader's tense face relaxed slightly.

"I'll chance it." A broad, strong hand reached out to shake hers in a firm grip. "I'm Coris. That was my wife who speared you with the spotlight." He grinned, a suddenly mischievous grin. "Did I fool you?"

"Fool me?"

"With all this padding. We find it useful to disguise our body outlines. I've been listed in official reports as a 'slightly obese middle-aged woman of medium stature.' " He had reached under his outer coverall to remove layers of rag stuffing, suddenly looking many pounds lighter and much more masculine. Off came a wig that Sassinak realized looked just like those in the costume shop, revealing a balding pate. "They don't worry as much about stray women in the tunnels. Although you, a Fleet commander, may give them a heart attack."

"I hope to," said Sassinak. She wasn't sure what to make of someone who cheerfully pretended to be the opposite sex. "But I'm a little . . . confused."

Coris chuckled. "Why wouldn't you be? Sit over here and have some of our delicious native cuisine and exquisite wine, and we'll talk about it."

He led her to an empty pile of blankets and gestured. She and Aygar sat. She was glad to let her aching legs relax.

"Delicious native cuisine" turned out to be a nearly tasteless cream-colored mush. "Straight from the food processors," someone explained. "Much easier to liberate before they put the flavorings or texture in . . . nasty stuff, but nutritious." The wine was water, tapped from a water main and tepid, but drinkable.

"Let's hear your side of it," suggested Coris.

Sassinak swallowed the last of the mush she'd been given and took a swallow of water to clear her throat. Around her, the ragged band had settled down, relaxed but alert.

"What if they are seaching for us?" she asked. "Shouldn't we . . . ?"

He waved his hand, dismissing the problem.

"They are looking, of course, but they haven't passed any of our sensors. And we do have scouts out. Go on."

Sassinak gave a concise report on what had happened from the arrival of Coromell's message. Highly irregular, but she judged it necessary. If she died down here, not that she intended to, someone had to know the truth. They listened attentively, not interrupting, until she told about entering the plea-sure-house.

"You went to *Vanlis*?" That sounded both surprised and angry.

"I didn't know what it was," said Sassinak, hoping that didn't sound critical. "It was the nearest door, and she helped us."

She told about that, about the woman's reaction to Fleur's name. She felt the prickling tension of this group's reaction. But no one said anything so she went on with the story until the group had "caught" them.

"Trouble, trouble, trouble," muttered Coris, now far less cocky.

"Sorry."

And she was, though she felt much better now that the tasteless food, the water and the short rest had done their work. She glanced at Aygar, who was picking moodily at the bandage on his face. He seemed to be over his fright.

"You're like a thread sewing together things we hoped they'd never connect," Jemi said softly. Coris's wife was a thin blonde. She looked older than either Sassinak or Coris, but it might be only worry. "Eklarik's shop . . . Varis's place . . . Fleur . . . Samizdat . . . they aren't stupid, you know. They'll put it together fast enough when they have time to think. I hope Varis has warned Fleur. Otherwise . . ."

She didn't need to finish that. Sassinak shivered. She could feel their initial interest fading now into a haze of fear and hostility. She had endan-gered their precarious existence. It was all so stupid. She had suspected trou-ble, hadn't she? She had known better than to go haring off into the un-known to meet some Admiral whose staff insisted he was off hunting. And because she'd been a fool, she and Aygar would die, and these people, who had already suffered enough, would die. And her ship? A vision of the *Zaid-Dayan* as it hung in orbit, clean and powerful, filled her eyes with tears for a moment. NO.

She was not going to die down here, not going to let the Paradens and Parchandris of the universe get away with their vicious schemes. She was supposed to be a Fleet *commander*, by Kipling's corns, and it was about time she started acting like it. The old familiar routines seemed to waken her mind as she referred to them, like lights coming on in a dark ship, compartment by compartment. Status report: resources: personnel: equipment: enemy situa-tion . . .

She was not aware of her spine straightening until she saw the effect in their faces. They were staring at her as if she had suddenly appeared in her white battle armor instead of the stained civilian coverall. Their response heightened her excitement.

"Well, then," she said, the confidence in her voice ringing through the chamber. "We'd better sew up their shrouds first."

Chapter Fifteen

Dupaynil stared at the bulkhead across from his bunk, and thought that luck was highly overrated. Human space aboard the *Grand Luck* meant this tiny stateroom, adjoining plumbing that made the *Claw*'s spartan head look and feel like a spa, and one small bare chamber he could use for eating, exercise, and what recreation his own mind provided. Most people thought the Seti had no sense of humor; he disagreed. The Commissioner's comments about the humbleness with which he would travel argued for a keen sense of irony, at the least.

He had had a brief and unhelpful interview with the Ambassador. The Fleet attache lurking in the background of that interview had looked unbearably smug. The Ambassador saw no reason why he should undertake to have Fleet messages transmitted to FedCentral when Dupaynil was headed there himself. He saw no reason why redundancy might be advisable. Was Dupaynil suggesting that the Seti, allies within the Federation, might interfere with Dupaynil's own delivery of those messages? That would be a grave accusation, one which he would not advise Dupaynil to put in writing. And of course Dupaynil could not have a final interview with Panis. Quite against the Ambassador's advice, that precipitous young man had already departed, destination unknown.

It occurred to Dupaynil that this Ambassador, of all the human diplomats, surely had to be in the pay of the conspirators. He could not be *that* stupid. Looking again, at the florid face and blurred eyes, he was not sure. He glanced at the Fleet attache and intercepted a knowing look to the Ambassador's private secretary. So. The Seti probably supplied the drugs, which his own staff fed him, to keep him so safely docile.

And I thought my troubles were over, Dupaynil thought, making his final very correct bow and withdrawing to pack his kit for the long trip. Not surprisingly, the Fleet attache insisted that anything Dupaynil asked for was unavailable.

And now he had the leisure to reflect on the Ambassador's possible slow poisoning while the Seti ship bore him to an unknown destination; he did not believe for a moment they were really headed for FedCentral. He forced himself to get up and move into the little exercise space. Whatever was coming, he might as well be fit for it. He stripped off the dress uniform that courtesy demanded and went through the exercises recommended for all Fleet officers. Designed, as he recalled, by a Fleet marine sergeant-major who had retired and become a consultant for adventure films. There were only so many ways you could twist, bend, and stretch. He had worked up a sweat when the intercom burped at him.

"Du-paay-nil. Prepare for inspection by Safety Officer."

Of course they'd chosen this time. Dupaynil smiled sweetly into the shiny lens of the surveillance video, and finished with a double-tuck-roll that took him back into the minute sanitation cabinet. No shower, of course. A blast of hot air, then fine grit, then hot air again. Had he been covered with scales, like a proper liz . . . Seti, they'd have been polished. As a human, he felt sticky and gritty and altogether unclean. He would come off this ship smelling like a derelict from the gutter of an unimproved frontier world . . . no doubt their intent.

He had his uniform almost fastened when the hatch to his compartment swung back, and a large Seti snout intruded. They timed it so well. No matter when he took exercise or was using the sanitary facilities, they announced an inspection. No matter how quickly he tried to dress, they always arrived before he was finished. He found it curious that they didn't interrupt meals or sleep, but he appreciated even that minimal courtesy.

"Aaahh . . . Commaanderrr . . ." The Safety Officer had a slightly off-center gap between front teeth. Dupaynil could now recognize it as an individual. "Iss necesssary that airrr tesst be con-duc-ted."

They did this every few inspections, supposedly to be sure that his pressure suit would work. It meant a miserable struggle into the thing, and a hot sweaty interval while they sucked the air out of his quarters and the suit ballooned around him. Dupaynil reached into the narrow recess and pulled out the suit. Not his choice of suits but, the Fleet attache had assured him with a smile, the only one in his size at the embassy. At least it had held up, so far, with only one minor leak, easily patched.

He pushed and wriggled his way into it, aware of the Seti's amusement. Seti faced the uncertainties of space travel without pressure suits. While they had such suits for those who might need to work on the outer surface of a ship, they did not stock suits for the whole crew. It made sense. Most of the time when a Fleet vessel lost hull integrity, the crew never made it into their suits anyway. And of course a Seti would have been disgraced for insisting on a way of cheating chance. Still, Dupaynil was glad to have a suit, even though the Seti considered it another example of human inferiority.

He dogged the helmet down snugly and checked the seals of the seam that ran from throat to crotch. The suit had an internal comunit which allowed him to speak, or more often listen, to the Seti. This time, he heard the Safety Officer's instructions with amazement.

"Come to the bridge?"

Humans were never invited to the bridge of Seti ships. No human had ever seen the navigational devices by which the gamblers of the universe convinced themselves they were being obedient to chance while keeping shipping schedules.

"At once."

Dupaynil followed, sweating and grunting. He had not had to put on his suit for this. Seti kept breathable, if smelly, atmosphere in their ships. No doubt they intended to make him look even more ridiculous. He had heard, repeatedly, what the Seti thought of human upright posture. It occurred to him that they might have insisted on his suit simply to spare themselves the indignity of a human's smell.

When he reached the bridge, it bore no resemblance whatever to that of a Fleet ship of the same mass. It was a triangular chamber—room for the tails, he realized—with cushioned walls and thickly carpeted floor, not at all shiplike. Two Seti, one with the glittering neck-ring and tail ornament that he had been told signified ship's captain, were crouched over a small, circular, polished table, tossing many-sided dice, while one standing in the remaining corner recited what seemed to be a list of unrelated numbers. He felt cramped between the table and the hatch that had admitted him and then slammed behind him. The Seti ignored Dupaynil and he ignored that, finally trying to figure out what kind of game they were playing.

The dice landed with one face flat up, horizontal. Three dice at a time, usually, but occasionally only two. He didn't recognize the markings. From where he stood, he could see three or four faces of each die and he amused himself trying to figure out what the squiggles meant. Green here, with a kind of tail going down. All three dice had this on the top face for a moment. Purple blotch, red square-in-square, a yellow blotch, two blue dots. The dice rose and fell, bouncing slightly, then coming to stillness. Green squiggles again, and on the other faces purple, blue dots, more red squares-in-squares.

The Seti calling out numbers paused through two throws. Dupaynil's attention slid from the dice to the Seti, wondering what the purple blotch on the napkinlike cloth around his neck meant. When he looked back at the board, the green squiggles were on top again.

Surely that couldn't be right, and surely they didn't just want an observer for the captain's nightly gambling spree. He watched the dice closely. In another two throws, he was sure of it. They were loaded, as surely as any set of dice that ever cheated some poor innocent in a dockside bar. Time after time the green squiggles came up on top. So why throw them? His mind wandered. Probably this wasn't the bridge at all. Some bored Seti officers had just wanted to bait their captive human. Then a fourth die joined the group in the air and down came three green squiggles and one purple blotch.

Three Seti heads swung his way, toothy jaws slightly open. He shivered, in his suit. If that was bad luck, and they thought he had brought it . . .

"Ahhh! Humann!" The captain's voice, through his comunit, had only the usual Seti accent. "It wass explained to me that you were ssent here by very sspecial luck. Ssso your luck continuess. As the luck fallss, you sshall be told, though it makess danger to usss."

Dupaynil could not bow. The suit gave him no room for it.

"Illustrious bringer of luck," he began, for that was part of the captain's title. "If chance favors your wish to share precious knowledge, my luck is great indeed."

"Indeed!" The captain reared back on massive hind legs, and snapped its jaws. A sign of amusement, Dupaynil remembered from handbooks. Sometimes species-specific. "Well, o lucky one, we ssshall sssee how you call your chance when you know all. We ssshall arrive even sssooner than you thought. And we shall arrive in forccce."

The Seti could not mean that the way a human would, Dupaynil thought. Surely not . . .

"Do you grasssp the flying ring of truth from tossssed baubles?" the Seti asked. Dupaynil tried to remember what *that* meant, but the Seti captain went on. "You ssshall sssee the ruin of your unlucky admiral, he who tossed your life against the wissdom of our Sek, in the person of the Commissioner of Commerce, and you shall see the ruin of your Fleet . . . and of the

Federation itself, and all the verminous races who prize certainty over Holy Luck. Sssee it from the flagship, as you would say, of our fleet, invincible unless chance changes. And then, o human, we ssshall enjoy your flesh, flavored with the smoke of defeat." The captain's massive snout bumped the screen of Dupaynil's helmet.

From the frying pan of Sassinak's displeasure, to the fire of the conspirators on *Claw*, he had come to the Seti furnace. If this was luck, he would take absolute determinism from now on. It couldn't be worse. He hoped the Seti could not detect the trickles of sweat down his back. He could smell his own fear, a depressing stench. He tried for a tone of unconcern.

"How can you be certain of this destination by throwing dice?" Not real thought, but the first words that came into his mouth, idle curiosity.

"Ahhh . . ." The captain's tail slapped the floor gently, and its tail ornament jingled. "Not pleass or argumentss, but ssense. As chance favors, I sshall answer."

His explanation of the proceedings made the kind of oblique sense Dupaynil expected from aliens. Chance was holy, and only those who dared fate deserved respect, but the amount of risk inherent in each endeavor determined the degree of additional risk which the Seti felt compelled to add by throwing dice or using random number generators. "The Glorious Chaos," as they named that indeterminate state in which ships traveled or seemed to travel faster than light, had sufficient uncertainty to require no assistance. So they tossed loaded dice, as a token of respect, and to allow the gods of chance to interfere if they were determined.

"War, as well," the captain continued, "has its own uncertainties, so that within the field of battle, a worthy commander may be guided by its own great wisdom and intuition. Occasionally one will resort to the dice or the throwing sticks, a gesture of courage all respect, but the more parts to the battle, the less likely. But you . . ." A toothy grin did not reassure Dupaynil at all. "You were another matter and judged sufficiently certain of unsuccess without our chance to place you in the toss. As your luck held, in the unmatched dice, so now I offer to chaos this chance for you to thwart us. I told you our plan, and you may ask what you will. You will not return to your quarters."

Dupaynil fought down a vision of himself as Seti snack-food. If he could ask questions, he would ask *many* questions.

"Is this venture a chance occurrence, or has some change in Federation policy prompted it?"

The captain uttered a wordless roar, then went into a long disjointed tirade about the Federation allies. Heavyworlder humans, as victims of forced genetic manipulation, roused some sympathy in the Seti. Besides, a few heavyworlders had shown the proper attitude by daring feats of chance: entering a Hall of Dispute through the Door of Honor, for instance. Some humans were gamblers: entrepreneurs, willing to risk whole fortunes on the chance of a mining claim, or colonial venture. That the Seti could respect. The Paradens, for instance, deserved to lay eggs. (Dupaynil could imagine what the elegant Paraden ladies would think of *that*.) But the mass of humans craved security. Born slaves, they deserved the outward condition of it.

As for the allied aliens . . . The captain spat something that Dupaynil was glad he could not smell. Cowardly Wefts, the shifters who would not dare the limits of any shape . . . Bronthin, with their insistence on mathematical limits to chaos and chance, their preference for statistical analyses. Ryxi, who were unworthy to be egglayers since they not only sexed their unhatched chicks, but performed surgical procedures through the shell. The Seti had the decency, the captain snarled, to let their eggs hatch as they would and take the consequences. The Ssli, who insisted on giving up their mobile larval form to become sessile, bound to one location throughout life: a refusal to dare change.

Dupaynil opened his mouth to say that Ssli anchored to warships in space could hardly be considered "bound to one location," remembered that not everyone knew about the Ssli in Fleet ships and instead asked, "And the Thek?"

This time the captain's tail hit the floor so hard its ornament shattered. "Thek!" it roared. "Disgusting lumps of geometrical regularity. Undifferentiated. Choiceless, chanceless, obscene . . ." The ranting went on in a Seti dialect Dupaynil could not begin to follow. Finally it ran down and gave Dupaynil a sour glance. "It is my good fortune that you will flavor my stew, miserable one, for you irritate me extremely. Leave at once."

He had no chance to leave under his own power. At some point, the captain must have called for Seti guards because they grabbed the arms of his suit and towed him along strange corridors much faster than he could have gone by himself.

When they finally stopped and released his arms, he was crammed in a smallish chamber with an assortment of aliens. The Bronthin took up the most cubage, its chunky horselike body and heavy head impossible to compress. A couple of Lethi were stuck together like the large yellow burrs which they greatly resembled. A Ryxi huddled in one corner, fluffing and flattening its feathers, and in a translucent tank, two Ssli larvae flutter-kicked from end to end. On one wall, a viewscreen displayed sickening swirls of violent color: the best an exterior monitor could do in FTL space. Beside it, a fairly obvious dial gave the pressure of various atmospheric components. Breathable, but not pleasant.

So the Seti had collected an array of alien observers to gloat over, had they? Dupaynil wondered who the human would have been, if he and Panis had not shown up. Certainly not the Fleet attache. Probably the Ambassador. Had they all been told what was going on? He cracked the seal of his helmet cautiously and sniffed. A tang of sulfur, a bit too humid and warm and clearly no shower in sight. With an internal sigh, he took off his helmet and attempted a greeting to his new companions.

No one answered. The Ryxi offered a gaping beak, which Dupaynil remembered from a training manual meant something like "Forget it, I don't want to talk to you unless you've got the money." He had never learned Bronthin (no human ever had) and the tubby blue mathematicians preferred equations to any other form of discourse anyway. Lethi had no audible communications mode: they talked to each other in chemical packages and could not interface with a biolink until they formed a clump of at least eight. That left the Ssli larvae, who, without a biolink, also had no way of communicating. In fact, no one was sure how intelligent the larvae actually were. They were in the Fleet Academy to learn navigational theory but Dupaynil had never heard of one communicating with an instructor.

He could try writing them a message, except that he had nothing to write with, or on. The Seti had not brought any of his kit from his compartment; he had only the clothes and pressure suit he stood up in.

It really wasn't so bad, he told himself, forcing cheerfulness. The Seti hadn't killed them yet. Didn't seem to be starving them, though he wondered if that slab of elementary sulfur was really enough for the Lethi clinging to it. He found a water dispenser, and even a recessed cabinet with oddly shaped bowls to put the water in. He poured himself a bowl and drank it down. Something nudged his arm and he found the Bronthin looking sorrowfully at the bowl. It gave a low, grunting moo.

Ah. Bronthin had never been good with small tools. He poured water for the Bronthin and held the bowl for it to drink. It swiped his face with a rough, corrugated lavendar tongue when it was done, leaving behind a faintly sweet odor. A nervous chitter across the compartment was the Ryxi, standing now with feathers afluff and stubby wings outspread. Dupaynil interpreted this as a request and filled another bowl. The Ryxi snatched it away from him with its wing-claws and drank thirstily.

"They for us water pour but one time daily," the Ryxi twittered, dropping the empty bowl. Dupaynil picked it up with less graciousness than he'd filled it. He had never been the nurturing type. Still, it was communication. The Ryxi went on. "Food at that time, only enough for life. Waste removal."

"Did they tell you where we're headed?"

An ear-spitting screech made him wince. The Ryxi began bouncing off the walls, crashing into one after another of them, shrieking something in Ryxi. The Bronthin huddled down in a large lump, leaving Dupaynil in the Ryxi's path. He tried to tackle it but a knobbed foot got him in the ribs. The Ryxi flipped its crest up and down, keening, and drew back for another kick, but Dupaynil rolled behind the Ssli tank.

"Take it easy," he said, knowing it would do no good. Ryxi never took it easy. This one calmed slightly, sides heaving, crest only halfway up.

"They told," came the sorrowful low groan of the Bronthin. Dupaynil had never heard one speak Standard before. "Wickedly dangerous meat-eaters. We told Theks what would come of it. Those who sweep tails across the sand of reason, where proofs of wisdom abound." The Bronthin had accomplished advanced mathematics without paper or computers, using smooth stretches of sand or clay to scribe their equations. Although their three stubby fingers could not manipulate fine tools, they had developed an elegant mathematical calligraphy. And a very formal courtesy involving the use of the "sands of reason." A colt (the human term) who used its whisk of a tail on someone else's calculations would be severely punished. Bronthin were also strict vegetarians—browsers on their world which had small and witless carnivores. They were pacifists.

Dupaynil eyed the calming Ryxi warily. His ribs hurt. He didn't need another kick. "Do you have any plan?" he asked the Bronthin.

"The probability of escape from this ship, in a nonviable state, is less than 0.1 percent. The probability of escape from this ship in a viable state i less than 0.0001 percent. The factors used to arrive at this include the . . ."

"Never mind," said Dupaynil, softening it with an apology. "My mathematical skill is insufficient to appreciate the beauty of your calculations."

"How kind to save me the trouble of converting to Standard that which can only be properly expressed in the language of eternal law." The Bronthin heaved a sigh, which Dupaynil took to mean the conversation was over.

The Ryxi, however, was eager to talk, once it had calmed enough to remember its Standard.

"Unspeakable reptiles," it twittered. "Unworthy to be egg-layers!" No again, thought Dupaynil, not anticipating the Ryxi side of that argument "Thick-shelled, they are. You can't even *see* a Seti in its shell. Not that i makes any difference, because even if something's wrong, they won't do anything. Just let the hatchlings die if they can't make it on their own. Som of them don't even tend their nests. Not even to warn away predators. They say that's giving Holy Luck the choice. I'd call it criminal negligence."

"Despicable," said Dupaynil, edging farther away from the dance of those powerful feet. Then a bell-like voice rang out, its source unidentifiable.

< <Sassinak friend?> >

Dupaynil tried to control his start of surprise, and glanced around. The Bronthin looked half-asleep which is the way Bronthins usually looked and the Ryxi had begun grooming its feathers with jerky strokes of its beak. The two Lethi were still stuck to each other and the slab of sulfur.

< <Do not look . . . in the tank.> > He managed to stare at the blank space above the Bronthin, while the voice continued and his own mind shivered away from it. He had never liked descriptions of telepathy and he liked the reality less. < <Sassinak friend you are. We greet you. We are more and less than we seem.> >

Of course. Ssli. So Ssli larvae could communicate! He could not "feel" anything in his mind when the voice fell silent, but that didn't mean it, or they, were not reading him.

< <No time to investigate your dark secrets. We must plan.> >

They were reading his surface thoughts, at least, to have picked up that distaste for internal snooping. He recognized the irony of that, someone whose profession was snooping on others, now being turned inside out by aliens. He tried to organize his thoughts, make a clear message.

"You stare at wall for a reason?" the Ryxi asked, its feathers now sleeked down.

Dupaynil could have strangled the Ryxi for breaking his concentration, and then he *did* feel a featherlight touch, soothing, and a bubble of amusement.

"I'm very tired," he said honestly. "I need to rest."

With that, he found a clear space of floor, between the wall and the Ssli tank, and curled up, helmet cradled in his arms. The Ryxi sniffed, then tucked its head back over its shoulders into the back feathers. Dupaynil closed his eyes and projected against the screen of his eyelids.

< <What can you do?> >

< <Nothing alone. We hoped they would bring a human.> >

< <What did you mean, 'more and less'?> >

Again the mental gurgle of amusement. < <We are not both Ssli.> >

The voice said nothing more and Dupaynil thought about it. If they were reading his thoughts, they were welcome. Not both Ssli? Another alien marine race? Suddenly he realized what it had to be and almost laughed aloud.

< <A Weft? > >

< <Seemed safer this way. Seti hate Wefts enough to kill them before the coup. But with this form come certain . . . limitations. > >

< <Which humans don't have? > >

< <Precisely. > >

< <Sorry, but I don't think they'll let me push that tank to wherever they keep the escape pods. Assuming they have any. > >

< <Not the plan. May we share? > >

It seemed an odd question from beings who could force mental intimacy, and already had, but Dupaynil was in the mood to accept any courtesy offered.

< <Go ahead. > >

He tensed, bracing himself for some unimaginable sensation, and felt nothing. Only information began to knit itself into his existing cognitive matrix, as if he were learning it so fast that it was safely in long-term memory before it passed his eyes. The Bronthin, he learned, had been hired by the Seti to provide them with mathematical expertise. On the basis of its calculations and models, they had defined the best time to attempt the coup.

And the Bronthin had had no way to warn the Federation. Bronthins could not manipulate Seti communications equipment, were not telepathic, and suffered severe depression when kept isolated from their social herds. As for the Ssli, it had been delivered, in its tank, after it had been stolen from a Fleet recruit depot. The Weft, a Fleet guard at the depot, had been shot in the burglary and survived only by shapechanging into the Ssli tank in a larval form. The thieves had not known the difference between Weft and Ssli larvae and had apparently supposed that two or more larvae were in each tank, in case one died.

< <But what can we *do*? > > Dupaynil asked.

< <You can talk to the Bronthin, and find out more of what it knows about this fleet. It had the information to make models with. It must know. It's depressed. That's why it won't talk. Later, when we drop out of FTL, you can see the viewscreen. We have no such eyes. But the Ssli can link with other Ssli on a Fleet vessel, and that Ssli has a biolink to the captain. > >

Cheering up the Bronthin took all of Dupaynil's considerable charm. It turned away at first, muttering number series, but the offer of another bowl of water helped. He watered the Ryxi, too, automatically, and this time the feathered alien handed the bowl back rather than dropping it. But it took many bowls of water, and a couple of sessions of picking the burrs from the dry grass the Seti tossed in for its feed, before the alien showed much response.

Finally it scrubbed its heavy head up and down his arm, took his hands in its muscular lips, and said, "I . . . will try to speak Standard . . . in thanks for your kindness . . ."

"Inaccurate as Standard is, and unsuited to your genius, would it be possible to recall how many ships this size the Seti have with them?"

The Bronthin flopped a long upper lip, and sighed.

"The ratio of such ships to those next smaller to those next smaller to the smallest is 1.2:3.4:5.6:5:4. An interesting ratio, chosen by the Seti for its ragged harmony, if I understood them." It shook its long head. "Alas . . . never again to roll in the green sweet fields of home or be granted the tail's whisk across the sands in the company of my peers."

"Such courage in loneliness," Dupaynil murmured. In his experience, praising the timid for courage sometimes produced a momentary flare of it. "And the total to which such a ratio applies?"

With something akin to a snort, the Bronthin's lovely periwinkle eyes opened completely.

"Ah! You understand that the ratio is theoretical. The fleet itself made up of actual ships, of which at any time some fraction is out of service for maintenance and the like. Of those actually *here*, in the sense that here has any meaning . . . are you at all familiar with Sere-kleth-vladin's transformational series and its application to hyperspace flux variations?"

"Alas, no," said Dupaynil, who didn't know such things existed—whatever they were.

"Unhhh . . . one hundred four. Eight similar to this, which would of course make you expect 22.6, 37.3, 35.9 ships of the other classes, but fractional ships are nonfunctional. Twenty-three of the next class, then thirty-seven, then thirty-six. And since it would be the logical next question," the Bronthin went on, its eyes beginning to sparkle, "I will explain that the passive defenses of the Federation Central System, if not tampered with, could be expected to destroy at least 82% of the total. Those remaining would be unlikely to succeed at reducing the planets or disrupting the Grand Council. But the Seti count on tampering, which will reduce the efficiency of the distant passive scans by 41%, and on specific aid whose nature I do not know, to disable additional defenses. This incursion is timed to coincide with the meeting of the Grand Council and the Winter Assizes, at which the presence of many ships could well cause confusion."

"They expect no resistance from Fleet?"

The Bronthin opened its mouth wide, revealing the square grinding teeth of a herbivore, and gave a long sound somewhat between a moo and a bray. "My apologies," it said then. "Our long misunderstanding of the nature of humans; our votes have long gone to reducing appropriations for what we saw as a means of territorial aggrandizement. These Seti expect that any Fleet vessels in Federation Central Systems space will be neutralized. And once again, we aided this, voting to require that all Fleet vessels disarm lest they overpower the Grand Council."

"A most natural error for any lover of peace," Dupaynil murmured soothingly.

Sassinak would be there with the *Zaid-Dayan*. Would she have disarmed completely, trusting in the disarmament of others to keep her ship safe? Somehow he doubted it. But with surveillance by the FSP local government, she wouldn't be able to have all the ship's scans on . . . and without warning . . . he realized he had no idea how fast the *Zaid-Dayan* could get into action.

< < We do appreciate the difficulty. > >

If mental speech could have tones, that would be dry wit, Dupaynil thought. He sent a mental flick of the fingers to the Ssli and Weft, still swimming with apparent unconcern in the tank. Easy for them, he thought sourly, and then realized it wasn't. He would be even more miserable if he'd been stuck in a tank like that.

Despite the rising tension, he had actually fallen asleep when a screech from the Ryxi brought him upright, blinking. The viewscreen showed what he presumed to be the real outer view, although he had no way of knowing which of the ship's outer sensors had produced the image. Darkness, points of light, some visibly moving. A Seti voice from the wallspeaker interrupted the Ryxi's tantrum.

"Captives, observe," it began, with typical Seti tact. "See your feeble hopes destroyed."

The view shown shifted from one angle to another. The outside of the *Grand Luck*, with a long pointed snout oozing from a recess to slide past, aimed at some distant enemy. A zooming view of nearby ships, lifting them from points of light to toylike shapes against a dark background. Then another view, of the star around which the Federation Central Zone planets swung, a star which now looked scarcely bigger than any of the others.

< < Share again! > >

Dupaynil tried to relax. He had already passed on all he'd learned from the Bronthin. Now he watched the screen, listened to the Seti boastful commentary and hoped the Ssli/Weft pair could contact another Ssli. Time passed. The view shifted every few minutes, from one sensor to another.

< <Contact.> >

Dupaynil wasn't sure if the triumphant tone came from the Ssli or his own reaction. He expected to hear more, but the Ssli did not include him in whatever link it and the Weft had formed with that distant Ssli. The Ryxi clattered its beak, shifted from one great knobby foot to another, fluffed and sleeked its feathers, staring wide-eyed at the viewscreen. The Bronthin refused to look. Its closed eyes and monotonous hum could be either sleep or despair. And the Lethi, as before, simply stuck to each other and the sulfur.

Dupaynil had the feeling that he should do something more to prepare for the coming battle. Now that the Ssli had warned its fellow. Now surely that alarm was being passed on. He felt free to consider more immediate problems. Could they possibly break free of this compartment? Could they steal weapons? Find some kind of escape vehicle? Or, failing escape, do something disasterous to this ship and destroy it? He and the Ryxi were the only two who might actually *do* something, for no one had ever heard of a Bronthin being violent. He edged over to the hatch, and prodded its complicated-looking lock.

A roar of Seti profanity from outside made it clear that wouldn't work. He was looking around for something else to investigate, when the viewscreen blurred, cleared, blurred, and cleared again after a couple of short FTL skips. Then it grayed to a pearly haze and the ship trembled.

"Battle started!" came the announcement in Standard over the speaker. Then a long complicated gabble of Seti that must be orders.

< <Sassinak is not aboard her ship.> > That fell into his mind like a lump of ice. < <She disappeared onplanet. Wefts can't land to find her.> >

< <Other ships?> >

He had assumed she would be aboard her ship. He had assumed she would be wary, as alert as he'd always known her. What was she doing, playing around onplanet with her ship helpless above, with its weapons locked down, with no captain? Without at least taking Wefts with her?

< <No other ships larger than escort insystem.> >

"Stupid woman!"

He didn't realize he'd said it aloud until he saw the Bronthin's eyes flick open, heard the Ryxi's agitated chirp.

"Never *mind!*" he said to them, glaring.

Here he had gone through one miserable hell after another, all to get her information she desperately needed, and she wasn't where she was supposed to be.

< < *Zaid-Dayan* moving. > >

That stopped his mental ranting. Then the *Grand Luck* lurched sharply, as if it had run into a brick wall, and as his feet skidded on the floor he realized his head had nowhere to go but the corner of the Ssli transport tank.

Chapter Sixteen

FedCentral

"You're joking." Coris stared at her. "You don't realize . . ."

"I realize precisely what will happen to all of us if we *don't* take the initiative." Sassinak was on her feet now and the others were stirring restlessly, not committed to either side of this argument. "If you'd wanted death, or a mindwipe, and the rest of your life at hard labor, you'd have managed it before now. It's easy enough, even yet. Just wait for them to come after me. Because Jemi is quite right. They will. I'm too dangerous, even by myself." She paused a careful measure, then added, "But with *you*, I could be dangerous enough to win."

"But we don't . . . We aren't . . ." Jemi's nervous looks around got no support. Most were staring fascinated at Sassinak.

"Aren't what? Strong enough? Brave enough? You've been strong and brave enough to survive and stay free. How long, Coris?"

"I been here eight years. Jemi, six. Fostin was here when I came . . ."

"Years of your lives," Sassinak said, almost purring it. "You survived capture, slavery, prison, all the disasters. And you survived this life below the city. Now you can end it. End the hiding, end the fear. End the suffering, your own and others."

They stirred. She could feel their need for her to be right, their need for her to be strong for them. Give them time and they'd revert, but she had this instant.

"Come on," she said. "Show me what you've got. Right now."

Slowly, they stood, eyeing her and each other with hope that was clearly unfamiliar.

"Any weapons? We've got this." She pulled out the snub-nosed weapon Aygar had taken from the first row. "How many are you, altogether?"

They had weapons, but not many and most, they explained, were carried by their roving scouts. Nor did they have an accurate count of their own numbers. Twenty here, a dozen there, stray couples and individuals, a large band whose territory they overlapped in one direction, and a scattering of bands in another. They had specialists, of a sort. Some were best at milking the mass-service food processors without detection and some had a knack for tapping into the datalinks.

"Good," Sassinak said. "Where's this godlike Parchandri you say is running the backscenes on FedCentral?"

"You're not going after *him*!" Coris's shock was mirrored on every face. "There'll be guards—troops—we can't do that! It's like starting a war."

"Coris, this became a war the second a warrior dropped into it. Me. I'm fighting a war. War means strategy, tactics, victory conditions." She tapped these off on her fingers. "You people can squat here and get wiped out as the enemy chases me or you can be my troops and have a chance. I don't promise more than that. But *if* we win, you won't have to live down here, eating tasteless mush and drinking bilgewater. It'll be your world again. Your lives! Your freedom!"

The big-framed man she'd noticed before shrugged and came up beside Coris. "Might's well, Coris. They'll be after her, after us. Using gas again, most likely. I'm with her."

"And me!"

More than one of the others; Coris gave a quick side-to-side glance, shrugged, and grinned.

"I should've slit you back up there," he said, jerking his chin in what Sassinak assumed was the right direction.

Aygar growled, but Sassinak waved him to silence. "You're right, Coris. If you're going to take out a threat, do it right away. Next time you'll know."

You can't wage war without a plan, one of the Command & Staff instructors had insisted. *But you can lose with one.* Sassinak found this no help at all as she chivvied her ragged troops through the tunnels to the boundary of their territory. She had no plan but survival, and she knew it was not enough. Find the Parchandri and . . . And what? Her fingers ached to fasten around his throat and force the truth testimony out of him. Would that do any good? They didn't really need it, not for Tanegli's trial. Even if she didn't make it back, even if Aygar didn't, there was evidence enough to convict the old heavyworlder. As for the status of Ireta, she doubted any non-Thek court would dare to question the Thek ruling she'd received which was already in official files.

Official files to which a powerful Parchandri might gain access. She almost stumbled, thinking that. Was nothing safe? She glanced around at her new fighting companions and mentally shook her head. Not these people, who were about as far from Fleet marines as she could imagine. Give them credit for having lived so long. But would they hold up in real combat?

Ahead, a quick exchange of whistled signals. The group slowed, flattened against the tunnel walls. Sassinak wondered if the battle would begin now, but it turned out to be the territorial boundary. She went forward with Coris to meet this second group. To her surprise, "her" people were now holding themselves more like soldiers. They seemed to have purpose, and the others were visibly impressed.

"What goes?" asked the second gang's leader. He was her age or older, his broad face heavily scarred. His eyes focussed somewhere past her ear, and a lot of his teeth were missing. So was one finger.

"Samizdat." The code answer.

"Whose friend?"

"Fleur's. And Coris's."

"Heh. You'd better be Fleur's friend. We'll check that. You have a name, Fleur's friend?"

"Sassinak."

His eyes widened. "She's got a call out for you. Fleur and the cops both. What you done, eh?"

"Not everything you've heard, and some things you haven't. You have a name?"

He grinned at that, but quickly sobered. "I'm Kelgar. Ever'body knows me. Twice bitten, most shy. Twice lucky, to be free from slavers twice." He paused, and she nodded. What could she say to someone like that, but acknowledge bad experience shared. "Come! We'll see what she says."

"She's down *here*?"

"She goes slumming sometimes, though she doesn't call it that. 'Sides, where she is, is pretty near topside, over 'cross a ways, through two more territories. We don't fight, eh?" That was thrown back to Coris, who flung out his open hand.

"We good children," he said.

"Like always," said Kelgar. "For all the flamin' good it does."

He led the way this time and Sassinak followed with Coris's group. She could tell that Kelgar had more snakes in his attic than were strictly healthy, but if paranoid he was smart paranoid. They saw no patrols while passing through his territory, and into the next. There she met another gangleader, this one a whip-thin woman who went dead-white at the sight of Sassinak's face. A Fleet deserter? Her gang had the edge of almost military discipline, and after that first shocked reaction, the woman handled them with crisp efficiency. Definitely military, probably Fleet. Rare to lose one that good. Sassinak couldn't help wondering what had happened, but she knew she'd get no answers if she asked.

They passed another boundary and Sassinak found herself being introduced to yet another leader. Black hair, dark eyes, brownish skin, and the facial features she thought of as Chinese. Most of his followers looked much the same, and she caught some angry glances at Aygar. All she didn't need was racial trouble; she hoped this leader had control of his people.

"Sassinak . . ." the man said slowly. "You had an ancestress Lunzie?" This was something new. How would he know? Sassinak nodded. The man went on, "I believe we are distantly related."

"I doubt it," Sassinak said warily. What was this about?

"Let me explain," he said, as if they had settled down in a club with all afternoon to chat. "Your grandfather Dougal was Fleet, as you are, and he married into a merchanter family . . . but Chinese. Quite against the custom of both his people and hers. He never told his family about the marriage, and she eventually left him to return to her family, with her daughters. His son they liked less, and when he married your *mother* and decided to join a new colony, it seemed the best solution for everyone. But your grandmother's family kept track of your father, of course, and when I was a child I learned your name, and that of your siblings, in family prayers."

"They . . . knew about us?"

"Yes, of course. When your colony was raided, your grandmother's ship was hung with white flags. When they heard you had survived . . ."

"But how could they?"

"You were honor graduate in the Academy. Surely you realized that an orphan rising to honor graduate would be featured in news programs."

"I never thought." She might have, if Abe's death had not come on the heels of that triumph, and her grief filled every moment until her first post-ing.

"The name is unusual. It had made your grandmother very angry for her son to choose a name like that. So they searched the databases, found your original ID. They assumed you had done the same, and would make contact if and when you chose." He shrugged, and smiled at her. "It has nothing to do with your purpose here, but I thought you might like to know, since circumstances brought us together."

If she had a later. "I . . . see." She had no idea what etiquette applied; clearly he expected something more from her than he would of another stranded Fleet officer. "I'm sorry. I don't know what obligations I would have under your customs . . ."

"You? It is our family that did not protect you. Our family that did not make sure you knew of us. What I am trying to say is that you have a claim on us, if you are not ashamed of the connection."

"I'm not ashamed." That much she could say honestly, with utter conviction. To have another segment of her family accept her brought her close to tears, but not with shame. "I'm . . . amazed, surprised, stunned. But not ashamed."

"Then, if it pleases you, we should go this way for you to meet Fleur again. She, too, was insistent that you must know about our family bond before you talked to her."

She tried to reorganize her thoughts as they went on. A family, at least her father's side. Now, why had she always thought her mother was the connection to Lunzie? Chinese didn't bother her. Why would it? And what kind of family had Dougal had, that he hadn't told them about his wife? Lunzie had said something about finding Fiona's children stuffy. She tried to remember, as she usually tried to forget, her parents. They had both been dark-haired, and she did remember that her father had once kidded her mother about her "Assyrian" nose, whatever that meant.

Her relative, in whatever degree, led her to into a huge room in which great cylinders hissed softly at one another. Pipes as thick as her waist connected them, code-striped for hot and cold water, steam, gas. Something thrummed in the distance. A narrow door marked "Storage" opened into a surprisingly large chamber that had evidently been used by the group for some time. Battered but comfortable chairs, stacks of pillows, strips of faded carpet. Sassinak wished she could collapse into the pillows and sleep for a day. But Fleur was waiting, as elegant as she had been in her own shop, in soft blues and lavenders, her silvery hair haloed around her head.

"Dear girl," she said, extending a hand with such elegance that Sassinak could not for a moment reply. "You look worn out. You know, you didn't have to get in this amount of trouble just to talk to me again."

"I didn't intend to."

Sassinak took the chair she was offered. Her new-found relative grinned at her and shut the door. She and Fleur were alone. She eyed the older woman, not quite sure what she was looking for.

"I suppose you could say that things . . . took off." Sitting down, in a real chair, she could feel every tired muscle. She fought back a yawn.

"I'll be as brief as I can." Fleur shifted a little in her seat and then stared at a space on the floor between them. "In the hopes that we will have time later to fill in what I leave out now." Sassinak nodded. "When Abe first met me, I had been captured, held hostage for my family's behavior and finally sold into prostitution." As a start, that got Sassinak's attention. She sat bolt upright.

"You?"

"My family were wealthy merchanters, rivals of the Paradens. Or so the Paradens thought. I'd been brought up to wealthy, luxury, society: probably spoiled rotten, though I didn't know it. The perfect hostage, if you look at it that way." Another pause. Sassinak began to feel a growing horror, and the certainty that she knew what was coming. "We were taken," Fleur said, biting off each word. "Me and my husband. Supposedly, it was independent pirates. That's what our families were told. But we knew, from the moment we were locked in the Paraden House security wing. I never knew the exact details, but I do know they asked for a ransom that neither my family nor his could have survived independently. His family . . . his family paid. And the Paradens sent him back, whole and healthy of body, but mindwiped. They made me watch."

Sassinak drew in a shaky breath to speak, but Fleur shook her head.

"Let me finish, all at once. My family thought they had proof of the Paraden connection. They tried to bring them to justice in the courts. In the end, my family lost everything, in court costs and countersuit damages. My father died, of a stroke; my mother's heart failed; my brothers . . . well, one went to prison for a 'vicious unprincipled assault' on the judge the Paradens had bribed so well. The other they had killed, just for insurance. And they sold me to a planet where none of my family had ever traded."

Sassinak's eyes burned with tears for the young woman Fleur had been. Before she realized it, she'd moved over to grip her hands.

"Abe saved me," Fleur went on. "He came, like any other young man, but he saw . . . something. I don't know. He used to kid me that whatever training my governness had given me couldn't be hidden. So he asked questions, and I was wild enough to answer, for I'd just heard of my sister-in-law's death. The Paradens took care to keep me informed. And he swore he would get me out, somehow. In less than a year, he had saved out my purchase price. How, on his salary, I'll never know. He wanted to marry me but I knew Fleet was strict about identity checks. I was terrified that the Paradens would find me again. So he helped me set up my first dress shop, and from there . . ."

She waved her arm, and Sassinak thought of the years of grinding work it must have taken, to go from that first tiny shop to the fashionable designer.

"Eventually I designed for the best families, including of course the Paradens. None of my friends recognized me. I had gray hair, I looked older, and of course I took care to look like a dressmaker, not a customer.

"Abe and I stayed in contact, when we could. He was sure there had to be a way to bring the crime home to the Paradens, and started digging. That was really the beginning of Samizdat. I knew a few people. I helped those I could. Passed him information, when it came to me, and he passed some back. We built up a network, on one planet after another. Then he was taken, and I thought . . . I thought I'd never survive his loss. So I swore that if he came back alive, I'd marry him, if he still wanted me."

She patted Sassinak's hands gently.

"And that's where you came in. When he came back, he had you: an orphan, in shock from all that had happened. I heard through our nets that he was back. I came to Regg to talk to him. And he explained that until you were on your way, he dared not risk your future with any more disruption."

"But I wouldn't have minded," Sassinak said. "How could he think I would?"

"I'm not sure, but we decided to wait, on marriage, that is, until after your graduation. And that, dear Sassinak, is what he wanted to tell you that night. I don't know whether you noticed anything . . ."

"I did! So—so *you* were his big secret."

"You sound almost disappointed."

"I'm not . . . but it hadn't occurred to me. I thought perhaps he'd found out more about the planet pirates."

"He might have. But he'd decided to tell you about me on graduation night. If all had gone well, he'd have brought you to the hotel where I was staying. We'd have met, and you'd have been the witness at our wedding before you went off on your first cruise."

Like light pouring into a darkened house as shutter after shutter came off the windows, she had wondered so long, so darkly, about the secret of that night.

"Did you come to his funeral? I don't remember any civilians at all."

Fleur's head drooped; Sassinak could not see her face.

"I was frightened again. I thought it was the Paradens, that they'd found me, and killed Abe because of me. You didn't need that and you didn't know about me, you wouldn't even have known why I was there. So I left. You can call it cowardice, if you like. I kept track of your career, but I never could find the right time to try telling you . . ."

Sassinak threw her arms around the older woman and hugged her as she cried.

"It's all right," she vowed. "I'll get the job done this time."

She could hear the steely edge in her voice herself. Fleur pulled away.

"Sass! You must not let it fill you with bitterness."

"But he *deserved* to get you!" Now she had tears in her eyes, too. "Abe deserved some pleasure. He worked so hard to save me . . . and you, and others, and then they *killed* him just when . . ."

She had not cried for Abe since her few tears the night of his death. She had been the contained, controlled officer he would have wanted her to be. Now that old loss stabbed her again. Through her sobs she heard Fleur talking.

"If you turn bitter, you've let them win. Whether you kill them or not, that's not the main thing. The main thing is to live as yourself; the self you can respect. Abe would not let me despair, the other kind of defeat, but he told me he worried that you might stay bitter."

"But they killed him. And my parents, and your family, and all the others . . ."

Fleur sighed. "Sassinak, I'm nearly forty years older than you, and I know that sort of comment makes prickles go up your spine." Sassinak had to chuckle. Fleur was so right. "And I know you don't want to hear that another forty years of experience means additional understanding. But!" Her beautifully manicured finger levelled at Sassinak's eyes. "Did Abe know more than you in the slave depot?"

"Of course. I was just a child."

"And if he were alive now, would you still respect his greater age and experience?"

"Well . . ." She could see it coming, but she didn't have to like it. Her expression must have shown that, because Fleur laughed aloud, a silvery bell-like peal that brought an answering laugh from Sassinak.

"So please trust me now," Fleur said, once more serious. "You have become what Abe dreamed of. I have kept an eye on you in the media; I know. But the higher you go in Fleet, the more you will need unclouded

judgment. If you allow the bitterness, the unfairness, of your childhood and
Abe's death, to overwhelm your natural warmth, you will become unfair in
your own way. You must be *more* than a pirate chaser, more than vengeance
personified. Fleet tends to shape its members toward narrow interests, rigid
reactions, even in the best. Haven't you found that some of your difficulties
down here arise from that?"

Put that way, some of them certainly had. She had developed the typical
spacefarer's distaste for planets. She had not bothered to cultivate the skills
needed to enjoy them. The various gangs in the tunnels seemed alien, even as
she tried to mold them into a working unit.

"Abe used to say to me," Fleur said, now patting at her hair, "that
growth and development can't stop for stars, rank or travel. You keep growing
and keep Abe's memory green. Don't let the Paradens shape the rest of your
life, as they shaped the first of it."

"Yes, ma'am."

"Now tell me, what do you plan to do with all this scruffy crowd?"

Sassinak grinned at her, half-rueful and half-determined.

"Chase pirates, ma'am, and *then* worry about whether I've gotten too
rigid."

But when it came down to it, none of them actually knew where The
Parchandri was located in a physical sense. Sassinak frowned.

"We ought to be able to get that from the data systems, with the right
codes," she said. "You said you had people good at that."

"But we don't have any of the current codes. The only times we've tried
to tap into the secure datalines, anything but the public ones, they've sent
police after us. They can tell where our tap is, an' everything."

"Sassinak?" Aygar tapped her shoulder. She started to brush him aside,
but remembered his previous good surprises. "Yes?"

"My friend, that student . . ."

"The one who boasted to you he could skip through the datalinks without getting caught? Yes. But he's not here and how would we find him?"

"I have his callcode. From any public comsite, he said."

"But there aren't any—are there? Down here?"

She glanced at the ragged group. Some of them nodded, and Coris
answered her.

"Yes, up in the public tunnels. There's a few we might get to, without
being spotted. Not all of us, of course."

"There's that illegal one in the 248 vertical," someone else said. "This maintenance worker put it in, patched it to the regular public lines so he could call in bets during his shift. We used to listen to him."

"Where's the 248 vertical?" Sassinak asked.

Not that far away, although it took several hours of careful zigging about to get to it. Twice they saw hunting patrols, one in the blue-gray of the city police, and one in the Pollys' orange. Their careless sweep of the tunnels did not impress Sassinak. They seemed to be content to walk through, without investigating all hatches and side tunnels. When she mentioned this to Coris, he hunched his shoulders.

"Bet they're planning to gas the system. Now they're looking for easy prey, girls down on their luck, kids . . . something to have fun with."

"Gas! You mean poison gas? Or knockout gas?"

"They've used both, before. 'Bout three years ago, they must've killed a thousand or more, over toward the shuttle station area. I was clear out here, and all it did to us was make us heave everything for a day or so. But I heard there'd been street crime, subways hijacked, that kind of thing."

Sassinak fingered the small kit in her pocket. She had brought along the detox membrane and primer that Fleet used against riot control gas, but would it work against everything? She didn't want to find out by using it, and she had only the one. She put that thought away and briefed Aygar on what to tell, and what not to tell, his student friend. If only she'd had a chance to evaluate that friend for herself. No telling whose agent he was, unless he was just a student playing pretend spy games. If so, he'd soon find out how exciting the real ones could be.

Two of the group went through the hatch into 248 vertical ahead of Aygar, and then called him through. This shaft, they'd explained, had enough regular traffic to keep the group out of it, except on special occasions.

Sassinak waited, wishing she could make the call. Aygar was only a boy, really, from a backwoods world: he knew nothing about intrigue. It would be like him to call up this "friend" and blurt out everything on an unsecured line. She kept herself from fidgeting with difficulty. She must not increase their nervousness. How many hours had slipped by? Would Arly be worried yet? Would anyone?

Aygar bounded back through the hatch, his youthful strength and health a vivid contrast to the underworlders' air of desperation.

"He wants to meet me," Aygar said. "He says the students would like to help."

"Help? Help what?"

Sassinak knew nothing of civilian students, except what the media reported. It was clear they weren't anything like cadets.

"Help with the coup," Aygar said as if that should explain it. "End the tyranny of greed and power, he says."

"We aren't starting a coup," Sassinak said, then thought about it.

While in one sense she didn't think she was overthrowing a government, the government had certainly sent riot squads after her, as if she were. Did they think she was working with a bunch of renegade students? Did someone else have a coup planned . . . and had they stumbled into it, and was *that* . . . ?

Her brain seemed to explode, as intuition and logic both flared. Aygar was giving her a puzzled look, as she went on, more quietly.

"At least, not the one he's thinking about. Exactly. Now, what kind of help can he give us? Can he find The Parchandri?"

"He just said to meet him. And where." Aygar was looking stubborn again; he could not fail to realize that he was being used, and no one liked that.

"In public territory. Great. And you're about as easy to disguise as a torn uniform at inspection."

"Fleur's the one who taught us all about disguises," Coris said. "Although, it won't be easy with *that* one."

Sassinak felt almost too tired to think, but she had to. She pulled herself together and said, "We'll go ask her. We certainly can't stroll out looking like this. *And* we'll get some rest before we go anywhere, because I notice that Aygar looks almost as exhausted as I feel. In the meantime, Coris, if you have any maps of the underground areas, I'd like to see them."

She hoped that would give them all the idea that she had a specific plan in mind.

Chapter Seventeen

FSP heavy cruiser Zaid-Dayan

"I do not like this." Arly tapped her fingers on the edge of the command console. One of its screens displayed the local news channel. "How could anyone think Sassinak would murder an admiral?"

The senior officers, including Major Currald, were ranged around her while the bridge crew pretended to pay strict attention to their monitors.

"Civilians." Bures looked almost as disgusted as she felt. "You know, if they're so scared of Fleet that they won't let us use our own shuttles up and down, then they probably think we're all born with blood in our mouths and fangs down to here." He gestured at his chin. "Long pointed ones. We go around covered with weapons, just looking for a chance to kill someone."

"News said the guy might not have been Coromell after all," said Mayerd who had come up to the bridge to watch the news with them. "Not that that helps. Good thing we don't have trouble in the neighborhood. It'd be worse if we had action coming."

Arly frowned at her. Doctors were the next thing to civilian, as far as she was concerned. "You know what she said. She thought there might be trouble . . ."

"Like what? An invasion of mysterious green-tentacled slime monsters?

We're at the center of as big a volume of peaceful space as anyone's ever known. Barring a few planet pirates, and I'm not minimizing that. But the last big stuff was decades back. Even the Seti haven't dared Fleet reprisals since the Tonagai Reef encounters. They may be gamblers, but they aren't stupid. I suppose, if the Paraden got all their pirate buddies to come blowing into FedCentral at once, they might cause us trouble, but they're not stupid either. They need a fat, peaceful culture to prey on. A shark has no advantages in a school of sharks."

Arly and Bures had crossed glances above Mayerd. Arly had to admit she had never considered a whole pirate *fleet*. They just didn't operate that way. Two or three raiders at once, more only in defense of an illegal installation. But now, with Sassinak lost somewhere below, the whole weight of the ship rested on her shoulders. She wished Ford would show up from wherever he'd been. She wished Sassinak would come back. *Blast that admiral,* she thought. Coromell, or whoever it had been, luring her away. And why? The trial? To have the *Zaid-Dayan* helpless?

The Fleet comline blinked at her, and she put the button in her ear. "Lieutenant Commander Arly, acting captain of *Zaid-Dayan*."

"Arly, it's Lunzie. Do you recognize my voice?"

Of course she did. She'd enjoyed meeting Sassinak's astonishing young ancestor. But why was Lunzie calling on the Fleet line? "Yes. Why?"

"You need to know I'm who I say I am. I'm on FedCentral. I can't tell you where."

Arly's heart skipped a beat. Could she be with the captain? Were they in hiding?

"Sass—Commander Sassinak?" She heard the rough edge to her own voice, and hoped it would not carry.

"We don't know. Arly, the *real* Admiral Coromell wants to speak to you. I know he's the real Coromell because I knew him years ago. Before my last session of coldsleep. Do you trust me?"

Something in the voice sounded different; something had changed since Arly had said goodbye as Lunzie left the ship back at Sector HQ. Arly considered. Lunzie sounded more mature, more confident. Did that matter? Did it mean anything at all? And even if she didn't trust Lunzie, she still wanted to hear what this mysterious Coromell had to say. She gestured to Bures, who bent close, and tapped out a message on her console: get Flag Officer Directory. Bures nodded. Arly spoke, hoping her voice sounded calm.

"I believe you're Lunzie if that's what you mean."

"It's not, but it'll do. Here he is."

A silence, then a deep voice that certainly had the expectation of command.

"This is Admiral Coromell. You're Lieutenant Commander Arly?"

"Yes, sir."

Bures handed her the Directory, and she flipped through it. Coromell: tall, silver-haired, bright blue eyes. A handsome man, even approaching old age. He had probably been very handsome when Lunzie knew him before. She wondered whether they'd had anything going, and forced herself to listen to him.

"As you no doubt realize, the situation is critical. Your captain has disappeared and the local law enforcement agencies were, until a few hours ago, convinced that she had killed *me*. I've been unable to find out what's going on, and some of my own staff have vanished as well."

"Sir, I thought the admiral was hunting over on Six. That's what Commander Sassinak was told."

"I was. I had an urgent message to return, and my return was complicated by Lunzie's . . ."

A flashing light on the console yanked Arly's attention away from Coromell; the Ssli biolink alarm. Could she interrupt an admiral?

"Excuse me, sir," she said, as firmly as she could. "Our Ssli has a critical message."

He didn't quite snort, but the sound he made conveyed irritation barely withheld. "Check it, then."

Arly touched the controls and the Ssli's message began scrolling across the console's upper screen.

"Enemy approaching. Seti fleet entering system, downwarping from FTL, expecting assistance in evading detection and system defenses."

Her hands trembled as she acknowledged that much. The message continued with details of the incoming menace. Number of ships, mass, weapons as known, probable crew and troop levels.

Bures, craning his neck to read this sideways, let out a long, low whistle. Mayerd, then Currald, joined him, their faces paling as they watched the long lists grow.

"Commander Arly?" That was the admiral, impatient of the long silence.

Arly answered, surprised that her voice was steadier than her hands.

"Sir, our Ssli reports an incoming Seti fleet, definitely hostile." She heard a gasp, but did not stop. "Apparently they've got Insystem help that's supposed to disable some of the system defenses. They're timed to arrive here during the Grand Council session. There's some kind of coup planned." The display had stopped. She tapped in a question to the Ssli, asking for the source of all this.

"But how do they know?" Coromell asked. The answer came up on the screen even as he asked.

"Sir, our Ssli says there's a Ssli larva, captive, on the Seti flagship, and a Fleet officer . . . *Dupaynil.*" Her own surprise carried to him.

"Who's that?"

"A Fleet Security officer assigned to us a few months ago. Then he was transferred, I think to go look up something in Seti space."

"Which he quite evidently found. Well, Commander, you have my permission to leave orbit and make life difficult for those Seti ships."

She opened her mouth to ask what about Sassinak and realized the futility. Even if the captain had been at the shuttleport, they couldn't have waited for her. Not knowing where she was, they certainly couldn't delay.

"Yes, sir," she said. Then, "Request permission to drop a shuttle and pilot in case Commander Sassinak shows up. She may need it."

"Granted," he said.

That was all. She was now more than acting captain: she had command of a warship about to fight an alien fleet. *This is impossible,* she thought, touching the button that set red lights flashing throughout the ship. She punched the ship's intercom.

"Ensign Timran to the bridge." And, off intercom, to Bures, "Get one of Sassinak's spare uniforms from her quarters and whatever else she might need. Get it up to Flight Two, fast."

More orders to give, evicting the Insystem Security monitor teams that had the weapons locked down, to Engineering to bring up the drives.

"Ensign Timran reporting, ma'am!"

He was very quick or he'd been lurking in the passage outside. She hoped he would be both quick and lucky with the shuttle.

"Report to Flight Deck Two. You'll be taking a small unit to the surface."

The admiral had said nothing about an escort, but whatever had happened to Sassinak, a few Wefts and marines couldn't make things worse. When she looked at Currald he nodded.

"Ten should do it," he said. "Leave room for her and that Aygar, coming back." He picked up another comset and called his own adjutant.

"Yes, ma'am!" said Tim, eyes gleaming. "Do I have permission . . . ?"

"You have permission to do whatever is necessary to assist Commander Sassinak and get her safely offplanet at her command. Bures will have some things for you to take. Check with him."

He saluted and was off at a run. She hoped she'd done the right thing. Whatever had happened to Sassinak, if she was still alive, she would think she had a cruiser waiting for her. And now we're leaving—*I'm* leaving, taking her ship, leaving her nothing but a shuttle.

Arly couldn't believe this was happening, not so fast, but it was. Through her disbelief, she heard her own voice giving orders in the same calm, steady tone she'd cultivated for years. Longscans on, undocking procedures to begin immediately, two junior Weft officers to report to Flight Two. A loud squawk from the Station Dockmaster, demanding to know why the *Zaid-Dayan* was beginning undock without permission.

"Orders of Admiral Coromell," said Arly. Should she tell them about the Seti fleet? "We'll be releasing one planetary shuttle."

"You can't *do* that!"

"We're releasing one planetary shuttle," she went on, as if she had not heard, "and request navigational assistance to clear your Station without damage." She punched the all-ship intercom and said, "Ensign Gori to the bridge."

"But our scans are showing live weapons . . ."

That voice abruptly stopped, and an Insystems Security Force uniform appeared on one of the viewscreens.

"You are in violation of regulations. You are requested to cease and desist, or measures will be taken . . ."

"Ensign Gori reporting, ma'am."

Not as quick as Tim, but eager in his own way.

"Ensign, the cap—Commander Sassinak said you knew regulations forwards and backwards." He didn't answer, but he didn't look worried, either. "You will discuss regulations with Insystems Security. We are withdrawing under threat of enemy attack, at the orders of a higher officer not in our direct chain of command." Gori's face brightened and his mouth opened. Arly pushed him toward one of the working boards, and said, "Don't tell *me*, tell *him*."

Yet another screen showed Flight Two, with the hatch closing on one of the shuttles. As the launch hatch opened, the elevator began raising the shuttle. Arly could just see some part of the Station through the open hatch.

". . . no authorization for such deliberate violation," the Insystem voice droned on. "Return to inactive status at once or regulations will require that force be used."

Arly's temper flared. "You have a hostile Seti fleet incoming," she said slowly, biting off each word. "You have traitors letting them past the defenses. Don't threaten me. So far I haven't hurt the Station."

Perhaps not all the Insystem Security were in the plot. This one looked as if he'd just been slugged.

"But . . . but there's no evidence. None of the detector nets have gone off . . ."

"Maybe someone's got his finger on the buzzer."

The shuttle cleared the *Zaid-Dayan*'s hull, and disappeared. Arly sent a silent prayer after it.

"If I were you, I'd start looking at the systems with redundancies."

By now, the *Zaid-Dayan*'s own powerful scans were unlocked. Nothing would show, yet. The enemy was too far out. Arly glanced around and saw that the regular bridge crew was now in place. It felt very strange to be in Sassinak's place, while 'Tenant Yulyin sat at "her" board, and stranger to see that board mostly dark, after a ship's alert. She pointed to Gori, who transferred the Insystems Security channel to his board.

"Ensign Gori will stay in contact with you."

"Fleet Regulations, Volume 21, article 14, grants authorization to commanding officers of vessels on temporary duty away from normal Sector assignment . . ." Gori sounded confident, and as smooth as any diplomat.

Arly left him to it. The combination of a surprise Seti fleet *and* Gori's zeal for regulations should keep trigger-happy fingers off the buttons until they could get away and raise shields.

"Docking bay secure, Captain!"

Arly nodded to Engineering. Critical as the situation was, she could not justify destroying the Station to jump-start the *Zaid-Dayan* and bringing the insystem drive up was a delicate operation. Centimeter by centimeter they eased away from the Station, adding just enough thrust at first to let rotational inertia begin their outward spiral.

"Weapons still locked down," Yulyin reported, at the two-minute tick.

"Right. Sassinak and I did some fancy stuff that should unkink by the time we can use them—" She wondered if this Ssli and that distant one were still in contact. And what was Dupaynil doing there? No time for that, though: her weapons had to come first.

She keyed in the code Sassinak had left with her, the captain's access to the command computers, the master controls of all weaponry. Then she explained what they'd done, and as quickly crew and marines began scurrying around the ship to restore it to full fighting capability. One hundred kilometers from the Station, Arly notched up the insystem drive.

So far, if the invaders were getting scan on her, she would look predictable. A rising spiral, the usual departure of a large ship from anything as massive as a planet. Then she engaged the stealth gear, and the *Zaid-Dayan* passed into darkness and silence, an owl hunting across the night.

FedCentral: Fleet Headquarters

Coromell swung to face Lunzie. "I never thought of *that*! My mind must be slowing!"

"What?" Lunzie hadn't heard what Arly said, had only seen its effect in the changes on Coromell's face.

"A Seti fleet, inbound—" He told her the rest, and began linking it to what they'd learned elsewhere. "This Iretan thing . . . you must have come very close to the bone somehow."

"Unless they had it planned and we just showed up in the middle of it."

"True. I keep forgetting you were sleeping away the past forty-three years. Like a time-bomb for them. Come to think of it, without the Iretan's trial, the Winter Assizes were mostly commercial cases this time. And nothing coming up before Grand Council but a final vote on some financial rules affecting terraforming. Not my field: I don't know a stock from a bond."

"So if they wanted a quiet session, they could have arranged that . . . and we really *are* a time-bomb."

"Which they set for themselves, I remind you. Very fitting, all this is."

"If they don't blow us away," said Lunzie. "That's not Sassinak up there."

"She'd have left the ship to her most competent combat officer. The best we can do now is make sure whatever was planned down *here* doesn't work."

Lunzie was unconvinced. "But what can one cruiser do against a whole fleet?"

"Buy us time, if nothing else. Don't worry about what you can't change. What we'll have to do is make sure Insystem has the alarm, and believes it, and get Sassinak out of whatever trap she's in."

The tiny clinic attached to Fleet Central Systems Command had but one corridor that opened directly into the back offices of the Command building. Lunzie followed Coromell, noticing that the enlisted personnel looked as stunned to see him as he had looked when he heard about the Seti fleet.

"Sir? When did the Admiral arrive?" asked one, almost but not quite barring the way to the lift marked "Admiral's use only."

"About thirty hours ago. Apparently our security confused at least a few people." He punched the controls and the lift door sighed open.

"But, sir, that commander . . . the murder . . ."

"Put a lock on it, Algin. Who's been speaking for us?"

"Lt. Commander Dallish, sir. He's up . . ."

But Coromell had closed the lift door, and now gave Lunzie a rueful smile.

"I knew that. But he doesn't know that Dallish is the one officer here I really trust. His father and I were close friends, years ago. Dallish has been covering for me."

"Shouldn't you have stayed under cover longer?"

"With Sassinak still accused of murdering me? No. Showing up alive should shake them up just as much as you shook the conspirators by waking up in the midst of their plot. Whoever *thought* he killed me will wonder who the victim was. And whoever sent the victim to take my place will wonder if we're onto him. We soon will be."

Lunzie found Coromell's office a relief after the pastel-walled, determinedly soothing atmosphere of the clinic suite. A great arc of desk took the place of the command module onboard a ship. He grinned when he saw her expression.

"Yes, it's an indulgence. But one which keeps me thinking like a deep-space admiral, and not a planet-dweller."

A younger man, whom Lunzie assumed was "Dallish," stood aside as they entered, then handed Coromell a sheaf of thin plastic strips. One wall had a window looking out across the city—Lunzie's first live view of the hub of interplanetary government. It looked, to her, like any other large city. Below, a broad street had both slideways and vehicular traffic: bright blue and green monorail trains. She glanced around Coromell's office again. The dark-blue flat-piled carpet that seemed to be favored by Fleet officers, a bank of viewscreens on the opposite wall, racks of datacubes, fichefiles, even a row of books bound in plain blue.

"Lunzie!"

She looked away from a row of exquisitely detailed model ships, displayed against a painted starscape. Coromell and Dallish had tuned in one of the civilian news programs, now showing a view that Lunzie realized was the docking tube of a ship at Station. At first she did not hear whatever the news commentator was saying. Over the tube, the electronic display had gone from green to orange; the ship's name *Zaid-Dayan* and status "Undock: Warning" blinked on and off.

A commentator stepped in front of the vicam, and Lunzie made herself listen to the sleek-haired woman with the professional frown.

"Most unusual behavior has prompted some to suggest that the missing captain of this dangerous ship may have been contaminated with a psychoactive agent, even a disease which has spread to crewmembers. We have just been informed that the Insystem Federation Security teams whose duty it is to ensure that these warships cannot fire their weapons at innocent civilians, these teams are being evicted from this ship. Even now," and the commentator's head turned slightly so that Lunzie could see out-of-focus movement behind her, up the tube toward the ship. "I believe, yes, here they are, quite against their will . . ."

Hands on heads, the men and women clumping down the length of the tube looked unhappy enough. Behind them were figures in ominous gray and green armor, helmets locked down, and very impressive-looking weapons in hand.

"Security team weapons," Coromell commented to Dallish. "Notice that? Their own are probably still locked up. They disarmed the warden teams." He sounded almost gleeful. "Probably Wefts, shifting on 'em."

"Excuse me," the commentator was saying, thrusting her microphone into the faces of the first to exit, while the camera zoomed at them. "Could you comment on the mental stability of the crew of this ship? Is there any danger that they might turn . . ."

"Bunch of flippin' maniacs!" snarled one of the men. He had a ripening bruise over one eye, and a split lip. "Gone totally bonkers, they have, hallucinatin' about invaders from the deep!"

"Krims!" Dallish glanced at Lunzie and back to the screen. "If they take that line . . ."

Coromell was already punching commands on his desk. Lunzie's gaze flicked back and forth between him and the newscast. She found it hard to concentrate on either. Those exiting the ship had clumped around the newscaster and her crew; behind them, the camera barely showed something moving again in the tube.

Suddenly a loud squeal made everyone on the screen jump and they moved back. The camera focussed on a large red hatch sliding across the tube opening, as the status board changed to "Undock: ACCESS CLOSED." The news program shifted to someone in a studio.

"Thank you, Cerise," said a male 'caster who then turned to the front. "As you can see, something ominous is going on with the Fleet heavy cruiser *Zaid-Dayan*, whose former captain, a Fleet officer named Sassinak, is sought in connection with a murder investigation on the surface of this planet. We have no explanation for the expulsion of the security teams or for the cruiser's apparent intention to undock from the Station. We have learned from sources close to the Federation Justice Department Prosecutor's office that valuable evidence and a witness in the upcoming trail of the heavyworlder conspirator Tanegli are also missing. Although we cannot speculate at this time on any connection between the two, our correspondent Li Tsan is standing by at the office of the Justice Department Chief Prosecutor, Ser Branik. Li, what can you tell us about the Justice Department's reaction to this latest Fleet outrage?"

"Well, the Prosecutor isn't saying anything. This situation is still too new. But we have heard suggestions that the *Zaid-Dayan* became contaminated with some kind of spore or viral particle, on the proscribed planet Ireta, which is affecting the mental processes of anyone exposed."

"And would that apply as well to the witnesses expected to arrive in the next day or so from the EEC vessel . . . the . . . uh . . . former co-governors, Kai and Varian?"

"It certainly could. We expect to hear that they may be quarantined and their transmitted testimony might well be scrutinized more closely. If such a disease did cause mental instability, that might even be a defense for the original alleged conspirators. Certainly Tanegli hasn't appeared normally healthy in any of the interviews we've seen."

"NO!" Lunzie startled herself as well as Coromell and Dallish with that explosion. They stared at her. She got her voice back under control, choked down the less acceptable phrases she wanted to use, and said, "It's ridiculous nonsense, and any doctor would know that at once. There's no disease that could make Sassinak and Arly crazy after a brief exposure, that wouldn't have affected the rest of us all those years. To the point where we couldn't have survived. Tanegli is *not* some innocent overcome by alien spores. He's as guilty as anyone could be, and I'll see him convicted."

"Not if this goes on," Dallish said, pointing to the screen. He had turned the sound down, but Lunzie could see that the mouths were still moving.

"He's right," Coromell said, putting down the comunit he'd been holding. "I can't convince *anyone* to listen to me. Even those who believe I'm who I say I am. Someone's put a lock on this thing, hard and fast. That," and he nodded at the unit, "was the Assistant Longscan Supervisor, and as far as he's concerned there's not a ship within a couple of light-years that he didn't have logged for scheduled arrival months ago. That's one I trust, normally as suspicious as I am, but he's believing his machines and his outstation crews. And someone had already reached him, insisting that it was his duty to squelch any panic in the week before the Grand Council and Winter Assizes open."

"Who?" asked Dallish. "I've never seen anything blocked that fast. It was as if they had everything in place."

"Of course they would have," Coromell said. "Once they knew about their time-bomb, about Ireta, they'd start setting up ways to counter anything we could do. I'm suddenly becoming very suspicious about that hunting trip."

"But, sir, you always go rhuch hunting."

"True, but you remember I thought of not going, with Sassinak coming in and the trial approaching. Then they had that 'cancellation' in Bakli Lodge. Well, no matter now. We can dig into that later, assuming we ensure a later."

"Sir, if I may suggest?" Dallish looked both embarrassed and determined.

"Go ahead."

"Lunzie's now the single witness in the Iretan case. She's an obvious target even if she hadn't brought back all that from Diplo."

"She ought to be safe enough here . . ." Coromell began, and then he shook his head. "Except that we've already passed word to the Prosecutor's office that she's onplanet."

"And we have to assume a leak in that office. Yes, sir."

"Mmm. We'll just have to make sure we have none here." His comunit buzzed and Coromell picked it up. "Ah . . . Mr. Justice Vrix. Yes, as a matter of fact, but you have her taped deposition on file. No. No, that's impossible. Because . . . yes. Precisely. And until that time, I'm not risking the government's remaining witness." He flipped a toggle and smiled at Lunzie. "You see? We must not let you out of our sight between now and the trial."

Fleet shuttle Seeker

This time, Ensign Timran told himself, he would do everything right the first time. Not by accident, but by the exercise of cool judgment and keen intelligence. He knew that he'd been chosen for this mission because he had a habit of being lucky. But *this* time he had a team of marines, a pair of Weft officers (that they outranked him hardly mattered: while he piloted the shuttle, he ranked everyone) and authorization to rescue his revered captain. He was going to do everything right. He would make *no* mistakes.

Tongue caught between his teeth, he eased the shuttle off its platform, remembered to key in the appropriate signal to the *Zaid-Dayan* to confirm liftoff, remembered to check the low-link and high-link connections with the cruiser's com shack. From this vantage, the Station looked as if a mischievous child had taken three or four sets of TekiLink toys and mismatched half the connections. As a habitat for gerbils, it might have a certain charm but it lacked the clean functional lines Timran approved of in Fleet installations. The cruiser had been docked at the outer end of one long arm; he had another such to dodge, with a row of boxy insystem transports.

Then he was clear, with an easy drop trajectory down to the shuttleport. Except that he was not going to the shuttleport. He hadn't told Arly: she was busy enough. And his orders said nothing specific about the shuttleport, just that he was to go render assistance to Sassinak. He was sure she wasn't at the shuttleport. If she had been, she'd have contacted the cruiser before now. So going to the shuttleport would only involve a lot of hashing around with civilians who didn't want a Fleet shuttle in their airspace anyway.

Beside him, one of the Wefts had tuned in the civilian newscast. Tim almost glanced at it when he heard the commentator's question to the evicted Security team and the answers, but he remembered what had happened last time he got distracted. More to the point were the angry questions from Airspace Control. They seemed to think he would interfere with scheduled traffic. He smiled to himself. Military shuttles would not have survived in service if they'd been blind to other craft. He knew where everything around him was at least as well as Airspace Control. And all of them knew, from hearing the smug Security teams brag about it, that FedCentral had no inner air defenses. The Bronthin had refused to allow them. From Tim's point of view, the only weapons down there were little stuff.

"We're not goin' to the 'port?" asked the Weft. Kiksi, her name was. If she was a she . . . Tim had never bothered to find out much about Wefts. He didn't dislike them, he just found his own amusements far more interesting than theoretical knowledge about aliens.

"No," Tim said. "They'll just try to impound us. And Commander Sassinak can't be there, or she'd have contacted us."

"Good thought," said the Weft. "Do you *know* where she is?"

"Nobody does," said Tim. He had punched up the mapping function and was now trying to decide just where he did want to land. FedCentral offered little open land close to where he thought Sassinak might be.

"Not strictly true," said the other Weft, 'Tenant Sricka. "Sassinak is not where the shuttle can reach her."

This time he did look away, though he kept his hands steady. "You know where she is? Why didn't you tell Arly?"

"She kept moving. She was under surface. We had no return contact."

"Under surface . . . like in a submarine?" FedCentral had only one ocean and Tim had not suspected it of submarine transport.

A chuckle from Kiksi, that made his ears burn. "No . . . under the city. Subways? Maintenance tunnels? We don't know. We don't *talk* with her in human shape. We're not made for it. It's direction sense only. When we are nearer, I can *shift*, and then perhaps touch her mind more directly. But you, where are you planning to land the shuttle? And how to prevent detection?"

"I'm not sure."

He knew his ears were bright red and the back of his neck, under his uniform. It had seemed like a good idea, and even before Arly called on him, he'd daydreamed about rescuing Sassinak, poring over the maps of the vast complex. The shuttle could land on unprepared ground, could even make a direct vertical drop of fifty to a hundred feet, although he'd never done it. But he couldn't land on the roofs of ordinary buildings or on slideways or monorail tracks.

Sricka reached over and tapped the map-control console; the area he'd been watching slid aside, and another came up. Open, not too rough, and fairly near the city. He didn't recognize the code.

"Landfill," the Weft said. "That end's already covered, and the replanting cycle's only up to grass. And that yellow line there, that's a subway tunnel for returning workers to their housing. It's your decision, but if I were flying this thing, that's where I'd go."

He had no better ideas, and he was not about to ask for a vote. He could almost feel the marines' amusement tickling his backbone.

"Looks good," he said, trying to sound casual. "And thanks."

"Will it alarm you if I *shift*?"

"No. Of course not."

Nonetheless, he had to gulp hard when the ordinary human figure beside him turned into a mass of extra joints, spiky protuberances, and all too many legs. And a row of bright blue eyes. Instead of staring, he entered his desired destination in the shuttle's navigational computer and saw to it that the course changes all went as planned. By the time he neared the landfill, flying the shuttle as if it were any aircraft, he knew that the *Zaid-Dayan* was long gone. He had to do it right this time. If he messed up, there would be no rescue.

Chapter Eighteen

For a moment, following Aygar up into the more public tunnels, Sassinak thought how she could explain all this to a Board of Inquiry, if she survived long enough. There were no Rules of Engagement covering this sort of thing. She remembered something about "accepting civilian volunteers into a military mission"—not recommended, but it did happen—and more than one passage strongly cautioning Fleet officers from involving themselves in local politics. And this was hardly local politics. She had taken on some part of the Federation itself and even though she considered the people involved to be traitors, they could say the same of her.

She dared not think too far ahead or the weight of it would crush her. A single Fleet captain against the most powerful families in the Federation, against the massed pirates, plus the Seti? And with nothing but a ragged bunch of crazies and losers? How could she even be thinking of this? Yet the thought daunted her for only a moment. She had survived the raid on her home, against odds as high. She had survived battle after battle in space where any mistake could have killed her, and some nearly had. She had survived the jealousy of other officers, a hundred mischances, to be where she was now. *If not you, who?* Abe had said more than once.

No time for letting her mind drift, not even to the things Fleur had told her. She would have time later for more such talks, for long reminiscences, for shared tears and laughter, or they would both be dead. For now, she had Aygar to get safely to the rendezvous with his student friend, and whatever came after. She patted her midsection where the extra bulk Fleur had insisted she stuff into the pale blue worksuit felt itchy and unfamiliar. Even worse was the slight dowager's hump that prickled when she twitched her shoulders, trying to remember to slump. Although she'd seen in the mirror that the gray streaks Fleur had added to her hair as well as decidedly wrong makeup made her look years older, she kept thinking a more complete disguise would have been better. Aygar, whose height and shoulders made him unmistakable, had been turned into a male fashion plate. A voluminous magenta shirt unlaced halfway down his chest and tucked into tight gray shorts made him look like anything but fugitive. His mapper button now looked like one of the jewels studding a huge medallion hung on stout chain around his neck.

The first "uptowners" they saw hardly glanced at them. The upsloping tunnel, linking one subway level with another, had streams of pedestrians scurrying in both directions. Most wore one-piece worksuits in grays, browns, and blues; the others were dressed as flamboyantly as Aygar. Homebound workers, Fleur had said, mingling with the pleasure-hunters who also tended to "change shifts" at rush hours. Sassinak trailed him, trying to look as if she merely happened to be going in the same direction. In that brief time below, she'd forgotten how noisy large groups could be. Announcements no one could have understood boomed from the levels below and above; the scurrying feet were overlaid by a constant roar of conversation. A flare of Ryxi screeched, threatening, and the humans parted around them. A gray uniform approached at a jog.

At the next level, the upbound stream bifurcated, a third veering left and two-thirds right. Even more noise broke over them. The synthesized voice of the transportation computers announcing train arrivals and departures, warning passengers away from the rails, repeating the same list of safety rules over and over. Friends met on the platforms with squeals of delight as if they had not seen each other at rush hour the day before. Less demonstrative workers glared at them or muttered brief curses. Aygar and Sassinak both turned right. Here, service booths backed the subway platforms: fountains, restrooms, public callbooths, even a few food booths. As he'd been directed, Aygar turned into the third of these. Sassinak paused as if to look over the menu displayed, then ducked in after him.

He was already shaking the hand of a much smaller young man with a milder version of the same outfit; small-flowered purple print shirt, and looser green shorts but higher-heeled boots. Backing him were two other young men, similarly dressed, and a girl who seemed to have stepped out of a Carin Coldae re-run. Her silvery snugsuit clung to the right curves, all the way down to sleek black boots, and her emerald green scarf was knotted casually on the left shoulder. Across the back of the bodysuit ran a stenciled black chain design and short lengths of minute black chain hung from her earlobes.

Sassinak managed not to snicker. Innocent bravado deserved a passing nod of respect, although she could have told the young woman that carrying a real weapon where she'd stashed her emerald-green plastic imitation needler would make it hard to draw in time for practical use. Her own hand checked the weapon Aygar had taken from the dead man behind the bar. She moved past them, up to the counter, and ordered a bowl of fried twists that were supposed to be real vegetables, not processor output. Whatever it was, it would taste better than her last meal. She paid for it from the money Fleur had given her and sat down at a largish table near the clump of young people. They were talking busily, waving their arms and looking like any other group of young people in a public place. Now they were moving up, ordering their own food, and then Aygar led them to the table she'd chosen.

"Can we sit here?" asked the darkest of the young men. He was sitting already. "We need a big table."

Sassinak nodded, hoping she looked like a slightly intimidated middle-aged office worker. She ate a couple of fries and decided that it didn't matter if they were real veggies or processed: they were delicious.

"I'm Jonlik," he said, smiling brightly at her. "This is Gerstan, and this is Bilis, and our Coldae clone is Erdra." The girl gave Sassinak a long stare intended to impress.

"I thought you were supposed to be a cruiser captain."

"I am," Sassinak said very quietly. "Did you never hear of disguises?"

They all looked unimpressed and she sighed inwardly. Had she ever been this young?

"I wore this for you," the girl said. "I thought . . ."

Sassinak laid a hand over the girl's wrist with strength enough to get a startled look. "I had a Coldae poster, in silver, when I was a girl. But that was a picture. Reality's different."

"Well, of course, but . . ."

Sassinak released the girl's wrist and leaned back, giving her stare for stare. The girl reddened suddenly.

"Erdra, you wouldn't have lasted a week in the slave pens. Most of my friends didn't."

Now their stares had a different expression. Jonlik's bottle of *drelz* sauce was dripping on his lap.

"Best wipe that up," she said, in the tone she used aboard ship.

He gaped, looked down, and mopped at his shorts with one flowing sleeve.

"I told you," Aygar growled. She wondered what else he'd told them. At least he was keeping his voice low.

Sassinak turned to Gerstan. "Is it true, what Aygar said, that you can patch into the secure links without being caught?"

Gerstan nodded, and gulped down his mouthful of fries.

"So far. We've gotten all the way up to H-level, and there's really tricky stuff from F-level on up. I've never been as far as H by myself. Erdra's done it, though."

"What's on H-level?"

Erdra tossed her head in a gesture not quite like Coldae's but close enough.

"Well, it lets you play model games with the lower levels. Like, what if all the water in the auxiliary reservoir is gone suddenly and the pumps on that line are about to seize. That's one thing, but it's not just games, because it's realtime, using their data, bollixing their sensors, overriding the safety interlocks. I've never done anything really dangerous . . ." The tone was that of someone who had indeed done something criminal, if not dangerous, but who wasn't about to admit it.

Bilis snorted. "What about the time you convinced the Transport Authority a train had derailed out on the Yellow Meadow line?"

"That wasn't *dangerous*. They had time to stop the following trains. I set it up that way."

"Cost the taxpayers 80,000 credits, they said," Bilis said to Sassinak. "Lost time, damage from the emergency halts, hours of hunting the 'bases, looking for tampering. Never did find her."

"Never did find the tap at all," said Erdra who sounded much smugger than someone faking a train derailment should. "And if something blows when a train has to make an emergency stop, it needs finding. If there *had* been a wreck, that number 43 would've plowed right into it. They should thank me for finding their problems."

Sassinak eyed the girl, wishing she had her on the *Zaid-Dayan* for a few weeks. With all that talent, she needed someone to straighten her out.

"By the way," Erdra said sweetly, popping a couple of fries into her mouth and crunching them. "How come your ship left without you?"

"I beg your pardon?" It was the only alternative to the scream that wanted to erupt from her gut.

"Your ship. That cruiser. Newscast says it broke away from the Station and went zipping off blathering about an invading fleet. The captain or whoever you left up there is supposed to be crazy with whatever drug or spore or something you caught on Ireta. Whatever made you kill that admiral?"

For a moment the whirl of Sassinak's thoughts found no verbal form. Rage: how dare they leave her! Fear: she had been so sure that if she could get a signal out, Arly would be there for her. Exultation: she had been *right*! There was more going on than anyone had thought and those blasted smug Internal Security fops were going to find something worse than a Fleet cruiser's guns to worry about.

She controlled all that, and her breathing, with an effort, and said, "I didn't kill any admiral." But I could cheerfully kill *you*, she thought at Erdra who clearly had no telepathic ability at all because she kept right on smiling.

"You nearly finished?" That came from an irritated clump of men in business jumpers, their fry packets leaking grease onto their fingers.

"Oh, sure." Gerstan stood up as quickly as the others did. "Let's go on to somewhere else and talk, huh?"

Sassinak felt very much the drab peahen among the flock but dealt with that by taking the lead. She trusted Aygar to keep them following.

Back down the sloping connecting tunnel to the narrow service tube and the unobtrusive door. Their last protest had been some distance back. Sassinak paid no mind to it. She had enough to think of. Arly would not have taken the *Zaid-Dayan* out without good reason. That she knew. But on top of her own concern, her own burning desire to *be there* when anything happened to her ship, the words "Court Martial" burned in her mind. There was no excuse short of death for a captain who was downside when her ship went into action.

She gave the signal knock to the door, and it opened at once. She led the others in, and when the door shut behind them, they faced the same weapons she had.

"What *is* this?" Gerstan demanded.

"Caution," Sassinak said. And to Coris, "No one noticed us and we had no problems. Some of these were fairly loose-tongued in a fry bar but the place was jammed with commuters. Shouldn't be a problem." She turned back to the students. "You wanted a conspiracy? You've just found one. These," and she waved an arm at her motley troop, "are fellow-conspirators. Refugees. Ex-slaves. The poor and homeless of this city which, according to Aygar, you hope to help by plotting a coup."

From their expressions, none of the students had actually *met* any of the undergrounders before. To their credit, none of them tried to bolt.

"You're sure about these four?" Coris asked.

"Not entirely, yet, but let's go down a bit and see if Erdra's as good as Gerstan says." Coris nodded, and waved Sassinak through the group. She spoke over her shoulder to Erdra. "Did they give any specifics about the ship leaving? Say *what* it was after?"

"Uh . . . not really." Erdra sounded much less smug. Perhaps the girl had recognized that those weapons were real. "Just that they—the people aboard—threw off the Security teams that make sure no weapons are usable. A shuttle was sent off and then the ship left the Station. They'd said something about an invasion, but there's been no word. But that got squashed. It's been confirmed that nothing's out there that shouldn't be."

"And *you* believe that?" Sassinak didn't wait for an answer, but let her annoyance work itself out. "You, who created a fake train wreck? Who could've hidden a real one as easily?"

"But I didn't. And that means someone *else* . . ."

"Is as smart as you are. Right."

"Then is there *really* something out there?" That was Gerstan, bouncing up alongside her. Sassinak refrained from slapping him back into place.

"Arly would not take the *Zaid-Dayan* without good reason. She's not any crazier than I am. So I think something's out there. What, I couldn't guess."

Actually, she could: a pirate incursion or a Seti fleet. Either one might be part of a larger conspiracy and she had to hope only one of them had materialized. Her mind reverted to something else Erdra had said. A shuttle? Why had Arly released a shuttle?

Then she grinned: obvious. And she would wager she could name the pilot aboard, but not what that very brash young man would do next.

"So you're saying," Gerstan went on, "that the Federation itself is involved in concealing the approach of some danger from deepspace?"

Sassinak nodded. "Yes, because some faction thinks that will give it control. In such cases you have two possibilities. The present rulers want to use force to give themselves absolute power because they fear a challenge, or a faction not quite in control wants to tip the balance its way."

"Which is it?"

"I don't know." She grinned at their confusion. "It doesn't really matter. If Arly detected the incoming fleet at the edge of the *Zaid-Dayan*'s scan range, it can't be here for days. It won't just launch missiles at the planet. To do that it could have lobbed a passive from far outside scan." Their faces were blank. Sassinak reminded herself that none of these people had military training. "Never mind," she said gently. "The point is that whatever's going on up there isn't our problem. *Our* problem is the group here that's concealing it. *That,* we can do something about, if we're quick enough. Then the existing defense systems should be able to handle the invaders." She wasn't at all sure she believed that. Would Arly think to call for more Fleet aid? Or would she be worried that what came might not be on their side?

"Now," she said, putting enough bite in it that they all, students and undergrounders alike, gave her their full attention. "First we must locate The Parchandri and neutralize him. That's your task, Erdra. Get into the links and 'bases, and find out where his hideyhole is. Get control of the lifesupport and communications lines. I'd wager next year's pay that he'll be underground but not completely self-contained."

"But . . ." The girl looked around. "Where's an access port? I've always used one of the Library carrels to get in."

"Coris. Take her down and help her get to one of the trunkline 'ports. Bilis can go with her and you'll need a tensquad for guards. If you run into trouble, run! And get her to another 'port. Two runners, for messages, until we get our communications set up. Gerstan, you told Aygar that there were a lot more students who wanted to get involved?"

"Yes, ma'am." That honorific came out slowly as if he hadn't planned it. Sassinak smiled at him.

"Good. We'll find you a 'port and you can let them know. We need communications links topside so we can keep track of what the media's saying and what's going down on the streets. We'll also need some small portable coms, like those the police have." From his expression, he was finding real action scarier than he'd expected. And he hadn't seen real action yet.

"You mean, steal . . . ? Like, from a . . . a policeman? A guard?"

"Whatever it takes. I thought you were eager to start a revolution. Did you think you'd do that without getting crossways with the police?"

"Well, no, but . . ."

"But talk let you feel brave without doing anything. Sorry, lad, but the time for that's all gone. Now it's time to act or go hide someplace *very* deep until it's over. Can you do it? Will your friends?"

"Well . . . yes. Some of 'em we've even had to sit on, practically, to keep from doing something stupid."

Sassinak grinned. "Change stupid to useful and get 'em rounded up. Let's go, everyone."

Coris had already left with Erdra and Bilis. Now Sassinak led the others at a good pace back to the lower levels. After the first shock of hearing that the *Zaid-Dayan* had left, she felt an unaccountable lift of spirits. The whole situation was impossible, but it would come out right.

In only a few hours, the fragile bond between the various groups began to strengthen. A trickle of students appeared, from one access tunnel and another, all with necessary equipment. Half a dozen standard 'phone repair kits, with the official connectors that wouldn't trip any alarms no matter where they were plugged in. Two police-issue belt-comps that included both communicators and tiny computers. Nineteen gas kits similar to the Fleet-issue one Sassinak carried.

"Where'd you get these?" she asked the short, chunky youth who brought them in. He blushed a deep rose and muttered something about the drama department. "Drama department?"

"We did Hostigge's *Breathless* last year and the director wanted realistic props. She's friendly with a guy at the local station who said these weren't really any good without the detox." At which point, he handed over a sackful of detox tubes. "Now these I got scrounging around in the junk stores over on Lollipi Street. Most of 'em have been used once, but I thought maybe . . ."

"How long have you been collecting them?" Something about the earnest sweating face impressed Sassinak. He reminded her of the best supply officers: longsided and sticky-fingered.

"Well, even before the play I thought maybe they'd be good for something, if somebody could synthesize the membranes. Then when we got the membrane masks and they didn't take 'em back, I thought . . ." His voice trailed away, as if he still didn't realize what he'd done.

"Good for you," she said.

She hoped he'd survive the coming troubles. He'd be worth recruiting. Of course, nineteen gas kits among hundreds didn't help much, but he'd had the right idea.

Meanwhile, with communications access to the topside, they knew what the news media were telling everyone. Erdra had tapped into the lower-level secured lines so they knew where the police patrols were. Sassinak found herself yawning again and when she counted the hours, realized she'd run over twenty-four again. Aygar was snoring in a corner of the crowded little maintenance area their group was in. She would have to sleep soon herself.

"Got it," came Erdra's triumphant cry.

Sassinak struggled up. She'd fallen asleep at some point and somebody had covered her with a blanket. She raked her fingers through her hair and wished she could have thirty seconds in her own refresher cabinet.

"Are you sure?" she heard someone else ask.

"Yes, because it's guarded like nothing else we've seen. It's *not* in the central city, though, where I'd have thought, but over here, map coordinates

13-H. Below the main tunnels. But look, it's not directly under any of them. So I got into an archive file and found the building specs." She was waving a hardcopy sheet and Sassinak grabbed it.

"It's a ship!" The others stared at her.

"It can't be," Erdra said. "It's underground."

"Silo construction." From the blank looks, none of them knew what that meant. "Look," and Sassinak pointed to her proof, "the stuff on top's designed to look like real buildings, but it's just shell. Probably even folds back. Down here, this is a lot more than self-contained habitat for a planet . . . this, and this," her finger stabbed at the plans. "Framing of a standard midsize personal yacht. My guess would be Bollanger Yards, maybe a hundred-fifty years ago. When was that section of the city built up?"

Erdra scowled, fiddled on the keyboard she now carried, and said, "Eighty-two years ago, subdivided for light industry. Before that, nothing but a single warehouse and . . . a derelict shuttle station, from back when private shuttles were legal."

"But a ship couldn't last that long, could it?" asked Gerstan.

"Easily, protected like that. They've maintained it. They'll have replaced obsolete equipment with new. No problem to them. And nothing wrong with the hull design. The question is, do they keep it fitted to launch?"

"Launch? From underground?"

Civilians! Did they not even know that *most* planetary defenses used some silo-sited missiles, often placed on moons or asteroids in the system, safe from random bombardment by stray rocks?

"Launch. As in, escape. If things get too hot. Which is precisely what we were planning to make them."

"How could we tell? And what will it do if it does launch? Will it start a fire?"

"Erdra, do you have a hardcopy of all the connection data?"

Wide-eyed, the girl handed over a sheaf of them. Sassinak began paging through as she talked.

"If it's the hull I think it is, and if it's got the engines it should have, then it will do more than start a fire if it launches. They won't have intended that silo to be used more than once. Its lining will combust to produce part of the initial lift and since they would only do it in an emergency, it's probably set to backblast down any communicating tunnels. Even though that wastes thrust, I doubt they'll care."

Her eyes scanned the sheets, translating into Fleet terms the different civilian notation. Yes. There. Solid chemical fuel, far more efficient than any in the dawn of the human space exploration, but still unstable and requiring replacement at intervals. So the hardened access tunnel for that alone, in case anything went wrong, would have blast hatches at both ends. He could still get away.

The old rage burned behind her eyes. So close, and he could still get away. She could almost see them getting near, breaking through one defense after another, only to be met by the blazing flare of the engines as the yacht lifted away from trouble to some luxurious hideyhole in another system.

< <Sassinak!> >

Her heart caught, then went on. A Weft—one of *her* Wefts—in range. She sent back an urgent query.

< <Ten marines, two of us, Timran piloting the shuttle.> >

The shuttle! Virtually helpless against real fighting craft, even a shuttle could take an unarmed yacht. Sassinak felt a rush of excitement. Now she had them trapped; The Parchandri and whoever his main conspirators were. She could block their escape. She could push them into it, make them commit themselves, show themselves. And then destroy them. She realized the others were looking at her oddly.

"Don't worry," she said. "That's not the disaster it seems like. In fact, when you know an enemy's bolthole, it becomes a trap."

"But if the ship goes up, how can we . . ."

Sassinak waved for quiet, and the babble died. "My cruiser dropped a shuttle, remember?" Heads nodded. She went on. "So if I get where I can contact them," and she waved her little comunit, "they can intercept it." She was not about to tell them she could talk to her Wefts. She'd heard enough racial slurs down here to convince her of that. "But there's plenty of work for the rest of you."

It would take pressure to make them run, pressure in the Grand Council, pressure underground. They must feel threatened every way but that. And she could not use these civilian lives freely. They were not hers to throw away, not even in such a cause.

Chapter Nineteen

FSP Escort **Brightfang**, *FedCentral Docking Station*

On the bridge of the escort vessel *Brightfang* by the courtesy of his old classmate Killin, Fordeliton had a startling view of the *Zaid-Dayan*'s departure as the escort approached the FedCentral Main Station. First he noticed that the Flight Bay was open, then he could see the elevator rising with a shuttle poised on its narrow surface. He wondered briefly if Sassinak were letting Timran run an errand as the shuttle lifted away, the Flight Bay closing in behind it. A few seconds later, the ship itself eased off the docking probe. He felt a great hollow open in his middle. He had counted on reporting to Sassinak the moment he arrived. He was in time for the trial. Why was she leaving? What would he do now?

"What's going on?" he asked.

No one answered. Killin looked angry as he spoke into his comset, but Ford could not quite hear what he said. The little ship shivered. Someone's tractor beam had swept it. He knew better than to ask anything more, and made himself as invisible as he could. Then Killin turned to him.

"They won't let us dock! They're holding us in position with the tractors and they're threatening worse."

"What's happened?"

"Your captain. According to them, she killed an admiral onplanet and whoever she left in charge of the *Zaid-Dayan* has gone completely bonkers, ghost-hunting. They think it's something catching, probably from Ireta."

"Arly! It'd be Arly if Sassinak left the ship. And Arly's *not* crazy. Patch me over to 'em."

Killin shook his head. "Can't. They've jammed us just in case. So far as they're concerned, Fleet personnel are all crazy until proven otherwise. They're not about to let us spread our damaging lies."

"They said *that?*" With astonishment came the sudden piercing loss. Where *was* Sassinak? In prison? Surely not dead! He realized that he did not want to deal with a world that had no Sassinak in it, not anywhere.

"They said it's worse than that. The Insystem Security officer I spoke to had been thrown off the *Zaid-Dayan*. By Wefts."

"But I've got orders. I've got to get this information down there in time for Tanegli's trial."

Killin shrugged. "Feel like space-swimming the last kilometer? And then I doubt they'll let you go down in a shuttle like a nice, harmless civilian."

"Why are they scared of you? They don't know you've got a deadly Iretan survivor with you."

Killin looked startled. "I forgot. You *were* there, weren't you? Snarks, if they figure that out . . ."

"We don't tell them. We don't tell them I have any connection to the *Zaid-Dayan* or Sassinak. I'm just a humble courier, carrying a sealed satchel from Sector HQ to FedCentral's Justice Center."

"I didn't pick you up at Sector HQ."

"And who knows that? Got a good reason for turning me over to these idiots?"

Killin shrugged. "No. But that still doesn't get you into the Station. If they relent . . ." He broke off as his comunit blinked at him and he cut the volume onto the cabin speakers.

". . . assurances that no member of your crew was at any time on the proscribed planet Ireta, which is believed to be the source of a plague affecting mental capacity, you will be allowed to dock and proceed with normal business."

Killin winked at Ford and spoke into the com. "Sir, this ship has never even been in the same sector as Ireta. We're a scheduled courier run between Sector Eight HQ and the capitol. We have a courier onboard, with urgent sealed messages from Sector to the Justice Center, as I believe your stripsheet will show."

A long pause, then another voice. "Right, Captain. You are on the sheet, listed as courier, with one passenger carrying papers under diplomatic seal. Is that right?"

"Yes, sir. The rest of the crew hasn't changed since the last run."

"Do you . . . ah . . . have any knowledge of the *Zaid-Dayan*'s crew? If any debarked at Sector HQ?" Killin raised his eyebrows at Ford, and Ford shook his head quickly, then scribbled a note to him. Killin began drawling his answer as he read.

"Well, only what we heard, you know, back at Sector. Whole crew was ordered to appear here as potential witnesses or something, is what I heard. Certainly didn't hear of anyone leaving the ship there."

Killin's grin at Ford was wolfish. He didn't like to lie, but this was not a lie. What Ford had told him in the week they'd been together was entirely separate from what he'd heard at Sector. More interesting, too.

"Very well. We will proceed with docking." Killin clicked the com off, and shook his head at Ford.

"You're going to have to be lucky to get away with this. And that captain of yours shouldn't be so trigger-happy. Admirals! I've known a few I'd like to blow away, but actually doing it gives such a bad impression to the Promotion Board."

Ford maintained the cool reserve expected of a courier all the way through Customs, an ordeal usually reserved for civilians, but in this instance imposed in its full rigor on every Fleet member. He gave his name, his rank, his number, and his current posting: special orders to Fleet Headquarters, FedCentral.

"Last ship posting?" This was almost a snarl.

Ford allowed himself a faint, sad smile. "I'm sorry to say, the *Zaid-Dayan*. I understand it's been a problem to you?"

He dared not try to conceal this, any more than his real identity. But the *Zaid-Dayan* had arrived in port without him, with someone else listed as Sassinak's second-in-command. He had a slight chance.

If the Insystem Security officer had had movable ears, they'd have pricked. He could feel the interest.

"Ah. And you served with Commander Sassinak?"

"Some time back, yes."

His tone indicated that the further back in time that association slipped, the happier he would be. The Security officer did not relax, but his eyelids flicked.

"And have you had contact with Commander Sassinak since?"

"No. I had no reason to contact the Commander once I left her . . .

command." Nothing so blatant as open hostility, just a chill. He had been
glad to leave her command, and no backward glances.

"I see." The officer looked down at a datascreen Ford could not see.
"This was before the Ireta incident?"

Ford nodded, tight-lipped, and muttered, "Yes."

They would have *his* files, but were unlikely to have the personnel history of the *Zaid-Dayan*.

"We show no ship assignments after that."

"I had special duty." It had indeed been special. "Plainclothes work;
I'm afraid I cannot comment on it."

"Ah. Duration?"

"Nor that, I'm sorry." Ford's regret was genuine. He'd have liked to tell
someone else about Madame Flaubert and her lapdog. "Some months, I can
say."

"And you've had no contact with Iretans since that assignment?"

Really it was too easy, the way the man asked all the wrong questions.
He didn't even have to lie.

"No. I reported directly, got my orders and boarded the next courier."

"Very well, then. We'll escort you to the next shuttle and to the Fleet
offices. There's been some unrest because of the . . . unfortunate incidents."

Ford gathered the details of the unfortunate incidents, at least as they
were known to the press, on his way downside. His escort, nervous at first but
increasingly relaxed as Ford showed no inclination to leap up and act crazy,
filled in what the news reports left out without adding any real information.

Sassinak had been onplanet and had killed someone. They were now
fairly sure it was *not* Admiral Coromell. Ford let his eyebrows rise. She and
the native Iretan had then disappeared, and nothing had been seen of them
since.

"Dear me," he said, stifling a yawn. "How tiresome."

His escort delivered him safely to the front door of Fleet offices. Ford
noticed that civilians did veer away from him, as if he might be contagious.
The marines on guard at the door saluted briskly and let him inside. So far, so
good, although he had no real idea what to do next. Still playing innocent
courier, he reported to the officer on duty and mentioned that he had important evidence for the Iretan matter.

"You! You're from *her* ship! How in Hades did you get through?" The
duty officer, a 'Tenant, had spoken loud enough to turn heads. Ford noticed
the quick glances.

"Easy, there," he said quietly, smiling. "I broke no laws and created no ruckus. Shall we keep it that way? And how about announcing me to the Admiral?"

"Admiral Coromell?"

"That's right." He glanced around and saw the eyes fall before his like wheat whipped by wind. Something wrong in *this* office, too. "I believe Commander Sassinak would have told him I was coming."

"N-no, sir. The Admiral's been offplanet, hunting over on Six. That's why we thought at first . . . why what they said . . . but the dead man wasn't Coromell . . ."

This made little sense. Ford tried to hack his way through the verbiage. "Is the Admiral aboard *now*?"

"Well, no, sir, he's not. He's en route, I've been told. No ETA yet. He was out hunting at the time of the—of whatever happened. That's why no one could reach him, you see, and . . ."

"I see." Ford would gladly have choked this blatherer, but he still had to find someone to share his information with. "Who's in charge, then?"

"Lieutenant Commander Dallish, but he's not available right now, sir. He was up all night, and he . . ."

Ford thought sourly that Dallish was probably a passed-over goofoff, lounging in bed in midafternoon just because he'd been up all night. Coromell had a good reputation, but if this office was any indication, he had quit earning that reputation some time back. He realized that the day's fatigues and surprises might have something to do with his attitude, but the planetside stinks had given him a headache. He wanted to hand over his highly important information, enjoy a decent fresh-cooked meal, and sleep. Now he could foresee that he was going to have to wait around for a lazy brother officer who would want to sit up and gossip about Sassinak. No. He would not play that game.

"Could you tell me where the Prosecutor's office is, then? I've got a hand delivery there, too."

The 'Tenant's ability to give clear directions met Ford's expectations, which were low. He accepted the offer of a marine guide and escort, and refused the suggestion that he would be less conspicuous in civilian clothes. He would take his evidence to the Prosecutor, he would find his own way back, by way of a decent restaurant. Surely the Prosecutor's staff would know of some.

By then, surely this Dallish would be awake, and if not . . . There was always a bunk in the Transient Officers Quarters. He had the uneasy feeling of being watched as he and his escort stepped onto the slideway, but shrugged it off. Of course he was being watched. The news had everyone paranoid about Fleet officers. But if he acted like a big, calm, bored errand-boy, nothing should happen to him.

Lunzie recognized his retreating back, but couldn't get Coromell's attention until Ford was out of sight.

"Who?" Coromell said, peering at the crowded slideway.

"Ford!" Lunzie was ready to cry with sheer frustration. It was impossible that *everything* could go so wrong. "Sassinak's Exec, from the *Zaid-Dayan*. He was *here!*"

"Omigod!" Dallish slammed his hand onto the windowframe. "It's my fault. You'd told us he was coming, but I was still thinking he'd report to his ship first. He must've gotten to the Station *after* . . ."

"We'll find him. Just call down and ask the duty officer where he went."

But although he told Dallish where Ford was going, they could not find him again. All communications to the Prosecutor's office were blocked.

"Lines engaged. Please call again later" in muted synthetic speech so sweet Lunzie wanted to gag.

"There's got to be a way," she said. "Can't you break into the line?"

"I'm trying. We don't want anyone to know the Admiral's here yet," Dallish said, "so I can't use his special code."

By the time they *did* get through, it was after hours as the computer's secretarial function insisted. When they worked their way through the multiple layers of authority and back down through the same layers trying to find the person to whom Ford would have reported if he'd been there, he'd already left. Without an escort. No, nobody knew where he'd gone. He'd been asking around for good places to eat, and the speaker thought he'd talked most to someone who had left even earlier. Sorry.

"He'll come back here," said Coromell, without much conviction. "It's standard procedure."

"Nothing in this entire situation is standard procedure," Lunzie said. "Why should he follow it?"

It came out sharper than she intended, and she realized all at once that she was hungry again and very, very tired.

Despite his confident insistence that he could certainly get something to eat and find his own way back to the Fleet offices, Ford was not entirely sure just where he was. After a long wrangle about what he considered minor matters, he had left the Prosecutor's office. It wasn't anyone's business but his captain's exactly when and where he'd left the *Zaid-Dayan* to visit his great-aunt. They'd had his original taped deposition; he hadn't wanted to repeat it.

The Prosecutor's staff gave him the distinct impression that Sassinak's disappearance with Aygar and Lunzie's non-appearance were somehow his fault. At least he was there to be griped at. He had pointed out that since the first report that the dead man was an admiral had been wrong, the report that Sassinak had anything to do with the murder might be wrong, too.

And where was she? he was asked, and he replied, with what he thought of as massive self-control, that he had no earthly idea, having arrived only that afternoon. He had parted from the staff in no mood to take the precautions they advised. It had been his experience on dozens of worlds that a confident walk, clean fingernails, and the right credit chip would keep him out of avoidable trouble, while good reflexes and a strong right arm would get him out of the rest. So he had walked along, working off the irritation until the right combination of smells led him into a dark little place which had the food its aroma promised.

Hot food, a good drink, and he felt much better about the world. He let himself wonder, for the first time consciously, where Sassinak was. What had *really* happened. He could not believe she was dead, stuffed in a trash bin down some sleazy alley. He wondered where Arly was going with the *Zaid-Dayan*, and what Sassinak thought about *that*, and if Timran had been piloting that shuttle, and who else might be in it.

Thinking about these things, he'd paid his bill with a smile and gone out into the darkening evening where the streets looked subtly different than they had in the sulfurous light of late afternoon. Of course he could stop someone and ask. Or he could go to any of the lighted kiosks and find his location on the display map. But he could always do that later, if he turned out to be really lost. At the moment, he didn't feel lost. He just felt that he wanted a good after-dinner walk.

When he realized that he'd walked far beyond the well-lighted commercial district where he'd had dinner, it was dark enough to make the next lighted transportation access attractive. Ford had walked off most of his ruffled feelings. He realized it much smarter to take a subway back to the central square. He was even pleased with himself for being so careful. Only a few dark shapes moved to and from the lighted space above the entrance. Ford ignored them without failing to notice which might turn troublesome as he rode the escalator down.

For a moment, he considered continuing to the lowest level, and seeing if he could find out anything about Sassinak. Every city had its denizens of the night, usually easy enough to find in tunnels and alleys at night. But he wasn't dressed for that. He would hardly fit in, and if Sassinak had plans of her own going forward, he would only get in her way.

At the foot of the escalator, he stood at the back of the platform, waiting for the next train to come. Only a small group, men and women both, who eyed his Fleet uniform and gave him room. When the train came in, he checked the number to be sure it would take him all the way in without a transfer, letting the others crowded into the first car. Ford shrugged, and stepped into the second without really looking. He had seen only a few heads in the windows. He was all the way in and the doors had thumped firmly behind him, when he realized what he saw. Thirteen Fleet uniforms, and two very nervous civilians who sat stiffly at one end trying to pretend they saw nothing.

"Ensign Timran," Ford said, as if he'd seen him only a few hours ago. And in a way, he had. "You do get around, don't you?" He let his eyes rest a moment on each one, and did not miss the very slight relaxation. Whatever they were up to, he had been instantly accepted as a help. Fine. When he found out what they were supposed to be doing, he would help. In the meantime . . . " 'Tenant Sricka, I presume you're in charge of this little outing?"

A quick flick of eyes back and forth made it clear what part of the problem had been. Timran, in command as long as he was piloting a ship, had not been quick to relinquish that command on the ground. Sricka, a tactful Weft, had not wanted to risk confusion by confronting him: not on what might be enemy territory, in front of the enlisted marines. Ford acknowledged that tact with a quirk of his mouth. Even Timran wouldn't argue with the Excc of the *Zaid-Dayan*, a Lieutenant Commander's stripes on his sleeves.

"Suppose I fill you in on a slight change of plans," he said. "After you fill me in on a few necessary details, such as where you left the shuttle and how many you left with it."

Timran leaned forward, keeping his voice low. Ford, who had been unconvinced of Tim's reformation after Ireta, approved.

"Sir, it's under shields on the replanted end of the landfill. 'Tenant Sricka recommended that site because it was remote from the city center but near a subway line. We left no one aboard, because we . . . I . . . we thought that we might need everyone to help the captain. Sir."

Which meant Sricka had tried to explain the stupidity of taking that many uniformed men into a situation where Fleet uniforms might precipitate panic, but Tim hadn't listened and now wished he had. Typical. Ford shifted his gaze to the Weft.

"Do you know where she is?"

"I believe I can find her, sir, given a chance to shift. It's easier that way."

"For which you need privacy, if we don't want to scare the horses. Right! Let me think." He tried to remember how many stops he'd passed during his walk. If only those civilians hadn't been in this car! They'd probably report this concentration of Fleet to someone as soon as they got out. That decided him. "We're getting off at the next stop. Just follow me."

He didn't know where the civilians would get off, but they didn't move when Ford stood and led the others off at the next stop. This one was no larger than the other, with only a narrow bridge to the outbound platform, and no privacy whatever. But if he led them all up to the street, they'd be just as noticeable. Unless, of course, he could get those uniforms out of sight. He got them all as far from the others on the platform as he could and explained.

"You marines are MPs, and I'm your commanding officer. These dirt-siders don't know one uniform from another. At least the civilians don't. These others are belligerent drunks that we're trying to get back to the city as quietly as possible."

The Wefts, consummate actors, nodded and grinned. Timran looked both worried and stubborn. Ford leaned closer to him.

"That's not a suggestion, Ensign; that's an order. Now say 'I'm not drunk' and take a swing at the sergeant there."

Timran said it in the startled voice of one who hopes it's not true, swung wildly, and the sergeant, grinning, enacted his role with vigor.

"Don't you bother 'im," Sricka said, tugging ineffectually at the sergeant's arm. "He's not drunk, it's just his birthday!"

"Happy *birthday* to him!" shouted the other Weft, entering into the game gleefully.

The marines grappled, struggled, and started their drunken charges up to street level with difficulty while Ford, still spotless, apologized coolly to the civilians on the platform.

"Sorry. Young officers, a long way from home. No excuse, really, but they're all like this at least once. Get 'em home, let 'em sleep it off, and they'll get their ears peeled in the morning."

With a crisp nod, he followed his noisy troop up the escalator. With any luck, they'd assume that this had nothing whatever to do with the *Zaid-Dayan*. Ford had never found a planet yet that didn't know about drunken young soldiers. On the streetside, his group wavered to a halt, waiting for his direction.

"That way," he said. "Just be prepared to do your act again if I signal. If it's official, let me do all the talking. I landed quite legally this afternoon by the official shuttle and all my papers are in order. Now tell me. Who's got the *Zaid-Dayan*, and what's going on up there?"

Sricka took up the tale, and in a few sentences explained what he knew. Little enough, but Ford agreed that a Ssli would be unlikely to make a mistake.

"If they say a Seti invasion, I'll buy it. What's Fleet have insystem?"

Sricka did not know that. Ford thought about the information lock put on the invasion news, and wished he could talk to his old buddy Killin. But at least Arly could call for help via the IFTL link. Ford decided not to worry about what he couldn't change. That brought his thoughts back to their uniforms, even more conspicuous as they came into better-lighted streets.

"And your orders?"

"Captain . . . Commander Arly told me to take a shuttle down in case the captain, Commander Sassinak, that is, needed it. To do whatever it took to help her."

"Well, then. First we'll have to find her, then we'll know what help she needs. And to do that, we'll have to look less like what we are. Here, hold up this lamppost for a minute." He had spotted a larger, much busier subway access, the kind that would have shops and other facilities on the platform below. "Sergeant, if anyone asks, tell 'em your officer went down to make a call to the office to get a vehicle."

Back down underground again. He found he was enjoying this much more than he should have. Even the contrast to Auntie Q's luxurious entourage cheered him. He found an automated clothing outlet where commuters who had just spilled something on their suit on the way to a conference could get a replacement. He dared not buy clothes for all of them, but two or three coveralls wouldn't be excessive.

No, four: the least expensive garment came in green, blue, gray, and brown. He inserted his card, punched the buttons, and caught the sealed packets as they came out of the slot. No one seemed to be watching. Back up the escalator, packages in hand, to find the group had put on a small show for a group of late diners who'd stopped to ask questions about Ireta's mysterious plague.

He took control, briskly and firmly, and marched his troops off as if to a definite destination. Half a block later, he slowed them down again. The Wefts wouldn't find much privacy in the subway tunnels of the inner city this early in the night. He glanced back at the marines, and met the wary glance of their sergeant. Who'd picked them? Arly? Currald? Whoever it was had had sense enough to send more than one NCO. Which should he peel off for Sassinak? The old rule held: don't tell 'em how to do it, just tell the sergeant what you need done.

"Sergeant, the Wefts'll need a couple of marines just in case someone comes after 'em while they're hunting the captain." Not that the Wefts couldn't outfight any three humans while in their own shapes, but he suspected that the mental concentration needed for hunting her could take the edge off their other abilities. "Take these clothes and the next dark patch we come to, put 'em on over your uniforms. That'll take care of three of you. One Fleet uniform shouldn't be too dangerous. Then take off. 'Tenant Sricka, you find the captain, and tell her where the shuttle is. Find out what she needs. If she can't contact me, you do or send one of the marines. Can you find *me*, the way you sense her?"

Sricka frowned, then smiled. "I was about to say we couldn't, sir, but you've changed."

"That's what I was told," said Ford, remembering the demise of Madame Flaubert.

"But it would be easier if one of us stayed with you."

Ford shook his head. "I know, but we don't know how bad her situation is. She may need both of you, or it may be harder than you expect to find her in a maze of tunnels. It's not like free space. If she knows she has you and a shuttle when she needs it. Which reminds me. Ensign."

"Sir?"

"You've got the toughest assignment. You're going to have to get back out to the shuttle—alone—and be ready for a call. Can't even guess when we're going to need you, or for what, but I know absolutely without a doubt we will, and we won't have time for you to take the subway back out there. D'you have rations on board for several days?"

"Yes, sir, but . . ."

"Ensign, if I could send someone back with you I would. I need all the rest of these in the city, nearby, in case she wants them. This is not an easy assignment for someone your age." That stiffened Tim's backbone, as he'd hoped. "But Commander Sassinak's told me you have potential, and if you do, young man, this is the time to show it."

"Yes, sir. Anything else?"

"Yes. Take this." The last package of civilian clothes. "Put it on first, then go straight to the subway, and back out to the shuttle. Try to look like a young man who's just been told he has to go back to work and fix a problem.

Shouldn't be too hard. Get some sleep. Whatever breaks won't break right away. Just be sure you're ready to get that thing up the instant we call for you. I'll try to patch a call to you from the Fleet offices when we get back, in an hour or so, but don't count on it."

"Yes, sir."

In the next darker patch, Ford got them into a huddle. When it opened again, one "civilian" headed back to the subway access, while three others and a marine continued to the next. Ford led the other nine on toward the center of the city. It was a lovely evening for a walk.

Chapter Twenty

Trial day. The early news reports had more speculation about the myste-rious shuttle that had disappeared "somewhere near the city" and the strange plague which supposedly afflicted anyone who'd been to Ireta. Riots in the maintenance tunnels, controlled by police with only minor loss of life.

Sassinak winced. She and Aygar and her crewmembers had just escaped the pitched battle that erupted when the Pollys tried gas on tunnel rats who had gas masks and weapons. She hoped the newssheet was right in reporting so few deaths. Only the knowledge that she *had* to fight the main battle elsewhere let her live with the decision to run for it. The lower third of the page mentioned the trial and Council hearing on Ireta's status.

Sassinak watched Aygar reading, his lips pursed angrily. She already knew what it said. No precedent for overturning a Thek claim. But at least he was alive, and if she could get him into the Council chamber that way, he should have a chance to testify.

Erdra had come back before dawn with a half dozen of the pearly cards that guaranteed admission, each one embossed with the name of its carrier. Sassinak had become "Commander Argray, Fleet Liaison" for the duration, and Aygar was "Blayanth, Federation Citizen." She hoped these faked IDs and the database entries backing them up would let them get into Council without being quarantined as dangerous lunatics. According to news reports, the lines for public seating had extended across the plaza by midnight. If the "invitations" didn't work, they wouldn't have a chance at open seats. A number of the student activists had been in the lines early, but no one knew which, if any, of those waiting would be admitted.

At least, Sassinak thought, she looked like herself again. Bless Arly for thinking of the clean uniform; familiar in every seam, comforted her almost as much as the bridge of her ship. So did the change in Erdra's eyes when Sassinak appeared in regal white and gold, now suiting the image Erdra had imagined.

"Should be starting now." Sassinak nodded to their guide without speaking. Aygar shoved the newssheet he'd been reading in a disposal slot, and came along.

"Do you think we'll get in?" he asked for the fourth or fifth time. After that he'd ask what they'd do if this didn't work. She was trying to be patient, but it got harder.

"No good reason it shouldn't work. It . . ." Internal and external communications layered in confusion for a moment. Then she realized that a Weft onplanet had managed to link her with a Weft on the *Zaid-Dayan*, and with its Ssli, and thence to Dupaynil on a Seti ship somewhere at the edge of the system.

"A *Seti* ship!" she muttered aloud, and caught a worried glance from Aygar. "Sorry," she said, and clamped her lips shut. < <What are you doing on a Seti ship?> > she asked Dupaynil.

< <Wishing I hadn't ever made you mad.> > Whether it was his mind, or the Weft linkage, that sounded both contrite and humble, qualities she'd never associated with Dupaynil.

< <Are you alone?> >

< <No. A Weft, a larval Ssli, two Lethi, a Ryxi, and a Bronthin are my companions in durance vile. The Seti want witnesses to their power. Then they'll eat us.> >

< <No way. We'll get you out.> >

How she was going to do that, while stranded onplanet with Aygar, in the middle of a Grand Council trial and hearing that was expected to turn into a revolution, she did not know. But she couldn't let him think she wouldn't try.

< <Don't fret . . . we're sending data to Arly. And I got what you wanted on the Seti, and more. That *Claw* escort was suborned. All but one of the crew were in with the pirates and in the pay of the Paradens.> >

Sassinak hoped he could interpret the cold wash of amazement tha took all the words from her mind. She had been furious with him, but she hadn't intended *that*.

Now his contact carried a thread of amusement. < <That's all right. I didn't think you knew. But if I live through this, you may have to fix some charges for me and a young Jig named Panis. > >

< <What charges? > >

< <Mutiny, for one. Misappropriation of government property, grievous bodily harm . . . > >

< <We'll get you out alive. I have *got* to hear this. > >

But right now she was too close to the Council buildings and she had to concentrate on her surroundings. Aygar strode along beside her, looking as belligerent as any Diplonian. Her Wefts from the shuttle, and two marines, had faked IDs as well. Would it work?

They came to a checkpoint in the angle between a colonnade and the massive Council building. One heavyworlder in Federation Insystem Security uniform stood behind a short counter. Behind it, lined against the wall, were five others. Sassinak handed over the embossed strip, saw it fed into a machine, and checked against a list. The heavyworlder's gaze came up and lingered on her in a way she did not like.

"Ah! Commander Argray. Your invitation's in order, ma'am. You may enter through that door." He pointed. As they had planned, Sassinak moved on, as if she had no connection with Aygar.

She heard the guard's voice behind her, speaking to Aygar and then Aygar's steps following hers.

The doorway fit the massive building; heavy bronze, centered with the Federation seal. Before Sassinak could reach, it opened flat against the wall for her. She entered the Grand Council chamber through a little alcove off the main room and just below the dais where the eight justices and the Speaker had their seats. Across from her, one wall appeared to be a single massive stone, a warm brown with gold flecks. Delegate seating curved around an open area below the dais, separated from the public seating behind by a tall barrier of translucent plastic. Each seat was actually the size of a sentry hut, or more, and in front of each delegate's seat, a colorful seal inlaid in the chamber floor gave the member's race and planet of reference. Sassinak could not see the public seating clearly, but it seemed to rake steeply toward a narrow balcony festooned with the lights and cables of recording and projection equipment.

Seating for invited guests was enclosed in a railing somewhat like an old-fashioned jury box, although much larger. Already this was filling up, with rather more heavyworlders than Sassinak would have expected. That fit the rumors of an impending coup. She found three seats together, and settled in, with Aygar between her and one of the Wefts. Aygar said nothing to her, and she watched her other crew come in. The other Weft and the two marines found scattered seats where they could catch her eye.

She had never really wondered what the Grand Council chamber was like. The few times she'd seen it on broadcasts, the focus had been on the Speaker's podium backed by the Federation seal. Now she looked up to see a high, ribbed ceiling, with dangling light pods. Behind the Speaker's podium and the justice's high-backed chairs, the great seal stood at least three meters high, its colors muted now in the dimmer light. From her seat, she could see through the plastic behind the delegates' seats more easily and realized that, early as it was, the public seating was nearly full. At the far end of the arc formed by the delegates' places, another enclosed seating area had only a sprinkling of occupants. She wondered if that was for witnesses. She could not see any of them clearly enough to know if Lunzie or Ford were there.

Soon the delegates began to come in, each preceded by an honor guard of Federation Insystem troops. Each delegate's seat, Sassinak realized, was actually an almost self-contained environmental pod with full datalinks. She watched as the delegates tested their seats. Colored lights appeared, to show the vote. A clerk standing by the Speaker's podium murmured into a microphone, confirming to the occupant the practice vote just cast.

A whiff of sulfur made her wrinkle her nose, as a *steth* of Lethi came in, looking like so many pale yellow puffballs stuck together into a vaguely regular geometric shape. They disappeared completely into their seat, closing a shiny panel behind them. Sassinak assumed they would open a sealed pack of sulfur inside, where it wouldn't foul the air for anyone else. A pair of Bronthin arrived, conversing nose-to-nose in the breathy whuffles of their native speech. She had never seen Bronthin in real life. They looked even more like pale blue plush horses than their pictures. Hard to believe they were the best mathematicians among the known sentient races. A Ryxi, loaded with ceremonial chains and stepping with exaggerated care, clacked its beak impatiently. A second Ryxi scuttled into the room behind it, carrying a mesh bag in the claw of its right wing and hissing apologies. Or so Sassinak assumed. The Weft delegate arrived in Weft form, to Sassinak's surprise. Then she was surprised at herself for being surprised. After all, as his race's representative, why should he try to look human?

She was surprised again when the Seti came in. She had not expected to see them except in battle armor. But here they were, tail-ornaments jingling and necklaces swaying, their heavy tails sweeping from side to side as they strolled to their seats. She could read nothing of their expressions. Their scaled, snouted faces might have been intended to convey reassurance. Sassinak wondered suddenly if the Seti had politics as humans understood them. Did all Seti support the Sek, were they all involved in this invasion? Could the ambassadors be ignorant of the Sek's plans?

She gave herself a mental shake. Interpreting Seti politics was someone else's responsibility. She had enough to do already. Rightly or wrongly, she had to assume they were part of it. She glanced around. Dark figures on the balcony slipped from one cluster of equipment to another. Lights appeared, narrowed or broadened in focus, changed color, disappeared again. The speaker's podium suddenly glowed in a sunburst of spotlights, then retreated into the relative dimness of the overhead panels.

The crowd's murmur grew, punctuated by a raised voice, a sneeze, a chain of coughs that began on one side and worked its way to the other. She could feel her skin tighten as the circulation fans went up a notch to maintain an even temperature. Now the legal staffs involved came in, bustling in their dark robes, each with the little gray curl of a wig that looked equally ridiculous on humans and aliens. She wondered who had ever thought up that symbol of legal expertise and why everyone else had adopted it.

Federation Court guards, also heavyworlders, brought in Tanegli who looked as if he could barely walk. Beside her, she felt Aygar stiffen and wished she could take his hand. Anger radiated from him, then slowly faded. Had he realized how useless his hatred of Tanegli was? As useless as her hatred of the Paradens.

She shouldn't think about that, not *now*, but the thought prickled the inside of her mind anyway. It was one thing to hunt them down for the wrong they had done, and another to let herself be shaped wholly by their malice. She couldn't ignore that. Abe had said it, had told the woman he loved, had urged her to find Sassinak someday and tell her. And Lunzie, who had admired her descendant the cruiser captain, would not be so happy with an avenging harpy.

The lights flared, then dimmed, and a gong rang out. Spotlights stabbed through the gloom to illuminate the door they'd come in, where two huge heavyworlders now stood with ceremonial staves, which they pounded on the floor.

"All rise!" came a stentorian voice over the sound system, "for the Right Honorable, the Speaker of the Grand Council of the Federation of Sentient Planets, the Most Noble Eriach d'Ertang. And for the Most Honorable Lords Justice . . ." The floor shook to another ceremonial pounding. The heavyworlder guards led in the procession.

The Speaker, a wiry little Bretagnan who looked dwarfed by the heavyworlders in front of him and the eight Justices behind him were each followed by a clerk of the same race carrying something on a silver tray. Sassinak had no idea what *that* was but overheard another guest explain to someone who asked that these were the Justices' credentials, proof that they were each eligible to sit on that bench.

"Of course it's all done by the computers, now," the knowledgeable one murmured on. "But they still carry in the hardcopy as if they needed it."

"And who are those men with the big carved things?"

"Bailiffs," came the explanation. "If I talk much more, they'll be after me. They keep order."

Sassinak found it very different from a military court. She assumed that part of the elaborate ceremony came from its combination with a Grand Council meeting. But there were long, flowery, introductory speeches welcoming the right noble delegate from this, and the most honorable delegate from that, while the lawyers and clerks muttered at one another behind a screen of hands, and the audience yawned and shuffled their feet.

Each Justice had an introduction, equally flowery, during which he, she, or it tried not to squirm in the spotlight. Then the Speaker took over. He began with a review of the rules governing spectators, then guests, then witnesses, any infractions of which, he said slowly, would be met with immediate eviction by the bailiffs, "—to the prejudice of that issue to which the unruly individual or individuals appeared to be speaking, if that can be determined."

Very different from court martials, Sassinak thought. She had never seen unruliness in a military court. Then came a roll call, another check of each delegate's datalink to the Speaker's podium, and the voting displays of all delegates and Justices. By now, thought Sassinak, we could have been through with an entire trial.

At last the Speaker read out the agenda on which Tanegli's trial appeared as "In the matter of the Federation of Sentient Planets vs. one Tanegli, and the related matter of the status of native-born children of Federation citizens on the planet Ireta!"

Sassinak felt Aygar's shiver of excitement. The moment the Speaker had finished, one of the bewigged and gowned lawyers stood up. This, it seemed, was the renowned defense counsel Pinky Vigal. He seemed tame enough to Sassinak, a mild-mannered older man who hardly deserved the nickname Pinky. But she heard from the industrious explainer behind her that it had nothing to do with his appearance, coming rather from the closing argument in a case he had won many years back. This explanation, long and detailed, finally caught the attention of a bailiff who shook his staff at the guest seating box, instantly hushing the gossiper.

A formal dance of legality ensued, with Defense Counsel and the Chief Prosecutor deferring to one another's expertise with patent insincerity, and the Justices inserting nuggets of opinion when asked. Pinky Vigal wanted to sever his client's trial for mutiny, assault, murder, conspiracy, and so on from any consideration of the claims of those born on Ireta, inasmuch as recent evidence indicated that a noxious influence of the planet or its biosphere might be responsible for his behavior. And that evidence was so recent that his client's trial should be put off until the defense had time to consider its import.

The Prosecutor insisted that the fate of Iretan native-borns, and of the planet itself, could not be severed from consideration of the crimes of Tanegli and the other conspirators. Defense insisted that taped depositions from witnesses were not adequate, and must not be admitted into evidence, and the Prosecution insisted that they were admissable.

During all this, Tanegli sat slumped at his attorney's side, hardly moving his head.

This boring and almost irrelevant legal dance seemed likely to take awhile. Sassinak had time to wonder again where the others were. Dupaynil she knew about, at least in outline, but what about Ford? She was sure that if Ford had been on a Seti ship, he'd have somehow taken control and arrived in time for the trial. But where was he? He was supposed to have acquired more backup troops. So far she'd seen nothing but heavyworlders wearing Federation Insystem uniforms.

And Lunzie? Had she not made it back from Diplo? Had something happened to her there? Or here? Aygar could testify about what he'd been told by the heavyworlders who reared him, damning enough to ensure conviction on some of the charges. But they needed Lunzie or Varian or Kai for the original mutiny.

Despite the briefings she'd had in both the local Fleet headquarters and the Chief Prosecutor's office, Sassinak really did not understand exactly how this case would be tried or whose decision mattered most. A case like this didn't fit neatly into any category although she'd realized that lawyers' perspective would be far different from hers. To them it was not a matter of right and wrong, of guilt or innocence, but of a tangle of competing jurisdictions, competing and conflicting statutes, possible alternative routes of prosecution and defense: a vast game-board in which it was "fun" to stretch all rules to their elastic limit.

She doubted that they ever thought of the realities: those people and places whose realities had no elasticity, whose lives were shattered with the broken laws, the torn social contract. Now the Justices finished handing down decisions on the initial requests and the Prosecutor opened with a history of the Iretan expedition.

Sassinak kept her mind on it with an effort. All the details of the EEC's contracts, decisions, agreements, and subcontracts wafted in one ear and out the other. Lunzie's version had been far more vivid. Display screens lit with the first of the taped testimony on data cube videos taken by the original expedition team, before the mutiny. There were the jungles, the golden flyers, the fringes, the dinosaurs . . . a confusion of lifeforms. The expedition members, going about their tasks. The children trying hard to look appropriately busy for their pictures.

A light came on above one of the delegate's seats and the translators broadcast the question in Standard.

"Are these the native born Iretan children making claim for the planet?"

"No, Delegate. These children's parents lived aboard the EEC vessel, and given this furlough onplanet as an educational experience."

The light stayed on, blinking, and another question came over the speaker system.

"Did the native born Iretan children send a representative?"

Sassinak wondered where that delegate had been for the past several days since Aygar's involvement in her escapades had been all over the news media. The Chief Prosecutor looked as if he'd bitten into something sour and it occurred to Sassinak that the delegate might be already in the defense faction.

"Yes, Delegate, a representative of these children did come, but . . ."

Aygar stood before Sassinak could grab him, and said, "I'm here!"

A chorus of hisses, growls, and the massive heavyworlder bailiff nearest their box slammed his staff on the floor.

"Order!" he said.

Sassinak tugged on Aygar's arm and he sat down slowly. The Speaker glared at the Chief Prosecutor.

"Did you not instruct your witness where he was to go and what the rules of this court are?"

"Yes, Speaker, but he disappeared in . . . ah . . . suspicious circumstances. He was abducted, apparently by a Fleet . . ."

The Chief Prosecutor's voice trailed away when he realized what that gold and white uniform next to Aygar must mean. Sassinak let herself grin, knowing that the media cameras would be zooming in on her face.

"Irregularities of this sort can precipitate mistrials," said Pinky Vigal, with a sweetness of tone that affected Sassinak like honey on a sawblade. "If the Federation Prosecutor has not readied his witnesses, we shall have no objection to a delay."

"No." The Chief Prosecutor glared. Defense Counsel shrugged and sat down. "With the indulgence of the Speaker and Justices, and all Delegates here assembled"—the ritual courtesy rattled off his tongue so fast Sassinak could hardly follow it—"if I may call the Iretan witness *and any other* from the guest seating?"

Above the Justices' seats, blue lights flashed, and the Speaker nodded.

"As long as you remember that it *is* indulgence, Mr. Prosecutor, and refrain from making a habit of it. We are aware of the unusual circumstances. And I suppose this may keep Defense from claiming your witnesses were coached excessively."

Even Pinky Vigal chuckled at that, throwing his hands out in a disarming gesture of surrender that did not fool Sassinak one bit. She felt the rising tension in the chamber. Would Aygar's presence make the conspirators here give their signal earlier or later? They must be wondering what other surprises could turn up. The delegate who had asked the original question had either understood this wrangling, or given up, because its light was out. The Prosecutor went on, outlining the events of the mutiny, of the attempted murder of the lightweights . . .

"*Alleged* attempted murder," interrupted Pinky Vigal.

The Prosecutor smiled, bowed, and called for "Our first witness, Dr. Lunzie Mespil."

Sassinak felt the surge of excitement from the crowd that almost overwhelmed her own. So Lunzie *had* made it! She saw a stir in the witness box, then a slim figure in Medical Corps uniform coming to the stand. Her pulse raced. Lunzie looked so *young*, so vulnerable, just like the younger sister that Sassinak had lost might have looked. Incredible to think that she had been alive a hundred years before Sassinak was born.

Lunzie began to give her evidence in the calm, measured voice that gradually eased the tension Sassinak felt. But a light flashed from one of the delegate's seats, this time with an objection instead of a question.

"This witness has no legal status! This witness is a thief and liar, a fugitive from justice!"

Sassinak stiffened and found that this time Aygar had grabbed her wrist to keep her down. Lunzie, white-faced, had turned to the accusing delegate's place.

"This witness pretended medical competence to gain entrance to Diplo, and then stole and escaped with valuable information vital to our planetary security. We demand that this witness's testimony be discarded, and that she be returned to the proper authorities for trial on Diplo!"

More lights flashed. As the Prosecutor tried to answer the Diplo delegate, others had questions, comments, discussion. Finally the Speaker got them in order again, and spoke himself to Lunzie.

"Is this accusation true?"

"Not . . . in substance, sir."

"In what way?"

"I did go to Diplo with a medical research team. My specialty and background suited me for the work. While there I was abducted, drugged, and put into coldsleep. I awoke here, on this planet, with no knowledge of the means of my departure from Diplo. I daresay it *was* illegal. I hope it was illegal to do that to a Federation citizen with a valid entrance visa."

"You lie, lightweight!" The Diplo delegate had not waited for the translator. He'd used Standard himself. "You seduced a member of our government, stole data cubes . . ."

"I did nothing of the sort!" Sassinak was amazed at Lunzie's calm. She might have been an experienced teacher dealing with an unruly nine year old. "It is true that I met an old friend, who had become a government official, but as for seducing him . . . Remember that I had lost over forty years in coldsleep between our meetings. The handsome young man I remembered was now old and sick, even dying."

"He's dead *now*, yes." That was vicious, in a tone intended to hurt, with implications clear to everyone.

Sassinak peeled Aygar's fingers off her wrist, one by one. He gave her a worried sideways glance and she shook her head slightly. Lunzie still stood calmly, balanced, apparently untouched by the Diplonian's verbal assault. Had she expected it? Sassinak thought not.

The Speaker intervened again. "Did you file a complaint about your alleged abduction?"

"Naturally, I informed the Prosecutor's office. They had me in for illegal entry."

"Well?" The Speaker was looking at the Prosecutor who shrugged.

"We took her information, but since she had no particulars to offer and we have no authority to investigate crimes on Diplo, we considered that she was lucky to be alive and took no action."

Sassinak might have missed the signal if Aygar had not reacted to it with an indrawn breath.

"What?" she murmured, turning to look at him.

"Tanegli's handsign. That guard just gave it and the other one . . ."

"Lying lightweight!" Again the Diplo delegate's bellow attracted all eyes. Or almost all. Sassinak saw the guard nearest the witness stand shift his weight, the reflections from his chestful of medals suddenly moving. What was he . . . Then she recognized the position.

"Lunzie! *DOWN!*" Her voice carried across the chamber effortlessly.

Lunzie dropped just as the guard's massive leg swept across the railing. It could have killed her if he'd connected. Sassinak herself was out of the guest box, with Aygar only an instant behind her. Lunzie popped back up and, with deceptive gentleness, tapped the guard on the side of the neck. He sagged to his knees just as Sassinak met the first bailiff's staff.

"ORDER!" the Speaker yelled into the microphone, but it was far too late for that.

The bailiff had not expected Sassinak's combination of tuck, roll, strike, and pivot, and found his own staff suddenly out of his hands and aimed at his head. Single-minded in his original rage, Aygar had launched himself across the Defense table to grapple with Tanegli. A gaggle of legal clerks flailed at Aygar with papers and briefcases, trying to save their client from summary execution.

The eight justices had rolled out of their exposed seats, and only the Ryxi's head peered out as it chittered furiously in its own language. Most of the delegates had shut themselves into their sealed seats, but the heavyworlders from Diplo and Colrin emerged, clad in space armor which they must have worn under their ceremonial robes.

Sassinak tossed Lunzie the bailiff's staff just as the guard Lunzie had hit came up again. Lunzie slammed the heavy knob onto his head, then swung the length violently to knock a needler free from a guard who aimed at Sassinak. When one of Sassinak's Wefts shifted to Weft shape, a Seti delegate stormed out of its seat, screaming Seti curses that needed no translation. Sassinak snatched at the Seti's neck-chain only to be slammed aside by the powerful tail. She rolled and came up on her feet to face a grinning heavyworlder with a needler who never saw the Weft that landed on his head and broke his neck.

Sassinak caught the needler and tried again to reach Aygar, but he and the defense lawyers were all rolling around in an untidy heap behind the table. She yelled, but doubted he could hear her. Noise beat at the walls of the chamber as the watching crowd surged up to get a better view, and then discovered its own will.

"Down with the Pollys!" came a scream from the upper rows as the students from the Library tossed paint balloons that splattered uselessly on the plastic screen.

"Lightweight scum!" replied a block of heavyworlders, followed by blows, screams, and the high sustained yelp of the emergency alarm system.

Down below, Sassinak faced worse problems, despite the defensive block she had formed with Lunzie, the Wefts and the two marines. The Speaker lay dead, his skull smashed by the Diplonian delegate who now bellowed commands into the microphone. Aygar crawled out of the ruins of the table and ducked barely in time to avoid a slug through the head.

"Over here!" Sassinak yelled. His head moved. He finally saw her. "Stay *down!*" She gestured. He nodded. She hoped he understood.

In through the door pounded another squad of Insystem Security heavyworlder marines. Three of the Justices tried to break for the door, falling to merciless arms, as Sassinak's group dived for what cover they could find. It wasn't much and the three staves and one small-bore needler they'd captured so far weren't equivalent weaponry.

This would be a good time for help to arrive, Sassinak thought.

"Yield, hopeless ones!" screamed the Diplonian. "Your fool's reign is over! Now begins the glorious . . ."

"FLEET!"

Something sailed through the air and landed with an uncompromising clunk about three meters from Sassinak's nose; it cracked and leaked a bluish haze. *I'm not sure I believe this,* she thought, reaching for her gas kit, holding her breath, remembering how to count, checking on Lunzie and Aygar. *This is where I came in but that shout had to be Ford's.*

The heavyworlder troops would have gas kits, too, of course. How fast could they move? She was already in motion, but again Aygar was faster, the blinding speed of youth and perfect condition. They hit the first heavyworlders before they had their weapons in hand, yanking them away and reversing without slackening speed. Sassinak leaped for the higher ground, the Justices' dais, and rolled behind its protective rail just as something splintered it behind her. She crawled rapidly toward the far seat, ignoring the unconscious Justices, and picked off the first trooper who came after her. Where was Lunzie? Which way had Aygar run? And did he even know what to do with that weapon?

A stuttering burst of fire, squeals and crashes, and high pitched screams suggested that he'd found out what to push, but she didn't trust his aim. She saw stealthy movement coming over the rail and fired a short burst: no yell, but no more movement.

"Sassinak!" Ford again, this time nearer. "Pattern six!"

Pattern six was a simple trick, something all cadets learned in the first months of maneuvers. Sassinak moved to her right, flattening to one side of the Federation Seal and wondered what he was planning to use for the reinforcements that pattern six sent down the center. The few marines he was supposed to have from the *Zaid-Dayan* wouldn't be enough. Something coughed, and she grinned. How *had* Ford managed to get a Gertrud into the Grand Council? The stubby, squat weapon, designed for riot control on space stations, coughed again, and settled to its normal steady growl. Sassinak put her fingers in her ears and kept her head well down. Behind that growl, Ford and whoever he had conscripted could edge forward, letting the sonic patterns ahead disorient the enemy.

But their enemies were not giving up that easily. One of them must have worn protective headgear, for he put his weapon on full automatic and poured an entire magazine into the Gertrud. Its growl skewed upward, ending in an explosion of bright sound. Sassinak shook her head violently to clear her ears and tried to figure out what next.

She could see through the paint-splashed protective screen from this height. The neat rows of public seating were the scene of a full-bore riot. No help there, even if her former accomplices were winning, and she wasn't at all sure they were. Higher up, she could see struggling figures behind the lights and lenses of the media deck. Down below, she saw the Diplonian delegate begin to twitch, waking up from the gas. Him she could handle and she let off a burst that flung him away from the podium, dead before he waked.

The witness box was empty. She did not see Ford, but she assumed he was still in the row below. But the guest box . . . from here, she could see its occupants, some dead or wounded, some frozen in horror and shock, and some all too clearly enjoying the spectacle. These had personal shields, translucent but offering safety from such hazards as the riot gas and small arms fire. Sassinak edged carefully along the upper level of the dais. No one else had come up here after her. Perhaps they'd assume she'd slipped off the far side to join her supporters. She wished she knew how many supporters, and with what arms.

In a momentary lull, one of the shielded guests glanced up and locked eyes with her. Sassinak felt her bones melting with rage. Age and indulgence had left their mark on Randy Paraden, but she knew him. And he, it was clear, knew her. She felt her lips draw back in a snarl. His curled in the same arrogant sneer, gloating in his safety, in her danger. Slowly, arrogantly, he stood, letting his shield push aside those near him and left the guest box. Still watching her, he came nearer, nearer, with that mocking smile, knowing her weapon could not penetrate his personal shield. Raised a hand to signal, no doubt to guide one of the heavyworlders to her.

And then fell, with infinite surprise, that expression she'd seen so often before on others who found reality intruding on dreams. It had happened so quickly the Weft was untangling itself from Paraden's body before she realized it. It had *shifted* across the shield and broken his neck.

<<Back to work.>> And it was gone, back into the fray.

She caught a glimpse of two other shielded guests departing, in considerable rush, and the Weft message echoed in her head.

<<Parchandri.>>

"You're sure?"

<<Parchandri.>>

If they were going, she was sure she knew where. She fished the comunit out of her pocket and thumbed it on. She had a message to send, and then a fight to finish.

Chapter Twenty-one

Timran had ignored the commotion around the shuttle's shields the morning after the landing. Nothing civilians could do would damage them or give access. He could tune in civilian broadcasts and spent the day watching newscasters ask each other questions on the main news channel. He'd rather have watched a back-to-back rerun of Carin Coldae classics, but felt he should exercise self-discipline. His second night alone in the shuttle he spent in catnaps and sudden, dry-mouthed awakenings. Keeping the video channels on did not help. He kept thinking someone had sneaked in to take control.

Morning brought the itchy-eyed state of fatigue. He turned the com volume up high and dared a fast shower in the shuttle's tiny head. A caffeine tab and breakfast. The news blared on about the trial which would start in a few hours. He had heard nothing from Ford since that brief contact giving him the coordinates to watch, the details of the ship he might encounter. That had been around dawn of the day before. He felt so helpless, and so miserably alone. How could he help the captain, stuck 'way out here? The memory of the last time he hadn't obeyed orders smacked him on the mental nose. But those had been the captain's orders and these were only the Exec's. He had a sudden memory of Sassinak and Ford coming out of her quarters when he'd been on an errand. On second thought, he had better not antagonize Ford.

He settled down to watch the news coverage of the trial. Another inter-view with another civilian bureaucrat concerning the Iretan plague. Tim snorted, squirming in his seat. They asked the stupidest questions and the experts gave the stupidest answers. He wished he could be interviewed. He'd do a lot better. None of them would ever say "I don't know" and stick to it. Of course, they'd probably quit asking the ones who did know.

When the coverage of the Grand Council finally began, with the Speaker formally greeting each delegate, Tim sat up straight. He had stowed all the litter of his solitary occupation, prepped the shuttle for emergency liftoff, and made sure that every system was working perfectly. What he didn't have was any kind of effective weapon, unless the ship he expected to meet had neither shields nor guns. He was trying not to think about that. He had his helmet beside him, just in case. Outside the shuttle's shields, a thin line of police kept the curious away. They would be safe at that distance when he lifted.

The view on screen flicked from one location in the chamber to another. He saw Lunzie and an admiral sitting together in the seats reserved for witnesses, then Ford coming in. The view shifted and he saw Sassinak on the other side of the chamber. Why over there? he wondered. Aygar, beside her, looked unhappy. Tim wanted to be there worse than he'd ever wanted any-thing. He liked the big Iretan and hoped he'd decide to join Fleet in some capacity. And everything was happening *there*! Not here.

When the trouble began, he sat forward, hardly breathing. He'd often said he wished he'd been there to see other fights, other adventures, but he found that watching was far worse. He couldn't see what he wanted, only what the camera showed, and it was all a lot messier than the stories. Then the screen blanked, streaked, and finally returned as an exterior view of the Grand Council hall with a rioting crowd outside. Again the views shifted; first one streetful of people screaming, then another of people marching in step, waving flags, then of orange uniformed police firing into the crowd.

He glanced outside. The police there shifted about, looking edgy. No doubt they had communication with the inner city, and wondered what to do about him. Suddenly one of them whirled, and fired point-blank at the shield. His companions pulled him away, yanked the weapon from him, and moved back. Tim did nothing. He was trembling, he found, far worse than he had been that time on Ireta, but he managed to keep his fingers off the controls. His mind clung to the thought that Sassinak would call for him, would need him: he must be ready.

Yet when the call came, he hardly believed it.

* * *

"*Zaid-Dayan* shuttle!" came the second time before he got his fingers and his voice working and thumbed the control.

"Shuttle here!" His voice sounded like his kid brother's. He swallowed and hoped it would steady the next time.

"Fugitives en route. As planned, launch and intercept."

Did that mean the others weren't coming? Was he really supposed to take off without them?

"Are you?"

"Now!"

That was definitely Sassinak, no doubt about it. *This is not like I imagined it would be,* he thought. His memory reminded him that so far it never had been. Helmet on, connections made. He looked at the fat red button and pushed it, then got his hands on the other controls just as the shuttle surged up, sucking a good bit of the landfill's carefully planted grass in its wake.

He was high over the city in moments, balancing on a delicate combination of atmospheric and insystem drives. He had time to enjoy the knowledge that he had made a perfect liftoff and was doing a superb job now in precisely the right position.

The coordinates he'd been given, entered into the shuttle's nav computer, now showed a red circle on a displayed map that matched what he could see below. Hard to believe that beneath that vast warehouse a silo poked into the ground ready to launch a fast yacht. But the displays were changing color. The IR scan showed the change first as the warehouse roof sections lifted away. Then the targeting lasers picked up the vibrations, translated as seismic activity.

The inner barriers lifted and the yacht's nose poked out, rising slowly, slowly. As if on an elevator lift, then faster, then . . . Tim remembered he was supposed to give one official warning and poked the button to turn on the pre-recorded tape. Sassinak had not wanted to trust his impromptu style.

"FSP Shuttlecraft *Seeker* to ship in liftoff. You are under arrest. Proceed directly to shuttleport. You have been warned."

Sassinak had said they *could* divert to the shuttleport, even immediately after liftoff. But she didn't think they would.

"Don't even try it, Tiny!" came the reply from the yacht. "You haven't got a chance."

He hoped that wasn't true. Supposedly, the constraints of taking off from a silo meant that the most common weapons systems couldn't be mounted until after the yacht was out of the atmosphere in steady flight. And his shields should deflect all but heavy assaults. The problem was how to stop the yacht. Shuttles were just that—shuttles—not fighter craft. He had a tractor beam which was not nearly powerful enough to slow the yacht and a midrange beamer designed to clear brush when landing in uncleared terrain. Could he disable the yacht's instrument cone? That's what Ford had suggested.

He got the targeting lasers fixed on the yacht's bow as he kept the shuttle in alignment, and pressed the firing stud. A line of light appeared, splashed harmlessly along the yacht's shields. It wasn't supposed to have shields. They were high in the atmosphere now. His displays told him the yacht should be planning to release its massive solid-fuel engine. This didn't worry him because the more massive yacht, with its limited drive system, could not possibly outmaneuver a Fleet shuttle as long as it stayed below lightspeed. But he still could not figure out how to stop it. If it made the transition to FTL, he could not follow.

Of course he could ram it. No shields on a ship that size could withstand the strain if he intercepted at high velocity. But what if he *missed*? How could he keep track of it, keep it from going into FTL, if he couldn't stop it cold? The yacht's booster separated and it surged higher. Tim sent the shuttle after it. What if it had more power then they'd thought? What if it *could* distance the shuttle? Then it would be free to go into FTL and disappear forever and he . . . *he* would get to explain his failure to Commander Sassinak.

Who had not explained, this time, exactly what to do. Who was not in her cruiser, this time, ready to come to his rescue. He found he was sweating, his breath short. He had to do *something* and, except by a kind of blind instinct, he had never been good at picking alternatives. The yacht opened a margin on him. Tim uttered a silent prayer to gods he couldn't name and redlined the shuttle to catch back up to it. If he was right . . . if he could remember how to do this . . . if nothing went wrong, there was a way to keep that yacht from making a jump. If things *did* go wrong, he wouldn't know it.

Sassinak picked herself out of the tangle of bodies with a groan. A dull ache in her leg promised to develop into real pain as soon as she paid attention to it. Tim should be on his way. Arly was out there somewhere doing something with the invasion fleet. And here . . . here was death and pain and carnage. One Lethi delegate smashed into amber splinters and dust that stank of sulfur compounds. A Ryxi whimpering as its broken leg twitched repeatedly. The singed feathers on its back added another noxious reek to the chamber. Aygar? Aygar lay sprawled, motionless, but Lunzie knelt beside him and nodded encouragingly as she looked up. Ford, gray around the mouth, held out his blistered hands for the medics as they sprayed a pale-green foam on them.

Sassinak limped over to Lunzie and thought about sitting down beside her. Better not. She didn't think she could get back up. "How bad is he?"

"Near as I can tell, a stunner beam got him. Not too badly. He should wake up miserable within an hour. What else?" Lunzie still had that intense stare of someone in full Discipline.

"The Paraden representatives here, the ones in the guest box, got away. To their yacht."

"*Blast* it!" Lunzie looked ready to smash through walls barehanded.

"Never mind. I had a trap for them."

"You . . . ?"

Sassinak explained briefly, looking around as she did. The surviving delegates were safely sealed into their places. She could just see them watching her. What must they be thinking? And what should she do?

"Sassinak. A statement?" One of the students had come down to the floor, with a camera on his shoulder. So they had secured the newslines. She frowned, trying to clear her mind, to think. She felt the weight of it all on her. She glanced around for Coromell who should, as the senior, make any statements. Then she saw his crumpled body in the unmistakable posture of the dead.

"I . . . Just a moment." Had Lunzie seen? What would she do? She touched Lunzie's shoulder. "Did you know? Coromell?"

Lunzie nodded. "Yes. I saw it. I'd just gone to full Discipline. Couldn't save him . . . and he was so *decent*." She blinked back tears. "I can't cry now, and besides . . ."

"Right."

Coromell dead. The Speaker dead. The Justices, if not dead, at least unable to take over. Someone had to do it. She limped up the step to the Speaker's podium and stepped gingerly between the bodies that lay at its foot: the Speaker, who had reminded her of her first captain, and the Diplonian delegate she herself had killed. The Speaker's podium had had status screens, an array of controls to record votes, and grant the right to speak. But none of that worked. Her own shots, most likely, had shattered the screens. Still, it was the right place, and she stood behind it as the student with the camera moved in for a close shot. She could imagine what it looked like. A tired, rumpled Fleet officer in front of the Federation shield, the very image of a military coup, the end of peace and freedom. But she would do better than that.

"Delegates, Justices, Citizens of the Federation of Sentient Planets," she began. "This Federation, this peaceful alliance of many races, will survive . . ."

Arly, in the command seat on *Zaid-Dayan*'s bridge, had the best view of what happened next. Although the Central System's defenses were concentrated along the three most common approaches from other sectors, the Seti had not chosen an alternative route. They had counted on most of the defenses being knocked out by collaborators. Once she realized that their approach was in fact along a mapped path, she had been able to use the *Zaid-Dayan*'s capabilities against them.

At first she had used the defense satellites as cover, taking out two of the flanking escorts, and one medium cruiser as if the satellites had been active. So far, the Seti commanders had assumed that the losses were, in fact, due to passive defense systems that had escaped inactivation. At least, that's what her Ssli told her they were thinking. She hoped they were also wondering if their human allies were double-crossing them.

When that got too dangerous—for the Seti clearly knew exactly where such installations were and they began attacking them—she used the stealth capability and the Ssli's precision control of tiny FTL hops to disappear and reappear unpredictably, firing off a few missiles each time at the nearest ship, and then vanishing again. She could not actually destroy the invaders, not with one cruiser, but she could inflict serious losses.

Now they were well into the system, inside the outer ranks of defenses, still in numbers large enough to threaten all the inhabited planets. It would be another day or more before any Fleet vessels could arrive, assuming the nearest had come at once on receipt of the mayday. By then FedCentral might be in range of the Seti ships.

She was just considering whether to sacrifice the ship by going in for close combat for she thought she might do the Seti flagship enough damage to force the invaders to slow, when the scans went crazy, doppler displays racing through color sequences, alarms flashing. Then the ship's drive indicators rose slowly from green to yellow with some strain as if a massive object had appeared not far off.

"Thek," said the very pale Weft, its form wavering before it steadied back to human.

"Thek?"

She had seen before the way Thek moved, and how it seemed to violate a lifetime's assumptions about matter and space. She had just not realized that her instruments felt the same way about it.

"Many, many Thek. They . . . more or less vacuum packed the Seti fleet."

The sensors reported the right density and mass for more Thek than Arly had ever seen, but what she thought of was Dupaynil. Dupaynil being squashed by granite pyramids.

"No," said the Weft, shaking his head. "Not *that* ship. That one's whole, but can't maneuver. The Thek have made it quite clear to the Seti that their prisoners had best stay healthy."

"What about us?" After all, humans had been involved in the plot, too.

"We're free to go, although they'd prefer that we picked up the prisoners from that Seti ship."

"Fine with me. I'm not arguing with flying rocks." She hoped the Thek wouldn't consider that disrespectful. "Are you . . . *talking* with them?"

He looked surprised. "Of course. You know we're special to them. They think we're . . . I suppose you'd say, cute."

"No one ever told *me* that you Wefts could talk to Thek."

"Not that many know we're telepathic with some humans, or most Ssli."

"Mmm. Right. So where does this Thek want us to go to pick up passengers?"

In the event, they sent a shuttle which the Thek guided through the interstices of the trap they'd shut on the Seti. While it was on its way, Arly remembered to prepare quarters for the alien guests, including a sealed compartment for the Lethi where the fumes from their obligatory sulfur wouldn't bother anyone else.

Arly decided the shuttle's arrival required a formal reception to reassure the allied aliens that Fleet was loyal to the FSP and not part of the plot. With the crisis over, she left the bridge to a junior officer and came to Flight Deck herself, with a squad of marines in dress uniform.

The *Zaid-Dayan* had no military band, but she had a recording of the FSP anthem piped in as more suitable to aliens than anything else. The shuttle hatch opened and two of the crew came out, carrying the Lethi. The Ryxi bobbed out on its own, fluffing feathers nervously, and chittered vigorously before greeting her in Standard with effusive thanks. Then came the Bronthin, its normal pastel blue fur almost gray with exhaustion and fear. Two more of the shuttle crew, with the larval Ssli's environmental tank. Finally, Dupaynil emerged.

Arly stared at him in frank shock. The dapper, elegant officer she remembered was a filthy, shambling wreck, red-rimmed eyes sunken.

"Commander!"

"Is Sassinak aboard?" That had an intensity she couldn't quite interpret.

"No. She's onplanet."

"Thank the . . ." he paused. "The luck, I suppose. Or whatever. I . . ." He staggered and the waiting medics came forward. He waved them off. "I don't need anything but a shower—a *long* shower—and some rest."

"But what happened to you?"

Dupaynil gave her a look somewhere between anger and exhaustion. "One damn thing after another, Arly, and the worst of it is it's all my fault for thinking I was smarter than your Sassinak. Now please?"

"Of course."

He did reek and she felt her nostrils dilate as he passed her. She wondered how long he'd been in that pressure suit. She hardly had all the survivors settled when the Weft liaison to the Thek called her back to the bridge. One last chore remained. The humans most responsible had escaped the planet in a fast yacht, and although a Fleet vessel had kept it in sight, it could not stop it.

"Tim and that shuttle!" Arly said. "I forgot him. Com, get us a link!"

Tim had the yacht's position and the Ssli flicked the cruiser in and out of FTL space in a minute jump that put them well in range. Her weapons officer reported that the yacht lacked anything to penetrate the cruiser's shields. Too bad Sassinak wasn't here. She would enjoy this. But she'd had the onplanet fun. Arly put their message on an all-frequency transmission.

"FSP Cruiser *Zaid-Dayan* to private vessel *Celestial Fortune*. Going somewhere?"

"Let us alone, or you'll regret it!" came the reply. "You're nothin' but a lousy little short-range shuttle tryin' to play big shot."

"Take another look," suggested Arly and cut back the visual screens. "Do you want to argue with *this*?"

She sent a missile past their bows, and heard a yelp from Tim on one of the incoming lines. A spurt of annoyance. He should have had sense enough to get out of the way.

"Get that shuttle back in here," she told him.

"Sorry, ma'am."

"What do you mean, *sorry*?"

"I . . . uh . . . It was the only way I could think of."

"What did you do?"

"I . . . locked shields with 'em."

Arly closed her eyes and counted to ten. So *that's* why they hadn't gone into FTL yet. But it meant that blowing the yacht would mean blowing the shuttle, and Tim. Nor could he pull away. Locking shields was hard enough going in. She'd never heard of anyone getting back out, unless both ships agreed to damp the shields simultaneously.

"Who's with you?" asked Arly.

"Nobody," came the reply.

From his tone he knew exactly what that meant. If Sassinak had been aboard . . . but one ensign, who had been unable to think of any way to impede the enemy but bonding to it? He was very expendable.

"You suited up?"

"Yes. But . . ." But what good would it do?

Shuttles had no escape pods, for the very good reason that in normal operation they were useless. And being blown out of an exploding shuttle was a little more than hazardous.

"I can flutter their shields, Commander. Give you a better chance of getting 'em with the first shot."

"Dammit, Tim, don't be so eager to die."

It would help, though, and she knew it.

"I'm not," he said. Was that a quaver in his voice?

He was not going to die if she could help it. But the yacht had meanwhile refused to cut its acceleration outsystem or change course. Its captain seemed sure he could make his FTL jump anyway.

"Even if I do scrape a louse off our hide."

"Do that and you're dead for sure. We've followed more than one through FTL flux." She flipped that channel off. "And why can't the blasted Thek help us now?" Arly demanded of the Weft at her side. "I hate the way they pick and choose. If these are the bigshots . . ."

The *Zaid-Dayan's* proximity alarms blared. The artificial gravity pulsed. Arly swallowed hastily, clutching the arms of her chair. Small objects tumbled about and a dust haze rose, to be sucked rapidly away by the fans.

"Do me a favor, Captain, and don't bad-mouth the Theks any more," said the Weft.

This time he'd shifted completely and hung now from the overhead, bright blue eyes gleaming at Arly. Then he shifted back, leaving a mental image of strings of innards trailing down in a most abnormal way to reassemble into a living person.

"I just said . . ."

"I know. But you people complain all the time about how slow the Thek are and how they don't pay attention. You should rejoice that they're now paying attention and you've had a demonstration of how they can move."

"Right. Sorry. But the yacht . . ."

The Thek had absorbed all the yacht's considerable inertia, flicking Tim and his shuttle off as a housewife might flick an ant off a plate. When he hailed them, Arly could hear astonished relief in his voice.

"Permission to land shuttle?"

Should she bring him in, or send him back to FedCentral? A glance at the readouts told her the shuttle wouldn't make it back safely.

"Permission granted. Bring 'er aboard, Ensign."

And he did, without any hotdog flourishes.

Arly looked around the bridge, and wondered if she looked as disshelved as the others. Far more ragged than Sassinak had ever looked, she thought. We'll have to get this place cleaned up before she sees it and everyone rested. But we still have to get back down there, just in case.

Convincing the Dockmaster at the FedCentral Station that the *Zaid-Dayan* was not an agent of doom required the rough side of Arly's tongue.

"We saved your tails from a 'catenated Seti *fleet*. And you're going to gripe at me because I left without your fardling permission?"

"It was highly irregular."

"So it was, and so were the Seti. So were the traitors in your system that wanted to let 'em in. It's not my fault you wouldn't believe the truth. Now you can let us dock or watch us sit out here using your station for target practice."

"That's a threat!" he said.

"Right. Going to take us up on it?"

"I'll file a complaint." Then his face sagged as he realized to whom that complaint would go: Sassinak, now in command of the loyal Federation forces onplanet, Acting Governor. "It's all *very* irregular . . ." His voice trailed away into a sigh. "All right. Bays twelve through twenty, orange arm."

"Thank you," said Arly, careful to keep her voice neutral. Never push your luck, Sassinak always said, and she felt her luck had been working overtime lately. "If you have any fresh forage for Bronthin, we have an individual in bad shape who's been a Seti prisoner."

This the Dockmaster could handle. "Of course. With so much diplomatic traffic, we pride ourselves on keeping full supplies for every race in the FSP. Any other requirements?"

"A Ryxi which is suffering from 'feather pit,' whatever that is, and a pair of Lethi who seem all right, although our medical team isn't familiar with Lethi."

"Only *two* Lethi? That's very bad. Lethi need to cluster in larger numbers."

"Plus a larval Ssli," Arly said. "It's complained that its tank needs recharging."

"No problem with *any* of that," said the Dockmaster, suddenly cordial. "If you'll send the allied races to bay sixteen, that'll be the quickest access for our specialty medical services."

"Will do." Arly shook her head as she looked around the bridge. "Can you believe that? He was willing to stand us off as if we were pirates, but he's got specialty medical teams for our aliens."

Arly had been in communication with Sassinak for the past several hours. The situation onplanet had stabilized with the loyalists firmly in control, and only scattered pockets of resistance.

"And I think most of that's confusion," Sassinak had said. "We're finding that many of the Parchandri/Paraden supporters had been blackmailed into it. Others just didn't know any better. Right now the Thek are calling for a formal trial."

"Not another one!"

"Not like that one, no. A Thek trial." Sassinak had looked exhausted. Arly wondered if she'd had any rest at all since her disappearance. "Another Thek cathedral is all I need! But considering what they've done, we really can't argue. They want those prisoners you rescued from the Seti, especially the Bronthin, Ssli, Weft, and Dupaynil."

So now, docked at the Station, Arly saw these turned over to special medical teams. Soon they'd be on their way to the Thek trial. She wondered about the crew and passengers of the yacht Tim had trapped. But she wasn't going to ask any questions. Two experiences with fast-moving Thek were quite enough.

It was impossible to overestimate the civilizing influence of cleanliness, rest, and good cooking, Sassinak thought. Back on the *Zaid-Dayan*, back in a clean uniform, with a stomach full of the best her favorite cook could do, with a full shift's sleep, she was ready to forgive almost anyone. Particularly since the Thek, in their unyielding fashion, had satisfied any remaining desire for vengeance.

For a moment, she felt again the pressure of those most alien minds. And marveled that she had survived *two* terms in a Thek cathedral. Never again, she hoped. The judgment process might be exhausting but it served its purpose admirably.

The guilty Seti were to be confined to one interdicted planet, guarded by installations whose crews were former pirate prisoners. Paraden family lost all its possessions, from shipping lines to private moonlets. Paradens and

Parchandris alike were given basic survival and tool supplies, the same they had sold to many a colony starting up, and deposited on a barely habitable planet.

With the single exception of Ford's Auntie Q. She lost nothing for the Thek considered her a victim, not a Paraden, despite her name.

And, thanks to Lunzie's partisanship and fierce arguments, heavyworlders were also considered victims. After all, they had been cheated by the wealthy lightweights who then blackmailed them into service. So the Thek required only that those conspirators in the governments of heavyworlder planets be expelled. The others, informed of the complex plot, were given shares in the liquidation of Paraden assets. They could use that to ease their lives.

In addition, FSP regulations changed to allow heavyworlder migration to any world open to humans. But that did not include Ireta: the Thek would not change their earlier decision. Aygar had been consoled, finally, by the knowledge that he would have a chance to see many equally fascinating worlds. And enough money to enjoy them.

Now the original team relaxed in Sassinak's office, with most of the tales untold and a long night ahead for telling them. Restored by a couple of sessions in the tank to heal his burns, Ford crunched another of the crispy fries. Sassinak met his eyes and felt indecently smug. They had private plans when the party broke up. He had told her just enough about Auntie Q and the Ryxi tailfeathers to whet her appetite.

Dupaynil, though, had lost some of his polish. Specklessly clean, as usual, perfectly groomed, he still had a hangdog tentative quality that she found almost as irritating as his former blithe certainty.

Lunzie, always tactful, had put aside her grief for Coromell to try to cheer Dupaynil up, but so far it hadn't worked. Timran, on the other hand, was indecently gleeful. He had taken the mild commendation she'd given him as if he'd been awarded the Federation's highest honor in front of the Grand Council. Now he sat stiffly in the corner of her office as if he would burst if he moved. She'd better rescue the lad.

"Ensign, there's an errand . . . a fairly special one . . ."

"Yes, *ma'am!*"

"We're having guests; I'd like you to escort a lady from the Flight Deck in here."

If anyone could settle a young man like Tim, it would be Fleur. He'd enjoy Aygar's student friend, too, and Erdra. Sassinak grinned wickedly at the thought of Erdra coming face to face with the reality behind her daydreams. *She* was no Carin Coldae and the sooner she quit playing games and went back to finish that advanced degree in analytical systems, the better. The riot had cured her of any thought that violence and glamor coexisted, and a visit to a working warship ought to clear out the rest of her nonsense.

Lunzie would want to meet her relative-of-sorts, from the Chinese family. It had been extravagant, in several ways, to send her own shuttle down for them, but she felt it important to build respect for Fleet. No more restrictions on the movement of Fleet personnel, and no civilian weapons monitors, either. The *Zaid-Dayan* was, as it always should be, ready for action. Now, while Tim was gone, she could try to penetrate Dupaynil's gloom again.

"I wanted to apologize to you," she began, "for pulling that trick . . ."

"It *was* a trick, then, with the orders?" He brightened a moment. "I was sure of it. You used the Ssli, right?"

"Right. But it was flat stupid of me not to know more about the ship I tossed you onto. I had no idea . . ."

"I know." He looked glum again.

"You said something about charges?"

"Well, the Exec of the escort and I had to overpower the crew, put 'em in custody . . ."

"On an *escort*? Where?"

"In the escape pod in coldsleep. They were going to space me."

Sassinak stared at him. He said it in a tone of flat misery entirely out of character for someone who had run a successful mutiny.

"I'm sure we can get the charges dropped. If anyone's dared filed them," she said. "Especially now. I've had contact with Admiral Vannoy, back at Sector, and he's rooting out the traitors around Fleet."

But that didn't cheer him up as it should have. Clearly impending charges weren't the burden he carried. Lunzie caught her eye and made a significant glance at Ford, at Dupaynil, then at Aygar. Sassinak let one eyelid droop in a near-wink.

"Ford, if you don't mind, I think I'd like a grownup to supervise that reception. Aygar, you might want to be there to greet your friends."

Aygar leaped up while Ford stood more slowly, grinning at Sassinak in a way that almost made her blush.

"You ladies take care," he said, with his own significant glance at Dupaynil. "No squabbling."

Then he left, shepherding Aygar ahead of him.

"Now, then," said Sassinak. "You've been brooding about as if you were about to be stuck in Administration forever. So, what's the problem?" She thought for a long moment he would not answer, then it burst out of him.

"It's ridiculous, and I don't want to talk about it."

Lunzie and Sassinak waited, saying nothing. Dupaynil looked up and met Sassinak's eyes squarely.

"I was so *furious* with you for pulling that trick. For getting *away* with that trick. I dreamed of outfoxing you again, coming back with what you needed, but making you pay for it. Then I had to escape those . . . those pirates on *Claw*, and realized that I didn't know one thing about actually running a ship. Panis had to train me as if I were a raw recruit. But I still thought, with what I'd found, that I'd have a chance of returning in triumph. A good story to tell, all that. But then the Seti . . ." He stopped, shaking his head, and Sassinak and Lunzie stared at each other over his bent head.

"What did they do?" asked Lunzie.

Sassinak was thinking that it was a good thing they'd died before she'd had the opportunity to skin their scaly hide off their live bodies.

"Arly didn't tell you?"

"She said you looked pretty dilapidated when you came aboard, but you wouldn't go to Medical—" Her skin crawled as she thought of reasons why he might not, which could explain his present mood. "Dupaynil! They didn't!"

This time he laughed, a genuine if shaky laugh. "No. No, they didn't actually *do* anything. It was just . . . Have you ever seen a Seti shower?"

What did that have to do with anything? "No," Sassinak said cautiously.

"It sprays you with hot air, grit, and more hot air," Dupaynil said with more energy than she'd heard from him yet. Bitter, but alive. "I'm sure it's what keeps their scales so shiny. Probably takes care of itchy little parasites on a Seti. But for a human, day after day . . . And then I had to stay in that blasted pressure suit for *days*." His expression brought a chuckle to Sassinak; she couldn't help it. "I'd planned on strolling in, cool and suave, to hand you what you needed. Instead, I was stuck in a stinking pressure suit in a crowded compartment full of terrified aliens where I could do not one damn thing, and had to be rescued like any silly princess in a fairy tale."

"But you did," said Sassinak.

"Did what?"

"Did do something. Kipling's corns, Dupaynil, *you* got the warning to us. You had evidence the Thek used."

"They could have got it straight from those slimebuckets' minds."

"Well, if the Thek hadn't been there, we'd have needed it. After all, they asked for you at the trial. They needed your evidence, too. I don't know what more you could want. You escaped one death-trap after another, you got vital information, you saved the world. Did you really think anyone could do that without getting dirty?" She thought of herself in the tunnels, even before Fleur's disguise.

"I wanted to impress you," he said softly, looking at his linked hands.

"Well, you did." Sassinak cocked her head at him. "Impress me? Was that all?"

"No." She would never have suspected that Dupaynil could blush, but what else were those red patches on his cheeks. "When I was on *Claw*, when I realized what you'd done, and I was so mad . . . I also realized I wanted . . ."

It was clear enough, though he couldn't say it.

"I'm sorry." That was genuine. He had earned it. She couldn't offer more. Her joyful reunion with Ford had revealed too much to both of them.

"Sorry!" Lunzie fairly exploded, her eyes sparkling. "You nearly get the man killed, he has to take over a whole *ship*, and then he saves us all from a Seti invasion, and you're just *sorry!*" She looked at Dupaynil. "She may be my descendant, but that doesn't mean we agree. I think she ought to give you a medal."

"Lunzie!"

"You wouldn't think so if you'd seen me getting off that shuttle." Dupaynil said. "Ask Arly."

"I don't have to ask Arly. I can see for myself." That came out in a sensuous purr. Under Lunzie's bright gaze, Dupaynil's grin began to revive.

Sassinak regarded her great-great-great with affectionate disdain. "Lunzie, I know where I inherited *some* of my propensities." If Lunzie stayed interested, she gave Dupaynil only a few more hours of freedom.

"Meow!" Lunzie stuck out her tongue, then leaned closer to Dupaynil.

Whatever else she might have said was interrupted by the arrival of the others: Fleur, who had worn one of her own creations in lavender and silver, Aygar and Timran in the midst of the students. Erdra, Sassinak noticed, wore the same kind of colorful shirt and leggings as the others. Perhaps she had grown out of her wishful thinking already.

"Have you?" Fleur asked, drifting close a little later, as the conversation rose and fell around them.

"What?"

"Grown out of your past?"

Sassinak snorted. "I grew out of Carin Coldae a long way back."

"You know that's not what I mean."

Sassinak thought of Randy Paraden's face, the instant before the Weft killed him, and of the faces of the other conspirators in the Thek cathedral.

She had looked long in her mirror when she came back aboard, hoping not to find any of the marks of that kind of character.

"Yes," she said slowly. "I think I have. I can't change what they did to me, but I can change what I do about it. It's time to be more than a pirate-chaser. But not less."